EVERYMAN'S LIBRARY

276

FICTION

Everyman, I will go with thee, and be thy guide,
In thy most need to go by thy side

HELIODORUS (3rd century A.D.), a native
of Emesa in Syria.

HELIODORUS
ETHIOPIAN STORY

TRANSLATED INTO ENGLISH
BY
SIR WALTER LAMB

LONDON J. M. DENT & SONS LTD
NEW YORK E. P. DUTTON & CO INC

INTRODUCTION

THE *Ethiopian Story of Theagenes and Chariclea*, composed by Heliodorus of Emesa in Syria about seventeen centuries ago, stands at the head of the abundant stream of prose romances which have recounted the adventures of pairs of lovers amid numerous distresses and dangers, and which have usually concluded with the final attainment of their safety and their peaceful enjoyment of a happy union. In earliest times, no doubt, popular lays and hymns supplied the materials for the later, far more expansive and accomplished verse compositions of the *Iliad* and the *Odyssey*; and the talents of the ablest bards could be relied on for the continual addition of fresh ballads, or extensions of the old, to the general stock. 'Men give the higher praise to the song that comes floating newest to their ears,' said Telemachus to Penelope when she asked the minstrel Phemius for a less doleful song than that of the Achaeans' return from Troy [1]— since this new song was especially grievous to her in her inconsolable sorrow; and it was from such lays of bards or minstrels at communal gatherings that the two most famous of the Greek epics were built up by the great poet or poets traditionally known to Europe as Homer.

Story-telling in ordinary speech, for its own sake as entertainment—one of the earliest and most valued arts of mankind—was highly developed in the Greek cities of Asia Minor, where oriental legends and fables had a fertilizing influence upon Greek imagination and ingenuity. Hence came, not only large extensions of the wonder-world of Greek mythology, but also the lively, though often licentious, diversions of the *Milesian Tales*, and the illustrative story-telling that enlivens here and there the serious recording of Herodotus. Through Miletus and others of the Ionian cities flowed strong currents of commerce from the East and from the West, bringing to their busy harbours and markets a great variety of adventurous travellers with tales of

[1] *Odyssey*, i. 351–2.

what they had seen and experienced, or heard from others, in Egypt, Syria and remoter regions. These cities, besides giving birth to European science and philosophy in the sixth century B.C., had surpassed Greece itself in the cultivation of architecture, the fine arts and poetry; not least, also, in the shaping of Greek prose, mainly for the impressive pronouncements of the early speculators on the truth about the universe, the earth, and man's nature and best social and political behaviour. A dark age, however, for Ionian culture came in the fifth century B.C., when the Greek cities of Asia succumbed to the westward advance of the mighty power of Persia, and Athens succeeded Miletus as the political and cultural centre of Greek civilization.

In the first half of the fourth century Plato composed the masterly narratives of his myths, bringing in persuasive literary art to enhance the appeal of his arguments. Xenophon, in his eloquent and edifying, though quite unhistorical, description of the education of Cyrus the Great, produced the first romantic stories of some extent and note in Greek prose that are known to us, in relating the ideal affections and loyalties of Araspes, Abradatas and Pantheia,[1] and those also of the king and queen of Armenia and their son Tigranes.[2] And there too the controversy and reconciliation of the proud Cyaxares with his nephew Cyrus are described in a highly romantic manner,[3] wholly regardless of history, that foreshadows the imaginative licence and engaging contrivance of the Greek novelists some six centuries later. Towards the end of the fourth century B.C. romantic attachments under difficulties were a popular theme in many of the skilful plots of Menander and other writers (in verse) of the New Comedy. The first known essay in poetic love-romance on an extensive scale appeared in the rather rambling epic of *The Argonauts' Expedition* composed by Apollonius Rhodius in the latter half of the third century B.C. The ardent passion of the young Medea for the gallant Jason is the main subject of the last two of the poem's four books. But no elaborate love-romance in Greek prose seems to have been produced till about A.D. 150, when a writer calling himself Chariton of Aphrodisias in Caria composed his story of *Chaereas and Callirrhoë*. As it has come

---

[1] Xenophon, *Cyr.* v. 1; vi. 1, 3, 4; vii. 1, 3.
[2] Ibid. iii. 1, 2, 4. [3] Ibid. v. 5.

down to us it begins with the lovers' marriage. Callirrhoë, in a deathlike swoon after being cruelly maltreated by her husband in a fit of furious jealousy, is entombed; she is discovered alive by a pirate, is sold as a slave in Miletus to an Ionian prince Dionysius, and enters the harem of Artaxerxes II, King of Persia, in the period 405–360 B.C. Her impetuous young husband is captured and made a slave of the Persian governor of Caria. He is brought to the royal court at Babylon, whence he makes his escape, and then becomes the leader of an Egyptian revolt.[1] He decisively defeats the Persian navy, and departs with his wife to Syracuse and the home of her father—the same historical Hermocrates who with Gylippus headed the Syracusan resistance to the ill-fated Athenian invasion of Sicily in 413 B.C. This partially preserved story is notable for the gentle restraint shown by Dionysius in paying court to his beautiful slave, and for the lucidity of the style in which it is written and for which it was admired in the Renaissance.

The entombment of another married heroine occurs in a certain later Xenophon's *Ephesian Story of Habrocomas and Anthia,* when the fair lady, in the course of adventures with her husband among pirates and bandits, takes a sleeping draught, and is carried off alive to Egypt by another band of pirates, who had come to plunder her tomb. She is rescued by a bandit of humane character who finally delivers her to her husband in Rhodes. The abundance of incidents—many of them either too similar or too improbable—crowding close upon one another, and a lack of any warmth or colour in the style—though it too found admirers in the Renaissance—place this romance in a quite secondary class of fiction.

The next surviving Greek novel of any importance is *Daphnis and Chloë,* a pastoral romance of two foundlings, by a writer named Longus, who probably lived in Lesbos during the first part of the third century A.D. The boy child is set to keep the goats of his foster-father, and the girl to keep the sheep of her foster-mother. The young pair gradually become enamoured amid scenes of rural beauty, without understanding the nature of their strong mutual attraction. The story proceeds through

---

[1] This successful revolt against Persian rule really took place in the preceding reign of Darius II (414 B.C.).

the seasons of the year, with charming descriptions of pastoral occupations and enjoyments interspersed with some violent irruptions of pirates and other marauders—Pan is one case opportunely arriving to rescue Chloë. After each alarming incident the pair become fonder of each other; and in the end the master of the shepherd appears and discovers that Daphnis is his son, while Chloë is found to be the daughter of one of the guests at a feast which he is holding. Nuptials of the young lovers ensue, and they continue to live a pastoral life together in perfect happiness.

This much admired novel is composed throughout in a sweetly poetic vein, and suffers from the somewhat cloying monotony of its highly artificial style; which, however, in spite of tricks of assonance and antithesis, succeeds in diffusing an atmosphere of true love ripening in conditions of tranquil wellbeing and seclusion from the busy ambitions and struggles of the mass of mankind. The main interest is centred in the personal feelings of two young human beings whose occupations and thoughts are bounded by the annual cycle of pastoral life, free from any concern with communal or public affairs. The attractive French translation by Jaques Amyot in 1559 brought this tale into wide and lasting favour in France and other parts of Europe. In the same year he produced the first edition of his famous version of Plutarch's *Lives*. But twelve years before, as a young professor of Greek and Latin in the University of Bourges, he had started his career of accomplished translator with the issue in his graceful French of *Theagenes and Chariclea*, which first attracted and afterwards shared with his other versions of Diodorus, Longus and Plutarch, the lively interest in later Greek literature that direct reading and retranslation of them aroused among poets, essayists and romancers in France, England and other European countries.

To Heliodorus, the author of this story, unquestionably belongs the credit of having produced for Europe the first well-constructed, humanly appealing and generally plausible prose romance of the strange adventures of a pair of young lovers. From his own statement at the end of his book we learn that he was 'Heliodorus, a Phoenician of Emesa, son of Theodosius, of racial descent from the Sun (Helios)'. It is possible that he was the person mentioned by Flavius Philostratus, a learned biographer in the first quarter of the third century A.D., as 'Heliodorus the Arab',[1] a sophist then spending his last years in Rome; but the novelist definitely calls himself a Phoenician. His words about his descent might perhaps be taken to mean that he was one of a family of priests devoted to the service of the Sun-god at Emesa. This city, in Syria Phoenice, stood on the east bank of the River Orontes, and was famed for its great temple of the Syro-Phoenician Sun-god, and for the worship conducted there by members of a priestly family. The town now standing on its site is known as Homs.

Syria, after Alexander's death in 323 B.C., had been ruled by his able successors, the Seleucidae, who made Attic Greek the civic and commercial language of their great Asiatic empire in the third and second centuries B.C. In the next century Syria passed under Roman control (65 B.C.), but continued to be ruled by a succession of petty sovereigns, while the Roman governor resided at Antioch. Emesa was founded as a 'colony'—in the then usual sense of a strong military centre—by the emperor Caracalla (A.D. 211–17). About this time a young priest Bassianus was serving in the temple: he was a son of Julia Soemias, a cousin of Caracalla; but his mother, and his grandmother Julia Maesa, sister of Julia Domna, the second wife of the emperor Septimius Severus (A.D. 193–211), had put it about that Bassianus was really Caracalla's son. The Roman army in Syria, after killing the interloper Macrinus, who himself had had Caracalla murdered in that region, made the young priest emperor in 218 under the name of the Sun-god Elagabalus or Heliogabalus. The vicious debauchery and outrageous caprices of this youth, and his murder by the praetorian guards in 222, were followed by the well-ordered, reforming government of his cousin, Alexander Severus (222–35), son of Julia Soemias's sister, Julia Mammea.[2]

Julia Domna, the wife of Septimius Severus and mother of Caracalla, was a woman of learning, ambition, shrewd policy and

---

[1] Philostratus, *Vit. Sophist.* 22.
[2] All four of these astute and ambitious Julias were descended from a Phoenician of humble birth named Bassianus, and Caracalla, Elagabalus and Alexander Severus all bore his name.

licentious life. She held a court of her own at Antioch till 217, when she put an end to herself after the death of her depraved and brutal son. It seems probable that Heliodorus figured in her literary circle, but composed, or at any rate completed, his novel about 230, after reading with deep interest the Life of the sage Apollonius of Tyana (c. 10–97), a Greek city in Cappadocia: this work was compiled by Flavius Philostratus from some materials given to him by Julia Domna, and also from various other writings available to him, including treatises and letters of Apollonius himself. It is evident that the Life was not published till after the death of the empress in 217, since it is not dedicated to her. The important character and pronouncements of the Egyptian priest and sage Calasiris in Heliodorus's story bear a close resemblance to those of Apollonius, who is described by his biographer as an abstemious person and admiring follower of the principles of Pythagoras, partaking of no wine or flesh; he also preached against animal sacrifices, dancing and the use of money, and travelled up the Nile to study the tenets and conduct of the Gymnosophists, or naked sages, who dwelt in the Thebaid by the Upper Nile. Like Calasiris, he had, or professed to have, foreknowledge of certain crucial events through dreams and intimations vouchsafed to him by supernal spirits.

The remarkable revival of Greek literature, and especially of Greek prose writing, in the second century A.D. had received its first impulse from the teachings of a few Greek scholars in Rome towards the close of the first century B.C. Some works of history and literary criticism then produced by one of them, Dionysius of Halicarnassus—the Greek city on the coast of Caria which had given birth to Herodotus some 450 years before—have come down to us. Of particular interest are Dionysius's treatises and epistles on the styles of the most famous Greek historians and orators in the great days of the past. Early in the first century A.D. appeared a treatise *On the Sublime* (in literature) traditionally attributed to an unknown 'Longinus', and another work on good prose style by a certain Demetrius, perhaps to be identified with a native of Tarsus in Cilicia who taught Greek at York about A.D. 80. The writings of the Evangelists and St Paul show the character of the Greek language in common use throughout the eastern Roman Empire: in some pieces of narrative they achieve a simple eloquence reminiscent, though rather dimly, of passages in the forensic speeches of Lysias and the early dialogues of Plato. The great popularity of Plutarch, a native of Chaeronea in Boeotia (A.D. 45–125), in the Roman world was the natural result of his skill in anecdote, his abundant and vivid recording of events in the lives of his fifty great men, together with their personal habits and pithy sayings, and his numerous speculations and discussions on moral, antiquarian and many other subjects set forth in his miscellaneous essays or *Moralia*.

The zealous Hellenism of the emperor Hadrian (A.D. 117–38) gave a special stimulus to the revival of Greek ideas and teaching, mainly through the activities of a new generation of sophists lecturing and speech-making on a diversity of themes. These professional men of letters strove to attain the level of learning, composition and eloquence which had brought fame and affluence to the leading sophists of the fifth century B.C.[1] The new aspirants came from all parts of the Roman Empire. Among the most successful of them was a contemporary of Plutarch, Dion Chrysostom of Prusa (Broussa) in Bithynia, who after extensive tours about the eastern Mediterranean settled and practised as an impressive apostle of moral improvement in Rome under Trajan (A.D. 98–117). His discourses contain occasional passages of vivid, entertaining narrative. The activities of the wealthy and brilliant Herodes Atticus of Marathon, the highly successful Polemon of Laodicea in Phrygia and the fine stylist Aelius Aristides of Adriani in Mysia also contributed greatly to a widespread popular interest in this revival of the old Greek vogue of rhetorical and descriptive displays. Lucian of Samosata in Syria (125–95), and Flavius Philostratus of Ionia (170–*c*. 250) especially, with their exceptional powers of lively narration, description and dialogue, and the attractive interplay of learning and imagination that ensured the success of their lecture tours and published writings, restored much of its bygone prestige to Greek prose.

Lucian, in his *True History*, a copiously inventive skit on the wondrous tales of travellers—which was doubtless congenial and suggestive to Rabelais—and also in parts of his *Dialogues of the Dead* and those *of the Gods*, shows that he was not far from

[1] e.g. Protagoras, Prodicus, Hippias, Gorgias.

becoming a satirically entertaining novelist. His friend Alciphron composed imaginary epistles which present in a fine Attic style a variety of characters and scenes set in the Athens of the years about 300 B.C. Arrian of Nicomedia in Bithynia (*c*. A.D. 100–80) wrote valuable accounts of the moral precepts of Epictetus, the slave-born philosopher from Hierapolis in Phrygia who taught in Rome *c*. A.D. 50–120; of the campaigns of Alexander; and of his own coasting voyage round the Black Sea: he also produced histories of Parthia and Bithynia which have not survived. Like Epictetus, he was befriended by the emperor Hadrian. One other writer of note was Athenaeus, a Greek born at Naucratis in Egypt and living in Rome during the early years of the third century, who composed a pleasantly informative record of social life in Greece, with its banquets and their accompaniments of music and dancing and story-telling, from the Homeric age to his own time.

No statement of any value can be made about the life and character of Heliodorus beyond his own words, already quoted, at the end of his book, and the strong probability that he was acquainted with Flavius Philostratus and the *Life of Apollonius* through some connection with the court of Julia Domna or with that of the enlightened but unfortunate emperor Alexander Severus (A.D. 222–35), who was a native of Arce on the Phoenician coast only forty miles to the west of Emesa. A statement was made in the fifth century by Socrates, a church historian of Constantinople, that it was reported of a Heliodorus who held the bishopric of Tricca in the west of Thessaly that in his youth he had written a love-romance which he entitled *Aethiopica*. Much later, at the end of the thirteenth century, Nicephorus, another church historian, after quoting the statement of Socrates, added that Heliodorus, on being ordered by ecclesiastical authority either to have his novel burnt, on account of its dangerous influence on young people, or to resign his sacred office, chose the latter course. It is possible that the novelist was a devout pagan in his younger days, and later became a Christian and rose to be a bishop of the early church: his paganism, as it probably appears in some tenets of the sages Calasiris and Sisimithres, seems to be a refined religion, condemning human, and perhaps even animal, sacrifice, and preferring to approach the deity or deities with only prayers and incense. The severe order for the destruction of his novel or the resignation of his bishopric is apparently a late and ill-considered invention, since there is nothing in either the religious or the moral import of the story that could be reasonably held to imperil youthful piety or virtue; and by the time that Heliodorus had attained the episcopate copies of his novel had probably spread too widely for its suppression or repudiation to be feasible. But whether there be any grain of truth in these hearsays or not, the fact remains that Heliodorus was the author of the first elaborate and persistently successful romance of lovers' perplexing and often dangerous adventures that has come down to us from the prose writing of the ancient Mediterranean world.

The opening scene of the *Aethiopica*, in agreement with the skilful scheme of the *Odyssey*, plunges the reader into a stream of events which, when traced both backwards and forwards from this point, is found to affect drastically the lives and fortunes of two young people of exceptional beauty, ability and courage. Curiosity is at once aroused by an extraordinary situation of persons and things which demands full explanation through the gradual unwinding and disentangling of fortuitous threads. The sustained interest of the experiences, feelings and actions of a handsome and gallant youth and a brave and beautiful maiden in their wide wanderings and dire straits; their own and their occasional companions' thoughts and speculations at moments of special anxiety; the timely recognition of the lovely Chariclea, in the midst of mortal peril to them both, as the long-lost child of the king and queen of Ethiopia; and the final fulfilment of their constant purpose—her marriage to Theagenes—all these, with a series of vivid scenes of life in Greece, Egypt and Ethiopia, secured for Heliodorus' novel a great popularity in Byzantium and generally throughout the Greek-speaking world. It makes no attempt at being a vehicle for political or philosophic theorizing, for any deep exploration of the inner springs of human thought and conduct or for the propounding of any particular 'message'. Rather it sets forth in clear and rapid succession the immediate reactions of two ideal persons when confronted with difficult and dangerous emergencies that try their simple human powers of courage, endurance, intelligence and ingenuity, as they strive towards their joint deliverance and ultimate happiness.

Some important new features are worthy of note in the revived Greek literature of the second and third centuries A.D. No longer is it mainly confined in authorship and subject to the Hellenic people and their legends, ideas and affairs. It is written now with ability and charm by many others besides Greeks, in no national spirit, but rather from an individual standpoint and the promptings of personal interest and feeling, though always much indebted to the influence, by this time widespread over the civilized world, of the old Greek powers of perception, intelligence and expression. There is now also to be observed a definite trend towards lively entertainment in prose writing, especially through following the fortunes of ideally attractive or distinguished persons in a great variety of localities and circumstances. No doubt this new departure was largely due to the impact of oriental fantasies, which continually rely more on the strange waywardness of an imagined Destiny than on the reasoned accounting of cause and effect. Most of the striking events in the *Ethiopian Story* are attributed simply to Fortune; but many of them are found, through the superior discernment of a priest or prophet, to be the work of a deep-designing Providence. The main purpose of course is to lead the reader's imagination and sympathy through a series of impressive and, in its author's day, just credible scenes and happenings, interspaced with reflections and consultations in times of special perplexity and suspense. But incidentally it seeks to suggest how the higher powers contrive, by the uncovering of long-hidden truth and the persistence of an ardent devotion between two lovers, to deliver and bless the hero and heroine in their hour of greatest danger.

A grimly repellent scene is presented in the account [1] of the impious resort to nocturnal magic by an old witch who conjures up to momentary life the dead body of one of her two sons, in order to gain knowledge of the other's chance of survival in a marauding excursion. When Chariclea, witnessing this infernal business unseen with Calasiris, impulsively suggests that they should approach the old hag and ask for information about the fate of Theagenes, the sage refuses, saying that prophets are

[1] vi. 14–15.

forbidden to take part in any such practices; their divination is procured by lawful offerings and righteous prayers. Nevertheless we are told that the resuscitated corpse, after chiding his mother for her interference with his peace, and predicting the evil fate which is about to overtake both her other son and herself, commends the devout virtue of the prophet, and foretells his successful intervention in a bitter quarrel of his two sons, and also the final happy union of the girl with her lover. It seems that in devising this weird episode Heliodorus was recalling the gruesome sorceries of Erichtho as related in profuse detail by Lucan[1] in the time of Nero, and also, perhaps, the bitter prophecy given to Saul by Samuel, called up from the dead by the witch of En-dor.[2] Far from seeking to discredit the pagan religions of the West and the East, Calasiris, who probably expresses in general the beliefs and feelings of his author, tends to combine in one vague, mystical system the three cults of the Egyptian Isis, the Greek Apollo with his famed Delphic oracle, and the Syrian Elagabalus or Sun-god. He is constantly pointing to the efficacy of divination through dreams, but warns against the vulgar interest in ghosts and belief in the possible forecasting or control of events by a resort to magical arts.

Perhaps the most striking innovation in the *Aethiopica* is the energetic, courageous and resourceful companionship of the heroine in each menacing or embarrassing situation. Again and again the lively Chariclea reveals the practical character of her devotion to Theagenes by a quick ingenuity that extends even to adroit deception in both word and action.[3] In many an alarming crisis she stands out as the leader and inventive thinker of the pair. This prominence of the heroine marks a notable change from the ordinary classical Greek conception of the relative positions and roles of women and men in the activities of daily life; [4] and it is not surprising that this novel was often

[1] Lucan, *Pharsalia*, vi. 507 ff.

[2] 1 Samuel 28—known to the Roman world through the Greek version of the Septuagint made in Alexandria some four centuries before. Samuel begins by saying: 'Why hast thou disquieted me, to bring me up?'

[3] Calasiris himself too, on occasion, takes cunning action in the good cause.

[4] The comic surprise in each of Aristophanes' two plays, *Lysistrata* and *Ecclesiazusae*, consists partly in his wild exaggeration of current ideas about the emancipation of women, but is mainly based on the general exclusion of women from the conduct of public affairs.

referred to by later authors simply as *Chariclea*. Love in this story arises and flourishes chiefly through visual impressions, and its onset and sway are almost limited to the attraction of physical excellence. Salient examples of this swift rapture are seen in the effects upon Chariclea of the athletic feats of Theagenes in his three contests with Ormenus of Arcadia, the runaway bull and the huge Ethiopian.[1] The characters are individually distinct in the main lines of their temperaments, but are not elaborately or subtly drawn, being on the whole less important in themselves to the general interest than the variety and cumulative impact upon them of scenes and events in which they become involved in the course of the beguiling complications of the artfully constructed plot.[2]

As background to the story we are given some vividly presented aspects of life in Egypt—particularly in connection with the Nile—under the dominion of Persia before its conquest by Alexander in 322 B.C. The title *Aethiopica* was doubtless chosen because the heroine's life and strange adventures began and, presumably, ended in Ethiopia, and because the Persian satrap of Egypt, Oroondates, went to war against the Ethiopians, whose king, Hydaspes, gained a decisive victory, and unwittingly brought the vicissitudes of the two young lovers to a happy solution of their last and most perilous crisis.

In the opening scene, and at other important turns in the plot, an engaging effect is produced by a minute description of facial expressions, gestures and motions, which provides a sort of visual characterization of the persons most concerned at the moment. Although there is little to be found here of the psychological kind of portraiture, the human interest is enhanced by various stirrings and outbursts of Chariclea's emotions in times of stress, which clearly distinguish her from the type of an unswervingly right-minded and self-controlled young woman. We are shown also the odd waverings of the nervous simpleton, Cnemon; the vicious and criminal proceedings of the women Demaenete, Arsace and Cybele; and the kindly welcome and

---

[1] iv. 3–4; x. 28–30, 31–2.
[2] We have here the beginning of the realistic, picturesquely detailed characterization which Le Sage exploited so successfully in France of the early eighteenth century, and was so finely filled out with a wealth of humanity and humour by Fielding and Smollett in England.

help given to Calasiris and the young lovers by the deaf fisherman, Tyrrhenus, at Zacynthus. In general, the graceful courtesy between casual acquaintances, and the fatherly concern of Calasiris for his two companions' success and happiness, add not a little to the attractions of the tale. Potent forces in the causation of events are the activities of pirates and brigands, and the elaborate siege operations of King Hydaspes and his Ethiopians at Syene, followed by their decisive victory over the Persian army. The character and conduct of Thyamis, the brigand chief whose succession in a priestly family had been usurped by his younger brother, are of striking effect at critical points, and the attitude of Hydaspes towards his captives and his gradual conviction of his daughter's identity, maintain a lively interest in the closing scenes. Touches of humour are sparse but brisk, and contribute to the actuality and warmth of the talk. The narrative style is lucid, often brightly eloquent. At times, in describing certain dazzling manifestations of Chariclea's beauty, or some ceremonial or momentous event, the writing verges on the elevation of poetry, with a few echoes of epic or dramatic lines from the great classics. Occasionally the author's indulgence in a fanciful conjunction of ideas or artificially balanced words or phrases betrays the influence of dramatists and rhetoricians of the past transmitted by the literary sophists who were flourishing in the second and third centuries of the Roman Empire. But in the main the style of Heliodorus is one of simple directness, enlivened here and there by specially elegant or resonant phrasing. The Athenian Cnemon's account of his stepmother Demaenete's wicked endearments and slander of him, with their grievous consequences, and the episode of the attempted seduction of Theagenes by the Persian satrap's wife, Arsace, are presented with admirable skill and verve.

An imitator of Heliodorus, Achilles Tatius of Alexandria, who wrote about A.D. 260, resorted to a more elaborate style than that of his model in *Cleitophon and Leucippe*, a romance which, in spite of absurd crudities in its contrivance of surprises and its character-drawing, is not lacking in varied interest and occasional passages of picturesque charm. The whole story is told by the hero Cleitophon who, enamoured of his cousin Leucippe, flees with her from his home in Tyre to Egypt. They are there captured by bandits; Leucippe is roughly handled by them, and the lovers pass through a series of dangers and narrow escapes from death, some of which appear to have been borrowed from Heliodorus. Cleitophon, believing Leucippe to have been killed, marries a supposed widow in Ephesus, whose husband reappears and prosecutes Cleitophon, while Cleitophon discovers Leucippe among the husband's slaves. After much tedious argument the lovers are liberated and happily reunited. Some of the incidents are pleasantly devised, but there is gross improbability and a too rapid succession in others. Parts of the work, which betray casual patchwork rather than a well-planned, cumulative design like that of the *Aethiopica*, give good descriptions of pictures and rural scenes—some taken from a younger Philostratus—but also inapposite digressions on matters of natural history and others not at all contributory to the main interest. As in Heliodorus' scheme, the hero's character is of less importance than the heroine's; but the progress of the passion and courtship of the pair is presented in gradual stages, unlike the immediate attraction and devotion to each other of Theagenes and Chariclea. This romance enjoyed much popularity in Constantinople, and was held in esteem there by the accomplished teacher and patriarch Photius in the ninth, and also by scholars and *littérateurs* in Europe generally during the sixteenth and seventeenth centuries.

Of greater import to literary history are the clear traces of the effects of Heliodorus' work on writers before, during and since the Renaissance. The numerous romances of adventure in the Middle Ages are notable for an increased use of supernatural agencies, in the shape of witches, enchanters, dragons, griffins and other fabulous monsters, introduced either by bards from the North or by crusaders and travellers returning from the East. Some of these romances also rely on substantial borrowings from old classical stories of the arts and practices of enchantresses like Circe and Medea, and of such monstrous creatures as the Cyclopes, Centaurs and Chimaeras—stories which had spread through the East after Alexander's conquests and returned thence in later times to the West with abundant accretions of marvels. With the rise of the feudal system came the accepted duty of nobles to go to the rescue of distressed damsels and other

victims of villainy, aided by squires from among the commonalty
who in time might become eligible for knighthood. The armed
combats of ancient days now took the form of tournaments, at
which knights displayed their prowess in tilting and impressed
more or less favourably the onlooking ladies whom they had
vowed to serve. The contest at Delphi between Theagenes and
Ormenus for the palm of victory to be bestowed by Chariclea [1]
manifestly gives the pattern for the later institution of the
tournament.

The vast, now much faded and almost forgotten, phantas-
magoria of the romances of chivalry doubtless served in their
day the purpose of literary entertainment, and had no little
effect on later relations between the sexes. In many of them
fragments of ancient Greek lore were expanded and embroidered
into fanciful tales of Achilles, Hercules, Jason and other heroes;
and among historical persons Alexander and Virgil were endowed with magical powers. These stories of wonderful adventures and valorous exploits provided Cervantes with material
for presenting to the world his immortal characters of Don
Quixote and his squire. Sir Philip Sidney's immature and
unevenly eloquent romance of *Arcadia*, in the true chivalric
tradition, bears upon its fabric of heroes' and heroines' adventures clear traces of familiarity with the *Aethiopica*; and the
activities of pirates and bandits, including the detention of an
important lady in a cave, seem to have passed from Heliodorus'
story through the Spanish fiction of the life of Maros de Obregon
to Le Sage's lively, skilful and widely popular romance of *Gil
Blas*. Tasso greatly admired the art with which the *Ethiopian
Story* is unfolded, and he reproduced almost exactly the account
of Chariclea's birth as the white daughter of the Ethiopian queen
Persinna in his lines on the birth of Clorinda in *Gerusalemme
Liberata* (xii); and in Guarini's *Pastor Fido* (v) the impending
sacrifice of a son by his father is averted in a similar manner to
that of Chariclea by her father, King Hydaspes. Rabelais,
besides his already suggested debt to Lucian, shows his acquaintance with our novelist by relating how Pantagruel (iv. 63)
slumbered in his ship holding a Greek text of Heliodorus in his
hand. Racine in his youth was quite captivated by the *Aethiopica*,

[1] iv. 1–4.

even to the extent of learning it, or perhaps most of it, by heart. His son Louis records that 'he had conceived in his childhood an extraordinary passion for Heliodorus: he admired his style and the marvellous art with which he tells his story'. During his sojourn at Uzès Racine began a play—*Theagène et Chariclée*—on that story, but later abandoned it, 'no doubt', his son says, 'because he felt that romantic adventures were not worthy of the tragic stage'. Although the force and refinement of the passions that actuate the dramas of his maturer years are on a plane more comparable to that of the greatest scenes in ancient Greek tragedy than to that of Heliodorus' ingeniously devised and conducted story, it may fairly be guessed that the passion of Phèdre, as it turns in her frustration to furious hate, owes something of its intensity to Racine's early emotion over the episodes of Arsace's consuming desire for Theagenes and Demaenete's attempted seduction and slander of her stepson Cnemon. To Heliodorus may also be attributed the first impulse of Racine's persistent and impressive exploitation for drama of the feminine mind and temperament, in striking contrast with the masculine tragedies of Corneille. And in yet another respect—the causation of events—we can reasonably regard the emphasis constantly given by Racine to an inscrutable, unalterable fatality governing human affairs as due in some measure to the early impression received from his admiring absorption in the varying fortunes and ordeals of Theagenes and Chariclea—all mysteriously designed by 'the higher powers'.

Cervantes, shortly after he had published the second part of *Don Quixote*, produced his romance of *Persiles and Sigismunda*, which he hoped would win a popularity equal to that of the *Aethiopica*. This story of his, in the serious vein of traditional romance, had an immediate, though for him an ineffectual, success: he died a poor man soon after its appearance in 1616. Shakespeare was doubtless alluding to the murderous act of Thyamis in the brigands' cave of the *Aethiopica* (i. 30) when he made the Duke in *Twelfth Night* say (v. 1):

> 'Like to the Egyptian thief at point of death
> Kill what I love—a savage jealousy
> That sometimes savours nobly.'

And Montaigne,[1] writing on *The Affection of Fathers to their Children*, after he has praised Heliodorus for choosing to lose his bishopric rather than his daughter (namely, his romance of *Theagenes and Chariclea*,[2] but with particular reference to his creation of the heroine), goes on with the gentle comment: 'A daughter that continues to this day very graceful and comely, but, peradventure, a little too curiously and wantonly tricked, and too amorous for an ecclesiastical and sacerdotal daughter'—Chariclea, at her first meeting with Theagenes, being a ministrant in the temple of Apollo at Delphi.

The Greek text of the *Aethiopica, or Theagenes and Chariclea*, was first printed by Vincent Obsopoeus of Basle in 1534. He had acquired a manuscript of the work that had been looted by a soldier who had taken part in the pillage of the great library of Matthias Corvinus, King of the Magyars, at Buda when the royal palace was sacked by the Turks after the battle of Mohacs in 1526. With the aid of other manuscripts that had come to light an improved text was produced in 1596 by H. Commelinus at Heidelberg; it was accompanied by a Latin translation made by a Polish scholar, Stanislaus Warschewiczki, which had appeared at Basle in 1552 and had been used by the Elizabethan Thomas Underdowne for his pleasant, rather free-and-easy English translation, best known in its revised edition of 1587. Another English version, by Nahum Tate, was produced in 1686, and was followed by an anonymous one of some distinction in 1791.

The editions mainly used for the present translation, in which verbal accuracy has been sought, together with some reflection of the revived classicism and the changes in mood of the author's style, are those of C. J. Mitscherlich, with its Latin translation (Strasbourg, 1798); Coray (Paris, 1804); and R. M. Rattenbury and T. W. Lumb, comprising an admirably documented and revised text, an introduction discussing the author, his work and the manuscript evidence, and a French translation, with another introduction, by J. Maillon (*Les Belles Lettres*, Paris, 3 vols., 1935, 1938, 1943).

W. R. M. LAMB.

[1] *Essays*, ii. 8. (transl. Charles Cotton).
[2] According to the late tradition (above, p. xii).

CONTENTS

CONTENTS XXV

BOOK I

*A strange scene around two young lovers, resulting from a feast
and a fray near the mouth of the Nile, is espied by some brigands.*

(1) The cheerful smile of day was just appearing, as the rays
of the sun began to light up the mountain tops, when some men
armed like brigands peered over the ridge that stretches alongside the outlets of the Nile and that mouth of the river which is
named after Hercules.[1] They halted there for a little while,
scanning with their eyes the sea that lay below them; and when
they had cast their first glances over the ocean and found no craft
upon it and no promise there of pirates' plunder, they bent their
gaze down upon the shore near by. And what it showed was this:
a merchant ship was moored there by her stern cables, bereft of
her ship's company, but full laden; so much could be inferred
even at a distance, for her burthen brought the water as high as
the third waling-piece of her timbers. The shore was thickly
strewn with newly slain bodies, some quite lifeless, and others
half dead whose limbs were still aquiver, thus indicating that the
conflict had only just ceased. That it had been no regular engage-
ment was betokened by what was visible; for there lay mingled
the pitiful remnants of a feast that had thus come to no happy
conclusion. There were tables still laden with their victuals;
some others, overturned on the ground, were held in the grasp
of those of the vanquished who had used them as armour in the
struggle, for it had been a fight on the spur of the moment; and
underneath others were men who had crept there in the hope of
concealment. Wine-bowls were upset, and some were slipping
from the hands of their holders—either drinkers or those who
had taken them up to use as missiles instead of stones. The
suddenness of the clash enforced innovations in the uses of things
and prompted the hurling of drinking-cups. Here lay a man
wounded with an axe, there one struck by a stone that the shingle
had provided on the spot, another mangled by a piece of timber

[1] The most westerly or Canopic mouth of the Nile, near the Libyan desert.

1

and another burnt to death by a firebrand; but most had fallen victims to darts and arrows. Countless were the varieties of sights that Fate had produced upon that small area—befouling wine with blood, thrusting battle upon banquet, with conjunction of killing and swilling, libation and laceration—so strange was the scene thus displayed to the Egyptian brigands. They had taken their places on that mountain height as spectators of this scene, but could not apprehend its meaning: they had the vanquished lying there, but nowhere could they see the victors. The conquest was clear as day, but the spoils were unseized; while the vessel, deserted and void of men, yet held its cargo intact, as though protected by a strong guard, and it rocked gently at its moorings as in a time of peace. But, although at a loss to know what could have occurred, they looked to the gain to be had in the booty, and assuming the part of victors they dashed on.

(2) When they had advanced to a little way short of the ship and the fallen, they came upon a sight more unaccountable than what they had seen before. A young girl was seated on a rock, so inconceivably beautiful as to convince one that she was a goddess. Though sorely anguished by her present plight, she yet breathed forth a high and noble spirit. Her head was crowned with laurel; a quiver was slung over her shoulder; and her left arm was propped upon her bow, beyond which the hand hung negligently down. The elbow of her other arm she supported on her right thigh, while on its palm she rested her cheek; and with downcast eyes she held her head still, gazing intently on a prostrate youth. He, cruelly wounded, seemed to be faintly awakening as from a deep slumber that was wellnigh death. Yet, for all that, he had upon him the bloom of manly beauty, and his cheek, stained red by the gushing of his blood, showed forth its whiteness all the more brightly. The sufferings of the youth were weighing down his eyes; but the sight of her drew them upward to her, compelled to see by merely seeing her. Then, collecting his breath and heaving a profound sigh, in a weak undertone he said: 'My sweet one, are you truly with me, still alive? Or have you too fallen by chance a victim to the fighting, and cannot any way endure, even after death, to be parted from me, but your wraith and your soul yet show concern for my fortunes?' 'On you,' she answered, 'it rests whether I live or die. Now, do you see this?'

she added, showing a sword that lay upon her knees. 'Hitherto
it has been idle, withheld by your breathing.' As she spoke she
sprang up from the rock: the men on the mountain, struck, with
wonder and alarm by the sight, as though by some fiery blast,
cowered under bushes here and there, for she seemed to them
to be something greater and more divine when she stood erect.
Her arrows rattled with her sudden movement; the inwoven gold
of her dress glistened in the beams of the sun, and her hair,
tossing below the wreath like the tresses of a bacchant, flowed
widespread over her back. All this and, more than what they saw,
their ignorance of what was happening, filled them with terror:
they either said she was some goddess—the goddess Artemis, or
Isis, the deity of that country—or supposed her to be a priestess
who, in a god-sent frenzy, had wrought the massacre that they
saw before them. Thus they opined, as yet unable to form a true
opinion. Then the maiden, descending swiftly upon the young
man and enfolding his whole person in her arms, wept and
kissed him, wiped his wounds and lamented, still in doubt of
her holding him. Seeing this, the Egyptians turned their thoughts
to other reasonings. 'How could these be the actions of a goddess?' they asked; 'how could a deity kiss a corpse with such
fervid passion?' So they urged one another to be brave, and by
advancing nearer learn the truth of the matter. They thus
recovered themselves, and running down they came upon the
maiden as she was still intent on the young man's wounds; then,
having come to a halt behind her, they did not venture to say or
do anything. The noisy clatter of the men, and their shadows
slanting across her view, caused the maiden to raise her head:
she looked, then bent it down again, not in the least dismayed by
their strange colour and brigand-like appearance—armed as they
showed themselves to be—but wholly engaged in tending the
prostrate youth. So it is that a true-hearted affection, a genuine
love, will despise all pains and pleasures alike that may intrude
from without, and will constrain the mind to regard and gratify
the beloved one alone.

(3) The brigands moved up, then stopped in front of the girl
and seemed to be on the point of taking some action. Again she
raised her head and, seeing their sable hue and unkempt appearance, said: 'If you are phantoms of the fallen, you have no right

to molest us, since most of you were slain by each other's hands; while those of you who were killed by us have met your fate through lawful self-defence and in retribution for vile assault on chastity. If you are among the living, your life, it would seem, is one of brigandage; but your coming here is timely. Release us from the sufferings that harass us by killing us and bringing to its close the drama of our destiny.' Thus she spoke to them, in high tragic vein; but they, unable to understand one word of what she said, left the young couple there, deeming their weakness a strong enough guard to be set over them. The brigands then hastened to the ship, which they proceeded to ransack for her cargo. Despising the rest of her contents, which were many and various, they bore off as much as each man could carry of gold, silver, precious stones and silken attire. When they thought that they had got enough—it was as much as might satiate even pirates' greed—they laid down their booty on the shore and divided it up into separate loads which they apportioned, not according to the value of each article seized, but to an equality of weight of burdens. As to what should be done with the maiden and the youth, this they would leave over to a later time.

A larger band of brigands arrives on the scene under their leader Thyamis.

At this moment another troop of brigands appeared, with two horsemen at its head. When the former band observed it, without showing any resistance or carrying off any of their spoils—so eager were they to evade pursuit—they fled as fast as they could run: they were but ten in number, and perceived the new-comers to be thrice as many. Thus were the girl and her companion a second time made captives before being captured. These brigands, however, despite their eagerness to be at the plunder, stayed their steps awhile in amazement at a sight that passed their comprehension. All that slaughter, they surmised, had been the work of the former brigands, while they saw the maiden dressed in resplendent foreign attire and ignoring the perils that beset her as though they did not even exist, so entirely concerned she was with the young man's wounds, and pained by his suffering as if it were her own. They admired her for her beauty and her spirit, and were amazed at him, wounded though he was, so fine and tall a figure he made lying there; for by now he was slightly revived, and was recovering the usual look in his eyes.

(4) After some little delay the brigand chief took hold of the girl and bade her rise and follow him. She understood no word of what he said, but guessing the sense of what he ordered she drew along with her the young man, who on his part would not let go of her; then, levelling her sword at her breast, she threatened to kill herself if they did not bring away the two of them. The brigand chief, understanding her not so much by her words as by her gestures, and also expecting to have the youth as an assistant, if he survived, in their major exploits, dismounted his henchman and himself from their horses and placed the prisoners on their saddles. He ordered the others to pack up the booty and follow him, while he ran on foot beside the prisoners and held them up when they might be losing their balance. There was something to count as glory in this proceeding: the master was to be seen acting as a slave, and the victor choosing to do a service to his captives. So it is that a noble presence and the sight of beauty have the secret of subduing even a brigand's nature, and the power to control even the most uncouth of creatures.

The two lovers, Theagenes and Chariclea, are carried off by the later brigands to their habitation on a lagoon, and are put in the charge of a Greek youth.

(5) After passing along the seashore for about two furlongs they turned and made straight for the mountain slopes, having the sea on their right. They climbed over the ridge with some difficulty, and then hastened on to a lagoon, which extended below the far side of the range and was of this nature: the whole region is named by the Egyptians 'Herdsmen's Home'; it is a low-lying tract in those parts which receives certain overflows of the Nile, so as to form a lake which is of immense depth at its centre but dwindles towards its edges into a swamp. What shores are to seas, swamps are to lakes. Here it is that Egyptians of the bandit kind have their city: one man has built himself a cabin on a patch of land that may lie above the water level; another makes

his dwelling in a boat which serves at once for transport and for habitation; upon this the women spin their wool, and also bring forth their children. When a child is born, it is reared at first on its mother's milk, but thereafter on the fish taken from the lagoon and broiled in the sun. When they observe the child attempting to crawl, they fasten a thong to its ankles which allows it to move to the limits of the boat or the hut, thus singularly making the tethering of their feet serve instead of leading them by the hand.

(6) Hence many a herdsman has been born on the lagoon, and reared in this manner, and so come to regard the lagoon as his homeland; and it fully serves as a strong bastion for brigands. Into it therefore flows a stream of men in that way of life, all relying on the water as a wall, and the abundant growth of reeds in the swamp as a stockade. By cutting a number of winding paths which straggle in many twists and turns, and by contriving exits which, while easy enough for them through their familiarity, are bewildering to strangers, they have ingeniously produced a fastness of surpassing strength to ward off harm that might come upon them from an onslaught. So much for the lagoon and the herdsmen who dwell within it.

(7) Towards the hour of sunset the brigand chief and his troop arrived at the lagoon. They dismounted the young pair from the horses, and placed the booty in their boats; while the main body of the brigands who had remained in the region, emerging from various parts of the swamp, were seen running together to greet their chief with a welcome suited to one who ruled over them like a king. When they saw the vast amount of the spoil and gazed upon the beauty of the girl as on something sublime, they supposed that some temples or gold-enriched shrines had been pillaged by their confederates, who moreover had abducted the priestess herself; or in their boorish simplicity they surmised from the girl's appearance that the living image of a goddess had actually been carried off. Showering praises on their chieftain for his steadfast valour, they escorted him to his dwelling-place: it was an islet lying at some distance from the rest, which had been assigned as a solitary retreat for him and his few companions. On retiring there he ordered the main body to depart to their homes, with the direction that they should all

come to him on the morrow. He himself, left alone with his few intimates, treated these to a brief repast, of which he also partook. The young captives he put in the charge of a Greek youth, taken prisoner by the brigands shortly before, through whom he might converse with them and to whom he allotted a cabin close to his own, commanding him to take due care of the young man, but especially to guard the maiden from any outrage. Then he, over-borne by the fatigue of his journeying, and feeling the strain of his present concerns, betook himself to sleep.

(8) Silence reigned over the swamp, and night had entered on the first watch;[1] the girl and her friend now, in the absence of any people likely to interfere with them, were given an opportunity for lamentation. Night, I imagine, stirred up their woes the more, because neither hearing nor sight distracted their reflections, and free scope was then allowed to their grief alone. So the girl, after wailing aloud by herself—for by order given she had been put in a place apart, and was lying on a low pallet bed—and having shed very many tears—'Apollo,' she said, 'with what excessive bitterness do you punish us for our offences! Are not the past events sufficient for your vengeance? Bereft of our kinsfolk, captured by murderous pirates, and after a thousand perils on the sea taken prisoners once again by brigands on the land, we have now the prospect of ordeals more severe than those that we underwent before. Where will you stay your hand? If it is to be at a death that I may meet unravished, sweet will be my end; but if anyone is to know me vilely, me whom not even Theagenes has yet possessed, I will forestall the outrage with a noose, having preserved myself then, as I have done till now, a pure virgin unto death, and taking with me my chastity as a noble winding-sheet. And I shall have no judge more severe than you.' As she was yet speaking she was stopped by Theagenes. 'Enough,' he said, 'my dearest, my very life, Chariclea! Your laments are natural, but you provoke the deity more than you are aware. He is not to be reproached, but en-treated; the higher power is appeased by prayers, not by accusations.' 'You are right,' she said; 'but tell me, how is it with you?' 'Easier and better since the evening,' he replied,

---

[1] The first of three periods taken in turn by Greek sentries during the night.

'thanks to this lad's attentions, which have relieved the inflammation of my wounds.' 'And also,' said the person charged with their custody, 'you will have even greater relief by the morning. I will supply you with a kind of herb that in two days' time will close up those gashes; I have tested its effect in actual use. For since these people brought me here a prisoner, whenever any of this chieftain's subjects came in wounded from an affray, their cure took only a few days' treatment with the herb of which I speak. My concern for the fortunes of you both should cause you no surprise: you appear to be sharing the same lot with me, and besides, being Greeks, you have my pity, since I am myself a Greek by birth.' 'A Greek? O Heaven!' exclaimed the two strangers together in delight; a Greek in very truth, by birth and by language! Perhaps we are to have some respite from our troubles.' 'But by what name are we to call you?' asked Theagenes. 'Cnemon,' he replied. 'And what citizenship do you claim?' 'Athenian.' 'What fortune have you met with?' 'Stop,' he answered; ' "why dost batter and unbar" all that?—as they say in tragedy.[1] This is no time to thrust in an episode of my troubles upon the drama of yours. Besides, the remainder of the night would not suffice for my story to be told, especially as you are in need of sleep and repose after all your hardships.'

The Greek youth Cnemon tells his distressful story to the two lovers, with the wicked devices of his stepmother Demaenete and her maid Thisbe.

(9) When they would not give way, but begged him by all means to speak on, expecting to find no small consolation in hearing of troubles like their own, Cnemon began his relation thus: 'My father was Aristippus, an Athenian by birth, a member of the Senate, and a man of moderate wealth. When in course of time my mother died, he let himself lapse into a second marriage, complaining that he had me as his one and only child to depend upon. He brought into the house a woman who was elegant indeed, but a fount of evil,[2] named Demaenete. For from the

---

[1] He quotes from Euripides, *Medea*, 137, where Medea, aloft in her magic chariot, bids Jason cease battering vainly at the doors of the house below.

[2] This rare epithet is applied by Homer, *Il.* v. 63, to the Greek ships that sailed against Troy.

moment of her arrival she was getting him entirely into her
power and persuading him to do whatever she wished, by
seducing the old man with her charms and coddling him in one
way or another, as clever a woman as ever lived at making a man
besotted with her, and marvellously expert in the art of seduction
—groaning at my father's goings-out and running to him at his
comings-in, reproaching him for his late return, and saying that
she would have died if he had delayed a moment longer, with
embracements at every word and tears mingled with her kisses.
Ensnared with all these wiles, my father made her absolutely his
life-breath, his eyesight. Me she at first affected to regard as her
son—another trick of hers to captivate Aristippus. Sometimes
she would come and kiss me, and continually begged that she
might have enjoyment of me. I bore with her behaviour, having
no suspicion of her real meaning, but only a feeling of wonder at
this display of a motherly attitude towards me. But when she
accosted me more recklessly, and her kisses were more ardent
than was seemly, and her glances so far passed the bounds of
modesty that I began to feel suspicious, I then made a rule of
shunning her and repulsing her advances. For the rest, why
should I trouble you with a lengthy account—of the persistent
attempts that she made upon me, the promises that she
held out, calling me now her little boy, now her sweet dear, and
then again, addressing me as her heir and, in the next moment,
her very soul? In short, she mingled the choicest terms with her
enticements, and was at pains to devise any and every means of
drawing me in to her. For, although in her more serious moods
she assumed the role of mother, in her more abandoned moments
she revealed herself actually in the glaring character of lover.

(10) 'In the end it came to this. The Great Panathenaean
Festival was being held, in which the Athenians carry the ship
to Athena in a procession overland.[1] I was a young man, just
come of age: after I had sung the customary paean to the goddess
and joined in the traditional procession, I made my way home,
still dressed up in the particular cloak and garlands of the

[1] This chief festival of Athens was held every four years in August, and
comprised musical, gymnastic, equestrian and rowing contests. The great
procession of victors to the Acropolis (partly shown in the sculptured frieze
of the Parthenon) brought a new robe for the statue of Athena Polias, and a
ship on which the robe hung like a sail.

ceremony. At her first sight of me she became quite demented, and dropped all artful concealment of her love. Laying bare her longing, she ran up to me and embraced me, saying: "My young Hippolytus!" What, do you suppose, was the effect of this on me? Even now I blush to relate it. Well, when evening came, my father was out dining at the town hall, where the festal assembly with its civic carousal would naturally detain him all night. She then took me unawares in the night time, and tried to obtain from me what was criminal. I made all the resistance in the world, and fought off every blandishment and promise and menace; then, with a deep and heavy groan, she left me and went away. No sooner had the abominable creature passed the night than she put in motion her plots against me. First, without rising that day from her bed, she pretended to my father, when he came to inquire what was the matter, that she was in a feeble state, and made no reply at first. On his pressing her and asking again and again what had happened to her, she said: "That wonderful pious young man, son to us both, whom—the gods are my witnesses—I have often treated with more affection even than you, perceived by some signs that I was with child. For the time I was hiding this from you till I could know it for certain. He watched for your absence and, while I was giving him my usual good advice, and admonishing him to be temperate and keep his thoughts off courtesans and drinking-bouts—for I was quite aware of these habits of his, but did not mention them to you for fear of being looked upon as a stepmother—while I was thus speaking to him, alone with me so that I should not put him to the blush, I am ashamed to repeat all the vile insults that he heaped on you as well as me; and then he rushed at me and gave me a kick in the stomach which put me in the condition that you see."

(11) 'After hearing her words he said nothing, he asked no question, he allowed me no chance of defence. Convinced that this woman, so well disposed towards me, could never slander me, in that instant and on the spot where he found me in a part of the house, while I knew nothing of the matter, he struck me with his fists, and summoning servants he had me cruelly flogged, though I lacked even the knowledge, that is commonly given, of the reason for my thrashing. When he had sated his

rage, "Oh, now at least, father," I said, "if I could not before, I may fairly be told the reason for this beating." His anger flared up then all the more and—"Ha, playing the innocent!" he said; "he wants me to tell him of his impious doings!" Then turning away he hastened to Demaenete. She, for her wrath was still not glutted, put in hand a second design against me, in this way. She had a young maidservant named Thisbe, who could sing to her own lute-playing and was not uncomely to look upon. This girl she set upon me with orders to make a show of loving me, and Thisbe promptly made love. Having frequently repulsed my advances, she was now seeking in every way to allure me—by glances, motions of the head and other tokens. I, in my vanity, believed that of a sudden I had become good looking, and at length I received her one night in my room. She came to me a second time, and then again, and after that she was continually paying me visits. Once, when I strongly urged her to take good care not to be detected by her mistress, she said: "Cnemon, I find you are too much of a simpleton: if you think it a bad business for me, a maidservant bought with money, to be caught in intercourse with you, what punishment would you say that woman deserves who, claiming to be well born, and having her lawful spouse, and knowing that death is the end in store for such transgression, commits adultery?" "Stop," I said; "I cannot believe you." "I tell you," she went on, "that if you were so minded, I could expose her gallant in the very act." "If only you would care to do so," I said. "To be sure I will," she replied, "not only for your sake, since she has caused you to be so grossly maltreated, but as much for my own, suffering as I do the vilest usage every day at the hands of that woman, who wreaks her senseless jealousy upon me. Now, mind that you play the man."

(12) 'I promised that I would so acquit myself; she then left me and departed. On the third night following she roused me from sleep and informed me that the adulterer was in the house: my father, she said, had gone on a journey into the country on some sudden call of business, and the gallant, by arrangement with Demaenete, had just then slipped in; I must be prepared to punish them, and must break in upon them, blade in hand, so that the rascal should not make his escape. I did as she bade me.

Dagger in hand, with Thisbe guiding me and lighting torches, I approached the bedroom. Stopping there I saw the gleam of some lamplight emanating from within. The door was closed: in the heat of my anger I burst it open, and rushing in I cried: "Where is the criminal, the dashing lover of this spotless chastity?"—and as I spoke I advanced to dispatch them both. From the bed, ye gods! my father, turning round, threw himself at my knees, saying: "My son, stay a moment! Have pity on him who begot you! Spare the hoary head that nurtured you! I have maltreated you, but not so as to deserve the penalty of death. Let not your wrath so possess you, nor pollute your hands with a father's blood!" With these and other appeals added to them he besought my mercy, while I, as though caught in a tornado, stood there, struck senseless as a stone, looking round for Thisbe —who had crept away, I know not how—and casting my eyes all about the bed and the room, utterly at a loss for words and incapable of any action. My weapon fell from my grasp; Demaenete ran forward and eagerly snatched it up; and my father, finding himself out of danger, laid hands on me and ordered me to be bound, while Demaenete continually fomented his rage, crying: "The very thing against which I cautioned you, when I told you to beware of the lad, as he would seize the first opportunity of doing us a mischief! I saw the look in his eyes, and read there his purpose." "You did caution me," he said, "but I did not believe it." For the time he kept me in bonds; I wanted to tell something of the facts, but he would not allow me to do so, or to speak a single word.

(13) 'At break of day he took me, bound as I was, before the people and, his head all bespattered with ashes, he said: "Nothing like this did I anticipate, men of Athens, in nurturing this person. Looking forward rather to his being a staff for my old age, I bestowed on him, as soon as he was born to me, a liberal upbringing. I taught him the rudiments of grammar; I made him a member of a clan, with the highest rank in it; I enrolled him in the class of adult students; and having thus established him as your fellow-citizen I anchored my whole existence upon him. But he, forgetful of all this, first outraged me with insults, and my wife here, my lawfully wedded housemate, with blows, and ended by attacking us at night, blade in hand, and was only

prevented from committing parricide by the fortune of a surprise alarm causing his weapon to fall from his grasp. I have turned to you for protection, and now denounce him to you. Our laws permit me to kill him myself, but I would not do it, preferring to leave the whole matter to your judgment, because I hold it better to punish a son through the law than by private slaughter." With that he shed tears, while Demaenete on her part lamented and made a great show, slyly enough, of grieving deeply over me, calling me a poor wretch now doomed to die, justly but before his time, who had been driven on by malignant spirits to assail his parents. So she wailed on—nay rather, testified against me with her wailing, as though confirming the truth of her accusation with her mournful cries. When I claimed to be allowed my turn to speak, the clerk came to me and put to me one bare question—whether I had attacked my father blade in hand. When I answered "I did attack him, but hear how this came about," with a great shout they all gave the verdict that I should not be allowed even to make a defence. Some were for stoning me, others for handing me over to the executioner and flinging me into the death-pit. And I, through all this uproar, and during the time of their voting to decide which punishment I was to suffer, kept on shouting: "A stepmother is the cause of my destruction! A stepmother is putting me to death untried!" My words reached the greater part of the assembly, and led them to suspect the truth. Even then I was not granted a hearing, so completely had the people been carried away by that ungovernable clamour.

(14) 'When the votes for the sentence were counted, those whose verdict was for death, either by stoning or by flinging into the death-pit, numbered about one thousand seven hundred; the rest, about a thousand, being those who inclined to a suspicion of my stepmother, condemned me to perpetual banishment. However, it was the vote of the latter that prevailed: for, although they were fewer than the whole body of the others, the thousand outnumbered either section of the divided vote of the rest. Accordingly I was expelled from the paternal hearth and the land of my birth. Yet Demaenete, with the gods' hatred upon her, did not remain unpunished. The manner of her fate you shall hear some other time; for the present you must take some

sleep, since the night is far spent, and you are in need of a long rest.' 'But you will only add to our distress', said Theagenes, 'if your story is to leave the pernicious Demaenete unpunished.'

'Well then, listen,' said Cnemon, 'since that is your desire. Immediately after that decision I went down without further ado to the Piraeus, and found there a vessel just putting to sea on which I voyaged to Aegina, because I had information that some cousins of my mother were there. I landed and found the people whom I was seeking, and at first the time went not unpleasantly for me. On the twentieth day of my visit I was strolling about in my usual way, and came down to the harbour, where a skiff was just coming in. So I stopped for a little to observe whence it hailed and what persons it had on board. The gangway had not yet been properly fixed when somebody leapt ashore, ran up to me and embraced me. It was Charias, one of my student group. "Cnemon," he said, "I bring you good news. You are avenged on your enemy. Demaenete is dead." "My best wishes to you, Charias," I said; "but why do you scamper so over this good news, as though it were something sinister that you were announcing? Go on and tell me how it happened, for I greatly fear she has met with a natural death, and eluded her deserts." "Not altogether", said Charias, "has Justice forsaken us, as Hesiod says: [1] at times, indeed, she may disregard some slight matter, drawing out the time for its requital; but sharp is the glance that she turns upon such unlawful acts as these, and so has she called to account the guilt-laden Demaenete. I have full knowledge of what was done or said, since Thisbe, as you are aware, was on intimate terms with me, and she told me the whole story. When that unjust exile had been inflicted upon you, your unhappy father, repenting of his actions, removed to a distant part of the country and there dwelt, 'devouring his own soul' —to quote the poem.[2] As for her, the Furies were not slow to drive her on: she loved you more madly in your absence, uttering ceaseless laments—over you, seemingly, but really over herself— and crying out 'Cnemon!' night and day, and calling you her darling boy, her very life; so that the women of her acquaintance who came to visit her were full of admiration; they praised this

---

[1] Referring to Hesiod, *Works and Days*, 197–200.
[2] Homer, *Il.* vi. 202, of Bellerophon, wandering in his exile from Argos.

instance of a stepmother showing the distress of a mother, and endeavoured to console and reassure her. But she replied that her misery was beyond consolation, and that other women could not know what a bitter shaft was infixed in her heart.

(15) '"Whenever she was alone, she poured out reproaches against Thisbe for not having served her dutifully, saying: 'Intent on mischief, she has been no helper in my love-suit. She has shown herself swifter than speech to bereave me of my dearest, and has not even allowed me a chance of changing my mind.' It became as clear as day that she would do some injury to Thisbe who, seeing her so deeply incensed and so sorely wounded that she was on the point of some action against her, especially as she was infuriated at once by wrath and by love, decided to forestall her and ensure her own safety by taking action against her in advance. So she came to her and said: 'What is the matter, mistress? Why do you make vain charges against your little handmaid? I have served you always, in the past as in the present, according to your wishes: if something has turned out contrary to your design, that is to be ascribed to Fortune; yet I am ready, at your bidding, to contrive some solution of the present trouble.' 'Ah, what could you devise, dear friend,' said Demaenete, 'when he who is able to solve it is now far from me, and the unexpected clemency of the judges has undone me? If he had been stoned, if he had been put to death, then my passion also would have wholly expired with him. For as soon as an object is past hoping for it has been withdrawn from one's soul; and when there can no longer be any looking forward to the thing desired it enables the sufferer to be relieved of his pain; whereas now I imagine that I see him, I have the illusion of hearing his voice near by, shaming me with reprobation of my criminal plot against him. I fancy to myself that I shall one day find him come secretly to court me, and that I am to have my pleasure of him, or that I am about to visit him myself, wherever in the world he may be. These things inflame one; they drive one mad. My suffering, ye gods, is deserved! Why did I persecute, and not rather entreat him? He refused me the first time, as was fitting; I was a stranger: but beyond that he was ashamed for his father's bed. Perhaps time and persuasion would have converted him to a softer mood. But I, with my savage,

merciless nature, more like a task-mistress to him than a lover, took it as an offence that he did not comply with my command and disdained Demaenete, whom he far surpassed in beauty. Now, darling Thisbe, what is the solution that you mentioned?' 'An easy one, mistress,' she replied. 'It is the general opinion that Cnemon withdrew from the city and travelled out of Attica in obedience to the judgment: but I, who seek by every means to serve your interest, have discovered that he is in hiding some- where just outside the city. You must surely have heard, I suppose, of Arsinoe the flute-player: he had been intimate with her, and after his misadventure he was taken in by this young woman. Promising him that she will go along as his fellow- traveller, she is keeping him concealed in her house until she has packed her baggage.' 'Happy Arsinoe,' said Demaenete, 'in her former intercourse with Cnemon and in this prospect of sharing his exile! But what is the good of all this to us?' 'A great deal, mistress,' said Thisbe. 'I will make a show of being in love with Cnemon, and will request Arsinoe, who is an old acquain- tance of mine through her profession, to bring me in to him by night instead of herself. If this could be arranged, it would be for you then to personate Arsinoe and visit him in her place. It will be my business to see that he goes to bed a little drunk. Should you attain your object, your love will most likely cool off: many a woman, after the first experience, has found her desire quite extinguished; for the sating of love is the ending of the trouble. If your love should still continue—which Heaven for- bid!—there will be, as they say, a second string to your bow, another plan. Meanwhile, let us make the most of the present chance.'

(16) '"Demaenete approved her plan, and begged her to act swiftly on their resolve. Thisbe asked her mistress to be allowed one day for carrying it out. She went to Arsinoe and said: 'You know Teledemus?' The other assented, and she went on: 'Take us in here today; I promised I would sleep with him. He will come first, and I later, when I have put my mistress to bed.' Then away she ran to Aristippus in the country and said to him: 'Master, I have come to accuse myself; deal with me in what way you please. I am in part the cause of your losing your son: it was against my will, but yet I was an accomplice. Observing

that my mistress, instead of leading an honest life, was defiling
your bed, and fearing that trouble might one day come upon
myself if another should detect the affair, and also being deeply
grieved that in return for all your care bestowed on the wife of
your bosom you received this treatment, I shrank indeed from
reporting it to you myself; but I went and spoke to the young
master at night, so that nobody should know, and told him that
an adulterer was sleeping with the mistress. Then he, who as
you know had already a grievance against her, thinking that I
meant that the adulterer was then in the house, was filled with
uncontrollable anger and snatched up his dagger. I tried my best
to restrain him, telling him that there was nothing of the sort
there at the moment; but he, taking little heed, or else having
expected me to back out of my words, rushed in fury to the bed-
chamber. You know the rest. And now you have the chance, if
you want to take it, to excuse yourself to your son, exile though
he be now, and to punish her who has done this wrong to you
both. For I will show you this day Demaenete lying with her
paramour in a house, and that a stranger's house, outside the
city.' 'Oh, if you could show it to be as you say,' cried Aristippus,
'the money for the purchase of your freedom shall be kept in
reserve for you; and I perhaps could enjoy a new life after
avenging myself on my enemy. For a long time now I have
had a smouldering doubt in my mind; I suspected that affair,
but for want of proofs I kept quiet about it. Now, what is
to be done?' 'You know the garden', she said, 'where stands
the Epicureans' monument? [1] Go there this evening and wait
for me.'

(17) '"With these words she at once ran off, and coming to
Demaenete she said: 'Make yourself fine; you must be in elegant
trim for your visit. I have made all the arrangements for you
that I promised.' So she dressed herself in the manner directed
by Thisbe. When evening had come Thisbe took charge of her
and led her to the place of assignation. As they approached it
she bade her mistress wait a moment: she then went ahead and
requested Arsinoe to move into another apartment and leave her

[1] In the famous garden in a central part of Athens Epicurus (342–270
B.C.) had his philosophical school, in which his teaching was continued by a
long line of successors.

to herself; for the youth, she told her, was bashful, being a mere novice in the ministry of Aphrodite. Arsinoe complied; then Thisbe returned and fetched Demaenete, brought her inside, saw her into bed, and took away the lamp, so that she should not be recognized by you—you, forsooth, who were staying in Aegina! After recommending her to satisfy her desire in silence Thisbe said: 'I am off now to the young man, and will bring him to you; he is drinking at a neighbour's house hard by.' She slipped out, picked up Aristippus at the appointed place and incited him to surprise and bind the adulterer. He followed her and suddenly dashed into the room. Making his way with some difficulty to the bed by a slight glimmer of the moon he said: 'I have caught you, accursed woman!' Just as he uttered these words Thisbe knocked on the door with all her might and cried out: 'What a strange thing! The adulterer has escaped us! Take care, master, that you make no mistake this second time!' 'Never fear,' he replied; 'I have got the villainous woman, her whom I wanted most.' He then seized hold of her and began leading her towards the city. Upon her mind, as might be supposed, came crowding all the troubles that beset her—the disappointment of her expectations, the public disgrace in what was in store for her, the punishment ordained by the laws. Aggrieved by being caught in such a situation and enraged at being so duped, when she came near the pit in the Academy garden [1]—you know it, of course, at which the Kings of Arms sacrifice by ancient custom to the heroes—she suddenly broke from the old man's grasp and threw herself headlong into the pit! As she lay there, in a plight as evil as herself, Aristippus said: 'You have paid me the penalty before the laws could exact it.' On the next day he declared the whole affair to the people, and with some difficulty obtained their exoneration. He then made a round of visits to his friends and acquaintances, seeking their advice on the prospect of his procuring your return. Whether anything in that way has been done I cannot say; before it could be I took ship for this place, as you see, on some private business. However, you can fairly count on the people's consent

[1] An enclosure with fine plane-trees by the stream Cephisus, named after the hero Academus and containing various monuments and shrines. Here Plato held his philosophic school.

to your return, and on your father's coming here in search of
you, for he was proposing to do so.''

*Thyamis, the brigand chief, prompted by a dream, announces
his intention of marrying Chariclea.*

(18) 'This was the report that Charias gave me. What occurred
next, how I came here and through what happenings by the way,
would be too long to tell and take too much time.' Upon this
Cnemon wept and the two strangers wept also, apparently for
his experiences, but each of them really reflecting on their own.
Nor would they have ceased lamenting, had not a spirit of sleep,
touched by the charm of their sad plaints, alighted upon them
and quelled their tears. And so they slumbered. Meanwhile
Thyamis—this being the name of the bandit chief—after taking
tranquil repose for most of the night, had been disturbed by
fitful dreams which suddenly robbed him of his sleep; and
puzzling over their explanation he was kept awake by his
anxious thoughts. It was about the hour when cocks crow—
whether moved, as they say, to address the sun by an instinctive
sense of this god's turning round to our region, or impelled by
his warmth, as well as by their desire to be stirring and feeding
betimes, to rouse up to work the people with whom they live by
their peculiar proclamation—about that time he had this heaven-
sent dream: at Memphis, his native city, he entered the temple
of Isis, which seemed to be lit throughout with a blaze of lamps.
Altars and braziers were laden with all kinds of animals and
were drenched with their blood. The portico and passages outside were thronged with people whose clatter and clamour filled
the whole place. When he came within the shrine itself, the
goddess advanced to meet him, leading Chariclea by the hand,
and said: 'Thyamis, I deliver to you this maiden: you will have
her and have her not; you will be a wrongdoer and will slay
your guest; yet she will not be slain.' The effect of this vision
was to put him in a state of perplexity, in which he kept turning
its indications this way and that, as he tried to make out their
meaning. Tiring at length of this, he shaped the solution to suit
his own desire. The words 'you will have her and have her not'
he supposed to mean 'as a woman, and no longer a virgin'; and

'you will slay' he took to signify the wounding to end virginity—
which would not be fatal to Chariclea.

(19) This was the sense in which he construed his dream,
according to the promptings of his passion. At break of day he
called to him the foremost men among his subjects, and ordered
the booty, which he dignified with the name of spoils of war, to
be brought before them. He then sent for Cnemon, whom he
ordered to attend together with the persons held under his guard.
As they were being brought: 'Now what turn of fortune are we
to encounter next?' they cried, plying Cnemon with appeals
for any support that he could give them. He promised his help,
and urged them to be of good cheer, engaging that the bandit chief
was not wholly a barbarian in behaviour, but even had something civilized about him; for he belonged to a distinguished
family, and had been driven by necessity to adopt his present
way of life. When they had been brought to the place, and the
main body of brigands had gathered there, Thyamis seated
himself in a prominent position above them and declared the
island to be in assembly. He directed Cnemon to interpret to the
captives what he was about to say; for Cnemon by then understood Egyptian, while Thyamis was not perfect in the Greek
tongue. He then spoke as follows: 'Fellow-soldiers, you know
well the sort of feeling which I have always had towards you. I
was born, as you are aware, a son of the prophet at Memphis;
but after my father's retirement I failed to obtain the priestly
office, which was unlawfully usurped by my younger brother. I
then took refuge with you, for the purpose of avenging myself
and recovering my high function. I was deemed worthy by you
to be your chieftain, and to this day I have continued without
once allotting to myself any larger portion than to each member
of our body. If it was money to be shared, I was content with an
equal division; if captives were to be sold, I paid all the receipts
into the common fund. For I consider that a captain so competent
as I ought to take the largest portion of the work, but an equal
one of the winnings. As to prisoners, I enlisted in our band all
the men among them whose bodily vigour made them likely to
be useful recruits, and sold off the weaklings. On women I have
committed no outrage, but have released those of good family
either on payment made or merely from the pity that I felt for

their plight. Those of meaner birth, for whom slavery, rather from habitude than from the fact of captivity, was inevitable, I distributed severally amongst us as servants. In the present case, however, I request of you one part of our booty—this foreign maiden here, whom I could assign to myself; but I consider it better to receive her from our body as a whole. It would be foolish indeed to seize this prisoner by force, and be seen securing an advantage against the will of one's friends. Moreover, I ask this favour of you, not as a free gift but in return for my resigning any share in the rest of the plunder. Since we of the family of the prophets disdain the popular Aphrodite, it is not for the purpose of enjoyment, but to provide offspring for the succession, that I have resolved to have this woman for myself.

(20) 'And I wish to explain to you my reasons for so doing. First, she appears to me to be of high birth, judging by the riches found about her person, and by her steadfastness under her present hardships and her maintenance of a brave spirit in face of all her previous fortunes. Next, I can discern her to be at heart both virtuous and chaste. For if, surpassing all other women in beauty of form, she restrains in awed respect every man who looks upon her by the modesty of her glance, how can she not produce with good reason the most favourable impression of herself? And, what is the most important point of her description, she seems to me to be the priestess of some deity. You can see how even in her calamity she does not think it permissible to put off the sacred vestments and chaplets.

(21) 'What marriage, I ask all here present, could be more appropriate than that of a prophet's son taking to wife the dedicated woman?' All in the assembly shouted their assent, and wished them a propitious wedlock. Then he, resuming his speech, went on: 'I thank you: but it would be reasonable for us to find out what are the maiden's feelings in the matter. For if I had had to avail myself of the chieftain's privilege, my desire alone was fully sufficient, since to those empowered to compel any such inquiry is superfluous. But where the matter in hand is a marriage both parties must give their willing consent.' Then, turning and addressing the girl, he asked her: 'Well then, how do you feel about being my wife?' And with that he requested her to state who she and her companion were, and of what

parentage. For a good while she kept her eyes fixed on the ground and shook her head a number of times, as though collecting her words and thoughts. At last, looking Thyamis full in the face and dazzling him more than ever with her beauty—for her cheek had flushed unwontedly from the nature of her reflections, and her glance had quickened to a quite awesome keenness— with Cnemon interpreting she said: 'It would be more fitting for my brother here, Theagenes, to be the speaker; for I think it proper for a woman to be silent, and for a man to make answer, before a company of men.

Chariclea gives a fictitious account of herself and Theagenes to Thyamis.

(22) 'But since you have granted to myself a part in the speaking, and are tendering this first token of a gentle heart in trying to make good your claims by persuasion rather than by force; and in particular, because the whole matter in debate is centred upon me; I am constrained to depart from the code observed by myself as well as every maiden, and to reply to our conqueror's inquiry about marriage, though it be before such a great assemblage of men. Here then is our story. We are of Ionian descent, born in the first place to Ephesian parents, and blessed with the affluence of a family from which children are called by law to service in the priesthood. I was assigned to the service of Artemis, and my brother here to that of Apollo. Our ministration was for one year, and when our term was completed we had to conduct a mission to Delos, where we were to arrange musical and gymnastic contests, and had then to resign our priestly offices in accordance with the national custom. So a ship was laden with gold and silver and vestments and everything else that would be required for the contests and the public banquet. Our parents stayed at home because of their advanced age and their fear of a sea voyage; but a large number of our citizens either embarked with us on the same ship or made use of boats of their own. When our voyage was all but accomplished we were struck by a sudden upsurge of waves and a violent blast of wind, with scurrying squalls and tornadoes that wildly lashed the sea and bore the ship off her course. The helmsman, quailing

before this tremendous turmoil, had abandoned all control of
the vessel under stress of the storm, and resigned the steering to
Fortune. And so we were swept along by the gale, which blew
for seven days and as many nights, till at last we were driven
ashore at the place where we were captured by you, and where
you have seen the great slaughter that was done when the sailors
set upon us as we were feasting in celebration of our coming safe
to land; it being their purpose to do away with us for the sake of
our riches. Huge was the havoc and destruction of all our people,
and likewise of the attackers themselves, as they slew and were
slain. In the end the victory fell to us two, surviving as a pitiful
remnant—would that it had been otherwise!—out of all that
number, with one sole benefit granted to us in our disasters, of
being brought by some deity into your hands and, when we were
in fear of death, being invited to consider a marriage which I am
by no means disposed to refuse. For that I, a prisoner, should
be deemed worthy of my conqueror's bed overtops the best of
good fortune; and that a maiden dedicated to the gods should
live united with a prophet's son who ere long, with the deity's
assent, is to become a prophet, cannot in any wise appear to be
other than the doing of divine Providence. One single thing I
ask, and you must grant, Thyamis: allow me first to go to a
town, or some place where an altar has been consecrated to
Apollo, and there deliver up my priesthood and its insignia. It
would be preferable to do this at Memphis when you have
regained your office of prophet; in this way our marriage would
be more joyfully performed, being connected then with victory,
and accomplished as the finishing touch to a successful enterprise. Whether it should take place sooner I leave for your
consideration: I only ask that I may first enact the rites that are
customary in my country. Indeed, I know that you will consent
to this, since you have been dedicated, as you say, from childhood to sacred observances, and hold in reverent regard the
worship of the gods.'

(23) With these words she ended her speech, and then began
to weep. Everyone present approved her request, and urged
Thyamis to do as she suggested, with shouts of their readiness
for the move. He also gave his approval, half willing and half
unwilling. In his desire for Chariclea he found even the present

hour an unending period of delay, while her words, holding him
with a charm like that of some siren's voice, compelled his
assent; and besides, he connected them with his dream, and felt
confident that his marriage would take place at Memphis. He
dismissed the assembly after distributing the booty, carrying off
for himself a quantity of the choicest goods which the others
willingly renounced in his favour.

(24) He issued an order to them that they should be fully prepared to make an advance on Memphis in ten days' time. To the
Greeks he assigned the same hut as before, which Cnemon was
directed to share with them again: his appointed duty was
thenceforth not to be their guard, but to keep them company.
And Thyamis not only provided them with food more refined
than their present fare, but occasionally brought Theagenes in
to partake of a meal with him, out of respect for the youth's
sister. Chariclea herself he had decided not even to see at all
frequently, lest the sight of her should add fuel to the flame of
his insistent longing and he should be driven perforce to disregard the decisions and declarations that he had made. For these
reasons then Thyamis declined to see the girl, feeling it impossible to look upon her without losing his self-control. Cnemon,
as soon as all the men had departed by slinking away into
different parts of the lagoon, went out for a little distance to look
for the herb which he had promised to Theagenes on the
previous day.

*Theagenes, alarmed by Chariclea's show of willingness to marry
Thyamis, is reassured by her.*

(25) Meanwhile Theagenes applied this vacant hour to weeping and lamenting. He spoke no word to Chariclea, but continually called upon the gods to witness his grief. When she
asked him whether he was mourning their common and accustomed situation, or had met with some new misfortune, he
replied: 'And what could be newer, what more nefarious, than
a violation of oaths and covenants, than Chariclea forgetting me
and consenting to wed another?' 'Fie on such words!' said the
girl, 'do not distress me more than do my misfortunes nor,
when past events provide you with ample proof of my loyalty in

my actions, take words uttered in an emergency as matter for suspicion of me; else you yourself, on the contrary, will appear to be changed, instead of your finding a change in me. I on my part do not deny that I am unfortunate; but no force on earth can shake me in my resolve to preserve my virtue. In one instance alone am I conscious of some immodesty—when I felt my passion for you; but even so it was a lawful feeling. For from the first I gave myself, not as yielding to a lover, but as affianced to a husband, and to this day I have continually kept myself pure from any intimacy even with you. Often I have repulsed your attempts, in order to make sure that the marriage agreed between us from the beginning and pledged with our most binding oaths, should eventually be solemnized according to law. It must therefore be absurd for you to believe that I could prefer the barbarian to the Greek, or the brigand to the man whom I love.' 'Then what was your design in all that fine harangue of yours?' asked Theagenes. 'To represent me as your brother, indeed, was exceedingly clever; it quite cleared Thyamis' mind of jealousy regarding us, and enabled us to keep each other company without anxiety. I also understood about Ionia and our straying to Delos, how this was all a device to conceal the truth and lead your hearers' minds astray.

(26) 'But to be so ready to consent to this marriage, to enter into the contract in definite terms, and to appoint a time—these steps I was neither able nor wishful to comprehend. I could only pray that I might sink into the earth rather than witness such a conclusion to all my endeavours and hopes for you.' Chariclea embraced Theagenes, gave him countless kisses and bedewed him with her tears as she said: 'What a delight to hear you expressing these fears for me! Those words are clear evidence that you have not slackened in your passion for me beneath the stress of so many misfortunes. But I assure you, Theagenes, that we could not at this moment be holding our conversation if those promises had not been made as you heard. For an impulse of dominant desire, you know, is augmented by a stubborn opposition, but words of compliance, meeting the lover's will half way, will repress the first effervescence of passion and lull to sleep the poignancy of his craving with the sweetness of the promise given. Indeed, I believe that lovers of

the rustic sort regard such a pledge as an earnest of success; they take the promise as a proof of a conquest and conduct themselves more calmly, buoyed up by their hopes. So I, anticipating this effect, bestowed myself in those words, entrusting the sequel to the gods and to the spirit who from the first was appointed to foster our love. Often have one or two days brought us ample means of deliverance, and Fortune has provided what an abundance of human counsels could not devise. So you see how in my case I have put off immediate action, and have averted certainties with uncertainties. We must be careful then to maintain this pretence as our defence, my darling, and to divulge it to nobody, not even to Cnemon. He is kindly disposed to us, and a Greek; but he is a prisoner, and more likely if he has occasion, to gratify his master than us. Neither duration of friendship nor obligation of kinship is there, to give us an absolute guarantee of his loyalty to our interest; and so, should he ever suspect something and get an inkling of the truth about us, it must be denied at once. For falsehood can be honourable when it assists the speaker without doing any real injury to the hearers.'

On the approach of a hostile force of bandits, Chariclea is imprisoned in a secret cavern.

(27) While Chariclea was making these and similar suggestions for their best advantage, Cnemon came running to them in great haste, and with a look in his eyes that attested much perturbation. 'Theagenes,' he said, 'I have come with that herb for you: apply it and cure your sores. But we must hold ourselves prepared for further wounds and renewed slaughter.' Theagenes begged him to state his meaning in clearer terms, but he said: 'This is no moment for listening; there is danger of words being overtaken by deeds. Follow me with all speed, and bring Chariclea too along with you.' He then took them both and brought them to Thyamis, whom he found furbishing his helmet and whetting a javelin. 'This is indeed the moment to be looking to your arms,' said Cnemon; 'now put on yours, and order the others to do likewise. A larger body of enemies than you ever met before is upon us: at so little distance are they that, when

I spied them clambering over the ridge near by, I ran to you to give you warning of their attack, not once slackening my pace, but also notifying as many men as I could in my passage to you here that they must make themselves ready.'

(28) At these words Thyamis leapt to his feet and asked again and again: 'Where is Chariclea?' seeming to fear more for her than for himself. When Cnemon pointed to where she stood shyly by the doorway, he said to him aside: 'Cnemon, take this woman away to the cavern in which our treasure has been stored for security: lead her down into it, my friend, and after closing its mouth as usual with the block, come to us as quickly as you can. The fighting shall be our concern.' [1] He then ordered his henchman to fetch a victim to be offered as a sacrifice to the gods of the country before they began the battle. Cnemon went to carry out his order, and led away Chariclea, who with much lamentation kept turning back to Theagenes; and so Cnemon deposited her in the cavern. This place was not a work of nature, like so many that become hollowed out of themselves either above or under the ground, but one wrought by the brigands' skill in imitating nature; it was the mining of Egyptian hands that had there elaborately scooped out a safe storehouse for their booty.

(29) It had been contrived after this fashion: it had a narrow, gloomy entrance situated beneath the door of a secret chamber, in such a way that the threshold stone served also as a door to the downward passage in case of need, and easily fell into position or opened up; and the space just beyond it was divided irregularly into a number of winding tunnels. The paths and cuttings that led to the inmost recesses in some parts kept to separate ways with artful meanderings; while in some they crossed each other and became intertwined like tree roots until they converged and opened out in the depths to a single spacious area, over which a dim light was shed through a small fissure close to the surface of the lagoon. Into this place Cnemon brought down Chariclea, leading her by the hand all the way, as he was acquainted with it, to the furthermost part of the cavern: there he gave her his best encouragement, and promised

[1] A reminiscence of Hector's farewell words to Andromache, Homer, *Il.* vi. 492 (parodied by Aristophanes, *Lysistr.* 520, 538).

to come and visit her with Theagenes in the evening; he would not allow him, he said, to engage in combat with the enemy, but would see that he made his escape from the battle. Chariclea spoke no word as though mortally wounded by this mischance, and bereft of life by the loss of Theagenes. Leaving her there in a breathless and speechless state, he ascended from the cavern, and putting to the threshold stone he shed some tears both for his own hard duty and for the fate of her whom he had all but buried alive, and had thus consigned Chariclea, brightest of human beauties, to night and darkness. He ran back to Thyamis, and found him all afire for the fray and clad, himself and Theagenes like him, in shining armour. The leader was addressing the men already mustered around him in words calculated to work them up to a height of furious ardour. Standing in their midst he said: 'Fellow-soldiers, I hardly think it necessary to exhort you at any length, when you yourselves need no reminder, being ever wont to regard warfare as your life. Moreover, this unexpected attack of the enemy precludes speaking at any length. To see the enemy moving into action, and not to aim a swift counterstroke in retaliation, is an absolute dereliction of one's duty. We know that it is no mere question of defending women and children—a reason indeed which alone may often suffice to spur one on to battle—for we shall now be enabled to hold it of less account, as also all the profit to be gained by victory; our fight being rather for very existence, for our own lives. A conflict between brigands never ends with a covenant or a treaty, but of necessity one must either survive as victor or die as vanquished. So, in face of our bitterest foes, let us whet the edge of our spirits and our powers, and come to grips with them.'

Thyamis, construing his dream differently, in distraction goes to the cavern and there kills a woman whom he supposes to be Chariclea.

(30) At the end of this speech he looked about him for his henchman, and called him repeatedly by his name, Thermouthis. When the man nowhere appeared Thyamis poured out angry threats against him and betook himself at a run to his boat. The

fighting had already broken out, and in the distance it could be seen how the dwellers on the farthest part of the lagoon, near to its inflow, were being overpowered. For the aggressors had set on fire the boats and huts of those who were being struck down or were taking to flight: the flames from these fires were blown far and wide over the adjacent swamp and devoured the huge, compact mass of reeds growing in it, so that an inexpressible, unbearable blaze flared full in men's eyes, while the loud noise of its crackling smote their ears. Every form of fighting was in operation and was resounding there: the inhabitants withstood the onslaught with their utmost zeal and vigour, but the enemy had an overwhelming advantage against them, both in their numbers and in the surprise of their attack, and were killing some on the land and sinking others, together with their boats and their dwellings in the lagoon. From all these happenings a confused rumbling arose in the air, as the battle raged at once ashore and afloat, men killing and being killed, reddening the lagoon with blood, and grappling with perils of fire and of water. When Thyamis saw and heard these things he reflected on the dream in which he had beheld Isis, and the temple all lit up and full of sacrifices; and supposing it to have signified the present events he construed his vision in a sense quite contrary to what he conceived before. That he 'would have and not have' Chariclea meant that she was destined to be taken from him by war, and his slaying and not wounding her meant that it would be with the sword and not by the usage of Aphrodite. Many were the reproaches that he uttered against the goddess for being so deceptive, and great his indignation that another man should gain possession of Chariclea. He ordered the men about him to halt for a moment, telling them that they must remain in that spot and continue to fight by lurking in ambush round about the islet, and from amongst its surrounding marshes making surprise sorties, well content if in this way they could hold out against the great numbers of the enemy. He himself, as though he were going in search of Thermouthis and to offer up prayers to their guardian deities, permitted no one to accompany him, and then turned his steps in mad distraction to the cavern cell. It is hard to withhold the barbarian temperament from any course on which it has set out: when it despairs of its own survival, it is wont first to destroy all beloved beings, either fondly believing that it will rejoin them after death, or wishing to rescue them from the danger of outrage at an enemy's hands. Such thoughts as these caused Thyamis to forget all his immediate concerns, even when the enemy had closed in around him like a net. Frantic with love and jealousy and wrath, he ran with all speed to the cavern and leapt down into it, uttering many loud cries in the Egyptian tongue. Just at the entrance he became aware of a woman's voice speaking to him in Greek. Following the guidance of the sound he came up to her, seized her head with his left hand, and drove his sword into her bosom close to the breasts.

(31) Thus cruelly was she struck down, as she sent forth a last pitiful shriek. Then he ran back, closed the doorway with the stone, and covered it with a small heap of earth. 'There you have my betrothal gift!' he said, weeping. When he returned to the boats he found his men just resolving on flight as the enemy were soon to be close upon them; while Thermouthis had arrived with a victim which he was holding ready for the sacrifice. Thyamis reproached him sharply, and said that he had fore-stalled him by offering up the finest of sacrifices. He then embarked in his boat with two others, Thermouthis and his oarsman; for the boats on the lagoon cannot carry more persons, being rudely hollowed in one piece from a stout tree trunk. Theagenes and Cnemon set out together in another boat, and all the rest followed likewise in their several vessels. When they had rowed a little distance from the island, and voyaged round it instead of away from it, they ceased rowing and ranged their boats in line of battle, so as to meet the enemy front to front. But on seeing their mere nearness to the foe, and finding that the dashing of oars alone was more than they could stomach, they all took to flight at first view of the enemy, some even being unable to bear the sound of their battle-cry. Theagenes and Cnemon retreated also, not, however, giving way in the main to fear. Thyamis alone—partly no doubt because he was ashamed to flee, but also perhaps because he could not bear to outlive Chariclea—dashed in among the enemy.

Thyamis is captured alive by the hostile bandits.

(32) As they were in the act of closing in combat someone called out: 'This is the man Thyamis; have a care, everybody!' Immediately the enemy turned their boats to form a circle round him on every side. He was defending himself, wounding some and slaying others with his spear, when a marvel of marvels occurred: not a single one of them either thrust or slashed at the man with his sword, but each endeavoured all he could to take Thyamis alive. He held his own to the utmost, until a number of them together seized hold of him and snatched away his spear; he was also deprived of his henchman, who after battling gallantly at his side had received what seemed to be a mortal wound. Giving way to despair, this man had plunged into the lagoon and, being an expert swimmer, came up to the surface beyond the range of missiles; then, with some difficulty, he swam away to the swamp where, moreover, nobody thought to follow in his pursuit. For now the enemy had possession of Thyamis, and regarded the capture of this single person as a complete victory. Though they had suffered the loss of so many comrades, they delighted more in escorting the slayer of their friends than they sorrowed for their decease. So true it is that brigands esteem riches more highly even than the very lives of men, and the words 'friendship' and 'kinship' have meaning for them only in respect of their profit. Thus it was in the case of these people.

(33) They were in fact a part of the band which had fled before Thyamis and his troop near the river mouth of Hercules. Annoyed at being deprived of the property of others, and as bitterly aggrieved by the loss of the booty as if it had belonged to them, they went and collected at home those of their body who had remained there, and made similar appeals to the surrounding villages, offering them a fair and equal share in the spoils that should be taken. They then took the lead in the raid on Thyamis, whom they were now capturing alive for a particular reason. He had a brother Petosiris in Memphis who, although his junior, had treacherously and against tradition deprived Thyamis of the prophet's priestly office. When he learnt that his elder brother was a chief of brigands, he feared that Thyamis might one day seize an opportunity of attacking him, or else that time might

bring disclosure of his treachery; and besides, he was becoming aware that in the minds of most people he was under suspicion, as there was nowhere any sign of Thyamis, of having done away with him. He therefore proclaimed by messengers sent to the villages of the brigands that large rewards of money and cattle would be given to those who brought in Thyamis alive. Prevailed on by these offers, the brigands did not allow even the ebullience of battle to expel the memory of the gain to be got, but as soon as he was recognized they took him alive, at the cost of many deaths. They bound him and conveyed him ashore, having chosen by lot one half of their number to be his guard, while he protested against their apparent humanity, more exasperated by his bonds than by death. The rest of the brigands went off to the island, expecting to find there the treasures and spoils that they were seeking. They ran about all over the place, leaving no part unsearched, but could discover nothing of what they had hoped for, or only some trifling remnants that had not been hidden underground but left lying near the cave. They then set fire to the cabins. As nightfall was approaching and gave warning against lingering on the island, lest they should be surprised there by the fugitives from the fighting, they departed to their kinsfolk at home.

BOOK II

*Theagenes laments the apparent loss of Chariclea in the foray,
but is assured by Cnemon that she is alive.*

(1) The island was being ravaged thus by fire; but Theagenes
and Cnemon, so long as the sun showed above the earth, did not
observe the calamity, because the aspect of fire is dimmed in
the day time by the rays of the Sun-god shedding their light
upon it. When, however, he was setting and drawing on the
night, the blaze regained its brilliance in unsubdued vigour, and
became visible over an enormous distance. Then the two men,
emboldened by the night, peered out from the swamp and saw
the island clearly overrun now by the fire. Theagenes smote his
head and tore his hair, saying: 'Away now with life, on this day!
Let all be brought to conclusion, to dissolution—fears, perils,
cares, hopes and loves! Lost is Chariclea; Theagenes has
perished! In vain, ill-fated wretch, did I turn coward and sink
to unmanly flight, that I might save myself, sweet girl, for you!
Nay, no longer will I seek my safety, when you, my dearest, are
laid low—not by the common rule of nature—O the bitterness
of it!—nor relinquishing your life in the arms that you had
wished to hold you. Instead, you have fallen a victim, alas, to
fire; such were the strange bridal torches that the deity lit for
you. Squandered is the choicest beauty amongst mankind, so
that not a relic of that unfeigned loveliness remains upon her
body, now that it is but a corpse. O the cruelty, O the unspeak-
able malignity of the divine will! I am deprived even of the last
embracements, bereft of the farewell, lifeless kisses!'

(2) As he spoke these words and looked for his sword, Cnemon
quickly thrust it away from his grasp, saying: 'What is this,
Theagenes? Why bewail her who is alive? Chariclea lives, and
is safe and sound; have no more fear.' 'That is a tale for idiots
or children,' he replied; 'you have undone me, in robbing me
of the sweetest death.' Then Cnemon, speaking now on oath,
gave him a full account of the order issued by Thyamis, of the

cavern, of his own descent into it, and of the nature of the excavation, which precluded any danger of the depths being reached by the fire, baffled as it would be by the countless windings of the tunnels. At these words Theagenes breathed again: he hastened away to the island, beholding in his mind his absent love, and picturing the cavern as his nuptial chamber, unaware of the lamentation that he was to make in that place. So they set forward with all speed in their boat, rowing themselves across the water; for their ferryman in the first clash of the fight had darted away, scared by the shouting as though shot off from a spring-board. Thus they went, diverging from a straight course, first to one side, then to the other, because in their inexperience they failed to pull together in their strokes, and were also buffeted by an adverse wind.

Theagenes and Cnemon enter the cavern in search of Chariclea, and stumble upon the dead body of a woman.

(3) But their fervent resolution overcame their lack of skill, and with great effort and sweat they brought their boat to the shore of the island and ran up as fast as they could to the cabins. These they found already burnt to ashes, and traceable only by their sites; the threshold stone, however, that concealed the cavern stood out clearly to their view. For the wind, bearing in that direction, had blown upon the cabins which, constructed of plaited reeds, and those too of the marsh-grown kind, were burnt up by the sudden sweep of its passage, and the area where they had stood now appeared to be almost level ground. The blaze had quickly died down and subsided into cinders: most of the embers had been scattered by the strong gusts of wind, and the small remainder had been almost entirely quenched on the spot by the draught and had been sufficiently cooled to be walked upon. The two searchers discovered some half-burnt torches and ignited some remnants of the reeds; they then opened the entrance to the cavern and ran down, Cnemon leading the way. When they had descended a little he cried out: 'O Zeus, what is this? We are undone! Chariclea is destroyed!' He dropped his torch on the ground, causing it to go out; with his hands held over his eyes he went down on his knees and

wailed. Theagenes, as if someone had forced him forward, fell down on the woman's body lying there, clasped it tightly and enfolded it so completely in his arms as to seem incorporate with it. Cnemon, observing him totally absorbed in his grief and overwhelmed by the calamity, from fear lest he should do himself some mischief, covertly withdrew his sword from its sheath slung at his side, and leaving him alone ran back to relight the torches.

(4) Meanwhile Theagenes was crying out in an agony of tragic distress: 'O unbearable blow! O god-sent disaster! What insatiable Fury can it be that has wildly revelled in our ruin, ejecting us in exile from our native land, subjecting us to perils of the sea and perils of pirate gangs, delivering us up to brigands, and despoiling us again and again of our possessions? A single one of all these yet remained to me, and it has now been snatched away: Chariclea has perished, stricken, she my dearest, by the hand of an enemy, holding fast, it is plain, to her virtue, and seeking to save herself, alas, for me! Yet, after all, the hapless girl has perished, having had no benefit herself of her maiden bloom, nor granted me any enjoyment of it. Ah, sweetheart, do but speak to me the usual last words! Lay on me now your behest, with what little breath still is in you! Alas, you are speechless; silence has hold of those prophetic lips which told of things divine; darkness has enveloped the torchbearer, and chaos the ministrant of the sacred shrine. Light has left the eyes which dazzled all men with their beauty, and which her assassin did not see, I am most certain. But what am I to call you? Bride? But you can have no wedding. Wife? But you have known no marriage bed. Then it must be the sweetest name of all, Chariclea! Ah, Chariclea, be assured; you have a faithful lover. In a little time you will have me again. See, I will offer up to you as libation the flow from my own wounding, and will pour out my own blood so dear to you. This cavern shall be our unintended tomb; at least we shall be allowed our union after death, even if the deity has not vouchsafed it to us in our lives.'

(5) As he was yet speaking he reached with his hand to draw his sword: not finding it, he cried out: 'Cnemon, you have destroyed me! And besides, you have done injury to Chariclea, by depriving her this second time of her greatest pleasure, our

companionship.' While he was thus speaking his mind, from the depths of the cavern the sound of a voice seemed to be heard calling 'Theagenes!' He, no whit perturbed, made answer saying: 'I will come, dearest soul; clearly you are still moving about the earth, partly because you could not bear to be separated from that body of yours from which you were by violence expelled, and partly perhaps because owing to your unburied state you are excluded by the infernal shades.' By this time Cnemon had arrived with lighted torches; then again the same sound could be heard, and the call it gave was 'Theagenes!' Cnemon cried out: 'Ye gods, is it not the voice of Chariclea? I think she is yet alive, Theagenes; for it comes from the farthest recess, from the part of the cave where I know that I left her, this voice that strikes my ear.' 'Oh, cease deluding me,' said Theagenes, 'as so often you have done before.' 'Well, then, in deluding you I delude myself no less,' said Cnemon, 'if we should find this woman lying here to be Chariclea.' With that he turned over the body to see its face, and as he looked: 'What is this,' he cried, 'ye wonder-working gods? It is the face of Thisbe!' He stepped backwards and stood there, trembling all over and dumbfounded.

Cnemon recognizes the dead woman as Thisbe, and they are happily joined by Chariclea.

(6) At Cnemon's words Theagenes recovered his breath and turned his thoughts to fresh hope. He roused Cnemon as he was swooning away, and begged him to lead him on with all speed to Chariclea. After a brief pause Cnemon came to himself, and began again to examine the corpse. It was in truth Thisbe, and he recognized by its hilt the sword, which had fallen out at her side after Thyamis, having dealt his stroke, in his rage and haste had left it in the wound. A tablet also was seen protruding from her bosom beneath the armpit: this he picked up, and then tried to make out some of the writing upon it. But Theagenes prevented him with importunate insistence, saying: 'Let us first retrieve my dearest one, unless some deity even now is making game of us. We can look into this writing later.' Cnemon agreed and, taking along the tablet and picking up the sword, they

hurried away to Chariclea. She, having clambered up with hands as well as feet to the light, came running to Theagenes and clung round his neck. 'I hold you, Theagenes!' and 'I have you alive, Chariclea!' they said to each other, again and again, and ended by falling both at once to the ground, where they lay clasping one another in a mute embrace, yet seeming to have become but one person, and were at a point very near to death. True indeed it is that an excess of joy will often turn to anguish, and an immoderate pleasure will beget a self-induced pain. So those two, surviving against all hope, were now endangered; until Cnemon by scraping opened up a spring from which came a trickle of water. Collecting some of it in the hollow of his hands, he brought it to them and, by sprinkling it on their faces and continually stroking their noses, he restored them to their senses.

(7) Then they, suddenly finding themselves prostrate in attitudes so different from those in which they met each other, at once stood upright and blushed—Chariclea especially—for shame that Cnemon should have witnessed such a scene, and besought his pardon. But he smiled at them, and to put them in blither mood he said: 'Your behaviour only merits praise, in my judgment and in that of anyone who, having wrestled with Love, has been pleasingly defeated in the struggle, and has been temperate in taking the inevitable tosses of that god. One thing, however, Theagenes, I could not commend—but was deeply ashamed, in truth, to see—your throwing yourself upon that strange woman, with whom you had no sort of connection, and abjectly bewailing her; and that too when I earnestly insisted that your beloved was still among the living.' 'O Cnemon,' replied Theagenes, 'do cease traducing me to Chariclea, whom I was bewailing in the body of another, supposing that it was she who lay there. But, since some god has graciously shown us what a mistake that was, it is time that you called to mind the surpassing manliness that led you in advance of me to bewail my lot, and then take to your heels on your unexpected recognition of the corpse, as though at the sight of spirits on the stage—you, an armed man, sword in hand, fleeing from a woman, and her a dead body! You, the stalwart Attic infantryman!'

Cnemon relates more about Thisbe to Theagenes and Chariclea.

(8) At these words they laughed, in a somewhat curt, constrained manner, and that not without some tears: indeed, in such a sorry plight as theirs, lamentation could not but claim the larger part. After a short pause Chariclea, chafing her cheek below the ear, said: 'Happy to my mind is she who has been bewailed by Theagenes, perhaps also kissed by him, as Cnemon tells, whoever she may really be. But—if you will not suspect me of being a little piqued by love—who pray was the fortunate person found worthy of Theagenes' tears, and how came it that you kissed an unknown woman in mistake for me? I should like to be told this, if you happen to know.' 'You will be surprised,' he answered, 'but in fact it was Thisbe, so Cnemon here says— that Athenian woman, the harp-player, and the hatcher of plots against him and against Demaenete.' Chariclea was astonished at his words, and said: 'How was it likely, Cnemon, that a woman from the middle of Greece should be transported into a remote corner of Egypt, as though by a stage-machine? And how was it that we did not see her as we came down here?' 'Those are questions that I cannot answer,' replied Cnemon; 'but what I do know about her I will tell you. When Demaenete, after she had been beguiled, had flung herself into the pit, and my father had reported the occurrence to the people, in the first place he obtained their exoneration; and he managed to procure from the people the grant of my recall and of his making a voyage in search of me. Then Thisbe, gaining freedom from occupation by his preoccupation, was at liberty to offer herself and her art for hire at banquets. In time she won a greater repute than Arsinoe —whose flute-playing was in slow measure—through the tripping rhythms of her own harp-playing and delicate singing to the lute: she unwittingly aroused against herself an intense jealousy in her comrade, and still more when a merchant of Naucratis,[1] a man almost made of gold, named Nausicles, took her to his arms. For in doing so he was casting aside Arsinoe, with whom he had been intimate before; but he had seen her

---

[1] A Milesian colony on the east bank of the Canopic arm of the Nile delta, about fifty miles inland, which became a great centre of Mediterranean commerce.

cheeks bulged out by her fluting and forced by her vigorous
blowing to protrude in an unseemly way to the length of her nose,
while her eyes all ablaze, were starting from their proper position.[1]

(9) 'Swelling with rancour at this treatment and inflamed
with jealousy, Arsinoe went to the kinsfolk of Demaenete and
informed them of the trap set for her by Thisbe, partly from
what she had herself surmised and partly from Thisbe's disclosures to her in the way of companionship. So the relatives of
Demaenete combined to attack my father, and with heavy bribes
put up the most skilful pleaders to appear as his accusers. They
clamoured that Demaenete had been done to death untried and
uncondemned; they made out that the adultery was invented to
screen her murder, and demanded that the adulterer be produced
either alive or dead, or insisted that at least his name should be
given. Finally, they called for Thisbe to be put to the torture.
My father undertook to hand her over, but was unable to do so,
since she, foreseeing this proposal while the case was being
drawn up, by arrangement with the merchant had made good
her escape. The people were so provoked that, although they did
not convict him of murder, since his deposition was deemed to
be a full and true account, they pronounced him to be an
accomplice in the plot against Demaenete and in my unjust
banishment, and condemned him to expulsion from the city and
confiscation of his property. Such was the joy that he had of his
venture upon a second marriage. And thus did the villainous
Thisbe sail away from Athens, and has now met this punishment
before my eyes. That is all that I have been able to learn from
the report of a certain Anticles at Aegina with whom I later
voyaged to Egypt, to see if I could find Thisbe somewhere in
Naucratis, bring her back to Athens, and not only dispel the
suspicions against my father, but also demand the punishment
of her machinations against us all. And now here I am, a sharer
in your ordeal: the cause of this, and the manner of it, and all
that I have undergone in the meantime, you shall hear later on.
But how Thisbe came to be in the cavern, and by whose hand

---

[1] So Athena, seeing her face puffed out by piping when reflected in water,
threw the pipes away: Athenaeus, xix. 7; Apollodorus, I. iv. 2. A painting
on a cup of about 470 B.C. in Corpus Christi College, Cambridge, shows a
flute girl with her face thus distorted.

she was killed, will require an intimation, I should say, from some deity.

(10) 'But, if you agree, let us examine the tablet that we have found by her bosom; it may well be that we shall get some further information from it.' They agreed, and he opened the leaves of the tablet [1] and began to read the writing as follows: 'To Cnemon, my master, from his enemy and his avenger, Thisbe. First I give you good tidings of the death of Demaenete, brought about by me for your sake; how—if you will admit me to your presence—I will recount to you in person. Next, I inform you that I have been in this island now for ten days, a captive of one of the brigands dwelling here who boasts of being the henchman of the chief of their band. He also keeps me in confinement, not permitting me so much as to peep out of doors, and imposing this restriction, in his own words, out of kindness to me but, as I conclude, for fear of somebody carrying me off. Yet, by the grace of some god, I have seen you, master, passing by, and recognized you; and I have secretly dispatched to you this tablet by means of the old woman who lives with me. I have bidden her deliver it into the hands of the good-looking Greek who is besides a friend of the Commander. Come then, rescue me from the brigands' hands, and receive your own little maid-servant. Save me, if you will be so good; and understand that the wrong which I seemed to do was done under duress, while the vengeance that I took on your enemy was the work of my own free will. But if you are filled with an implacable wrath, expend it upon me to your heart's content: only let me return to your service, even if I should have to die. For it would be better to perish by your hand, and be granted a Greek funeral, than to endure a life more grievous than death, and a barbarian's endearments, more baneful to an Athenian woman than his enmity.'

(11) Such was the message that came from Thisbe in her tablet. Then Cnemon said: 'Thisbe, you have done well to die, and to be yourself the informant of your own misfortunes by delivering the relation of them to us through the very wound of

---

[1] A writing tablet usually consisted of two or more flat pieces of wood hinged together and coated on the inner sides with coloured wax, which was scratched through with a pointed metal instrument or 'style'.

which you died. Thus an avenging Fury, it would seem, has
driven you from land to land, not ceasing to ply the scourge of
justice until I, chancing to be in Egypt, am here the injured
person made a witness of your punishment. But what, I wonder,
was the further artful scheme which you were devising against
me in writing this letter, and which justice has been quick to balk
of execution? For I, even when you lie dead, still hold you
suspect, and greatly fear that the death of Demaenete is a mere
fiction, and that I was deceived by those who reported it, while
you came far across the ocean to enact even in Egypt another
scene of Attic drama for my undoing.' 'Come, cease overplaying
the unmanly fellow,' said Theagenes, 'with your apprehensions
of spectres and shades. For you cannot say that I too, and these
eyes of mine, have been bewitched by her; I have no part in
your play. Now, in simple fact, she lies there, a lifeless corpse,
so on that score be absolutely reassured, Cnemon; but who could
have done you the good turn of killing her, or when was she
brought here? These are questions that leave me extremely
perplexed and astonished.' 'There is much of which I can see no
explanation,' said Cnemon; but, all things considered, her slayer
is Thyamis, if we are to judge by the sword that we found close
to the mortal wound: I recognize it as his by this notable feature
of the hilt, an ivory carving of an eagle.' 'And could you say',
asked Theagenes, 'how and with what motive he committed this
murder?' 'How could I know that?' he replied. 'This cavern
did not transform me into a soothsayer, as the sanctuary of
Pytho might.' Suddenly Theagenes and Chariclea wailed aloud
and cried out in mournful tones: 'O Pytho! O Delphi!' Cnemon
was astonished, and could not guess what it was that so affected
them at hearing the name of Pytho.

*Thermouthis, henchman of Thyamis, comes to the cave in search
of Thisbe, finds her corpse, and meets Theagenes, Chariclea and
Cnemon.*

(12) While they were thus occupied, Thermouthis, the henchman of Thyamis, after being wounded in the fight had made his
escape by swimming to land. At nightfall he happened upon a
boat that was drifting through the swamp from among the

wreckage, and embarking in it he made with all speed for the
island in search of Thisbe. She, a few days before, as she was
being taken along by her merchant Nausicles, had been carried
off from him by Thermouthis, who had ambushed him in a
narrow pass of the mountain range. When Thermouthis, amid
the tumult of the battle that raged as the enemy attacked, was
sent by Thyamis to fetch the sacrificial victim, he took her out
of the reach of missiles and, purposing to preserve her for
himself, brought her down unobserved into the cavern; and
there in his distraction and haste he left her at a point just within
the entrance. There, in the spot where she had been thrust
inside, she remained for the moment, from fear of the perils all
about her and from ignorance of the passages leading to the
cavern; and there Thyamis came upon her and slew her, Thisbe,
supposing her to be Chariclea. To this same woman hastened
Thermouthis, in the belief that she had safely evaded the dangers
of the battle: as soon as he had landed on the island he ran as
fast as he could to the cabins. These were now no more than
ashes, and he had difficulty in detecting by its stone the entrance
to the cavern. He lit some reeds that happened to be left still
smouldering, and ran down with all speed calling out Thisbe's
name—the only word of Greek that he knew. At the sight of her
prostrate body he stood for some length of time dumbfounded;
till finally he became aware of a sound of voices borne like a
murmur from the hollow depths of the cavern; it came from
Theagenes and Cnemon talking together, and he surmised that
they were the murderers of Thisbe. He was perplexed as to what
he should do: his brigand's fierceness and barbarian's rage,
exasperated now by the frustration of his love, urged him to
close there and then with the supposed authors of the deed; but
his lack of armour and sword constrained him against his will to
refrain and control himself.

(13) It seemed to him better not to meet them as an enemy
but, if he could provide himself with some means of defence, to
go then and set about his enemies. With this resolve he halted
near Theagenes and his companions, darting wild, wrathful
glances from eyes that betrayed the purpose lurking in his heart.
When they beheld a naked man suddenly appearing before them,
wounded and with blood-stained face, Chariclea withdrew into

the farther recesses of the cavern, partly, no doubt, as a precaution, but more of course from virgin modesty at the sight of
a nudity so indecorous. Cnemon slunk back a little way: he
recognized Thermouthis, whose unlooked-for presence suggested that he was bent on some desperate act. But his aspect
did not scare Theagenes; it rather provoked him to brandish his
sword at the man, in readiness to strike if he should attempt any
affront. 'Stop, man,' he said, 'or you will be struck; that you
have not been struck already is because I partly recognized you,
and because your purpose in coming here is still dubious.'
Thermouthis threw himself down before him, entreating him in
supplication born of the moment, rather than his mood, and
beseeching Cnemon to come to his aid. He said he could rightly
claim to be spared his life at their hands, earnestly protesting
that he had done them no wrong; that he had always been
friendly to them up to the previous day, and had come to them
now as his friends.

(14) Moved to pity by these words, Cnemon drew near to
him, raised him up from clasping the knees of Theagenes, and
asked him repeatedly where Thyamis was. He then gave a full
account of how Thyamis got to grips with the enemy; how
rushing into their midst he fought without sparing either them
or himself; how he continued to kill whoever came in his way,
but was himself safeguarded by an order directing everyone to
spare his life. He finally stated that he was unable to tell what had
become of him: he himself was wounded, and swam away to land;
and he had now come to the cavern in search of Thisbe. They
asked him what interest he had in Thisbe, or how he had got
hold of her, that he should be searching for her. Thermouthis
explained this also, by relating how he had carried her off from
some merchants, had fallen madly in love with her, and had kept
her hidden all the time until, on the attack of the enemy, he had
taken her down into the cavern. He now found her slain by some
persons of whom he had no knowledge but whom he would much
like to discover, that he might learn the reason of their action.
Then Cnemon, speaking with extreme earnestness, so eager was
he to clear himself of possible suspicion, said 'Thyamis is her
slayer', and showed him as evidence the sword which they had
found by the body of the slain. When Thermouthis saw it still

dripping with her blood—the steel spitting it yet warm from the recent slaughter—he recognized it as Thyamis' sword, and heaved a deep and long-drawn sigh. At a loss to comprehend the truth of the affair, smitten with misted sight and muteness, he crept up to the mouth of the cave, and coming beside the dead woman he laid his head upon her bosom and said: 'O Thisbe!' —and repeatedly spoke the name, and nothing more, till he began to curtail it somewhat, and so, his voice gradually failing, insensibly he fell asleep.

(15) The thoughts of Theagenes and Chariclea, and of Cnemon also, turned quickly to the general state of their concerns. While they seemed wishful to give this some consideration, yet the multitude of their sufferings in the past, the perplexities of their present misfortunes, and the uncertainty of what the future held for them in prospect, obscured the light of reason in their minds. For a great while they looked at one another; each of them, expecting someone else to speak and being disappointed, turned eyes to the ground, and then lifted head again to take fresh breath and relieve emotion with a sigh. At length Cnemon lay down on the ground; Theagenes sank down on a rock; and Chariclea flung herself upon him. For no little time they re-pelled the onset of sleep, in their desire to settle on some expedient for their present straits; but yielding to faintness and exhaustion they obeyed, despite themselves, the law of nature, as the excess of their grief caused them to slide into a pleasing slumber. Thus it is that at times even the intelligence of the soul is content to come to terms with the sensations of the body.

(16) When they had snatched a little sleep—just enough to close up smoothly the rims of their eyelids—Chariclea was visited by a dream of this tenor: a man with shaggy hair, stealthy looks and blood-stained hand struck at her with his sword and cut out her right eye. At that moment she screamed, and she called to Theagenes, telling him that her eye had been plucked away. He turned to her in the instant of hearing her call, and was deeply distressed by her suffering, as though he shared even the sensations that she had from visions in sleep. She clapped her hand to her face and felt it all over, searching for the feature that she had lost in her dream. Finding that it was a dream she said: 'It was a dream: I have my eye. Do not be

alarmed, Theagenes.' Hearing this, Theagenes breathed again and said: 'How fortunate that you have preserved those rays of sunshine! But tell me, what was it that happened to you? What was that sudden fright about yourself?' 'A violent, reckless man,' she said, 'undeterred by even your irresistible strength, made a savage assault on me, sword in hand, as I rested upon your knees, and I thought that he robbed me of my right eye. Would that it had been a waking reality and no dream, Theagenes, that I beheld!' 'Fie on such words!' he said, and asked her why she said that. 'Because it were better,' she replied, 'that I should be deprived of one of my eyes than be anxious on your account; for I greatly fear that the dream points to you, whom I have come to regard as my eye, my soul, my all.' 'No more of that,' said Cnemon, who had been roused from sleep by Chariclea's first outcry and had overheard everything. 'To my mind the dream is plainly to be construed in another way. Tell me, are your parents still alive?' She told him that they were and asked: 'And what if they should be?' 'Well then', he said, 'you must take it that your father has died; and this is how I make it out. We owe our coming forth into this life on earth and our sharing in the light of day to those who begat us; so it is likely that our dreams subtly present our father and mother in our wedded pair of eyes—our luminous sense, enabling our perception of the visible world.' 'A grievous meaning, this also,' said Chariclea. 'Yet I would rather it were true than the other. May the tripod of your oracle prove to be the more accurate, and I a false prophetess!' 'So it will turn out; only have faith,' said Cnemon; 'but we, in truth, seem to be dreaming, since we inquire into visions and apparitions instead of advancing some kind of scheme for our own future—and that too while we are free to do so in the absence of that Egyptian' (meaning Thermouthis) 'while he is refashioning and lamenting loves that are dead and gone.'

It is decided that Cnemon and Thermouthis shall go in search of Thyamis.

(17) Theagenes then spoke up. 'Well, Cnemon,' he said, 'since some deity has linked you with us, and made you a fellow-voyager through our misfortunes, you shall be the opener of our

consultation. You have a good knowledge of this region and of languages, whereas our wits are altogether too addled to devise what ought to be done; for we are overwhelmed by a huger surge of troubles.' After a short pause Cnemon answered him thus: 'Of troubles, Theagenes, it is doubtful who can claim to have the larger share, because the deity has deluged me also with a profusion of disasters. But since you both request me, as your senior, to speak of our present situation, this island, as you see, is deserted, having nobody on it but ourselves. Of gold, silver and apparel it has an abundance; many articles are stored here in this cavern, stolen from you and stripped from others by Thyamis and his men; but of grain and other provisions not the merest hint remains. There is a danger, if we stay on here, of perishing from starvation, or of perishing in an onslaught either of the enemy, should they return to the attack, or of the band with whom we were, if they should join up together again and, mindful of the treasure hidden here, come in search of this wealth. In that event we should inevitably be destroyed out of hand, or exposed to their maltreatment, if some humaner feeling prevailed. For in general these herdsmen are a faithless race, and more so than ever now, when they are deprived of the leader who restrained their minds to more temperate measures. We must therefore abandon this island, and avoid it as we would some snare or jail, having first dispatched Thermouthis on the alleged errand of inquiring far and wide for any news that he may gather of Thyamis. For it will be easier for us, when we are by ourselves, to consider and carry out our plan of action; and besides, it will be well to rid ourselves of a man who is by nature unreliable and a brigand of quarrelsome temper; one who is also inclined to have some suspicion of us on account of Thisbe, and who will surely not rest until he can find an opportunity of discomfiting us.'

(18) His advice was approved, and they resolved to act upon it. They advanced to the mouth of the cavern—for they reckoned that it was now day time—and roused up Thermouthis, who was wholly sunk in slumber. They explained to him as much as was suitable of the plans that they had made, and found it easy to persuade his somewhat volatile mind. They laid the body of Thisbe in a cavity, and heaped over it, instead of earth, some of the ashes from the cabins; and they performed all the customary

funeral rites that were possible on the occasion, paying the
tribute of their tears and lamentations in default of the full
honours of the traditional offerings. Then they dispatched
Thermouthis on the errand that they had arranged for him. He
went off on his way for a short distance, and then turned back.
He said that he would not travel alone, nor would venture upon
such a dangerous investigation, unless Cnemon agreed to bear
a share in the undertaking. Theagenes, observing that Cnemon
shrank from this proposal—for, while reporting what the
Egyptian had said, he was obviously in great trepidation—
remarked: 'I see; you are sturdy enough in opinion, but rather
feeble in resolution: I have noted some signs of your character,
and most clearly in this present instance. Come now, whet the
edge of your spirit, and raise your mind to more manly thoughts.
At this moment it seems necessary to agree to his terms, that he
may not conceive some suspicion of our intended flight, and to
accompany him for the first part of his journey. Surely there is
no danger in going along with an unarmed man, when one has a
sword in one's hand and armour on one's body, and then, at a
favourable moment, quietly giving him the slip and coming to
join us at an agreed place. Let us agree, if you like, on some
village near by, which may be known to you as a civilized one.'
Cnemon thought well of his suggestion, and mentioned a village
named Chemmis, a wealthy place and populous, built along the
banks of the Nile on high ground, so as to be fortified against
the herdsmen. The distance, he said, after one crossed the
swamp, was a little under a hundred furlongs, and they must
make for it with faces turned due south.

(19) 'Hard going,' rejoined Theagenes, 'at least for Chariclea,
for she is unaccustomed to walking any great distance. Nevertheless we will make the journey, assuming the guise of beggars and
strollers who show tricks to get food.' 'Yes, by Zeus,' said
Cnemon, 'you both do look grossly disfigured, especially
Chariclea since she had her eye knocked out, just lately. In your
present state, I should say, you will be asking, not for scraps, but
for falchions and cauldrons.' [1] At this they smiled a faint, forced

---

[1] A reminiscence of Melanthius' words about Odysseus when he appeared
in beggarly guise (Homer, *Od.* xvii. 222). Swords and cauldrons were among
the usual gifts presented to heroes.

smile, that merely flitted over their lips; then, after confirming with oaths their joint resolve, and calling the gods to witness that never of their own will would they forsake one another, they proceeded to do as their plan required. Cnemon and Thermouthis crossed over the swamp at sunrise, and made their way through a dense forest whose tangled growth much impeded their passage. Thermouthis led the way, at the request purposely made by Cnemon, who gave as his pretext the other's acquaintance with that difficult region, and his reliance on Thermouthis as guide; but more truly he was concerned to ensure his own safety, and wished to prearrange an opportunity of making his escape. As they progressed they came upon some flocks of sheep —the shepherds ran away and lay hidden in the denser part of the forest. They slaughtered one of the rams and set it to roast over the fire prearranged by the shepherds; and they gorged themselves on the meat without waiting for it to be properly roasted, so hard pressed by hunger were their bellies. Like wolves or jackals they devoured the pieces of flesh as they were cut off, only slightly scorched by the fire, and the half-roasted meat, as they ate, dripped its blood down their cheeks.[1] When they had gorged their fill, they gulped down some milk, and then pursued their intended route. The time was now about the hour of the unyoking of oxen. As they were ascending a ridge, Thermouthis stated that below it was the village in which he guessed that Thyamis, after his capture, was confined or had been put to death. Cnemon began complaining that his belly was disordered by his overeating, and said that the milk had brought on a troublesome flux of the bowels: he bade Thermouthis go on ahead, saying that he would soon overtake him. When he had made this move once, twice and thrice, he was judged to have spoken the truth; and he added that he had difficulty in catching up. Having brought the Egyptian to the point of being used to his halts, he finally stayed behind, well out of sight, and by dashing headlong down the hill into the more difficult parts of the undergrowth he made good his escape.

(20) When the Egyptian reached the crest of the ridge, he rested awhile on a rock, awaiting the evening and nightfall, after which they had agreed to enter the village and inquire up and

---

[1] Another reminiscence: cf. *Il.* xvi. 156–9, of wolves devouring a stag.

down for Thyamis. At the same time he looked about to see if
Cnemon were coming up from anywhere, for the fellow was
forming a sinister plan against him. The suspicion rankled in his
mind that Cnemon was the slayer of Thisbe, and he was considering how he might at some time take his life; while his fury
impelled him, after dealing with Cnemon, to make an attack also
on Theagenes. As Cnemon nowhere appeared, and it was now
the dead of night, Thermouthis betook himself to sleep—a sleep
heavy as bronze, so prolonged as to become his last, through the
bite of an asp; and thus by the will, no doubt, of the Fates he
sank to a sudden end not inappropriate to his character. Cnemon,
from the moment of parting from Thermouthis, sped away in his
flight without pausing for breath, till the darkness of night came
on and hindered his further progress. On the spot where he was
thus overtaken he hid himself beneath as large a pile of leaves as
he could heap together. As he lay beneath the pile he passed most
of the time without sleeping and in sore distress, supposing
every sound, a gust of wind or a stir of leaves to be Thermouthis;
and when he had yielded a little to the onset of sleep, he seemed
to be fleeing, and kept turning round to look behind him to see
if he could spy a pursuer who was not anywhere. He wanted to
sleep, yet prayed to be spared what he wanted, since the dreams
that visited him were more dire than the truth of his case. He
felt like being angry with the night, accounting this a longer one
than any others. Gladdened by the sight of day, he first cut off
so much of the overgrowth of his hair as he had purposely
produced to accord with a brigand-like appearance among the
herdsmen, in order that he might not arouse aversion or suspicion in anyone who came across him. For herdsmen, among
various ways of presenting a formidable aspect, draw their hair
down upon their eyebrows, and toss it about as it falls over their
shoulders, well knowing that the hair makes love-makers more
winsome, but freebooters more fearsome.

*Cnemon, having parted from Thermouthis and come to the Nile,
meets with the Egyptian sage Calasiris at Chemmis.*

(21) So Cnemon cut away enough of his locks to reduce them
from the brigands' style to one of some refinement; and he then

made haste to reach the village of Chemmis, where he had appointed to meet Theagenes. As he drew near the Nile, and was about to cross over to Chemmis, he observed an old man roaming along the bank: he was continually running up and down for quite a distance beside the flowing water, and seemed to be imparting to the river some matters preying on his mind. His hair hung down in the priestly fashion, and was perfectly white: his chin had a bushy beard of venerable length; and his gown and other attire tended somewhat to the Grecian style. Cnemon halted for a moment: the old man ran past him again and again, without seeming to notice that anyone was there, so completely, in fact, was he absorbed in his train of thought, his mind being occupied solely with his meditation. Cnemon advanced to meet him face to face, and began by bidding him good day. The man replied that it could not be such for him, since he was not being so treated by Fortune. Surprised at his words, Cnemon asked if the stranger were a Greek. 'Not a Greek,' he answered, 'but an Egyptian of these parts.' 'How comes it then that you are wearing Greek dress?' 'Calamities', he said, 'have put me in this brilliant change of costume.' Cnemon wondered that a man should brighten his appearance on account of calamities, and requested to be informed of these. 'You summon me from Troy,'[1] answered the old man, 'and stir up against yourself a swarm of troubles and their incessant buzzing. But whither are you bound, young man, and whence? Why this Greek speech in Egypt?' 'How absurd!' said Cnemon. 'You explain nothing of your own business, though the first to be questioned about it, and seek information of mine.' 'Well then,' said the other, 'since you look like a Greek man, and some turn of Fortune, belike, is disguising you also, and you are filled with a desire to hear my story, and I on my part am with child to relate it to somebody— I would perhaps have told it to these reeds here, like the fellow in the legend,[2] if I had not met with you—well now, let us leave

---

[1] To tell the sad tale of the siege and sack of Troy by the Greeks; cf. Introduction, p. i.

[2] Midas, King of Phrygia, was given ass's ears by Apollo for judging Pan to be the better musician. The King's hairdresser discovered the ears under the King's Phrygian cap, and confided the secret into a hole that he dug. Huge reeds then grew up and whispered it abroad (Ovid, Metamorph. xi. 174, 193).

these banks of the Nile, and the Nile itself, for there can be no pleasure in listening to narrations of some length in a place that is being burnt up by the midday sun. Let us go to the village that you see situated just opposite, unless you have some more pressing affair on hand. I will lodge you, not in a house of my own, but in that of an honest man who took me in myself at my entreaty. Under his roof you shall hear as much of my tale as you desire, and in your turn shall recount your own adventures.' 'Let us go,' said Cnemon; 'for in any case I am anxious to make my way to that village, as I have an appointment to wait there for some special friends of mine.'

(22) So they embarked in one of the boats that lay moored by the bank in readiness for travellers who paid to be ferried over. They made the passage to the village, and arrived at the lodging where the old man stayed. They did not find there the master of the house, but were cordially welcomed by a daughter of their host—a young woman of marriageable age—and by all the maidservants in the house, who treated their lodger just as they would a father, on instructions, I conceive, from the proprietor. One of them washed his feet and wiped away the dust from his shanks; another attended to his bed, and got ready a soft couch on which he could recline; another fetched a jug of water and kindled a fire; while another brought in a table laden with wheaten bread and all sorts of the season's fruits. Marvelling at all this, Cnemon said: 'Surely we have come to the abode of Zeus the Hospitaller—so it would seem from these open-handed attentions, revealing a disposition of such warm kindliness.' 'Not the abode of Zeus,' said the other, 'but of a man exact in his devotions to Zeus the Hospitaller and Patron of Suppliants. His life also, my son, is a roving one: he is a merchant, whose experience of many cities and the behaviour and cast of mind of many people has taught him, it would seem, to receive strangers under his roof, as he received me a few days ago, restless wanderer that I am.' 'And why all this wandering, father, that you mention?' 'Robbed of my children by brigands,' he replied, 'and knowing the offenders but unable to obtain my rights, I roam around this region and utter forth my grief in moaning, like some bird, I imagine, whose nest is ravaged by a snake and, while her brood is being devoured before her eyes, is afraid to

go near, yet cannot bear to flee away. Affection and affright do battle in her breast, and with shrill cries she flutters about her beleaguered young, addressing to savage ears, that nature has not made acquainted with pity, the ineffectual appeal of a mother's laments.' [1] 'Then will you please relate', said Cnemon, 'how and when you were a victim of this grievous assault?' 'Later on,' he replied; 'for it is time now for us to attend to the stomach—which Homer, glancing at the fact that it makes all things wait upon its pleasure, admirably called 'baneful'.[2] But first let us follow the rule of the Egyptian sages, and pour libations to the gods; for even the belly shall not induce me to transgress, or ever let any suffering succeed in dispelling the memory of one's duty towards the divine.'

(23) Having thus spoken he poured from his drinking-bowl some pure water, for that was his habitual drink, and said: 'Let us offer libation to the gods of this land, and to those of Greece besides, and especially to the Pythian Apollo; also to Theagenes and Chariclea, those most excellent persons, seeing that I number them too in the company of the gods.' With that he shed some tears, as though rendering to that pair, in those mournful drops, an additional libation. Cnemon was astounded at hearing their names and, after gazing up and down at the old man, he asked: 'What is this you say? Are Theagenes and Chariclea in very truth your children?' 'Children, good sir,' he replied, 'born to me motherless. It was my fortune that the gods presented them to me: they were brought forth by the travail of my soul; my inclination towards them was regarded as natural affection; and this led to their both regarding and addressing me as their father. But tell me, how came you to know them?' 'Not only have I come to know them,' said Cnemon, 'but I can give you the happy news of their being still alive.' 'Apollo!' cried out the other; 'ye gods! Where on earth are they? Oh, tell me! I will look upon you as my saviour, and esteem you as on a par with the gods!' 'And what will be my reward?' said Cnemon. 'For the present,' he replied, 'gratitude, which to my mind is the

---

[1] A reminiscence of the more elaborately described portent of a snake at a sparrow's nest in Homer, *Il.* ii. 308–16.

[2] 'A ravening belly may not be put down, a baneful thing, that brings many woes upon mankind' (Homer, *Od.* xvii. 286–7).

handsomest guest-offering to a man of good sense; I know many a one who has laid up this gift as a treasure in his soul. But if we should once set foot in our native land—an event which the gods foreshadow to me—you will have your fill of a plentiful draught of riches.' 'These are future, uncertain things that you promise me,' said Cnemon, 'while you have the means of requiting me here and now.' 'Point out to me anything that you see here and now, for I am ready to give up even a part of my body.' 'No need of any amputation: I shall consider myself amply repaid if you will please make clear to me whence that pair came, of what parentage they are, how they arrived here, and what manner of experiences have been their lot.' 'You shall have your reward,' replied the old man, 'in good measure, such as you would not get even if you went so far as to ask for all the money in the possession of mankind. But for the moment let us taste a few morsels of food; for the tale will require a lengthy spell of listening on your part and of relating on mine.' They then ate heartily of nuts, figs, fresh-gathered dates and other such things as the old man had for his daily food, for he never killed any animal for a meal; and for his drink he had water, while Cnemon took some wine. The latter, after a little while, said—'Dionysus, as you know, father, delights in tales, and loves comedies: he has now taken up his abode in me, and disposes me to be a hearer of something, and he impels me to claim the payment that you promised me; so now it is time for you to produce the drama of your story, as it were, upon the stage.' 'You shall hear it,' he said; 'but note that we chanced to have here the worthy Nausicles, who many a time has pestered me to unfold my narrative to him, but whom I have fobbed off each time by one shift or another.'

(24) 'And where might he be now?' asked Cnemon, as he called to mind the name of Nausicles. 'He has gone a-hunting,' he said. To Cnemon's next question: 'After what sort of quarry?' 'Wild beasts', replied the other, 'of the most dangerous kind: they are called men, and herdsmen, but they are brigands in their way of life, and extremely hard to catch in the swamp which provides them with lairs and hollow places.' 'And with what offence does he charge them?' 'The seizure of an Attic woman,' he answered, 'whom he loved, and whom he called

Thisbe.' 'Alack!' said Cnemon, and of a sudden fell silent, as though checking himself. 'What ails you?' asked the old man; but Cnemon changed the subject and said: 'I wonder how, or relying on what support, he was moved to make this attack.' To which the other answered: 'The Great King,[1] sir, has as his satrap over Egypt Oroondates, by whose authority Mitranes has been assigned the command of the garrison of this village. Now this man has been paid a great sum by Nausicles to accompany him with a strong body of cavalry and men-at-arms. Nausicles is aggrieved by the abduction of the Attic girl, not merely as being the object of his love and a most admirable singer, but because he intended, in his own words, to convey her actually to the King of Ethiopia, to be the future play-fellow and companion of his consort, after the Grecian fashion. Deprived of the very handsome price which he was expecting to be paid for her, he is casting about for any expedient that will assist him. I myself have incited him to this action, in the hope that he might also be the means of preserving my children's lives.' Here Cnemon broke in, saying: 'Enough of herdsmen and satraps, yes, and even of kings! Before I was aware of it, you were almost leading me on and on to the end with such talk. Here you have trundled in this old scene which, as they say, has "nothing to do with Dionysus."[2] So bring back your story to its promised course. I find you behaving like Proteus of Pharos—not assuming as he did, a delusive, fluid form, but still attempting to lead me astray.' 'You shall be told the tale,' said the old man; 'I will relate to you my own history first, quite briefly, not complicating my narrative as you imagine, but providing an orderly, consecutive account for your hearing.

Calasiris recounts his adventures to Cnemon.

'I belong to the city of Memphis. My father, and I myself, were named Calasiris. My life now is a wandering one, but was not such aforetime, for in the past I was a prophet. I took to me

---

[1] Egypt was under the dominion of Persia from its conquest by Cambyses in 525 B.C. till its subjection to Alexander in 332–331 B.C.

[2] This saying was originally a protest against novel or irrelevant matter introduced into Attic drama, which was traditionally produced in honour of Dionysus.

a wife according to my country's law; I lost her by the ordinance of nature. After her dissolution and passage into her next allotted state, I lived for some time unmolested by troubles, priding myself on two children that I had by her. But a few years later the fated revolution of the luminaries of heaven caused a change in my fortunes. The eye of Cronos [1] cast a glance upon my house, which brought upon me the alteration for the worse that my learning had foreshadowed, but had not enabled me to escape. For, while it is possible to foresee the inflexible determinations of the Fates, to evade them is beyond our reach. Yet foreknowledge in such matters is an advantage, since it mitigates the fiery effect of the dread event. An unexpected disaster, my son, is intolerable, but one foreknown is more easily borne: for in the former case the mind, gripped by fear, cowers down; in the latter, habituation reconciles us through cool calculation.

(25) 'What befell me was this: a Thracian woman, in the full bloom of her age, in beauty second only to Chariclea, whose name was Rhodopis,[2] but who was sent forth, I know not whence or how, by a Fate intent on harming all who came acquainted with her, went roaming about Egypt and paraded herself even as far as Memphis. She was escorted by a great train of attendants, was possessed of great wealth, and was a perfect adept in all amatory seductions. It was impossible to meet her and not be captivated, so inescapable and irresistible was the kind of lascivious drag-net that she trailed with the glances of her eyes. She often visited the temple of Isis, whose priest-in-charge I was, and constantly made offerings of sacrifices and votive gifts of great price. I am ashamed to tell it, but it shall be spoken: the frequent sight of her came to be too much for me; she began to break down my lifelong practice of continence. For some time I opposed the eyes of the soul to those of the body, but at last I had to own my defeat and submit to the burden of amorous passion. I discerned in that woman the origin of the future distresses foretold to me by the divine power, and understood that there my destiny was producing a scene in which the spirit

[1] The youngest of the Titans, and father of Zeus and other Olympian deities, Cronos was identified by the Romans with Saturn, who according to some had on mankind the baleful influence of the evil eye.
[2] 'Rosy face': a famous courtesan from Thrace thus named, who amassed a fortune in Egypt, is discussed by Herodotus, ii. 134–5.

then appointed to play the part had seemingly assumed the character of Rhodopis. I resolved not to disgrace the priestly service in which I had been reared from childhood—and I did resist—nor to profane the rites and the shrines of the gods. On my offence—not one of acts, which Heaven forbid!—but only of appetite, I imposed a fitting penalty. Setting up my reason as my judge, I punished my lust with exile. Ill-starred wretch that I was, I went forth from my native land, submitting to the constraints of the Fates and resigning my life to whatever treatment they might choose to give it, and at the same time escaping from the accursed Rhodopis. For I feared, good sir, that under the oppression of the star then dominant over me I might be reduced even to the viler course. But what more than all and on all accounts drove me forth was my children, of whom the inexpressible wisdom vouchsafed to me by the gods often gave me forewarning that they would clash with one another in armed conflict. So, to exclude from my eyes such a cruel sight—one which I imagine the very sun would avoid by veiling his rays in a cloud —and to deliver a father's vision from the spectacle of his children's slaughter, I expelled myself from the land and home of my fathers, without speaking a word to anyone of my departure. I made a pretext of voyaging to Great Thebes,[1] in order to see the elder of my two sons, who dwelt there at that time with his maternal grandfather. That son's name, good sir, was Thyamis.' Once again Cnemon started back, as though his ears had been struck a blow by the name of Thyamis: while he refrained from speech so as to hear the sequel, the other completed his story thus:

Calasiris relates how he visited Delphi, received a prophecy from the oracle, and met Charicles, the priest of Apollo, who told his story to Calasiris.

(26) 'I pass over the middle stages of my wanderings, young man, since they contribute nothing towards your inquiry. I learnt that there was a city in Greece named Delphi, sacred to Apollo

---

[1] The important and populous city on the Upper Nile: the impressive relics of its former splendour at its eastern quarters of Luxor and Karnak are well known.

and containing shrines of other gods; and that it was a centre for
the work of learned men in a situation apart from the madding
crowd. Thither I betook me, deciding on it as a suitable resort
for a prophet, dedicated as it was to sacred rites and ceremonies.
I crossed the Crisaean Gulf, and putting in at Cirrha I hastened
from shipboard to the city. As I halted before it, a holy voice,
in tones truly divine, came to my ears on the very spot; and the
city impressed me in general as an abode of the higher powers,
but especially from the nature of its site. For, precisely like a
fortress, the inartificial acropolis of Mount Parnassus, impending
aloft, closely enfolds the city within its flanks.' 'Admirably
spoken,' said Cnemon, 'as by one who actually felt upon him the
Pythian afflatus. So it was that my father used to describe the
position of Delphi, after the citizens of Athens had sent him as
recorder to oversee the ceremonies.' 'Are you then an Athenian,
my son?' 'Yes,' he said. 'And your name?' 'Cnemon,' he
replied, and added: 'As for my story, you shall hear it another
time: for the moment, continue with yours.' 'I will do so,' said
the old man, and resumed the account of his ascent to the city.
'Highly pleased with the city's public walks and squares and
fountains, and with the Castalian spring itself, from which I duly
besprinkled myself, I hastened on to the temple, incited by the
talk of the crowd, who were saying that it was the time for the
prophetess to have her tremor. I entered in, and prostrate before
her I was uttering some words of private prayer, when the
Pythia pronounced these words:

> "Thou hast brought thy footsteps from the fruitful land
>   beside the Nile,
>   In flight from the spinnings of the predominant Fates.
>   Persevere, for I will give thee soon the soil
>   Of dark-furrowed Egypt. Meanwhile, be thou my friend."

(27) 'When she had delivered this oracle, I flung myself
prone upon the steps of the altar, and besought the god to be
gracious to me in all things. The large gathering of bystanders
loudly praised the god for the prophecy vouchsafed to me on my
first appeal to him; and they congratulated me and paid me
thenceforward all manner of kindly attentions, saying that I was
the first man to be received by the god as a friend since a certain

Lycurgus of Sparta.[1] They gave their consent to my dwelling at my pleasure within the precincts of the temple, and decreed that I be provided with sustenance at the public expense. In short, I enjoyed every advantage without stint. I either took part in the ceremonies or officiated at the sacrifices daily offered by foreign as well as native peoples in great number and variety to gratify the god, or else I held converse with philosophers; for not a few in that walk of life gather about the temple of the Pythian Apollo. Indeed, the city is quite a school of the Muses, being inspired by Phoebus, divine leader of the Muses. For some time at first these persons plied me with questions on various matters. One would ask how we Egyptians worship our country's gods, while another wished to know how it came about that different animals were adored by different sections of our people, and what was the reason of each cult. Some wished to know about the construction of the Pyramids, others about the subterranean mazes. In brief, they omitted not a single point of interest in their inquiries concerning Egypt; for listening to any accounts of Egypt is what appeals most strongly to Greek ears.

(28) 'At length a day came when one of the more accomplished of them brought me a query concerning the Nile—as to what are its sources, and what is the peculiarity distinguishing it from other rivers, whereby it alone of them all overflows in the summer season. I told him what I knew of these matters, giving him all the information which is recorded in sacred books about this river and which prophets alone may read and learn. I described how it has its sources in the highlands of Ethiopia on the borders of Libya—that is, in the region where the zone of the East has its end and that of the South its beginning. The river increases its height in the summer season not, as some have supposed, because its flow is repelled by opposing currents of the monsoons,[2] but through the action of these same winds which, about the summer solstice, drive and hustle all the clouds from the north to the south until they are crowded into the torrid

---

[1] Herodotus (i. 65) gives the four lines of the oracle spoken to Lycurgus, the mythical law-giver of Sparta, in words declaring him to be a friend of the gods and more a divine than a human person.

[2] Periodic winds blowing from the north-west throughout the summer.

zone. There they are repelled in their onward course by the extreme fierceness of that region: all the moisture that until then has been gradually collected and condensed is evaporated, with the result that heavy rains are precipitated. The Nile then swells up and, disdaining to be a river, rebels against its banks and transforms Egypt into a sea, fertilizing in its passage all the arable land. That is why its water is so very sweet to drink, being furnished forth by the showers of heaven, and so very agreeable to the touch, being no longer so hot as at its outset, though still tepid from its earlier warmth. For this reason it alone of rivers gives off no vapours, as it doubtless might be expected to do if, as some persons, I am informed, of high repute in Greece have held, it derives its brimming flood from the melting of snows.

(29) 'While I was expounding these and other such matters, the priest of the Pythian god, with whom I had become intimate, and whose name was Charicles, said to me: "A most excellent statement, with which I am myself in agreement; for I have had the same information from the priests at Catadoupa[1] on the Nile." "Then, Charicles," I said to him, "you have been there?" "I have, learned Calasiris," he replied. When I asked him next "What purpose drew you thither?" he answered: "Ill fortune in my domestic affairs, which yet has been a cause of good fortune also for me." When I showed surprise at this inconsequence he went on: "You will not be surprised if you learn the course of events; and you can learn it whenever you wish." "Then it is time that you told me," I said; "for I wish to hear it now." "Listen then," said Charicles, after he had dismissed the rest of the company; "indeed, I have long been wishing to let you hear my experiences, for a certain benefit that it may bring to me. I married, but had no children, until at long last, when I was advanced in years, my many entreaties to the god were answered: I was declared father of a daughter, who according to the forewarning of the god would be born under no fair auspices. She came to be of marriageable age, and I bestowed her upon the man among her suitors—and they were many— whom I judged to be of the highest merit. On the very night of her going to bed with her bridegroom, the unfortunate girl met

---

[1] A town at the first Cataract, near Philae, now known as Assuan.

her death from a thunderbolt, or a fire caused by man, that
seized on our sleeping-quarters. The nuptial song was suddenly
succeeded by lamentation; from her bride-chamber she was
escorted to her tomb; and the same torches that had so brightly
lit up her wedding feast now kindled her funeral pyre. My Fate
added a further woeful scene to this tragedy, by carrying off my
girl's mother, worn out by her mourning. This divine visitation
of misery was too much for me. I did not remove myself from
life, in deference to the theologians' opinion that such a course
is unlawful, but crept away from my native land, fleeing from the
desolation of my house. For it is a great help towards oblivion
of one's troubles to screen from one's soul any visual reminders
of them. I wandered in many regions, and came at length to your
Egypt, and even to Catadoupa, seeking knowledge of the
Cataracts of the Nile.

(30) '"So there, my friend, you have the explanation of my
travelling thither. But there is something incidental to my
account, or rather, to speak more truly, the main point in it,
which I would have you know. As I was strolling about the city
and availing myself of my leisure for buying some articles that
are scarce in Greece—for by then the severity of my grief was
being softened down by time, and I was feeling an eagerness to
return to my native country—I was approached by a man of
serious mien whose eyes shone with a quick intelligence. He
had but newly emerged from adolescence; his colour was perfectly black. He greeted me, and stated in halting Greek that he
wished to tell me something in private. I readily complied, and
having led me into a temple near by he said: 'I have seen you
buying leaves and roots of Indian, Ethiopian and Egyptian plants.
Now, if you should have a mind to buy things that I have of pure
quality, with no deception about them, I am ready to supply
them.' 'I am so minded,' I said; 'show me some.' 'You
shall see them,' he went on; 'but you must not be a haggler
over their purchase.' 'On your part,' I said, 'you must pledge
yourself not to put too high a price on them for their sale.' Then
he drew forth a small pouch that he had under his arm, and
showed me some marvellous specimens of precious stones: in it
were pearls of the size of a small nut, developed to a perfect
roundness and shining with the whitest lustre; also emeralds,

hyacinths—some green like corn in the spring, and gleaming
with a smooth polish like drops of olive oil, while others suggested the colour of the sea shivering slightly beneath some sheer
headland and showing in its depths a violet tinge. In brief, they
combined to make such a sparkling medley of various colours as
was highly delightful to the eye. When I saw them I said: 'You
had better go, sir, and find other purchasers of these things; for
I and all my resources could hardly balance in value a single one
of the stones that I see there.' 'But even if unable to buy,' he
said, 'you can at least accept a gift.' 'I am not incapable,' I
replied, 'of accepting a gift, but for some purpose or other you
are jesting with me.' 'I am not jesting,' he said; 'I am quite
serious; and I swear by the god who has his abode in this place
that I will give you all these things if, besides them, you consent
to take possession of another gift much more precious than
these.' At this I laughed: when he asked me why, I answered:
'Because it is laughable that, while gravely promising me gifts
of such great value, you propose in addition to enrich me with
something far more valuable even than those.' 'Only trust me,'
he said. 'Come, swear that you on your part will make the best
use of my gift, in the way which I myself shall indicate to you.'
Surprised and bewildered, I yet swore to this, in the hope of
acquiring such fine things. When I had taken the oath in the
terms that he required, he took me to his house and showed me
a girl of inconceivable, celestial beauty. He said that she was
seven years old, but to me she seemed to be approaching the
marriageable age—so much, you know, does exquisite beauty
tend to magnify one's impression of stature. I stood dumbfounded, alike from incomprehension of the whole proceeding
and from a desire to feast my eyes more and more on what I was
beholding.

(31) '"The man then started to tell this story: 'The girl whom
you see here, sir, was still in her swaddling-clothes when her
mother exposed her, for a reason that you will learn a little later,
committing her life to the vacillations of Fortune. I discovered
her and took her up; for it had been a wrongful thing for me to
suffer a soul once invested with human existence to remain in
peril—this being one great precept of our Naked Sages, a
disciple of whom I have lately been counted worthy to become.

Besides, I was there and then aware of a radiant, heavenly light that shone from the infant's eyes, so awe-inspiring, and at the same time so fascinating, was the gaze that it turned on me as I was inspecting it. Exposed with the child was a necklace of stones—that which I showed you just now—and a swathe of spun silk in which were inwoven characters of our native script, so pricked out as to relate the child's story: the mother, I suppose, had the forethought to provide these tokens for her daughter's identification. When I had read the writing and learnt where and to whom the infant belonged, I carried it to a farm in a situation remote from the city, and handed it over to my shepherds to rear, sternly warning them not to tell anyone. The articles exposed with it I kept in my hands, lest they should occasion an attempt upon the girl. At first she continued in this way unnoticed; but when with the passage of time the fullness of her maidenhood was seen to display a more than ordinary bloom, and her beauty, even if hidden underground, could not have escaped notice, but would, I believe, have shone forth even thence, I feared that knowledge of her might come to light; she might be put to death, and I in turn might be faced with some unpleasant consequences. I therefore contrived to be dispatched as an envoy to the Satrap of Egypt, and came here, bringing her along with me in the hope of settling her in life. I am to speak with the satrap forthwith on the business of my mission: he has notified me that I am to have an audience today. To you, and to the gods who have so ordained, I commit the girl on the terms of the sworn agreement between us: that you will keep this girl free, and give her in marriage to a free man, together with this swathe which I convey to you from my own hands, or rather from those of the mother who exposed her. I have confidence that you will carry out in full the purpose of this transaction; for I take courage from the oaths that you have sworn, and I have also been at pains during the many days of your sojourn here to take note of your character as one that is truly Greek. This is what I had to tell you, in concise terms at this moment of my being called away by the duties of my mission. A clearer and more particular account of the girl shall be given you tomorrow, when I meet you at the temple of Isis.'

(32) '"Proceeding as had been agreed, I took charge of the

girl and brought her veiled to my house. During that day I
tended her with care and constant kindliness, and rendering
many thanks to the gods I have ever since considered and called
her my own daughter. The next day, at dawn, I went off in great
haste to the temple of Isis, where I had the appointment to meet
the stranger. After walking about there for a great while and
failing to see him anywhere, I presented myself at the satrap's
palace and inquired whether anyone had seen the envoy from
Ethiopia. I was informed that he had departed, or rather, had
been expelled, the satrap having threatened him with death if
he had not passed over the frontier before sunset. When I asked
the reason of this my informant replied: 'Because he ordered
the satrap to keep his hands off the emerald mines, since they
belonged to Ethiopia.' I returned, greatly annoyed, like one
who had received a heavy blow, at not having obtained any
knowledge concerning the girl—as to who she was, whence
she came and what was her parentage."' 'You ought not
to wonder at that,' said Cnemon. 'I too am vexed at having
heard nothing, but perhaps I shall hear.' 'You shall hear,'
said Calasiris.

Calasiris continues the story told to him by Charicles.

(33) 'I will now relate,' he went on, 'how Charicles continued
with the rest of his story. "When I arrived at my dwelling," he
said, "the young girl came to meet me and, without saying a
word—for she was not yet familiar with the Greek tongue—gave
me her hand in greeting. The mere sight of her relaxed my mind
to a more cheerful mood. I marvelled also that, just as fine, well-
bred dogs will fawn upon everyone, even at a short acquaintance,
this girl was so quick to perceive my goodwill towards her, and
honoured me as a father. So I resolved not to linger on at
Catadoupa, for fear lest some malign visitation should bereave
me of this my second daughter; and I voyaged down the
length of the Nile to the sea, where I found a vessel that took
me on my homeward way. And now the child is here with me,
as my own child, bearing my name; for my life is anchored upon
her, and in every respect she excels, surpassing even all that I
could pray for, so rapidly has she absorbed the Greek language,

and rapidly also sprung up to her prime like a shoot of some thriving plant.[1] And so far has she outstripped all the other girls in the fresh bloom of her person, that every eye, Greek or foreign, is turned upon her; and wherever she appears, in temples, walks or squares, like some statue upheld as an exemplar of beauty she attracts to herself the sight and mind of everybody. Yet, with all this excellence, she afflicts me with a harassing distress: for she has renounced marriage, and is intent on remaining a virgin all her life; and having devoted herself as a ministrant to Artemis she spends most of her time in hunting and practising archery. My life is now a misery, because I hoped to give her in marriage to my sister's son, a youth of rare refinement and charm in both speech and disposition; but I am now frustrated by the girl's heartless decision. Neither by kind attentions, nor by promises, nor by appeals to reason, have I been able to persuade her. Hardest blow of all, she has aimed, as they say, my own shafts against me, and brandishes over me her accomplishment in the arts of speech—the subtleties of which I have imparted to her—to demonstrate that she has chosen for herself the best life—glorifying the virgin state which, she declares, is next to the immortal, and calling it unspotted, untainted, incorruptible. Love, Aphrodite, and all nuptial celebration she utterly consigns to the crows! In this situation I appeal to you for your help; and it was for this reason that I seized an opportunity, a happy chance that somehow came my way of its own accord, and so was led to tell you my story at this undue length. And now indulge me, my good Calasiris: bring to bear on her something of the Egyptian lore and enchantment. Persuade her, whether by words or by works, to know her own nature and to be conscious of her womanhood. If you consent you will find it an easy matter; for she is one who has not lacked converse with learned men, but has come to maidenhood in constant company with them. She shares the same dwelling with you there, I mean within the precincts and shadow of the temple. Do not disregard my entreaty; do not assent to my continuing a childless and disconsolate man, to live out a burdensome old age bereft of descendants, I beseech you by Apollo and by the gods

---

[1] So in Homer, *Il.* xviii. 437. Thetis says that her son Achilles sprang up like a new shoot of a plant.

of your country!" I wept, Cnemon, at hearing those words; for he too shed some tears as he pressed his petition, and I promised to give him any succour that I could.

(34) 'While we were still considering the matter, a man came running to us and reported that the leader of the Aenianes' [1] mission had been waiting a long time at the door, and was loudly calling for the priest to attend and begin the sacred ceremony. When I asked Charicles who the Aenianes were and what was their mission and their sacrificial oblation, he replied: "The Aenianes are the noblest people in the region of Thessaly, having a distinct Hellenic descent from Hellen, son of Deucalion. Altogether they are spread along the whole extent of the Malian Gulf; but they take especial pride in their capital, Hypate, so named, they will have it, from its supremacy and authority, but according to others because it is situated below Mount Oeta.[2] The sacrifice and pious mission take place in every fourth year, when the Pythian Games are being held, as they are now, to your knowledge. The Aenianes do this in honour of Neoptolemus, son of Achilles; for it was here that he was treacherously murdered, close to the very altar of the Pythian Apollo, by Orestes, son of Agamemnon. The present mission surpasses all that have come before, as its leader prides himself on being a descendant of Achilles. I met the young man yesterday, and truly I thought him worthy of the lineage of Achilles, so distinguished he is in form and stature, which visibly attest his kinship." I wondered at this, and asked how, belonging to the clan of the Aenianes, he could declare himself to be a descendant of Achilles, seeing that the Egyptian Homer's poem informs us that Achilles was of Phthiotis. "This young man," said Charicles, "contends that the hero was entirely of the stock of the Aenianes, insisting that Thetis came from the Malian Gulf to be wedded to Peleus; that of old the region bordering on the gulf was named Phthia; and that the other peoples, because of Achilles' great renown, fictitiously appropriated him. And, apart from this, the youth accounts himself one of the Aeacidae, adducing as his forefather

---

[1] These people inhabited the country to the south of Thessaly, in the upper valley of the River Spercheius.

[2] 'Hypatos' was an epic word for 'supreme' or 'supernal'; the other view combined 'hypo' (under) with the name 'Oeta'.

Menesthius, son of Spercheius and Polydora, daughter of
Peleus—Menesthius, who with Achilles was a leader in the
expedition against Troy and, as being his kinsman, commanded
the first rank of the Myrmidons.[1] And he clasps and clings
tightly to Achilles, and tries in every way to embody him among
the Aenianes; citing as proof, besides other grounds that he
alleges, this sacrificial offering to the spirit of Neoptolemus, in
which service the Thessalians, he says, gave the preference to
the Aenianes, thus attesting their close kinship with the hero."
"One can have no objection, Charicles," I said, "either to their
being thus favoured or to their claim being vindicated. Now,
order the leader of the mission to be called in here, for I am in
quite a mad flutter of eagerness to see him."

(35) 'Charicles made a sign to have him called, and the youth
came in, diffusing something truly Achillean about him. His
looks and spirit recalled the hero: his neck was held erect, and
his hair was thrown back from his forehead and tossed up high
like a mane; his nose bespoke courage, and its nostrils had a
gallant way of respiring the air; while his eyes, not quite a light
blue, but darkish with a light blue gleam, gave glances at once
haughty and apt for love, like the sea when it is just beginning
to settle down from a swell into a calm. After giving us the usual
greeting and receiving ours in return, he told us that the moment
had arrived to offer the sacrifice to the god, so that there might
be time enough thereafter for the rite of atonement to the hero [2]
and the procession in his honour. "It shall be done," said
Charicles. He then stood up and said to me: "You will see
Chariclea also today, if you have not seen her already: precedent
requires that the ministrant of Artemis shall take part in the
procession and the propitiation of Neoptolemus." Now, Cnemon, I had often seen the girl before, when she joined me in
conducting sacrifices, and sometimes sought to learn parts of the
liturgy: however, I was silent, in eager expectation of what would
ensue. Meanwhile we made our way towards the temple, where
all the preparations for the sacrifice had already been made by
the Thessalians. When we reached the altars, and the young
man was beginning the performance of the ritual, and when the

[1] This passage is based on Homer, *Il*. 155–78.
[2] Neoptolemus.

priest had offered the opening prayer, from the inmost sanctuary the Pythian priestess delivered these words:

> "Mark well, ye Delphians, her who hath first, Grace and last, Glory;
> Also him, the Goddess-born.[1]
> These shall depart from my fane and, after cleaving the waves,
> Shall arrive at the swarthy land of the Sun.[2]
> There they shall win and wear about their temples, as the noble prize of virtuous lives,
> A white coronal from darkling brows."

(36) 'When the god had thus pronounced, a deep perplexity possessed the company gathered there, who were at a loss to tell what was the meaning of the oracle. Each of them strained the message to a different sense, making some conjecture to suit his own desire; but none at that time could apprehend the truth of it, for oracles and dreams in general are tested only by the event. And besides, the Delphians were in a flutter of excitement to see the procession, which had been magnificently equipped, and they would not trouble themselves to search out the exact meaning of the oracle.'

---

[1] Chariclea is indicated by the words *charis* (grace) and *cleos* (glory); Theagenes by *thea* (goddess) and *genetes* (begotten son).
[2] 'Ethiopia' in Greek means 'swart-faced country'.

BOOK III

Calasiris describes to Cnemon the solemnities at Delphi in honour of the hero Neoptolemus, and how Theagenes and Chariclea became enamoured there.

(1) 'When the procession and the whole ceremony of the propitiation had been performed——' 'Stay, father,' interrupted Cnemon, 'not all performed: at least, your account has not yet made me a viewer of the spectacle. Here I am, utterly consumed with impatience to hear your recital, and am all ardour to be an actual witness of the festival; and there you go rushing past me, so that I arrive, as they say, too late for the party. No sooner have you opened your theatre than you close it!' 'I am far from wishing, Cnemon,' said Calasiris, 'to pester you with incidental matters such as these; I am for pressing on to the more momentous points in my relation, and to the questions that you raised with me at the beginning. But since you have set your heart on being a casual spectator, revealing thereby your Attic character,[1] I will give you a concise description of that procession—a famous one as few have ever been, both on its own account and for its consequences. It was headed by a hecatomb, brought along by male initiates of a somewhat rustic way of life and attire: each had a white tunic trussed up into a looped fold by a girdle; and his right hand, bared—as also were his shoulder and breast—waved on high a two-edged axe. The oxen were all black, with brawny necks rising in a gentle curve; their horns were sharp-pointed but not overlarge or crooked, some having them gilded, while others had them entwined with garlands of flowers; their forelegs were stocky, and their dewlaps hung down as low as their knees. The hecatomb numbered exactly one hundred, fulfilling the true sense of the term.[2] These

[1] Athenians and their neighbours in Attica were noted for their love of spectacle.
[2] *Hecaton* (100) and *bous* (ox) combined to form the word *hecatombé*, which as early as Homer had lost its precise meaning, and sometimes comprised 50 or a smaller number of oxen selected for sacrifice.

were followed by a varied assortment of other victims, each kind of animal being made to proceed in a separately marshalled troop, while flute and syrinx struck up a mystic air in announcement of the sacrifice.

(2) 'The cattle and their herdsmen were succeeded by Thessalian maidens with handsome girdles worn low in the waist and their hair flowing loose. They were divided into two companies. In the first they carried small baskets full of flowers and fruits; in the other they bore large baskets containing cakes and incense balms that breathed sweet fragrance about the place. In this group they kept their hands disengaged, bearing their burdens on their heads, and they went linked together in a figure of oblique lines, so that they were able to pace onward and dance at the same time.[1] The other group marked the time for them with the keynotes of the tune, it being enjoined on this group to chant the whole of the hymn, the theme of which was praise of Thetis and Peleus, and also of their son Achilles and his son Neoptemon. After the maidens, Cnemon——' 'Why "Cnemon?"'' asked the other, 'when you are going to deprive me once more, father, of a rare pleasure, by omitting to recite the hymn, as though you had invited me to be only a spectator and not also a hearer of this procession?' 'You shall hear it,' replied Calasiris, 'since you so desire. The chant went somewhat like this:

Thetis I sing, golden-haired Thetis,
Immortal daughter of Nereus of the briny wave,
Wedded to Peleus on the prompting of Zeus,
Bright glory of the waves, our own Lady of Paphos;[2]
Who from her womb brought forth
The furious spearman, the god of battles,
The thunderbolt of Greece,
Divine Achilles, whose glory rose to heaven;
To him Pyrrha bore a son, Neoptolemus,
Destroyer of the Trojans' city, saviour of the cities of the
    Greeks;

[1] This dance seems to be a *hyporchema*, or dance with song, such as the 'crane dance' connected with the worship of Apollo at Delphi.
[2] That is, 'our Aphrodite', the goddess who had a great temple, the centre of her widespread cult, at Paphos, in the south-west corner of Cyprus.

Be gracious unto us, O hero Neoptolemus,
Thou who art blest in lying now beneath the earth of the
   Pythian; [1]
Receive with favour this mystic sacrifice,
And ward off all threatened peril from our city.
Thetis I sing, golden-haired Thetis.

(3) 'Somewhat after this fashion was the hymn, Cnemon, so
far as I can recollect it. So harmonious was the music accompanying the dancers, and so exactly did the beat of their footfalls
accord with the rhythm of the tune, that one's eyes were induced
by one's ears to neglect what one was beholding; and those
present followed along with the maidens as they passed on from
point to point, seeming to be impelled by the ringing tones of
their chant, until close behind them a mounted troop of youths
with their captain flashed forth, presenting a vision of beauty
that prevailed over any charm of hearing. In number the young
men amounted altogether to fifty: they were divided into two
companies of twenty-five, escorting the leader of the mission as
he rode midway between them. They were shod with boots of
red leather strapping interlaced and fastened above the ankle,
and they wore white cloaks gathered into their chests by gold
clasps and edged all round with a border tinted blue. Their
mounts were all from Thessaly, with the gallant glance of steeds
bred in the plains of that country: they chafed at the bit as a
tyrannous master, spitting upon it and foaming amain; and yet
they suffered themselves to be guided by the rider's intent. They
were richly adorned with silver or gilded head-bosses and
frontlets, as though the youths had made this a matter of emulation amongst them. But their splendid appearance, Cnemon, was
disregarded and forsaken by the eyes of the onlookers, which
were all turned upon the captain of the troop—upon my heart's
darling, Theagenes; and you might have supposed that a lightning
flash had bedimmed all that had appeared before, so brightly did
the sight of him illumine us. He too was mounted indeed, but
armed like a foot-soldier he brandished an ashen spear tipped
with bronze: he did not wear his helmet, but rode gravely along
bare-headed, and clad in a cloak of purple dye which was

[1] Apollo.

embroidered at large with gold thread depicting the Lapithae
in combat with the Centaurs, while its clasp was in the form of a
wreath encircling an Athene of amber, showing forth to shield
her the Gorgon's head upon her breast. A special grace was
added to the scene by some fresh puffs of wind; for blowing
lightly upon him they softly dispersed his hair over his neck
while they drew his locks away from his forehead, and trailed the
border of his cloak over the back and haunches of his horse.
One would have said that the horse himself was sensible of the
bloom and beauty of his master, and felt the glory of bearing so
glorious a rider, to see the undulation of his neck as he tossed up
his head with ears pricked, and haughtily twirled his brows above
his eyes. Exulting in him whom he bore and in his own bearing,
he paced onward obedient to the rein: balancing himself on
either shoulder in turn, and lightly tapping the ground with the
tips of his hoofs, he adapted his paces to the rhythm of a gentle
motion. All were astonished at the spectacle, and all accorded to
the youth the prize for pre-eminence in manliness and beauty.
And promptly the women of the common folk, such as were
unable to restrain and conceal their emotion, tossed to him
apples [1] and flowers, thinking thus to attract to them some sign
of his favour. For this single verdict prevailed amongst all
present—that nothing could be found in all mankind to surpass
the beauty of Theagenes.

(4) '"But when the daughter of the morning, rosy-fingered
Dawn, appeared," as Homer would have said—when from the
temple of Artemis drove forth the fair and sagacious Chariclea,
we were then made aware that even Theagenes could happen to
be excelled, though only inasmuch as the purest feminine beauty
has a stronger attraction than the greatest comeliness to be found
amongst men. For she rode in a covered car drawn by a pair of
white oxen in charge of a driver; and she was attired in a purple
robe reaching to her feet and bespangled with golden rays. She
wore a girdle set close up to her bosom, on which the craftsman
had brought to bear the full power of his craft: never before had
he fabricated its like, nor would be able ever to repeat it. For he
wrought two serpents so that they twined their tails behind her

---

[1] Apples, the fruit dear to Aphrodite, were commonly thrown to betoken
amorous inclination.

back, while their necks crossed below her breasts and were plaited into a complex knot from which their heads were allowed to emerge and hang down on either side as the loose ends of the girdle. You would have said that the snakes not merely seemed to creep, but were actually creeping; they struck no terror with grim and cruel looks, but were relaxed in a melting languor, as though lulled to repose by the sweet charm of the maiden's bosom. Their material was gold, but their colour was dark; for the gold had been skilfully so blackened that the mingled yellow and black should represent the rough surface and varying sheen of the scales. Such was the maiden's girdle. Her hair was neither wholly plaited nor flowing loose; the greater part of it, behind her neck, fell in waves over her shoulders and her back, while the rest, on her crown and forehead, was held by a garland of tender sprays of laurel, binding it close as it gleamed like roses amid sunbeams, and keeping it from being tossed about more than was seemly by the breeze. In her left hand she bore a gilded bow, and the attachment of her quiver passed over her right shoulder; in her other hand she held a small lighted torch, yet even so she flashed from her eyes a brighter light than any torch could shed.'

'It is they—Chariclea and Theagenes!' cried Cnemon. 'And where in the world are they? By the gods I beg you, tell me!' said Calasiris, fancying that they were visible to Cnemon. 'I thought that I had sight of them, father,' he replied, 'although they were not there, so vividly, so truly as I recall seeing them, has your description brought them before me.' 'I doubt', said Calasiris, 'if you saw them as they were beheld on that day by Greece and the sun—so admired by all, so kindly congratulated, answering the dearest wish, she of men and he of women. A union with either of those two they deemed equal to immortality, except that the people of that country admired more the young man, and the Thessalians the maiden, each more impressed by what he saw for the first time; for a strange sight is more apt to astonish than a familiar one. But oh, the pleasing deception! Oh, the sweet idea! How wildly you excited me with the fancy that you saw and could point out my darlings, Cnemon! And indeed it seems that you are altogether deceiving me: at the beginning of my relation you undertook that they would be coming and showing themselves at any moment, and on those terms you claimed the reward of my informing you about them; evening has now come on, and night also, and nowhere can you indicate their presence.' 'Bear up', said Cnemon, 'and be of good heart, for in truth they will come. It may be the fact that some hindrance has arisen, and they may arrive rather behind the appointed time. In any case, even were they here, I would not have pointed them out before I had obtained my full reward. So, if you are eager for the sight of them, make good your promise, and complete your narration.' 'I shrink in any case', said Calasiris, 'from a subject that recalls painful events to my mind; but I also considered that I must be wearing you out with such an overdose of garrulity. Since, however, I find that you are so fond of listening, and have an insatiable appetite for good discourses, come now, let us step into the story where I quitted it, first lighting a lamp and pouring our bedtime libation to the gods of night, so that after performance of the customary rites we may pursue our night-hour narrative with our minds at ease.'

(5) After the old man had thus spoken, a lighted lamp was brought in by a young maidservant at his bidding. He poured the libations, invoking several gods and especially Hermes; he asked for a night of pleasant dreams, and entreated that his dearest ones might appear to him, if only in his sleep. Having finished his prayers he said: 'Now, when the procession, Cnemon, had made a circuit round the tomb of Neoptolemus, and the young horsemen had ridden around thrice, the women raised the ritual call, and the men the martial chant. Then, as at one concerted signal, oxen, lambs and goats were sacrificed; it was as though the slaughter of them all were done by the stroke of a single hand. On an altar of great size they heaped a vast amount of cleft wood and placed upon that, according to custom, all the extremities of the victims; they then called upon the priest of Pythian Apollo to begin the libation and kindle the altar fire. Charicles replied that it was his office to perform the libations, but he said: "The leader of the mission must kindle the altar fire with the torch handed to him by the ministrant; that is the practice ordained by ancestral custom." So saying he began to pour the libations; and Theagenes was about to take the torch, when, my dear Cnemon, we were convinced by what occurred of the divinity of the soul and its kinship with the powers on high.

For at the moment of meeting the young pair looked and loved, as though the soul of each at the first encounter recognized its fellow and leapt towards that which deserved to belong to it. At first they stopped short, in consternation; then, with a lingering motion, she proffered and he received the torch, with eyes intently fixed on each other, as if they had had some previous knowledge or sight which they were recalling to memory. Next, they smiled slightly and furtively, a smile traceable only by the light shed forth by their eyes. Then, as though ashamed of what they did, they blushed; and again, their passion, I conceive, having seized hold also of their hearts, they turned pale and, in short, a thousand changes of expression in that brief moment spread over the features of them both, as every variation of hue and look declared the agitation of their souls. These effects, naturally enough, escaped the notice of the multitude, since everyone was absorbed in one or another interest or considera-tion of his own: they escaped even Charicles, who was pro-nouncing the traditional prayer and invocation. I was occupied solely with my observation of the young pair, ever since, Cnemon, the oracle was chanted concerning Theagenes as he sacrificed in the temple; and I had been moved by hearing their names to speculate on what would befall them. But I still could not make out any distinct meaning of the latter part of the prophecy.[1]

(6) 'At length and, it seemed, with a struggle, Theagenes tore himself away from the young girl. When he had applied the torch and ignited the altar, the procession was disbanded. The Thessalians then betook themselves to feasting; the rest of the people departed, each one to his own home. Chariclea clad herself in a white robe and made her way with her few female companions to her lodging in the temple precincts; for she was not dwelling with her supposed father, since the sanctity of her office obliged her to keep herself entirely apart. So then, my curiosity keenly aroused by what I had both heard and seen, I chanced to fall in with Charicles—just what I had been intend-ing. "Have you seen", he asked me, "my glory, and the glory

[1] Calasiris had understood the play made with the two names by the oracle in ii. 35, but could not discern precisely what fortunes awaited the young pair.

also of the Delphians—Chariclea?" "Not now for the first time," I answered. "Many a time before have I seen her, whenever she met me in the temple, and not just, as it were, by the way. And besides, I have sacrificed with her not a few times, and she has questioned me and received my instruction on various divine and human matters that happened to perplex her." "And what was your opinion of her on the present occasion, my good Calasiris? Did she add some grace to the procession?" "Fie on such words, Charicles," I said; "as well ask me whether the moon outshines the other stars." "Well, you know," he said, "there were some who praised the Thessalian youth also." "Awarding him the second or the third prize," I said; "but the crowning glory, indeed the bright eye, of the procession was acknowledged to be your daughter." Charicles was delighted with this, while I by speaking the truth was attaining the object that I had in view—of getting the man in some way or other to feel at ease with me. He smiled and said: "I am going to her now: if you like, come, share my solicitude and my observation as to any unpleasantness from the crowd that may have discomposed her." I gladly nodded my assent, and made it clear to him that I accounted no other business so important to me as his.

(7) 'When we arrived at her dwelling, we entered and found her lying listless on her bed, with her eyes all bedewed with love. She greeted her father with her habitual embrace: when he asked what ailed her, she replied that she was suffering from a severe headache, and would like to keep quiet, if this could be allowed her. Charicles was greatly disturbed by her words; he stole out of the room with me, directing the maidservant to leave her in peace. When he had passed outside the house he said: "What can this be, my good Calasiris? What is the meaning of this weakness that has stricken my little daughter?" "Do not be surprised", I answered, "that by her figuring in a procession before so great a concourse she has drawn upon her a glance of the evil eye." He laughed ironically and said: "Why, you too, like the multitude, have come to believe that there is such a thing as the power of the evil eye!" "There is nothing more real," I said; "it works in this way. This air enveloping us makes an entrance through our eyes, our nose, our windpipe and our other apertures into our inmost parts, and brings in with it

portions of the external qualities, and there it implants in the recipients a passion of like quality to that which it has when it flows in. Hence whenever anyone looks with envy upon beautiful objects, the ambient air becomes charged with a malignant quality, and that person's breath, laden with bitterness, blows hard upon the person near him. This breath, made up of the finest particles, penetrates to the very bones and marrow, and engenders in many cases the disease of envy, which has received the appropriate name of the influence of the evil eye. With that too you should consider, Charicles, the many instances of people who have been infected with ophthalmia or symptoms of the plague, without having touched diseased persons at all, or even shared bed or board with any such, but have only partaken of the same air. And to give you good proof of this theory, let me cite in particular the generation of love—how things taken in by our sight produce in us its beginning by shooting the passionate feelings like wind-borne shafts through our eyes into our souls. That this should be so is reasonable enough: for of all our bodily vents and senses the most constantly mobile and fervid is our sight, and hence is especially receptive of the effluences of things, attracting by its igneous fume the transits of the feelings of love.

(8) '"I can also adduce for you, if you require it, by way of example, a fact of natural history, set forth in the sacred books on the subject of animals. The plover cures sufferers from jaundice: the patient has only to look at this bird, and it turns away, fleeing from him, with its eyes shut—not, as some suppose, that it begrudges him the relief it can give, but because its gaze has the property of attracting and transferring his disease in a sort of flux to itself; and hence it shuns the sight of him like the infliction of a wound. And you have doubtless heard how the serpent called 'the basilisk' by its mere breath and glance will shrivel and cripple whatever comes in its way. Nor is it surprising that some people cast a spell over others who are most dear to them and to whom they wish well; for being naturally inclined to jealousy they act thus, not from their will, but from their nature."

(9) 'At this Charicles paused for a while; then he said: "You have cleared up the question in a most sagacious and convincing way. May she likewise feel one day in herself a lover's longing!

I should then have satisfied myself that she was in good instead
of ill health: you know it was to this end that I called upon you
for help. But as things are, there is no risk of her being so
affected—this enemy of wedlock, this stranger to love! Rather,
I should say, she is in fact labouring under a malignant spell, and
I am sure that you will wish to clear up this trouble also, being
my friend and a man of comprehensive knowledge." I promised
to do my utmost to relieve her of whatever malady I might find
afflicting her.

(10) 'While we were still discussing the matter a man hurried
up to us and said: "Gentlemen, you are loitering as though you
had been summoned to the field of battle instead of a banquet
which is being provided by that most handsome of youths,
Theagenes, and presided over by that greatest of heroes,
Neoptolemus. Come along; do not stretch out the festivity till
evening, for you are the only ones missing from the party."
Charicles leant over to me and said in my ear: "This fellow has
come with an invitation backed by a cudgel: how very un-
Dionysiac he is, although in a fairly tipsy condition! But let us
go, for I fear he may end by treating us to a drubbing." "You
are joking," I said; "however, let us go." When we had arrived
Theagenes seated Charicles next to himself, and put me also, I
may say, in a place of honour, on Charicles' account. There is
no need for me to overburden you with all that passed at the
banquet—the maidens' dances, the flute-girls, the war-dance of
young men under arms and other performances with which
Theagenes enhanced the sumptuous provision of victuals, and
so rendered the festivity a sociable and unusually joyous carousal.
But there was one particular feature of it which you must be
told, and which will be more pleasant for me to mention: it was
this. Theagenes made a show of gaiety, and constrained himself
to pay kind attentions to the guests; but I detected the direction
in which his mind was working. At one time his eyes rolled to
and fro, at another he heaved a deep sigh for no apparent
reason; now he was downcast and seemed lost in thought, now
of a sudden he changed to a more cheerful expression, as though
recovering his senses and recollecting himself, thus easily passing
from one variation into another. For the mind of a lover, not
unlike that of a drunken man, is mutable and intolerant of any

settled state: both alike have their souls tossing on the tide of passion; and hence it is that the lover is inclined to drinking, and the drunkard to loving.

(11) 'When he was seen to be seized with an oppressive fit of yawning, it became obvious to the rest of the company that he was unwell; so that Charicles, having observed his disorder, said quietly to me: "I do believe that he too has been looked upon by the evil eye; he seems to me to have met with the same misfortune as Chariclea." "Yes," I said, "the same, by Isis; quite rightly and reasonably too, since in the procession he came second to her in distinction." These remarks we made to each other. When the time came for the cups to circulate, Theagenes drank to each person from the loving-cup, though unwillingly. As it came round to me I said that I welcomed his friendly compliment, but I declined the offer of the cup. He gave me a sharp, heated look, conceiving himself to be slighted. Charicles understood, and told him: "He abstains from wine and the flesh of animate creatures." Theagenes asked the reason, and he replied: "He is of Memphis, an Egyptian, and a prophet of Isis." When Theagenes heard mention of Egyptian and prophet, he was at once filled with delight and, like one who had discovered some treasure, stood up, called for water, drank some and said: "O paragon of wisdom, please accept this toast that I have drunk to you with the liquor most agreeable to you; and may this table solemnize our pact of friendship!" "So be it," I said, "handsome Theagenes; it is a friendship that I have long felt on my part for you." I received the cup and drank. With this incident the festivity came to an end. We took our departure, each to his own home, after Theagenes had embraced me repeatedly, with remarkable fervour considering the time in which he had come to know me. On reaching my dwelling I lay awake for a while on my bed, turning over and over in my mind the concern that I felt for the young pair, and trying to make out the meaning of the last part of the oracle. When midnight came I saw Apollo and Artemis—so I thought, if I was merely thinking so, and not really seeing them—the one leading up to me Theagenes, and the other Chariclea. They called me by name and said: "It is time now for you to return to your native land: this is the dictate issued by the Fates. Depart hence, therefore,

and take these twain with you in your charge, to be your fellow-travellers, and to be treated as your children; and then conduct them out of Egypt to such region and in such wise as may be pleasing to the gods.''

Calasiris, after having a vision in the night, discusses its meaning with Cnemon.

(12) 'Thus they spoke, and then departed, leaving me in no doubt that what I had seen was no dream, but a waking vision. In the main I grasped the meaning of the apparition; but I was at a loss to know to what people or to what country it pleased the gods that the young pair should be conducted.' 'You acquired that knowledge yourself later on, father,' said Cnemon, 'and later too you will tell it to me: but in what way did the gods convince you, as you said, that they came, not in a dream, but in visible presence?' 'In the way, my son,' he answered, 'which sapient Homer expresses, in a riddling fashion overlooked by ordinary folk:

> '' The traces left behind him'' (he says somewhere) ''of his feet and legs
> I easily discerned as he departed; the gods are not hard to discern.'' [1]

'It seems, in truth,' said Cnemon, 'that I too am one of the ordinary folk, and it was doubtless with the purpose of exposing me as such, Calasiris, that you have recalled those verses. Their superficial sense I have known ever since I was taught to know the words; but the theological lesson implanted in them I have not comprehended.'

(13) After a brief pause, in which Calasiris uplifted his mind to the mystic aspect of things, he said: 'Gods and divine spirits, Cnemon, in their comings and goings on visits to us, assume but rarely the forms of common animals, and most frequently those of human beings, so that their likeness to us may aid in producing in us the impression of their presence. The uninitiated must fail

---

[1] Homer, *Il.* xiii. 71–2: Ajax, son of Oileus, tells Ajax, son of Telamon, that he has discerned the presence of Poseidon.

to observe them, but they will not escape the perfection of the
sage: he will recognize them by their eyes, with which they
maintain a steady gaze, never closing their eyelids; and still more
by their gait, which does not proceed with the feet parted, or one
before the other, but in a sort of aerial gliding, with an un-
impeded motion, as they cleave rather than tread the atmosphere.
For this reason the images of the gods are fashioned with the feet
joined together, as though forming a single limb. All this was
well known to Homer, as he was an Egyptian and was well
schooled in the sacred lore; and he wrapped it up in symbolical
verses, leaving it to be discerned by persons able to understand.
He says of Athene:

> "Her two eyes shone forth,"

and of Poseidon:

> "The traces left behind him of his feet and legs
> I discerned as he departed *flowing*,"

as it were, flowing in his onward motion; for so should the
words to be taken, and not, as some do in error, "I *easily*
discerned."' [1]

(14) 'You have admitted me here to a mystery, most reverend
sir,' said Cnemon, 'and as you keep calling Homer an Egyptian
—a thing which I dare say nobody in the world has heard until
this day—I cannot venture to disbelieve you. At the same time
I am so struck with surprise that I beg you not to pass on
without giving me the precise reason for this statement.'
'Cnemon,' he said, 'although this is not the moment for a
detailed exposition of the matter, I will nevertheless give you a
summary of the case. Let Homer be styled, my friend, a native
of this or that country by different people, and let any city claim
to be the birthplace of the sage; but in truth he was our countryman, an Egyptian, and his city was Thebes, "which hath a
hundred gates",[2] as he himself tells us. His reputed father was a
prophet, but was actually Hermes, whose prophet that reputed

---

[1] The Greek word *rhei* has the two possible meanings of 'easily' and 'was
flowing'.
[2] Homer, *Il.* ix. 383.

father was. For, when the prophet's wife had the duty of performing some traditional rite, and was sleeping in the temple,
the god lay with her and begot Homer, who bore upon him a
mark attesting this unequal union. From the time of her delivery
one of his thighs was overspread with hairs of great length,
whence he received his name [1] as he wandered and chanted his
poems among various nations, and especially among the Greeks.
He himself did not mention his real name, or even that of his
city or of his race; but those who knew of that growth affecting
his body fabricated his name from it.' 'And what was his object,
father, in keeping silence about his native land?' 'It was either
because he was ashamed of being an exile—for he was cast out
by his father when he was about to be selected as one of the
young men consecrated to divine service, the blemish on his body
having caused him to be deemed a bastard—or else it was a skilful expedient that enabled him, in concealing his real city, to
win favour in every place.'

(15) 'I have accepted your statement of the matter as sound
and true,' said Cnemon, 'judging by the man's quite Egyptian
way of giving us in his poems dark sayings mingled with all
kinds of delight, and also by the pre-eminence of his natural
powers, which could never have set him above everyone else if
he had not partaken, in truth, of some divine, some supernal
influence. But after you had caught sight of the gods in person,
Calasiris, as they appear in Homer, what happened next?' 'The
same kind of thing as before, Cnemon: more wakefulness, more
speculations and more anxieties—those friends of Night. I felt
very glad, hoping that I had been granted an unlooked-for boon,
and looking forward to my return to my own country; but I was
also pained by the thought that Charicles would be deprived of
his daughter; and I was perplexed as I bethought me in what
manner I should take the young people along with me and contrive our departure. I was harassed with doubts as to how we
could make our escape unobserved, in what direction we should
travel and whether by land or by sea. In short, I was tossed on a
surge of anxieties, and had no sleep during the remainder of an
exhausting night.

(16) 'Day had not fully dawned when there came a knocking

[1] *Ho meros* is Greek for 'the thigh'.

at the inner door,[1] and I heard someone calling "Boy!" When my servant asked who knocked and what he wanted, the caller answered: "Announce that it is Theagenes the Thessalian." I was delighted to hear the young man announced, and ordered that he be invited in; for I conceived that here of itself was coming my way an inception of the scheme that I had in hand. I surmised that, having heard at the banquet that I was an Egyptian and a prophet, he had come to obtain my assistance in his love-affair—labouring, I imagine, under the common, ignorant misapprehension that the love of the Egyptians is a single, invariable knowledge. Now, one kind of it is popular—moving, one might say, along the ground, ministrant to images, and wallowing among corpses; addicted to simples, and relying on incantations. It neither attains any good end itself, nor brings any good to those who use it; most often it finds itself at fault, such successes as it may achieve being painful and meagre—merely the presentation of unrealities as realities, and the disappointment of hopes; a deviser of unlawful actions and purveyor of licentious pleasures. But the other knowledge, my son, the true wisdom, of which this has spuriously assumed the name, and in which we priests of the prophetic line are trained from our youth, looks upward to the heavenly region: companion of the gods, partaker of the nature of the higher powers, it traces the motions of the stars and gleans foreknowledge of the future.[2] Standing aloof from all our earthly evils, it devotes itself to the pursuit of what is honourable and beneficial to mankind. It was the cause of my absenting myself from my native land in time for me to see if I could give a wide berth to the events that it foretold to me, as I have already recounted to you, and the conflict between my two sons. So now I must commit these matters to the care of the gods, and especially of the Fates that have power to decide our doing or not doing: for they enjoined on me this exile from my native land, not merely, it would seem, because of those events, but equally for my discovery of Chariclea, the manner of which you will learn in the next part of my story.

---

[1] This door closed off the inner rooms of the house from the court and servants' quarters.

[2] Calasiris seems here to be imbued with the ascetic doctrine on divinity and astrology set forth by Lucian, *On Astrology*, and Philostratus, *Life of Apollonius of Tyana*.

Theagenes confesses to Calasiris his love for Chariclea.

(17) 'When Theagenes came in I exchanged greetings with him, and seated him beside me on the bed. "What business brings you so early to see me?" I asked. He stroked his face for some length of time, and then said: "I am in great anxiety about my whole position, but I blush to explain why," and was silent. I decided that the moment had come for me to play the mountebank with him, and appear to divine what I actually knew. Looking at him with a more cheerful expression I said: "Though you are shy of speaking, still nothing is unknown to our wisdom and to the gods." I paused for a little, arranging on my fingers some counters that bore no numbers, tossing out my hair and imitating some person possessed by a spirit; then I said: "You are in love, my child." He started up at my divination, and when I added "With Chariclea", he believed these words to be the very promptings of a god: and he was on the point of falling down and worshipping me. When I prevented this he stepped up to me, covered my head with kisses, gave thanks to the gods for not having been disappointed, as he said, of what he expected, and besought me to be his saviour: his life could not be saved, he declared, if he failed to get help, and that quickly, so serious was the attack from which he suffered and so fierce the flame of his passion, in what was, moreover, his first experience of love. He affirmed with many oaths that he had never yet had intimacy with a woman. He had spurned all women, and marriage itself, and any love-affairs that were mentioned to him, until the beauty of Chariclea had proved to him that he was not by nature obdurate; but up to the previous day he had never beheld a woman worthy of being loved. With these words he wept, as though for his thus confessing himself overcome against his will by a girl. Wishing to reassure him I said: "Take courage, now that you have turned to me for succour: she will not win a similar victory over our wisdom. She is indeed somewhat austere, and stubbornly resists subjection to the sway of love; for she despises Aphrodite and marriage—nay, the mere mention of their names. But to help you every means must be tried; art can find a way to compel even nature. Only be of good cheer, and follow the advice that I shall give you on what is to be done."

He promised to comply with all directions that I gave him, even if I bade him walk over swords.

(18) 'He was still entreating me about his affair, and promising to reward me with his whole fortune, when a messenger came from Charicles and said: "Charicles requests you to come to him: he is there, near at hand, in the temple of Apollo, where he is offering up a hymn to the god, after being alarmed by something in his sleep." I rose at once, sent Theagenes away and repaired to the temple, where I found Charicles seated in a stall, overcome with grief and uttering groan upon groan. I went up to him and asked: "Why so gloomy and doleful?" "How should I be otherwise", he replied, "when dreams have filled me with alarm, and my daughter's condition, as I have heard, has taken a more serious turn, and she has not had a wink of sleep all night? And I am the more distressed by her ill health because the occasion for the contest has been fixed for tomorrow: it is the custom then for the female ministrant of the goddess to present torches to the armed runners and award the prize. One of two things must happen: either her failure to appear will be an outrage on the tradition, or by attending under constraint she will greatly aggravate her illness. So, if you have not already done so, pray go now to her aid, and bring her some remedy; you will be doing what we and our friendship may fairly claim of you, and it will be a pious service to the gods. I know that it would mean no great effort to you, if you were so minded, to cure what you yourself called a case of the evil eye: prophets do not lack the power to deal successfully with even the greatest difficulties." I acknowledged my remissness, artfully dissembling with him also; and I requested him to allow me the space of that day, since I had to concoct something to apply as a remedy. "Meanwhile", I said, "let us go to the girl, in order to examine her more closely, and comfort her as much as we can. At the same time, Charicles, I should like you to use such language about me to the girl, as will make it plain that you commend me to her better acquaintance, so that, having become familiar with me, she may receive my curative treatment with the greater confidence." "Agreed," he said; "now let us go."

(19) 'When we had come in to Chariclea—why tell it all at length? She had become completely subjugated by her passion,

and the bloom was now banished from her cheeks, the fire in her eye seemed to have been quenched, as it were, in the flood of her tears. Nevertheless she tried to recover herself on seeing us, and strove her utmost to resume her wonted looks and speech. Chariclea embraced her, gave her countless kisses, and lavished on her every mark of tenderness. "My little daughter, my child," he said, "will you hide your trouble from me, your father? You have fallen under a malign influence, and will you keep silent, as though you had done wrong, and were not rather wronged by the evil eye that has looked upon you? Come, have no fear: this wise man, Calasiris, has been called in to provide us with a remedy. He is an adept, excelling all others in divine science; for prophecy is his vocation, and he has been dedicated to the sacred service from childhood; more important than all, he has in addition the most affectionate regard for us. It is only reasonable, then, that you should welcome him without reserve, and submit yourself to the spells and other remedies that he proposes to apply: it is not your habit to shun converse with men of the learned sort." Chariclea was silent, but nodded her assent, however, seeming glad to accept consultation with me. This settled, we parted from each other, after Chariles had reminded me that I would give careful attention to the subject of his previous appeal to me, and take thought how I could produce in Chariclea some appetite for marriage and male company. So I sent him off in good spirits, having promised him that it would not be long before his wish was fulfilled.'

BOOK IV

Calasiris continues his story to Cnemon, telling him what occurred on the last day of the Pythian Games at Delphi.

(1) 'On the following day the Pythian contest was to end; but the contest of the young couple was then coming to its height. The god of love, I imagine, was acting as their marshal and umpire, and was determined to prove, through the particular case of these two athletes, paired off by him, that his own kind of contest is the greatest of all. What came to pass in chief was this. All Greece was present to see the games, and these were managed by the leagues of the various states. When the other events had been duly performed in magnificent style—close-run races, clinches of wrestling and buffets of boxing—at the end the herald called out: "Forward, the armed men!" The ministrant of the goddess,[1] Chariclea, then shone forth at the far limit of the stadium, having come, though reluctantly, in obedience to tradition—or rather, I should suppose, in the hope of somewhere getting sight of Theagenes. In her left hand she bore a flaming torch, in the other she held before her a branch of palm; and as she appeared she attracted to herself the gaze of the whole assembly, but of no one, I should say, more quickly than that of Theagenes; for a lover has sharp sight for the object of his desire. And he of course having already heard what was to take place, had his whole mind so intent on his first glimpse of her that he could no longer be silent, but said to me softly—for he had purposely seated himself close to me—"That is she, Chariclea!" I requested him to keep quiet.

(2) 'At the herald's call there came forward a man in light armour, of haughty mien and, it seemed, of particular distinction. He had already been crowned in a number of contests, and now he had no competitor to challenge him, since no one, I suppose, was bold enough to encounter him. So the leagues' officers were for sending him away, on the ground that the law

---

[1] Artemis.
86

did not grant a crown to one who had not engaged in a contest. But he claimed that the herald should call for anyone who offered to come and contend with him. The managers gave the order, and the herald announced that any intending competitor should come forward. Then Theagenes said to me: "He is calling me." "How do you mean?" I asked. "Just as it shall be, father," he said; "for no one else, in my presence and in my sight, shall obtain the victor's crown from the hands of Chariclea." "But failure," I asked him, "and the consequent disgrace, are those of no account to you?" "And who", he said, "is so madly eager to behold and approach Chariclea as to outstrip me? Who, like me, can be so elated by the sight of her as almost to take wing and be borne into the upper air? Do you not know that Love himself is given wings by painters, who thus allude to the mobility of those whom he has mastered? And, if I am to add a little boast to my remarks, nobody to this day has plumed himself on outrunning me in a race."

(3) 'With these words he started up, and advancing into their midst announced his name and stated his nationality; he was allotted his position on the course, and then put on a complete suit of armour, and took his stand at the starting line, panting and barely able in his impatience to wait for the signal call of the trumpet. It was a grand and impressive spectacle such as Homer presents in Achilles' feats of arms at the River Scamander.[1] Thrilled by this unlooked-for challenge, the whole of Greece there prayed for the victory of Theagenes, as though each man present were himself engaged in the contest; for beauty has something that compels goodwill in one at the very first sight. Chariclea's excitement knew no bounds; and I, who had been observing her for some time, saw continual changes occurring in her demeanour. When, for all to hear, the herald had proclaimed the names of the entrants for the race, calling out "Ormenus of Arcadia and Theagenes of Thessaly", and when the cord was let fall and the race was started at a speed which almost defeated the quickest vision, then the young girl was no longer able to keep still: her legs quivered, her feet danced, as if, to my thinking, her soul were floating away with Theagenes and were zealously supporting him in the race. The

[1] Homer, *Il.* xxi.

spectators, to a man, were in suspense to see the outcome, and filled with a great anxiety—and I more than any, since I had made up my mind to be concerned for him as for a son.' 'No wonder', said Cnemon, 'that the spectators on the spot were anxious when I am myself in fear now for Theagenes; so I beg you to go on and tell me quickly whether he was declared the winner.'

(4) 'When he had completed half the course, Cnemon, he turned a little and looked askance at Ormenus; he then lifted up his shield on high, threw back his head, and fixing his gaze full on Chariclea he sped onward like a dart to its mark, and came in so many yards ahead of the Arcadian that the measure of the interval was taken afterwards. He ran up to Chariclea, flung himself with intense energy into her bosom, as though he were unable to check the impetus of his pace; and as he received the palm I observed that he kissed the girl's hand.' 'You have brought me back to life', said Cnemon, 'by telling of his victory and his kiss; but what happened next?' 'Ah, Cnemon, you are not only an insatiable listener to tales, but also an elusive truant from sleep: already no small portion of the night has gone by, and you hold out, wide awake, while my narration, for all its long continuance, does not exasperate you.' 'I blame Homer, father, for saying that one becomes sated with love as with other things.[1] In my opinion it is a thing that induces no repletion, either when its pleasures are being enjoyed or when a tale of it is told. If anyone should relate the love of Theagenes and Chariclea, what heart of steel or iron would not be charmed by the story, even should it last for a year? So please continue with the sequel.'

'Theagenes, as I said, Cnemon, was crowned and proclaimed the victor, and he was applauded, as he passed along, by the whole assembly; while his conquest of Chariclea was decisive, and she was now in greater subjection to her passion than before, from having this second view of Theagenes. For the exchange of looks between lovers revives the fervour in their souls, and sight can rekindle their minds like logs upon a hearth. The girl, when she returned home, passed the same sort of night as those

[1] Homer, *Il.* xiii. 636–7: 'There is satiety of all things, of sleep, and love, and excellent dancing.'

preceding, or one even more anguished; while I again lay sleepless, considering in what direction we should take our flight to avoid being observed, and wondering to what country the god intended the young couple to be conducted. I could only conclude that our escape must be made by sea, taking as a clue the words of the oracle: [1]

"After cleaving the waves they shall arrive at the swarthy
    land of the Sun."

(5) 'But for the problem of where I should conduct them I could see but one solution—to discover, if somehow I could, the swathe which was exposed with Chariclea, and on which was embroidered the statement about her, as Charicles said he had been told; for it was likely that I should ascertain from it what the girl's country was, and who were the parents already guessed at by me as hers; most probably it was there that the young people were being sent by Destiny. So at an early hour I went to see Chariclea. I found the whole household in tears, especially Charicles. I went up to him and asked: "What means all this upset?" He replied: "The malady has been increasing its hold on my daughter, and she has found the past night a more troublous one than the former." "You must withdraw," I said, "and all the others must go away too. I wish only to be provided with a tripod, some laurel, fire and incense, and to be disturbed by nobody whatever, until I call for someone to come in." Charicles gave orders accordingly, which were carried out. When I was left in peace I began what you might call a piece of play-acting business. I burnt the incense and, after muttering some pretended prayers with my lips, I shook the laurel briskly over Chariclea, up and down, from head to foot; then, yawning at her in a drowsy, or rather, an old-womanish fashion, at long last I ended my performance, having bespattered both myself and the girl with a fine lot of twaddle. She kept on shaking her head, with a wry sort of smile, to signify that I was hopelessly adrift, with no inkling of her sickness. I sat down beside her and said: "Have no fear, daughter; your disease is a slight matter, easily cured. The evil eye lighted upon you, no doubt when you were in the procession, and still more when you were presenting

[1] At the end of Book II.

the prize. And I guess who chiefly cast the spell—Theagenes, he who raced in armour: I noticed how he was constantly watching you and turning on you an ardent glance." "Whether that person looked at me as you say, or not," she said, "much good may it do him. What is his parentage or his country? I saw indeed that many people were in a flutter about him." "That he is a Thessalian by birth", I said, "you have already heard, by the herald's announcement of him. He traces his ancestry back to Achilles, and there, I dare say, he speaks the truth, to judge by the youth's stature and beauty, which seem to attest his exalted kinship with Achilles—except that he is not haughty or headstrong like that hero, but has a sweetness that tempers the high dignity of his mind. Yet, with all these qualities, may he suffer severer pains than those which he has inflicted on you, for the envious vision that he possesses and the spell of an evil eye that he has cast upon you." "Father," she said, "my thanks to you for your sympathy in my sore distress; but why curse at random a man who may well have done no wrong? My sickness comes from no evil spell; it is seemingly some other disease." "And so you hide it away, my child," I said, "and will not be brave and tell it me, so that we might find some effective means of relieving you. Am I not a father to you in years, and still more in affection? Am I not well known to your father and at one with him in mind? Reveal what it is that ails you. You can take me into your confidence—if you wish, under oath. Be brave and tell me; do not augment your pain by your silence. For every disorder, if quickly recognized, is amenable to treatment; but, neglected for a time, it is wellnigh incurable. Silence is a nourisher of disease; trouble divulged is quickly assuaged."

(6) 'At this she paused for a moment, showing by her looks the countless rapid changes and impulses of her mind. Then she said: "Grant me this day, and you shall be told afterwards, if you do not learn the truth meanwhile by the divination that you profess." I rose at once and went out, to allow the girl in the interval to come to terms with her maiden modesty. I was met by Charicles, who asked: "What news have you?" "All favourable," I replied; "tomorrow she will be rid of the trouble that so oppresses her, and then another effect very agreeable to you will follow. And there is nothing to prevent us from calling in a

doctor." So saying I ran off, to stop Charicles asking any more questions. I had not proceeded far after leaving the house when I saw Theagenes there by the temple, pacing about the precinct and talking to himself, as though he were content merely to be observing the dwelling-place of Chariclea. So I turned aside and went past him, as if I had not seen him. "Good day, Calasiris," he said, "now listen: I was waiting for you." I turned round quickly and said: "Ah, the handsome Theagenes! I did not see you." "How can he be handsome", he said, "who is not agreeable to Chariclea?" I assumed an air of annoyance and said: "You must cease insulting me and my science, by which she has already been captivated, and compelled to love you and pray for a sight of you, as if you were a visitant from on high." "What is that you say, father? Does Chariclea love me? Why then do you not at once lead me to her?" And as he spoke he was dashing away. I got hold of his cape and said: "Stop now, swift runner though you be. This affair is no catch, or a thing to snatch up like a cheap bargain laid out for sale to anyone who may fancy it; rather it is something that requires much consideration for its suitable accomplishment, and much prearrangement to avoid mishap in carrying it through. You must surely know that the girl's father has the highest position in Delphi, and keep in mind the laws that visit such attempts with death?" "To me", he replied, "even loss of life is indifferent, if I have obtained Chariclea: however, if you think fit, let us go to her father and ask her in marriage; for I surely am no unworthy person to become a kinsman of Charicles." "We should not obtain her," I said; "not that any fault can be found with you, but Charicles has promised the girl some time ago to his sister's son." "He shall rue it", said Theagenes, "whoever he may be; for no other man, while I live, shall take to bed Chariclea. This arm of mine, and this my sword, will not be so indolent as to suffer that." "Peace!" I said; "there will be no need of such action. Only obey me and do as I direct you. For the present go away, and take care not to be seen continually in my company: see that you meet me in quiet and alone." He went away downcast.

(7) 'Charicles met with me on the following day. As soon as he saw me he ran to me and kissed me on the head many times, exclaiming repeatedly: "Here is wisdom, here friendship! You

have achieved a great work; she is caught who defied capture, she, the invincible, is vanquished! Chariclea is in love!" At these words I bridled up, raised my eyebrows, and moving at a sauntering pace I said: "It was clear enough that she would not withstand even my first onset, without any harassing action by my stronger forces. But how, Charicles, have you discovered that she is in love?" "By following your advice," he replied. "I summoned, on your own suggestion, the most renowned physicians and brought them in to examine her, promising to reward them with my whole fortune if they succeeded in curing her. As soon as they came in they asked her what ailed her. She turned away from them, and would not answer them a single word, but kept loudly repeating the verse of Homer:

'O Achilles, son of Peleus, most valiant of the Achaeans!' [1]

The learned Akesinus—you doubtless know the man—seized hold of her wrist despite her resistance, and seemed to be diagnosing her illness from her pulse and its indication, I conceive, of the beating of her heart. For some length of time he pursued his accurate investigation, thoroughly observing her condition in one part after another, and then said: 'Charicles, it was superfluous to call us in to this case; medicine can do nothing at all to help her.' 'Ye gods!' I cried, 'what do you say? Then I have lost my daughter, lost her beyond all hope?' 'No need for agitation,' he replied; 'listen to me.' And taking me aside, at some distance from the girl and the others, he said: 'Our science undertakes to treat disorders of the body, not those of the soul particularly, but only when the soul suffers together with an afflicted body and is relieved equally with it under the treatment. The condition of this girl is one of disease, but not in the body; there is no excess of fluids, no oppressive headache, no burning fever, and no other bodily ailment, either local or general, so it seems. This, and this alone, is the correct opinion.' At my earnest entreaty that he would tell me if he had discovered anything he said: 'Why, a child could perceive that the trouble is in her soul, and that her malady is obviously love. Do you not see how her eyelids are swollen, her glances dis-

[1] Homer, *Il.* xvi. 21: spoken by Patroclus to Achilles at a crisis in the fortunes of the Greek army.

tracted, her face pallid, while she complains of no internal pain; whereas she wanders in her mind, utters whatever comes into her head, suffers from an unaccountable insomnia, and has suddenly lost flesh? You must go in search of her healer, Charicles; and he can only be the man of whom she is enamoured.'

'"This said he departed; and here I have come running to you, my saviour, my god, who alone are able to assist us, as the girl herself understands. For indeed, when I begged and pressed her to tell me what ailed her, she merely answered that she did not know her disorder, but felt sure that Calasiris alone could cure her; and she besought me to call you in to see her. This inevitably led me to the conclusion that she has been captivated by your wisdom." "Then can you tell me, besides the fact of her being in love," I asked, "who it is that she loves?" "No, by Apollo," he said; "how and by what means could I know that? Rather than all the wealth in the world I was longing to have her in love with Alcamenes, my sister's son, whom this long time I have intended to be her future husband, so far as my own wishes are concerned." I suggested that he might easily try the effect of bringing the lad to her dwelling and showing him to her. He approved and went off. Later on, about noontide, he met me again and said: "I have painful news to give you: the girl seems to be possessed, her manner is so very strange. I brought Alcamenes in to her, as you bade me, and presented him in attire of due elegance: but she, as though she had looked on the Gorgon's head or something yet more monstrous, uttered a loud and piercing shriek, and averted her eyes to the other side of the room. Pressing her hands like a noose around her throat, she threatened, and swore an oath, to destroy herself if we did not instantly depart. We removed ourselves from her presence more speedily than words can tell; for what in fact was to be done when we saw such extraordinary behaviour? To you I come once more with an entreaty—that you will neither allow her to perish, nor suffer me to be disappointed of my earnest hopes." "Charicles," I said, "you were not far wrong in stating that the girl is possessed; for she is irritated by the powers that I myself drew down upon her—powers of no little influence, but such as might be expected to force her into actions prompted neither by her nature nor by her inclination. It seems, however, that some hostile deity is hindering my operation and contending with my assistants; so now the right moment has come for you to show me the swathe that was exposed with the girl child and which you said you had received with the other means of identification. For I fear the thing may be full fraught with sorceries, and perhaps inscribed with cabbalistic signs which are turning her heart to a savage harshness, through some device of an enemy aimed at her living through all her days a stranger to love and offspring."

Charicles brings to Calasiris the swathe which was found with the infant Chariclea, and which bears an inscription worked upon it by her mother, Persinna, queen consort of Ethiopia.

(8) 'He assented, and came soon after with the swathe. I asked him to grant me some leisure and, as I found him agreeable, I went to my lodging. Without losing a moment I began reading the script on the swathe. It was pricked out in Ethiopian characters, not in the popular but in the royal hand, which resembles that of the so-called sacred writings of the Egyptians. As I proceeded I made out this statement from the script: "I, Persinna, Queen of Ethiopia, to her who has yet to bear a name, my daughter only until the travail of her birth, I inscribe as my parting gift these letters of lamentation." I was astounded, Cnemon, at the mention of that name, Persinna; but yet I went on and read what followed: "It was owing to no guilt of mine, my child, that I exposed you thus at your birth, and concealed you from the sight of your father, Hydaspes; as witness to this I would invoke the founder of our family, the Sun. I can, however, justify myself to you one day, my daughter, should you survive, to him who may be divinely appointed to take you up, and indeed to the whole of mankind then alive, by revealing my motive in exposing you. Our ancestors were, among the gods, the Sun and Dionysus, and among demigods, Perseus and Andromeda, and also Memnon. Now those who from time to time constructed the several parts of the royal palace adorned them with pictures relating to those ancestors; representations of them and their deeds were depicted in the men's apartments and the galleries, and the bed-chambers were decorated with the

love-making of Andromeda and Perseus. There one day it chanced that Hydaspes and I, having had no children born to us after the passage of ten years since our marriage, were taking our noonday rest, relaxed in summer-time slumber. Your father then had intercourse with me, as he had been bidden to do, he solemnly averred, in a dream; and immediately I was aware that I was pregnant by his engendering. The period from that day to my delivery was devoted to public festival and sacrifices of thanksgiving to the gods for the king's expectation of a successor in his line. But when I brought you forth white, gleaming with a light complexion alien to the Ethiopian race, I understood the cause. During the intercourse with my husband the picture of Andromeda presented her image to my eyes, showing her entirely nude, just as Perseus was taking her down from the rock, and it had thus by ill fortune given to the seed a form similar in appearance to that of the heroine. I therefore decided to save myself from a shameful death, being convinced that your colour would subject me to a charge of adultery—for nobody would believe my account of that miraculous change—and that it was better to give you the advantage of the hazard of fortune than the certainty of death or, in any case, of being called a bastard. I pretended to my husband that you had died at the moment of birth, and I exposed you in complete and utter secrecy, placing with you as large a store of riches as I could, to be a reward for whoever should preserve your life. I decked you out finely, and wound this swathe about you, to tell your pitiful story, yours and my own, with the marks that I made on it of the tears and blood shed over you by me, whose first child labour brought me so much lamentation. But, my sweet daughter of only an hour, if you should survive, be mindful of your noble descent; honour chastity, the distinguishing mark of woman's virtue; and cultivate a regal spirit that will bespeak your parentage. Remember, from all the treasures exposed with you, to select and cherish especially for yourself a ring which your father presented to me at my betrothal: it has the royal emblem engraved round it, and is hallowed by a stone, pantarbe, set in a bezel, which exerts a secret influence. This account I have given you, availing myself of the service of script since the deity has deprived me of living and visual converse with you.

Perchance my words will be mute and futile, perchance they will one day stand you in good stead; the hidden issues of fortune are not to be known by men. You, whose charms are wasted, you, whose beauty smirched me with imputation, will have in this writing, if you should survive, the means of your recognition. But if that befalls which I pray may never come to my hearing, it will serve as your epitaph and your mother's funeral tribute of her tears."

(9) 'When I had read these words, Cnemon, I recognized and admired the wise dispensation of the gods. Filled with mingled feelings of pleasure and pain, I went through the singular experience of weeping and rejoicing at the same moment. My soul felt relaxed by the discovery of the unknown facts and the conclusive explanation of the oracle; but it was greatly harassed with thoughts of what result the future might bring, and stirred with pity for the instability and infirmity of human life, swayed now towards one thing and now towards another— as was then supremely evidenced in the fortunes of Chariclea. My mind was beset by many reflections: what an origin was hers, and with what parentage had she been credited! How great a distance had she been brought from her native land, she to whom Destiny had allotted a spurious daughterhood after being deprived of her genuine one in Ethiopia and in the royal house! For some time I stood there with my mind divided—inclined to feel pity for the past, yet not daring to be happy about the future —until, recalling my reason to sober thought, I decided that I must set to work without further dallying. I went to see Chariclea; I found her alone, quite prostrated now by her passion. Her spirit urged her to recover herself, but her body bore her down altogether by yielding to her malady and failing through weakness to hold out against its attack.

(10) 'I therefore dismissed the persons who were with her, and ordered that no one should disturb us, pretending that I wished to resort to some prayers and invocations for the girl. "It is time now, Chariclea," I said, "that you told me what ails you, as you promised to do yesterday, and that you ceased to conceal it from a man who is your well-wisher and is quite able to know all about it, even if you keep silence? She took my hand and kissed it, shedding some tears; then she said: "O wise

Calasiris, let your first kind service be to leave me to bear my sad lot in silence, after taking such note as you wish of the nature of my sickness; and let me at least profit enough from my sense of shame to conceal what is shameful to feel, and more shameful to utter. For I am suffering from the full pressure of my disease, and still more from my failure to subdue it in its first onset and my surrender to a passion which I have continually renounced hitherto, and which defiles by its mere mention the proud name of virgin." Then, to encourage her, I said: "Daughter, on two accounts you do well to conceal your condition: I on my part have no need to be told what I have long known through my special skill, while you, from a natural feeling, blush to speak what it is more seemly for women to conceal. But now that you have experienced the passion of love, and at first sight Theagenes has captivated you—for so much has been imparted to me by the divine voice—be assured that you are not the only or the first woman to submit to this passion, but are sharing the experience with many women of distinction and with many a maiden of irreproachable virtue. Love is the mightiest of gods; indeed, he is even said to vanquish at times the gods themselves. Now, consider what is best to be done in regard to your present case. There is happiness in having remained altogether free from experience of love; but if once you have been caught, the wisest course is to guide your desire safely into the way of sobriety. And so, if you agree to trust this advice, it is feasible for you to fend off the shameful repute of mere lust and, by deciding on a legal contract of union, convert your malady into marriage."

(11) 'At these words of mine she perspired profusely, Cnemon, and was evidently moved by a great mixture of feelings—of joy over what she heard me say, anxiety for the chances of her hopes and bashful shame for being so captivated. For some time she remained silent; then: "Father," she said, "you mention marriage, and urge me to decide on it, as though one were certain that it will meet with my father's consent, or with my enemy's aspirations." "As to the young man," I replied, "we can depend upon him: he on his side is probably more captivated than you, and has been stirred by feelings similar to yours. It seems that your souls, at your first meeting, had somehow a cognisance of each other's quality, and were swept along into a

mutual affection. Out of kindness to you I have applied my skill to heightening his desire. But your supposed father is providing you with another husband, Alcamenes, who is not unknown to you." "For Alcamenes", she said, "let him provide rather a tomb than wedlock with me: I shall either be bride to Theagenes or be overtaken by my destined fate. But, as to your remark that Charicles is not my real but my supposed father, tell me, I beseech you, how you discovered that." "By means of this," I replied, displaying the swathe. "From whom, and how, did you get it? For ever since he received me from my foster-parent in Egypt and brought me—how, I cannot tell—to this place, he has taken and kept it from me, stowed in a casket, to save it from suffering injury in the course of time." "How I procured it", I replied, "you shall hear later on; for the moment tell me if you are aware of what is inscribed on it." She owned that she did not know. "How could I?" she asked. "It declares your family," I went on, "your nation and what befell you." She implored me to disclose everything that I was able to learn, and I told her all, going through phrase after phrase of the script and translating it word for word.

Calasiris tells Chariclea of his acquaintance with her mother, and how he undertook to search for her.

(12) 'When she had learnt who she was and, her spirit now raised more in keeping with her birth, she stepped up to me quickly, asking "What now is to be done?" I then and there entered on a more open kind of counsel, revealing to her all the facts of the matter. "I had gone, daughter," I said, "as far as to the Ethiopians, from a longing to acquire their wisdom. I became acquainted with your mother, Persinna, for that royal court always welcomes the learned sort of men, and besides, I enjoyed there the enhanced credit of sanctifying my Egyptian wisdom by adding to it the Ethiopian. When the Queen understood that I was about to depart for home, she related to me the whole of what happened to you, after obtaining my sworn pledge of silence, for she said that she dared not tell it to the sages of her country. She begged me to ask the gods first, whether you had survived your exposure, and next, in what part of the world

you were living: she could not hear of any girl like you in her nation, despite her many persistent inquiries. I was informed of everything by the gods, and told her that you were alive and where you were. She then besought me to seek you out and induce you to come to your native land; not once, she said, had she conceived or borne any child since the travail of your birth, and she was prepared, if you should one day appear, to confess to your father what had happened. She knew that he would believe her story, as he had tested her integrity in the years of their wedded life, and would then be attaining beyond all expectation his ambition of being succeeded by offspring of his own.

(13) ' " That is what in her talk with me she begged me to do, conjuring me repeatedly by the Sun, an oath that may not be violated by any of the sages. I have come here in order to perform the duty laid on me by the vow that I took at her supplication; not that this was the actual cause of my hastening to reach this place. It was through an intimation from the gods that I have reaped this richest gain from my travels, and for a long time now, as you are aware, I have been close to you here, without ever neglecting any careful attention that I ought to pay to you. I have been silent about the truth, waiting for the right moment and means for obtaining the swathe that should attest the statement which I was to make to you. So now, if you will be persuaded, and decide to join us in our flight from here before you are forced to submit to some arrangement contrary to your own choice—for Charicles even now is busied with your marriage to Alcamenes—you have the prospect of regaining your kinsfolk, your native land and your parents, and of being united to Theagenes, who is prepared to accompany us wherever we may go. Thus you may exchange the life of a stranger beneath an alien roof for one that is truly your own in a ruling house, where you will share the royal throne with him whom you love best, if we are to place any confidence in the gods, and especially in the oracle of the Pythian Apollo." And with that I reminded her of the oracle's words and explained to her their meaning: Chariclea was not ignorant of them, as they were chanted and discussed by many of the people. She was petrified by my words, and said: "Since that is the purpose of the gods, as you say, and I believe

it, what then are we to do, father?" "Make pretence", I replied,
"of consenting to the marriage with Alcamenes." "It would be
a burdensome, and besides a degrading, thing for me", she said,
"merely to profess my preference of another to Theagenes; but
yet, as I have committed myself to the gods and to you, father,
what is the object of such pretence, and by what means could one
be disentangled before the fact is upon one?" "The facts will
inform you," I said; "it sometimes happens that the prediction
of them causes a certain wavering in women, but the performance of them on the spur of the moment often results in
a quite gallant achievement. Only follow my instructions in all
things and, just for the present, concur in Charicles' plan for
your marriage; for he has done nothing without my guidance."
She consented to this, and I left her in tears.

(14) 'Hardly had I come out of the house when I saw Charicles
in a state of extreme distress and utterly sunk in dejection. "You
marvellous man!" I said. "When you ought to be wearing a
crown, and rejoicing, and offering up sacrifices of gratitude to
the gods for granting your oft-repeated prayer—now that
Chariclea has been at long last converted to a desire for marriage
by my powerful art and my lore, you choose this moment to be
gloomy and despondent, and all but lamenting over goodness
knows what trouble." "And why should I not," he asked, "when
she who is dearest to me is ready, it seems, to rid herself of life
sooner than enter, as you say she will, into the bond of wedlock
—if one is to have regard to dreams, and particularly to those
which have terrified me last night? It appeared to me that an
eagle was released from the hand of Apollo, and swooped down
and suddenly snatched up my darling daughter, alas! from my
embrace, and then bore her away to the farthest corner of the
earth, a place all crowded with dusky, shadow-like phantoms. In
the end I failed to make out what the bird could have done with
her, because the immense distance that separated it from me
baffled the efforts of my sight to keep up with it in its course."

(15) 'After he had told me this I understood the intention of
his dream; but to recall him from his despondency and to make
sure that he would be far from suspecting what was to ensue I
said: "For a priest, and one moreover who serves the most
prophetic of the gods, you seem to me no adept at construing

dreams. These visions in your sleep foretell to you the future marriage of your daughter: by the eagle they darkly intimate the husband who will take her to himself, and they announce to you the good tidings that so it will befall, with Apollo approving and almost leading to her by the hand her destined spouse; and you are distressed by this vision, and make your dream a reason for being despondent! Now, Charicles, let us keep our lips from uttering inauspicious words, and concur in the purpose of the higher powers by applying ourselves with still greater zeal to persuasion of the girl." He asked me what he should do to make her amenable. "If you have some precious article that you treasure," I said, "a robe inwoven with gold, or a valuable necklace, bring it to her as a wedding gift from her bridegroom, and by its presentation conciliate Chariclea. Indefeasible is the spell cast by gold or gems upon a woman. And now you must get everything in readiness for the celebration: it will be best to clinch the marriage while the girl is still feeling the unabated urgency of the desire effected by my treatment." "You may take it that I shall neglect nothing that lies in my power," said Charicles, as he ran off in joyful haste to act upon his words. He did indeed, as I learnt later, just what I had put to him, without any putting off: he brought to Chariclea not only garments of great price, but also the very Ethiopian necklaces that had been exposed with her by Persinna for her identification—all represented to be wedding gifts from Alcamenes.

Calasiris tells of his meeting with some Phoenician traders, and how he planned to escape from Delphi with Theagenes and Chariclea.

(16) 'Then, meeting with Theagenes, I asked him where the persons who formed the procession with him had their dwelling. He replied that the girls had taken their departure, having been sent on in advance because of their less speedy rate of walking; while the youths were showing their impatience by making a disturbance as they mustered in a body to start their return journey. On learning this I enjoined on him what he should say to them and what he was to do; and I bade him be on the alert for the signal that I would give him when the right time and

moment had arrived. I then left him, and was making my way towards the temple of Apollo, intending to entreat the god to guide me by an oracle on my flight with the young pair. But in truth the divine nature moves more quickly than any human mind in coming to the support of what is done in accord with its will, and often anticipating one's prayer with an unsolicited benignity. And so it was then; for Apollo gave the answer to my inquiry before I could present it, and signified his guidance of me by the incidents that followed. For, while I was busied with the matters that weighed upon my mind, and was hastening, as I have said, to consult the prophetess, I was stopped on my way by some visitors calling out to me: "Join us in our libations, dear sir." They were, it seemed, about to hold a ceremonial banquet with some flute-playing, in honour of Hercules. I stopped in my onward course when I perceived what this was, for it was not permissible for me to disregard a sacred call. When I took some incense and offered it up, and poured a libation of water, they showed surprise at the costliness of my offering; [1] but still they accepted me as a worthy partaker of their banquet. I complied in this also, and reclined on the couch strewn for their guests with myrtle and laurel; and I tasted such portions of the fare as were habitual with me. "Now, my good sirs," I said to them, "I have here no lack of delectable dishes, but as yet I am uninformed of your repute in the world; so it is time for you to tell me who you are and whence you come. For I look upon it as the vulgar way of uncultivated people when, after sharing in the libations and the meal at table, they part without becoming acquainted with one another—after they have partaken of the salt that is sacred to the forming of friendship." So then they told me that they were Phoenicians of Tyre, and were sea-traders voyaging to Carthage in Libya, in a vessel of very large tonnage freighted with Indian, Ethiopian and Phoenician wares. At the moment they were dedicating their banquet to the Tyrian Hercules in celebration of a victory; for the young man there—they showed him reclining there opposite to me—had won the garland in the wrestling at Delphi, and had made Tyre renowned among the Greeks for its victory. "This man," they said, "when we had passed by Cape Malea and,

[1] Probably a sarcastic murmur among the strangers.

meeting with contrary winds, had put in at Cephallenia, declared to us on oath taken in the name of this our national god [1] that a dream foretold to him his coming victory in the Pythian Games; and he persuaded us to turn aside from our intended route and put in at this place. By his exploits he has proved the truth of the prophecy, and he who till now was a mere merchant stands forth a glorious victor. And he makes this feast-offering to the god who gave him that intimation, to signalize both his victory and his gratitude, and also to obtain a blessing on our voyage. For at dawn tomorrow, my very good friend, we mean to set sail, if the winds should blow in favour of our wishes." "You really mean to do so?" I asked. "Yes, we do," they replied. "Then will it be agreeable to you to have me as your passenger? I intend to make the voyage to Sicily about some business: that island, you know, lies on your route, as you are bound for Libya." To which they answered: "If it should be your pleasure, we shall consider ourselves most fortunate in having with us a man who is a sage and a Greek and who, as our impression indicates, is probably in high favour with the gods." "It will be my pleasure", I told them, "if you will allow me a single day to make ready." "You shall have tomorrow," they said; "only be by the waterside, at any rate, by the evening: for the night time is most advantageous for sailing, because vessels are then sped on their way by land breezes which raise no great swell." I agreed to do as they said, after I had made them pledge their word on oath that they would not put to sea before the appointed time.

(17) 'I left them there at their flute music and their dancing, in which they frisked to a tripping time given out by pipes in an Assyrian measure; now lightly springing aloft, and now crouching close to the ground and spinning the entire body round and round like possessed persons. I went and visited Chariclea: she was still holding in a fold of her dress and examining the heirlooms that she had received from Charicles. From her I passed on to Theagenes, and having imparted to them what each had to do and at what hour, I went home and meditated on what lay before us. On the following day things fell out thus: while midnight steeped the city in sleep an armed

_____
[1] Hercules.

band invaded the dwelling of Chariclea; the leader of this
amorous foray was Theagenes, who had formed the young men
of the procession into a fighting troop. With a sudden uproar
of shouting and a clashing of shields, which utterly dismayed
even those who heard it but faintly, they dashed with lighted
torches into the house, breaking their way through the outer
door without difficulty, since the bolts had been purposely
tampered with in order to facilitate an opening. They snatched
up Chariclea, who was in readiness and had knowledge before-
hand of the whole plan, and willingly submitted to this violent
proceeding; and they also carried away such belongings as the
girl desired them to take. As soon as they came outside the house
they raised loud shouts of victory, made a mighty clatter by
beating on their shields, and marched through the length of the
city, filling its inhabitants with inexpressible alarm; for it had
been their plan to cause a thorough panic by doing this in the
dead of night, Parnassus the while re-echoing their outcry together with the brazen clang. In this manner they traversed
Delphi, continually calling out in quick reiteration the name of
Chariclea.

(18) 'When they had got outside the town they took horse
and rode at full speed to the heights of Locris and Oeta.[1] Theagenes and Chariclea, acting on the prearranged plan, parted
from the Thessalians and took refuge in secret with me: together
they fell down at my knees and clung to them for a long time,
trembling all over and exclaiming again and again: "Save us,
father!" Chariclea indeed said this and no more, bowing her
head to the ground and blushing for the strange action that had
just been taken; but Theagenes went on to make a further
appeal, saying: "Calasiris, save suppliants who are in a foreign
land, stateless, dispossessed of everything, so that having lost
all else they may gain only each other! Save two creatures left
as chattels to the disposal of Fortune, two captives of chaste
love! Save two fugitives, voluntary but guiltless, who rest on
you all their hopes of salvation!" I was confounded by this
appeal, and wept more in my mind than with my eyes over the
young pair, so much as, unobserved by them, might relieve my

---

[1] The mountain range extending northwards from the country west of
Delphi to Mount Oeta.

own feelings. I raised them up and encouraged them; then, having advised them of the good hopes we should have of our coming adventure, undertaken from the start with the god's blessing, I said to them: "I leave you now, and go to see to the next steps to be taken. You two must wait for me in this spot, taking the utmost care that nobody shall see you." With these words I was hurrying away. But Chariclea took hold of my cloak and stopped me, saying: "Father, you are heading for wrong-doing, nay, even betrayal, if you go away and leave me here alone, with my fortunes committed to Theagenes, and do not reflect how untrustworthy a guardian is the lover who is dominant in the love-making, especially when he is freed from the presence of those who could give him a feeling of shame. For his ardour blazes up the more, I conceive, when he sees the object of his longing at his mercy, with none there to defend her. So I will not let you go before assurance is obtained from Theagenes under a binding oath, as a safeguard for the present, and still more for the times to come, that he will have no amorous connection with me before I regain my family and home; or, if this is denied me by Fate, at least until he can take me with my full consent to be his wife; otherwise, not at all." I admired this speech of hers, and decided that we should certainly proceed as she wished. I lit a fire on the hearth, using it as an altar, and burnt on it some incense. Theagenes then swore an oath, stating indeed that it was an injustice to take this solemn precaution whereby the fidelity of his character was discredited in advance, since he was now unable to prove that he could do of his own choice what he was regarded as forced to do by fear of a supernal power. However, he swore by the Pythian Apollo and Artemis, and by Aphrodite herself and the Loves, that he would in all things act according to the wishes and bidding of Chariclea.

(19) 'To this mutual agreement they added some others besides, praying the gods to be witnesses to their vows. I then hurried off to see Charicles, and found the house full of tribulation and wailing. The servants had already come to him with reports of the girl's abduction, and a great throng of citizens was streaming in. Charicles, as he lamented, was hemmed in on all sides by these people, who were bewildered by ignorance of what had happened and perplexity as to what should be done.

Thereupon with a loud voice I called out to them: "You poor wretches, how long will you remain sitting here like senseless creatures, speechless and inert, as though in the presence of misfortune you had suffered the loss of your wits! Why not arm yourselves forthwith and go in pursuit of the enemy? Why not capture and punish the ruffians?" "Surely it is useless", said Charicles, "to struggle against this disaster; for I can see that it is the wrath of the gods that has brought upon me this penalty, of which I had warning from Apollo for having once entered his sanctuary at an incorrect time, and having allowed my eyes to behold a forbidden sight: such an improper view was to be requited by my losing sight of my darling. Nevertheless there is nothing to prevent us from battling, as the saying goes, even against divinity,[1] if we could but know whom we are to pursue, and who it is that has launched this grievous assault." "It is the Thessalian," I said, "so greatly admired by you, whom you would have me also accept as a friend; it is Theagenes and his young companions. You will not find in the city now a single one of that troop who were staying in it up to last evening, so you must rise and call on the people to assemble for a consultation." This was done, and the commandants proclaimed by trumpet throughout the city the summoning of a special assembly. The people attended immediately in the theatre, putting it in use for their nocturnal debate. Charicles came forward in the view of all; the mere sight of him at once moved the multitude to cries of grief. He stood there clothed in black, his face and head bespattered with ashes, and said: "You may well suppose, people of Delphi, that I have come before you, and have convened this assembly, in order to make some announcement concerning myself; so much may be suggested to you by my extraordinary misfortunes. But that is not the case. My fate indeed is tantamount to many deaths: I am destitute, and am pursued by divine rancour; my house henceforth is desolate, being emptied all at once of my dearest intimates. However, hope, that vain illusion shared by all mankind, persuades me still to hold on to life, suggesting to me the possibility that my daughter may be found; and even more than this, the city bids me stay, that I may see it take vengeance on those who

[1] The bold words of Menelaus in Homer, *Il.* xvii. 104.

have committed this gross outrage—that is, if your spirit of liberty, and your indignation for your native and ancestral gods, have not been abducted also by these Thessalian youngsters. For the most grievous feature of the affair is that a handful of young dancers, attendants on a sacred mission, have got away after trampling on the first city of Greece, and robbing Apollo's temple of its most precious treasure, Chariclea—the light, too, alas, of mine eyes! Oh, the implacable enmity of Fate against us! It extinguished my first, my own begotten daughter, as you know, together with her wedding torches; it carried off from me her mother at the first shock of her grief; and it drove me forth from my native land. Yet all these things could be borne after I had found Chariclea. Chariclea was my life, the hope of succession in my family; Chariclea, my only solace and, one may say, my sheet-anchor. And now this anchor has been cut loose and swept away by whatever may be the destined tempest that, in no light or casual manner, but in its wonted course, has chosen this untimely moment to make cruel sport of me, by snatching her almost from her very bridal chamber, just when her coming marriage had been announced to you all."

(20) 'While he was yet speaking these words, completely carried away by his grief, the commandant Hegesias stopped him and, thrusting him aside, said: "Hear me, all present: Charicles will be at full liberty to lament, both now and hereafter; but let us not be engulfed with him in the depths of his distress, nor be unwarily swept along, as it were, in the torrent of his tears, thus throwing away opportunity, a thing which in every affair, and especially in war, tips the scale. For if we now leave this assembly there is hope of the enemy being taken by surprise, in a time when their expectation of our being still engaged in our preparations causes them to be quite leisurely in their progress. But if, in pitying ourselves, or rather playing the woman's part, we allow our delay to put them farther ahead of us, the only result must be that we shall be laughed to scorn, and that too by a number of lads whom, in my opinion, we should capture with all speed and crucify, and then, by outlawing their descendants, carry over our retribution to the whole of their posterity. This could easily be done if we were to excite the indignation of the Thessalian people against any of these same persons who might

escape us, and against their descendants, by our decreeing that Thessalians be forbidden to perform the sacred mission and sacrifice to the hero, and resolving that this service shall be maintained from our public funds."

(21) 'These proposals were no sooner approved and sanctioned by resolution of the people than the commandant went on to say: "Let this also be voted by show of hands, if it be thought fit—that henceforth the ministrant maiden shall not be brought into view of the runners in the armed race; for I see reason to suppose that it was from such view that Theagenes derived the impulse to his sacrilege and, from his first sight of the maiden, apparently, conceived the idea of her abduction. It will be well, therefore, to preclude any similar enterprise on future occasions." When this resolution also had been passed unanimously by show of hands, Hegesias gave the signal for departure. The trumpet sounded the call to arms, and the meeting in the theatre broke up to go to battle. All made a headlong rush from the assembly to engage in the fight; not only men at arms of robust age, but many boys also and youths just on the threshold of manhood, who made up the tale of years with their zeal, and thus emboldened themselves to join in that expedition. Many women besides showed a more manly spirit than beseemed their nature and, snatching up any weapon that came to hand, ran after them—in vain, for falling behind in the race they had to acknowledge the inherent weakness of their sex. One could have seen also, struggling against his senility, an old man whose mind seemed in his zeal to drag his body along and upbraid its feebleness. Thus the whole city showed its deep resentment of the abduction of Chariclea: all, as if stirred by a single emotion, launched themselves in one body upon the pursuit at the first call to battle, without waiting for daylight.

BOOK V

After hearing Calasiris' story Cnemon discovers Chariclea in the house at Chemmis where Calasiris and he are staying.

(1) ' Such then was the state of things in the city of Delphi, and such the action that it took; with what result I am unable to tell. But to me that pursuit of theirs indicated the moment for our flight. I took the young pair with me in the direction of the sea, just as they were, while it was still night, and put them on board the Phoenician ship, finding her on the very point of casting off. For indeed, as a glimmer of dawn was already appearing, the Phoenicians did not consider that they were breaking their sworn agreement with me—that they would wait for a day and a night only.[1] They greeted our arrival with much pleasure, and immediately moved out of harbour, at first by rowing; but as a gentle breeze began to blow from the land, and low waves came running under the stern, seeming to smile at it, they then handed over the ship to the power of the sails. The gulf of Cirrha, the foothills of Parnassus, the headlands of Aetolia and Calydon in turn passed by the vessel as she almost flew along; and the Pointed Isles, so named from their shape, and the sea of Zacynthus came into view just as the sun dipped to its setting. But why am I relating all this at such length and out of season? Why do I heedlessly send my narrative sailing out upon the veritable ocean of what ensued? Here, I think, we may well halt my story and snatch a little sleep; for however resolute a listener you may be, and however stoutly you may fend off sleep, Cnemon, I fancy you are already beginning to sink down under the tale of my experiences, drawn out by me to such a late hour of the night. And besides, I on my part, my son, am feeling now the weight

---

[1] If the text is correct it would seem that the author has forgotten that Calasiris was to embark on the evening of the day after his talk with the Phoenicians (iv. 16); or perhaps the Phoenicians had only a hazy memory of the agreement made during their joyous festivity.

of my many years, while the recollection of my misfortunes prostrates my mind and inclines it to sleep.' 'Stay, father,' said Cnemon; 'it is not that I wish to jettison your narrative, for I believe that even if you were to continue for a long string of nights, and a longer one of days, I should never come to that, so uncloying, so bewitching, is the matter of your story. But for some time now I have heard a kind of murmur, like the buzzing of a crowd, resounding through the house: I could not help being disturbed by it, but I refrained from saying anything, I was so enticed by my desire to hear each new incident that you had to tell me.' 'I did not notice it,' said Calasiris, 'I dare say because my old age has made me somewhat hard of hearing— for deafness is one of the ailments of advanced years—and also, I suppose, because I was preoccupied with my narration. I should think it will be Nausicles, the master of the house, who has come in; but, O ye gods, what has he succeeded in doing.' 'Everything as I wished,' said Nausicles, suddenly appearing before them. 'I did not fail to observe, my good Calasiris, that my operations were much on your mind, and that in a sense you were adventuring abroad with me in your thoughts; and now, apart from what I have perceived in your general behaviour towards me, I have come upon clear evidence of your feeling in those words that I caught you uttering here, as I entered. But who is this stranger?' 'A Greek,' said Calasiris. 'You shall hear more about him later on. If your efforts have happily succeeded, make haste to let us know, so that you may bring us in to share your joy.' 'Well,' said Nausicles, 'you shall hear about it all at daybreak; but for the moment it will suffice you to know that I have got hold of Thisbe, now in better trim. As for me, I must have at least a short sleep, to relieve the fatigue of my journeying and my many anxieties.'

(2) With these words he hurried away to do as he had said. Cnemon had been stunned when he heard the name of Thisbe, and in his helpless bewilderment was revolving thought after thought in his mind. Continually heaving deep sighs, he spent the rest of the night in great distress, so that at length even Calasiris, sunk though he was in a deep slumber, became aware of his trouble. The old man then raised himself up and, leaning on his elbow, asked Cnemon what ailed him, and what was the

cause of his being so strangely distracted in a manner hardly differing from that of mad people. To this Cnemon replied: 'How should I not be mad, when I have heard that Thisbe is still alive?' 'And who is that Thisbe?' said Calasiris; 'how come you to know her name, or be concerned at the report of her being alive?' To which he answered: 'You shall have a full account later on, when the time comes for me to tell you my own story; but with these eyes I discovered that woman lying dead, and with these hands of mine I buried her in the herdsmen's haunt.' 'Go to sleep,' said Calasiris; 'we shall know quite soon how it may have happened.' 'That I cannot do,' he said; 'you must have quiet rest; but I feel that I cannot live if I do not slip away immediately and search out by hook or by crook what illusion has taken hold of Nausicles, or how it is that only among Egyptians do the dead come to life again.' Calasiris showed a slight smile at this, and betook himself to sleep once more. But Cnemon left the room, and found himself in the natural difficulty of one who wanders in the darkness of night about an unknown house. Yet he went on undeterred, so eager was he to rid himself of his terror of Thisbe and the imaginings of his mind. At length, as he took many turns through the same parts of the house, which seemed to him each time to be different, he became aware of a woman weeping and wailing in secret, like the nightingale when it sobs out its nocturnal song of woe in the spring time. Guided by this mournful sound, he made his way towards the room whence it came and, on applying his ear to where the doors met and listening, he caught these words of the woman's continuing lamentation: 'What boundless misery is mine! I thought that I had escaped from the clutches of the brigands and evaded the brutal murder that I was expecting, so that I could live thenceforth with my darling the life indeed of a wandering exile, yet made delightful by his company; for no burden could be so irksome that I would not be able to bear it with him at my side. But now the Fate-appointed spirit, still unsated, though in charge of me from the first, has allowed me a little taste of pleasure only to disappoint me. I thought that I had escaped from slavery, and I am a slave once more; from prison, and I am in custody. I was held in an island, and in darkness; my present lot is no better than the former or, to speak more truly, more painful, now that he who has both the will and the power to assuage my pain is parted from me. Till yesterday a brigands' cave was my lodging: an awesome chasm, a veritable tomb, was my dwelling. Yet even these hardships were relieved by the presence of him who is dearer to me than all the world. There he lamented over me while I lived, and bewept me when, as he supposed, I was dead; he mourned for me as perished from the earth. Now I am deprived even of his plaints; gone is my comrade in misfortune, he who shared with me the burden of my sufferings. I am alone, deserted, a captive ever in tears, a prey to the designs of a bitter Destiny, only enduring life itself because I hope that my darling may still be alive. But, O my soul, where, where can you be? What fortune has befallen you? Can it be that you yourself, alas, are enslaved—the one high spirit that was free and unenslaved, except by love? Oh, if only you may remain alive, and behold one day your own Thisbe! For by this name shall you call me, even though it be against your will.'

(3) Cnemon, on hearing these words, lost all power to restrain himself any longer. He did not wait to hear what else might be said; for, although the first words had given him a different impression, the last that he heard convinced him that it was in truth Thisbe, and he came near collapsing close to the very door. With a great effort he held himself up; then, in fear of being caught there by someone—for the cocks were already crowing for the second time—he hurried away, stumbling as he went, now getting his feet tripped up, now suddenly running into the walls: here it was against a lintel, there against some utensil hanging by chance from the roof, that he knocked his head; till after much wandering he reached the apartment where they were lodged, and there flung himself prone upon his bed. His body was quivering, his teeth chattered aloud, and he would probably have sunk into a most critical condition had not Calasiris, on perceiving his disorder, hastened to chafe him assiduously and done all that he could to rouse him with words. When Cnemon had a little recovered himself, Calasiris earnestly asked him to say what was the cause of his trouble. 'I am done for, I tell you,' he replied; 'that vile creature, Thisbe, is in truth alive!' With these words he swooned away again.

*How it came about that Chariclea was separated from Theagenes
and was found in the same house as Calasiris and Cnemon.*

(4) Calasiris once more was hard put to it in efforts to revive
him. And indeed it seemed that Cnemon had become the play-
thing of some divinity that makes a practice of treating human
affairs altogether as a jest and a sport. It would not permit him to
enjoy even his greatest pleasures without incurring some pain,
but promptly interwove a strand of anguish with what was ere
long to bring him delight; and belike it was giving an example of
its practice in this instance, though perhaps the truth is that human
nature is incapable of any joy unmixed and pure. And so on this
occasion Cnemon shrank from that which he preferred to all the
world, and viewed with terror what gave him most delight. For
the wailing woman was not Thisbe, but Chariclea. Now, what
had happened to her was this. When Thyamis had been captured
alive and was held as a prisoner, and the island had been set
ablaze and had been evacuated by its herdsmen inhabitants,
Cnemon and Thermouthis, the henchman of Thyamis, crossed
over the lagoon at dawn to discover in what way the enemy
had dealt with the brigand chief. How it fared with them has
already been told.[1] Theagenes and Chariclea were left alone in
the cavern, and turned their extremely perilous situation to the
best advantage. For this was the first time that they found themselves together in private, freed from any irksome presence; and
they took their fill of unhindered ardent embraces and kisses.
In a moment they were plunged in oblivion of everything: for a
long time they clung to each other as though grown into one
person, satiating themselves with a devout, virginal love, com-
muning with one another through the flow of hot tears, and
commingling only by the chaste means of their kisses. For
Chariclea, when she found Theagenes making some too impulsive
advance of manly ardour, restrained him by recalling his oaths,
and his attempt was easily checked. It was a light matter for him
to be temperate, for although mastered by love he could be
master of his pleasures. But when at long last they came to
reflect on what they had to do, and were forced into thinking
that they had had their fill, Theagenes began their consultation

[1] In ii. 19.

thus: 'To be united with each other, Chariclea, and to possess
what we have deemed more precious than anything else, and for
which we have endured all things—that is the object of our
prayers, and may the gods of Greece bestow it. But human
nature is an unstable thing, ever veering this way and that: we
have undergone much, and expect to undergo more. It is now
our duty, under our agreement with Cnemon, to go with all
speed to the village of Chemmis. There is no knowing what kind
of fortune will next attend us, and we have a long, a seemingly
infinite distance yet to travel before we reach the land of our
hopes. So come, let us devise some tokens by which we can
convey information without speech when we are together, and
if we should ever chance to be separated we can search for each
other. For it is a wise provision, in case of going astray, to have
a sign agreed between friends as a ready means of finding
themselves again.'

(5) Chariclea approved his suggestion, and they resolved, if
they should be separated, to inscribe on temples, notable statues,
boundary pillars or stones set at partings of the ways, these
words: The Pythian man (for Theagenes) or The Pythian
woman (for Chariclea) has passed on to the right, or to the left,
making for such and such a town or village or people; and besides
this to specify the day and hour. If they should meet at some
place it would be enough for them merely to be seen by each
other; for no lapse of time could avail to erase from their souls
the marks of identity made by love. Nevertheless Chariclea
showed her father's ring that was exposed with her, and Theagenes the scar on his knee that he had from a boar hunt; and to
save words they agreed to use two emblems, she a torch and he a
palm. Upon this they embraced one another again, and again
they wept, offering up their tears, I conceive, as libations and
their kisses as solemn vows. Their compact thus made, they
crept out of the cavern, not touching any of the treasure stored
within it, since they regarded as unclean those riches gained by
rapine. But the articles which they had themselves brought from
Delphi, and which the brigands had taken from them, these they
packed up for their journey. Chariclea changed her dress,
putting away in a small satchel her necklaces, her garlands and
her sacred robe and, to hide these from view, placing on top

some other articles of small value. Her bow and quiver she handed to Theagenes to carry—a most pleasant burden to him, as they were the arms associated with the god who was his master. Then, just as they reached the lagoon and were about to embark in a boat, they saw a large body of armed men crossing over towards the island.

(6) Staggered by this sight, they stood for a great while dumb-founded, as if they had become insensible to the despiteful treatment that they received unceasingly from Fortune. At length, however, when the newcomers were just on the point of putting in to land, Chariclea urged that they should take to flight and hide themselves in the cavern, on the chance of avoiding discovery, and she started at once to run off. But Theagenes stopped her, saying: 'How far are we to continue fleeing from the Fate that everywhere pursues us? Let us yield to Fortune, and meet half way the flood that would sweep us along. Let us spare ourselves these futile strayings of a nomad life, and the deity's persistent mockery of us. Do you not see how eagerly he endeavours to lengthen the chain, linking ordeals to exile and adding to misadventures at sea the greater hardships of the land, and now, in quick succession, producing battles after brigands? But lately he had us in captivity; then he returned us to solitude; and after giving promise of deliverance and freedom in flight, he sets our destroyers upon us. Thus he diverts himself with battling against us, as though he had made our fortunes the plot of a drama on the stage. Why then do we not cut short his tragic scheme, and give ourselves up to men intent on our destruction, lest in his eagerness to bring his play to some monstrous conclusion he should drive us to laying violent hands on ourselves?'

(7) Chariclea did not agree with everything that he had said. His upbraiding of Fortune, she said, was just; but she did not approve of voluntarily yielding themselves up to the enemy, since there was no evidence to show that they would be put to death when taken. The divinity against whom they were contending was not so kind as to grant them a quick deliverance from their troubles. Nay, rather, it was possible that he might desire to preserve them for a life of slavery; and what death would not be less bitter than that? To be subjected to the infamous and abominable outrages of murderous barbarians—

'that we must avoid by every means in our power,' she said,
'counting our past trials as so many hopes of success, since we
have often come through still more desperate straits.' 'Let us do
as you wish,' said Theagenes, following her lead as though
drawn along by her. However, they were unable to reach the
cavern in time. While they were observing the advance of the
men in front of them, they failed to see that they had been
enveloped by a detachment of the enemy which had disembarked
behind them in another part of the island. They both stood still,
in consternation; Chariclea had crept close to Theagenes so that
if indeed she had to die it should be in his arms. Some of the
assailants pressed forward as if about to strike at them; but when
the gaze of the young pair shed its radiance on them as they
dashed up, the spirit of each man sank down and his right hand
fell limp by his side; for even a barbarian's arm, it seems, will
falter in the presence of human beauty, and the sight of loveliness
can pacify even an alien's eye.

(8) So they seized hold of the pair and led them before their
commander, full of eagerness to be the first to bring in the finest
piece of plunder. But in fact this was the only piece that they
were to bring, because not a man of them found anything else
about the place, although they scoured the island from end to
end, sweeping it thoroughly in every direction, as it were, with
the drag-net of their weapons. It had been altogether devastated
by fire that arose in the previous fighting; only the cavern
remained, and it was not discovered. The two captives were thus
hurried before the commanding officer. Now he was Mitranes,
a prefect under Oroondates, the satrap set by the Great King
over Egypt. This officer, for a large sum paid to him by Nausicles, as has been related,[1] had invaded the island in search of
Thisbe. When Theagenes and Chariclea, continually calling
aloud for divine deliverance, were seen approaching under
guard, Nausicles, conceiving a commercial and practical plan,
started up and ran to them, crying out: 'This is the woman
Thisbe, whom those pestilent herdsmen stole from me, and
whom I now hold, thanks to you, Mitranes, and the gods!' He
took firm grasp of Chariclea, making a show of extreme delight,
and urged her to acknowledge that she was Thisbe, if she wished

----

[1] In ii. 24.

to save her life, speaking aside to her in a low voice and in Greek, so as not to be understood by the persons there present. His ruse was successful: for Chariclea, hearing the Greek language, and surmising that she might obtain some advantage from this man, became an accomplice in his scheme and, when Mitranes asked her what her name might be, she agreed that it was Thisbe. Thereupon Nausicles ran to Mitranes and kissed his head again and again. He expressed immense admiration of the commander's good fortune, puffing up the barbarian with praises of his numerous successes in war, and especially of the happy result of his present expedition. The other, swollen with pride by these compliments, was at the same time deluded by the name into believing the case to be really as pretended; for, although astonished at the girl's beauty, which shone forth even in her simple attire like a moonbeam from among clouds, he yet had his shallow mind so overborne by the swiftness of the deception that he left himself no time to reconsider, and said: 'This girl is yours: receive her again, and take her away.' So saying he handed her over to Nausicles, gazing fixedly at her the while and clearly signifying that his renunciation of the girl was against his will and on account of the prepayment made to him. 'As for this fellow, whoever he may be,' he said, referring to Theagenes, 'he must be our booty, and be brought along under guard. He is to be sent up to Babylon, for he is suitable for the service of the King's table.'

(9) After this parley they all crossed over the lagoon and then separated, Nausicles proceeding to Chemmis with Chariclea, while Mitranes diverged to visit other villages in his domain; and without a moment's delay he dispatched Theagenes together with a letter to Oroondates, who was then at Memphis. The terms of his message were these: 'To Oroondates, satrap, Mitranes, his prefect: this young Greek, superior to the quality of persons in my service, and worthy to be in personal attendance on the celestial Great King alone, I have taken prisoner and now send over to you, yielding to you the presentation to our common master of this fine and valuable gift—an adornment such as the royal court has never seen before nor will ever see again.'

*The Egyptian merchant Nausicles offers a sacrifice and holds
a feast, at which Calasiris presents him with a marvellous jewel.*

(10) These were the terms of his message. Day had not yet
fully dawned when Calasiris went together with Cnemon to see
Nausicles, in quest of some news of doings as yet unknown to
him. On being asked what he had accomplished, Nausicles told
the whole story: how he went to the island and found it deserted;
how at first he met with nobody; how he beguiled Mitranes with
a pretence and received, claiming her as Thisbe, a girl who had
been discovered; and how he had done much better for himself
by happening upon her than if he had found the girl whom he
had been seeking. For there was no small difference between
them: it was as much as set a god above a man, so incomparable
was this girl's beauty, so beyond any power of his to describe in
words; moreover, she was there at hand: he could readily show
her to them.

(11) On hearing his words they at once conceived a notion of
the truth, and begged him to have her summoned as quickly as
possible; for they called to mind the indescribable beauty of
Chariclea. When she was brought in she at first kept her head
bent down and her face covered to her eyebrows. Nausicles
urged her to have no fear; she raised her head a little, and saw
and was seen by them, to the great surprise of both parties. At
once all three gave way to tearful sobbing and doleful cries,
as though at one signal or the shock of a single blow. One
could hear, for the most part, only the words 'O father!' 'O
daughter!' and 'It is really Chariclea, and not Thisbe!' Nausicles
was struck dumb, as he gazed at Calasiris embracing Chariclea
and continuing to weep over her for so long; he wondered what
to make of this recognition scene, enacted as though in a drama.
At length Calasiris said to him, after saluting him for a great
while with kisses: 'O best of men, for this deed may the gods
grant you all the desires of your heart, to its full contentment!
You are the saviour of my daughter when I had abandoned all
hope of her; you have enabled me to behold what is to me the
sweetest sight in all the world. But O daughter, O Chariclea,
where have you left Theagenes?' She uttered a wail at this
question and, after pausing awhile, said: 'He has been captured

and taken away by whoever the man may be that handed me
over to this person.' Calasiris then begged Nausicles to relate
what he knew about Theagenes—who was now his master, and
whither he was being taken. Nausicles told him everything, for
he now understood that the young pair were the persons of
whom the old man had so often spoken to him, and in search of
whom he knew Calasiris to be pursuing his sorrowful wanderings. But he added that their case was none the better for this
intelligence, as they were without any resources; it would be
astonishing if Mitranes should be willing to give up the young
man for even a large sum of money. 'We have money,' said
Chariclea aside to Calasiris; 'promise as large a sum as you please.
I have preserved the necklace that you know of, and have it here
with me.'

(12) Calasiris was encouraged by these words; but he feared
lest Nausicles should get some suspicion of the facts and of the
articles that Chariclea carried with her. 'My good Nausicles,'
he said, 'a sage is never in want: he confines his desires to what
is essential, and obtains from the highest powers only so much
as he can honourably ask. So now, just tell us where is the master
of Theagenes; for the divine power will not ignore us, but will
succour us as fully as we desire, to the discomfiture of the Persian
love of money.' Nausicles smiled at this and said: 'You will
induce me to believe that you are able to become wealthy all of
a sudden, as by some miracle, if and when you pay me first the
ransom of this girl: you must in any case bear in mind that
merchants, no less than Persians, are lovers of riches.' 'I am
aware of that,' said Calasiris, 'and you shall be paid. Why should
you not, indeed, when you show no lack of generosity, and even
forestall my appeals by your spontaneous assent to the restora-
tion of my daughter? But first I must offer up a prayer.' 'No
objection,' said Nausicles; 'or rather, come now, if you will—
for I am about to offer a thanksgiving sacrifice to the gods—and
speak the prayer at this oblation, as one dedicated to the service:
ask the gift of riches for us, and then receive it for yourself.' 'Do
not jest or be so unbelieving,' Calasiris said to him; 'go on
ahead and make the preparations for your sacrifice: we will
attend when all has been got ready.'

(13) They proceeded accordingly: a little later a messenger

from Nausicles bade them come without delay to the sacrifice. They had by now agreed on what they should do; and they set forth in joyful mood, the two men along with Nausicles and a company of others whom he had invited, for it had been arranged as a public sacrifice. Chariclea went with the daughter of Nausicles and the other women, whose many appeals and requests had with some difficulty prevailed on her to walk along with them. It is probable that they would never have succeeded if she had not bethought her of using the ceremony as a cover for her intercession for Theagenes. When they arrived at the temple of Hermes—to whom Nausicles was offering the sacrifice as the god of commerce and traders, and whom he singled out from all the gods for his personal devotion—and as soon as the victims had been slain, Calasiris briefly inspected the entrails, and indicated by his facial expressions an intimation of future fortunes chequered with both pleasures and pains. He then reached out with his hands over the altars, uttering some words and making pretence of having drawn out of the fire what he had all the time been carrying with him. 'Here', he said, 'you have the ransom of Chariclea, Nausicles; the gods bestow it through me.' Therewith he put into the merchant's hands a ring of regal splendour, a miraculous work of divine art. The circlet was a hoop of amber, and in the bezel blazed an Ethiopian amethyst, as large in contour as a maiden's eye, and in beauty far surpassing the stones to be found in Spain or Britain, which have a faint reddish bloom like that of a rose just opening out its petals from the bud and beginning to blush under the rays of the sun. But the amethyst of Ethiopia glows in its depths with a pure gleam that has a fresh, spring-like charm: if you turn it round in your hand it gives forth a golden beam which, instead of dazzling your eyes with a fierce glare, sheds all around it a gladdening light. And yet there also resides in it a potency more sovereign than is found in many of those that come from the West: for it does not falsify the import of its name,[1] but is in truth preventive of intoxication in its wearer, and preserves his sobriety in wine parties.

(14) This is the quality of all amethysts coming from India and Ethiopia; but that which Calasiris then offered to Nausicles

[1] The Greek word means 'avoiding drunkenness'.

far excelled even those in merit. For it was finely worked with a
design which had been carved into a representation of live
creatures. The subject was a young boy tending sheep; he stood
on a low rock, so that he could look all around him, and he was
regulating the pasture of his flock with the music of his cross-
fluting. They appeared to be submitting obediently to the
guidance of their feeding given by the keynotes of his flute. One
would have said that they were heavy-laden with fleeces of gold:
not that this was a happy effect of the artist's skill; it was rather
that the amethyst shed over their backs the flower-like brightness of its natural flush. The design included the limber friskings
of the lambs: some were running upwards in troops at the rock,
while others wheeled in stately circles round their shepherd,
treating this outcrop of stone as the platform of a pastoral
theatre; while others, delighting in the sun-like blaze of the
amethyst, scraped the rock with the tips of their hoofs as they
bounded against it. Those of earliest birth, bolder than the rest,
seemed eager to leap outside the circle of the gem, but to be
prevented by the art with which the bezel had been made to
enclose both them and the rock as in a golden fold. The rock was
a real stone, and no imitation of one; for the artist, to make it
real, had so marked off a portion of the gem's border as to
produce his effect in the actual material, considering it over-
curious to impose by craft one stone upon another. Such was
this ring.

(15) Nausicles, besides being quite taken aback by the surprise of the jewel, was even more delighted with its great value,
which he judged to be equal to that of a man's entire fortune.
'I was jesting, my good Calasiris,' he said; 'my request for her
ransom was mere talk, whereas my purpose was to deliver your
daughter to you free of any payment. But since, as you say, "not
to be cast aside are the glorious gifts of the gods",[1] I accept this
heaven-sent jewel, convinced that it has come to me from
Hermes, best and kindest of the gods, in his wonted manner.
He has in fact conveyed this treasure trove to you through that
fire—indeed, one can see it beaming far and wide with the flame.
And besides, I judge the finest kind of gain to be that which
enriches the recipient without causing a loss to the donor.'

[1] Homer, *Il.* iii. 65.

When he had thus spoken and acted he bade the whole company join him at the banquet: he disposed the women by themselves in the interior of the temple, while the men he set at table in the vestibule. When they had taken their fill of enjoyment of the viands, the pleasures of the table gave place to those of the wine-bowl; the men poured libations singing a hymn to Dionysus for a blessing on their voyage, while the women danced to a chant of thanksgiving to Demeter. But Chariclea withdrew for her own devotions, and prayed that she might survive for Theagenes, and he be preserved for her.

(16) The drinking-bout was now in the full flow of its gaiety, and each man was making merry as he felt inclined, when Nausicles offered a cup of water free from any admixture to Calasiris, saying: 'My good Calasiris, we drink to you this virgin draught,[1] as being congenial to you; it has had no association with Dionysus, and is still truly in its maiden state. If you would respond to our toast with the story that we are longing to hear, you would be entertaining us with a draught of the most exquisite of liquors. You hear how the women have arranged for a dance as their pastime during our potations; but for us your adventures, if you would be so good as to relate them, would make a most admirable accompaniment to our festivity, pleasanter than any dancing or piping. You have often, you know, put off recounting them to me, as you were still immersed in the flood of your experiences; but you could not possibly reserve them for a fitter occasion than the present, when of your two children the daughter here is saved and visible to your eyes, and the son will at any moment, with the gods' aid, appear before you—the more surely, if you do not annoy me by a further deferment of your story.' 'A thousand blessings light upon you, Nausicles,' interjected Cnemon; 'for, after having called in all manner of musical instruments for our banquet, you despise them at this moment, renouncing the more popular kinds of entertainment, and show yourself eager to hear of matters truly mystical and, in fact, imbued with heavenly pleasure. To me you seem to have the finest understanding of the divine nature, linking as you do the cult of Hermes with that of Dionysus, and mingling the flow

[1] The Greek word here, 'nymph', came to be used by late Greek writers for 'water' as well as for the maiden deity of a spring or stream.

of sweet-savoured words with the draughts of our wine. I have been filled with admiration of the whole of your sumptuous celebration of this sacrifice; but how could one better propitiate Hermes than by raising from among the company some discourses as a festive contribution most appropriate to the god?' Calasiris complied, since he wished to gratify Cnemon, and also to oblige Nausicles, with an eye to what the future might bring. He told them the whole story, but abridged the first part, already told to Cnemon, only giving it in a sort of summary, and purposely omitting portions which he did not consider advantageous for Nausicles to know. When he came to the yet untold sequel of what he had related, he thus took up the tale.

Calasiris tells how he, Theagenes and Chariclea sailed with the Phoenicians to Zacynthus, and lodged there with a deaf fisherman named Tyrrhenus.

(17) When they had got on board the Phoenician vessel, he said, in their flight from Delphi, the beginning of their voyage was quite agreeable, as they were borne along by a following wind of moderate strength. But when they entered the strait of Calydon [1] they were subjected to a severe tossing by the naturally turbulent waters that they met with there. Cnemon requested him not to pass over this fact itself, but to tell of any particular observation that he might have made of the cause of the sea's prevailing roughness in that part. 'The Ionian Sea', he answered, 'is there contracted from a wide expanse and, pouring through a sort of bottle-neck into the Crisaean Gulf and speeding on to meet the Aegean Sea, is thrust back from its onward flow by the Peloponnesian Isthmus: Divine Providence, it would seem, has erected the bulwark of this neck of land as a barrier against inundation of the lands confronting the current. Thence arises, of course, a reflux of the waters, which are more constricted in this passage than in the rest of the gulf. It often happens that the main stream, still moving on, meets the returning flow, and causes the water to boil up as it is roused into a seething surge and piled up by the clash of currents into high-crested billows.'

[1] Between the Corinthian (or Crisaean) Gulf and the Gulf of Patras (part of the Ionian Sea).

This account of his was warmly applauded and approved by his hearers, who testified to the truth of his explanation. Calasiris then pursued his narrative thus: 'We made our way through the strait,' he said, 'and when we had lost sight of the Pointed Isles we fancied that we could distinguish the headland of Zacynthus [1] creeping into our view like a dark cloud. The pilot ordered some sails to be furled: when we asked him why he was slackening the ship's motion when she was running so well before a fair wind—"Because", he answered, "if we continued under full sail before this breeze, we should be coming to anchor by the island about the first watch, and in the dark there is a risk of running our ship aground in a place full of hidden and rugged reefs. So it will be best to pass the night well out to sea, and make now but a moderate use of the breeze, calculated so as to suffice us for a landing at daybreak."

(18) 'These words of the pilot, Nausicles, were not confuted by the event; for the sun was rising at the moment when we dropped anchor. The people of the island dwelling about the harbour, which is not far distant from the town, came streaming towards us as though to some strange new sight. They were evidently filled with wonder at the easy management of our vessel and the combined beauty and loftiness of the lines which her builders had given her. They recognized, they said, the subtle skill of the Phoenicians, but wondered more at the singular good fortune which had enabled us to make a tranquil and unharassed voyage in the winter time, and just as the Pleiads had begun to set. Hardly had the hawsers been made fast when almost all the passengers left the ship and hurried to the town of Zacynthus to do their marketing. But I, having chanced to hear the pilot say that they were going to make the island their winter quarters, went to look for a lodging somewhere near the shore; for I rejected the ship as a dwelling-place, made unsuitable as it was by the rowdiness of the sailors, and the town as unsafe in view of the young couple being refugees. After proceeding for a little way I saw an elderly fisherman seated in front of his door and at work on the repair of some broken meshes of a net. I went up to him and said: "Good day, my friend; tell me, where

[1] A large fertile island about twenty miles off the north-west coast of the Peloponnese.

can one find a lodging?" "By that near headland," he replied;
"it was caught on a sunken rock yesterday and was badly torn."
Then I told him: "That is not what I wished to know; it would,
however, be good of you, and I should take it kindly if you would
either provide a lodging yourself, or direct me to someone else
who would." "It was not I," he said; "I was not in the boat: may
Tyrrhenus never make such a bad mistake, or be so broken down
by old age! No, it was a blunder of my little boys who, unacquainted with the reefs, put down the nets where they should
not have done." At last I understood that he was somewhat hard
of hearing; so I raised my voice and shouted: "I bid you good
day, sir; and would you tell us strangers of a lodging?" "Oh,
good day to you too," he answered; "do stay with us, if you
will, unless mayhap you are one of the sort who go looking for
houses with many beds, or bring along with them a train of
attendants." When I told him that we were three—my two
children and myself—"The quota is agreeable," he said, "for
you will find us but one more than that. I also have still two
children boarding with me; my elder sons are married and
heads of their own households; and my children's nurse makes
the fourth in mine. Their mother died not long ago. So, my very
good sir, do not hesitate, or be in any doubt of our giving a
warm welcome to a man who, from the moment of one's meeting
with him, shows the marks of good breeding." I took him at his
word, and after a brief interval I came along with Theagenes
and Chariclea. The old man received us gladly, and allotted to
us the sunnier side of the house; and, I may say, we passed quite
pleasantly there the first part of the winter season. Our rule was
to spend the day time together, but to separate at bed time:
Chariclea took her rest with the nurse, and I and Theagenes ours
by ourselves; while Tyrrhenus retired with his children to
another room. We shared common table with them, and we
provided most of the food; but Tyrrhenus brought in from the
sea abundance of fish for his young guests' entertainment, in
part the product of his personal fishing, but some also caught at
times when we employed our leisure in assisting at the haul. In
this pursuit he had become a perfect adept, varying his method
to suit the changes of the seasons. This brought him such happy
success in securing great catches that the skill which he had

acquired by long practice was commonly accounted to a special benignity of Fortune.

(19) 'But it was not possible, as the saying is, for unfortunates to avoid misfortune anywhere; and even in her lonely retreat Chariclea's beauty was not without its embarrassments. That merchant of Tyre, who had been victorious in the Pythian Games and our fellow-voyager, frequently pestered me with coming to see me in private and wearying me with importunate requests that, as her apparent father, I would let him have Chariclea in marriage. He gave himself great airs, first pointing out the distinction of his family, and then recounting in detail the riches that he had with him; how the ship was his own property and the main part of the wares that she carried belonged to him—gold, stones of many talents' worth and silken stuffs; and, as no small enhancement of his fair fame, he spoke of his victory at Delphi and many other successes besides. I pleaded my present poverty, and said that I would never consent to give my dear daughter to anyone residing in a foreign land, and among people so far remote from Egypt. "No more of that, father!" he said; "I shall regard the girl herself as a fully paid dowry of many talents' value, amounting to absolute opulence; and I will adopt your people and your country as my own. I will abandon my voyage to Carthage, and will be your shipmate wheresoever you may choose to go."

Tyrrhenus warns Calasiris against a threatened attack of pirates.

(20) 'Seeing that the Phoenician, instead of relinquishing his purpose, continued to pursue it with the utmost fervour, and did not cease for a single day from pestering me on the same subject, I decided to put him off for the present with fair promises, lest we should become victims of some act of violence in the island. So I promised that I would do all that he desired when I arrived in Egypt. Hardly had I thus disposed of the man for a while, when Fate drove one wave after another, as they say, upon me. For Tyrrhenus, a few days later, drew me apart into a little cove in the coast and said: "Calasiris, I swear to you by Poseidon, lord of the ocean, and all the other deities of the sea, that I truly look upon yourself as a brother, and upon your

children quite as though they were my own. I have come now
to tell you of a certain matter that is raising its head—a troublesome affair, but such as I could not rightly keep to myself, since
I have had you sharing my hearth and home, and such as it is
absolutely necessary for you to know. A gang of pirates, lurking
in the hollow fold of the flank of this headland, is lying in wait
for the Phoenician vessel, and is posting scouts in relays to watch
for her departure. Look out then; be on your guard, and think
out your plan of action; for it is on your account, or rather on
that of your daughter, that they are meditating this stroke—so
brutal, but common enough among those people." "May the
gods reward you," I said to him, "as you deserve, for doing
this! But how, Tyrrhenus, have you got hold of their design?"
"Through my business", he said, "I have become known to
those men: I supply them with fish, and they pay me more for it
than I get from any other people. Yesterday, as I was collecting
some wicker creels round the cliffs, the pirate chief met me and
questioned me earnestly, saying: 'Tell me, have you heard
when the Phoenicians intend to sail?' I, perceiving the hidden
purpose of his question, replied: 'Trachinus, I cannot say
exactly; but I believe they will depart about the beginning of
spring.' 'Well, and will that girl,' he asked, 'who is staying
with you, accompany them on the voyage?' 'That is uncertain,'
I replied; 'but why are you so curious?' 'Because I am madly
in love with her,' he said, 'from a single sight that I had of her.
I do not recall having come across such beauty before, though I
have made many girls my prisoners who were not unattractive.'
Then, that I might induce him to reveal the whole of his design,
I said: 'Now why should you get yourself embroiled with these
Phoenicians, instead of possessing yourself of the girl without
bloodshed, before she goes to sea, by abducting her from my
house?' 'Even among brigands', he replied, 'there still
survives something of conscience and kindly feeling towards
their acquaintance. So, besides sparing you the trouble caused
to you by an inquiry being made concerning your guests, I
propose to achieve at one blow two paramount objects—
possession of the riches in the ship and marriage with the girl.
I must certainly fail of attaining one of these if I set about the
action on land; and besides, any such proceeding so close to the

town would be exposed to a real risk of immediate detection and pursuit.' After complimenting him profusely on his sagacity I parted from him; and, in bringing you this information of the plot which is being hatched by those accursed villains, I beseech you to take serious thought for the safety of both yourself and yours."

(21) 'I went away depressed by this news, and was turning over all manner of plans in my mind, when by sheer chance the merchant met me again: as he kept on conversing in the same strain, he gave me my cue for a certain plan of action. I concealed from him part of the information that I had from Tyrrhenus, as seemed best to me, and disclosed only the news that an abduction of the girl was contemplated by a local inhabitant by whom he was sure to be outmatched in a conflict. "I would much prefer", I told him, "to betroth her to you, because of what I already know of you as well as your affluence; above all, for your prompt undertaking, if you had her to wife, that you would live in our country. So, if this is absolutely your desire, we must hasten our voyage hence before we are surprised by some very unwelcome experience." He was overjoyed at hearing this and: "That is fine, father!" he said, as he came and kissed my head; then he asked me what time I appointed for putting to sea. Although the season might be too early yet for navigation, he said, we might shift to another anchorage where we could both avoid the suspected attack and await the full advent of spring. "Well then," I said, "if my order is to decide it, I should like to sail away this coming night." "So shall it be," he said, and went off. I returned to the house and, without saying a word to Tyrrhenus, told my children that after nightfall we had to re-embark in the ship. They wondered at this sudden resolve and asked me the reason of it. I put off telling them till later and only said: "This is the best course for us in the circumstances."

(22) 'After having a little supper together we betook ourselves to sleep. Then in a dream an old man appeared to me whose form was withered away, except that where his doublet was trussed up he showed in his thigh muscles some relics of the robustness of his prime. On his head he wore a leathern cap; he looked about him with glances at once sagacious and wily; and he dragged a limping leg, as though he had been wounded. He

drew near to me and said with a cunning kind of smile: "Reverend sir, you alone have treated us as persons of no account. From all who have voyaged past the island of the Cephallenians,[1] and who have taken note of my house and made it their concern to acquaint themselves with my renown, you alone have distinguished yourself by such disdain that you did not show me even the courtesy of an ordinary greeting, although I was dwelling in the neighbourhood. Consequently it will not be long before you pay the penalty of this behaviour. You will meet with sufferings similar to mine, at the hands of enemies on both sea and land. Give this message from my wife to the girl who accompanies you: she blesses her for prizing chastity above all things, and assures her that all will end happily for her." I started up trembling with fright at this vision. When Theagenes asked what had so affected me, I said: "Surely we are too late now for the ship's departure—the thought of this has upset me when I awoke. Come, get up yourself, and help to pack our things; I will go and fetch Chariclea." My daughter appeared at my call, and Tyrrhenus, on hearing it, rose also and asked what was happening. "It is the happening", I told him, "that you recommended. We are trying to elude our would-be assailants. May the gods preserve you also, who have proved yourself such an excellent friend to us. Now do us this final favour: sail over to Ithaca, and sacrifice to Odysseus on our behalf, begging him to abate his wrath against us. He appeared to me this night to declare his resentment of our negligence." He promised to do this, and accompanied us to the ship, shedding abundant tears and praying that we might have a prosperous and satisfactory voyage.

'Why weary you with a drawn-out tale? The morning star was just beginning to shine out when we put to sea. The crew at first made many objections to sailing, but were at length persuaded by the Tyrian merchant telling them that he was evading an attack of pirates, of which he had had warning—little knowing how true was his feigned explanation. We then met with such boisterous winds, and had to contend with such an

---

[1] This large island is about twenty miles to the north of Zacynthus; and Ithaca—with the former palace and later cult of Odysseus who is the old man in this dream—lies close to the north-east coast of Cephallenia.

overwhelming surge of billows, beyond all description, that after nearly losing our lives we ran the ship inshore by a promontory of Crete. One of our rudders had been carried away and most of the yard-arm shattered. We therefore decided to remain in that island for a few days, in order to repair the vessel and refresh ourselves. When we had done so word was given for setting sail again on the first day of the new moon's shining after its conjunction with the sun. We put out to sea and, to the humming sound of the vernal zephyrs, were borne along night and day, the pilot setting the vessel's course for the Libyan coast. For he declared that with this favouring breeze he could cross the sea on a direct line throughout, and that he was making all haste to reach a harbour in some mainland, since he suspected the small boat showing astern of us to be a pirate craft. "Ever since we left the Cretan headland", he said, "it has been following in our wake and persistently running along the line of our course, just as though by some connection it were sharing the same motive power. I frequently detected it varying its movement in accord with ours, whenever I purposely turned our ship, now and then, off her straight course."

The ship bearing Calasiris and the young lovers from Zacynthus is chased and captured by pirates led by Trachinus. Nearly overwhelmed by a storm, they land at length near the mouth of the Nile.

(23) 'The effect of his words was to spur some of the men to action, and these called for measures to be taken for resistance: but others made light of the matter, asserting that it was usual in the open seas for lesser craft to follow those of greater size, as though to have the guidance of their more expert navigation. The contest between these two opinions continued till the day had advanced to the hour when the husbandman unyokes his oxen from the plough. The wind was abating its vehemence, and gradually gave way to a breeze of ineffectual feebleness which, as it came upon the sails, rather stirred than propelled the canvas, and at last subsided into a calm. It was as though the wind were setting in company with the sun or, in words nearer to the truth, were bent on serving the ends of our pursuers. For the people in the boat, so long as the wind sufficed to keep us on

our course, naturally lagged a good distance behind our ship, since her larger sails took the wind in greater strength; but when the calm had smoothed the sea, and there was need to employ the oars, they made up to us faster than words can tell, all of those on board, I suppose, being oarsmen and working a light craft that was more responsive to their strokes.

(24) 'When they were coming quite close to us one of the persons who had embarked with us at Zacynthus cried out: "There you are, friends, we are done for! It is a pirate craft; I recognize the boat of Trachinus." A great tremor ran through our ship at this news and, although becalmed, it was filled now with a storm of the men's clamours, laments and hurry-scurry that burst upon it; some hiding themselves below in the hold, some calling on each other to stand and fight on the deck, while others urged that they should jump into the cockboat and make their escape; till the conflict caught and held them as they were hesitating and shrinking, and forced them to take up any chance objects as weapons for their defence. I and Chariclea held Theagenes enclosed in our arms; he was in a frantic state, boiling with desire to fight, and we were hardly able to restrain him; she was striving, as she declared, not to be parted from him even in death, and in that to share with him a like fate by the same stroke of the same sword; while I, aware that our assailant was Trachinus, was devising a plan that would serve us well in what might follow. And so in fact it turned out to do. For the pirates came close up to us and, passing athwart our bows, reconnoitred to see whether they might be able to get possession of our ship without bloodshed. While they refrained from launching any missile, they circled round us in a manner that kept us from making progress in any direction, just as though they had us under siege and were desirous of taking the ship by capitulation. "You hapless creatures," they said, "why be so mad as to lift your hands in resistance to such invincible and preponderant force, and at the hazard of evident death? We still prefer the humaner part; we permit you to take to your cockboat and make off with your lives to wheresoever you please." These were the terms that they offered: yet the men in our vessel, so long as they were in a conflict free from danger, a bloodless war, made bold to say that they would not quit the ship.

(25) 'But one of the pirates, the most daring among them, leapt aboard our ship, and striking with his sword at those who came in his way gave proof that war is decided by slaughter and death. Then all the rest of his fellows leapt aboard after him. This quickly brought the Phoenicians to their senses, and on their knees they begged the enemy to spare them in return for their compliance with any terms that might be imposed on them. The pirates, though now at their work of slaughter—for the sight of blood is a hardener of valour—on the order of Trachinus, and beyond all hope, had mercy on the prostrate suppliants. An unstipulated armistice ensued by which, under the false appellation of peace, the bitterest war was in fact unleashed, with conditions imposed which were more distressing than any battle. For command went out that each man was to quit the vessel wearing only a single short tunic, under threat of death to any who disobeyed. But it would seem that men value life above all else; and so, for its sake, on this occasion, the Phoenicians, while they were cheated of the riches that they hoped to gain from their ship, seemed as though instead of being robbed they were in the way to make a profit. They pressed forward to get before one another in embarking in the cockboat, everyone struggling to be the quickest in making sure of saving his life.

(26) 'As soon as in obedience to his order we came before Trachinus, he seized hold of Chariclea and said: "It was not at all against you, dearest one, but for you, that this battle has been fought; all this time I have been following you, ever since you left Zacynthus, and it is for your sake that I have undertaken this long voyage with all its perils. Take heart, then, and know that with me you will be mistress of all this booty." At these words of his she, as clever a creature as ever lived, with her quickness in turning a situation to the best account, and also getting some advantage from my promptings, threw off the downcast look caused by her present predicament and, forcing herself to show a more engaging expression, said: "Ah, thanks be to the gods for inclining your mind to humaner intentions towards us! But if you wish to have and keep me truly enheartened, give me the first impression of your goodwill by saving the lives of this brother of mine, and of my father here, and do not allow them to leave the ship; for it will not be possible to live if they are

parted from me." With these words she threw herself down at his knees and clung to them for a long time in supplication, while Trachinus, luxuriating in the clasp of her entwining arms, purposely delayed in giving his promise. Moved at length to pity by her tears, and subdued by her glances to absolute compliance, he raised up the girl and said: "I grant you your brother, with the greatest pleasure, for I see that the young man is full of valour and competent to play his part in our way of life. As for this old man, he is a useless burden; but, solely as a favour to you, he may remain."

(27) 'While all this was being spoken and enacted, the sun completed his round and came to his setting, thus bringing on the hour of twilight, that limbo betwixt day and night. The sea then suddenly became rough, perhaps affected by the change of hour, or perhaps unsettled by the design of some Fate. One heard a booming of the wind as it swept down, and instantly a blast of unprecedented fury and force struck us, and filled the pirates with all the confusion caused by a sudden surprise. They had left their own boat, and were caught as they were busied with pillaging the cargo of the merchant ship, and they lacked any experience of managing a vessel of her large size. Consequently the several tasks of her navigation were taken up casually by each man as he chanced to be at hand, and each made bold to improvise what skill he could for his task. Some tugged distractedly at the sails, others ignorantly handled the ropes; one, quite unqualified, was posted in the prow, while another in the stern had charge of the tiller. Indeed, what chiefly exposed us to extreme peril was not the violence of the storm, which had not yet reached the full height of its tumult, but the inexpertness of the pilot, who held out as long as the beams of daylight continued to shine around us, but resigned his task when darkness prevailed. Finding themselves now all awash and on the point of foundering, some of the pirates at first attempted to transfer themselves to their own boat. But they quickly desisted when they were beaten back by the surge, and were also persuaded by Trachinus that they could be wealthier by the value of a multitude of such boats if they preserved the merchant ship and her rich cargo; and he ended by cutting the cable with which their boat was attached to the ship, averring that it was like dragging

another storm along after them. He also pointed out that they must take thought for their future safety; for suspicions would be aroused by their sailing into any place with both of the vessels, and inquiry would surely be made after the passengers embarked on one of them. His words carried conviction, and at one stroke he gained credit, for the moment, on both counts. They were sensible of some little relief as soon as their boat was parted from them, though they were still not wholly clear of their danger. Huge waves, one close upon another, drove them hard; they jettisoned much of the cargo, and were menaced with every kind of danger until, having barely survived the passing of that night and the following day also, towards evening we ran the ship in to land by the Herculean mouth of the Nile.[1] There we, unhappy creatures, set foot by no wish of ours on Egyptian soil: while the pirates did so gladly enough, we in our sore distress poured out reproaches against the sea for preserving our lives. For its waves had begrudged us a death clear of human outrage, and had abandoned us to the greater terrors of the land and what it held for us in prospect, exposed as we were to the lawless purposes of pirates. Such in fact were the dealings of those miscreants from the moment of their stepping ashore. Professing a specious desire to sacrifice in thanksgiving to Poseidon, they fetched some Tyrian wine with other fare from the ship, and dispatched a party of men to purchase cattle from the inhabitants of the district: these men were amply supplied with money, and were ordered to pay the first price that was demanded.

Calasiris finally tells how the pirate chief Trachinus held a feast to celebrate his intended marriage with Chariclea; how Pelorus, his second-in-command, quarrelled with him over possession of the girl; and how a murderous fight ensued between partisans of the two men, the result of which was described at the beginning of Book I.

(28) 'The men returned very soon, driving a whole flock of sheep and pigs. The pirates who had stayed behind met them, lit an altar fire, flayed the victims, and were preparing the banquet.

[1] See note to i. 1, p. 1.

when Trachinus took me aside privately, so as not to be overheard by the others, and said: "Father, I have set my heart on
taking your daughter to wife and, as you see, I am going to hold
the marriage feast this day, thereby combining with this sacrifice
to the gods the sweetest of festivities. So, in order that you on
your part should not, from lack of this information, cut a somewhat sullen figure at our banquet, and that your child, by
learning it from you, should welcome with joy her new condition,
I have thought it right to tell you my intention beforehand. It is
not that I desire to have it confirmed by you, since I hold full
warranty for my purpose in my freedom of action; but I consider that in any case it is propitious and seemly to secure the
ready compliance of one's bride by having her informed of it
beforehand by her parent." I warmly commended his statement,
and made a show of being delighted; and I rendered a thousand
thanks to the gods for having vouchsafed that the absolute
master of my daughter should become her husband.

(29) 'I retired for a little while and tried to think out by
myself some plan for what had next to be done. I then returned
and begged of him that a greater solemnity be given to the performance of the ceremony by using the merchant ship as the
girl's bridal apartment, and ordering that no one else should
enter it or disturb her there, so that she might be able to attend
in good time to her wedding attire and her other adornment
befitting the occasion. "For it would be most extraordinary," I
said, "if with the pride that she takes in her high birth and great
fortune and, above all, with this prospect of being the wife of
Trachinus, she should not even bedeck herself with the things
available to her, when we are deprived by time and place of the
more brilliant equipage of a bridal procession." At these words
Trachinus' features relaxed, and he assured me that he would
gladly issue this command. So he then commanded his men to
fetch at once everything that they required from the ship, and
thereafter not to go near it. They carried out his orders, and
brought away tables, wine-bowls, carpets, hangings—handi-
works from Sidon and Tyre—and everything else in abundance
for furnishing forth a banquet, all displayed in a jumble on their
shoulders; and so the rich store amassed by long, parsimonious
industry was abandoned now by Fortune to the rude ill usage of

a party of dissolute revellers. Taking Theagenes with me, I went to look for Chariclea, whom I found all in tears. "Daughter," I said, "you have here nothing unusual or strange. But tell me now, are you, however, lamenting old bygones or something quite new?" "Everything," she replied, "and most of all, the prospect that I have of Trachinus' repugnant affection, which the luck of the moment, no doubt, has heightened in him; for it is the way of unexpected success to call forth acts of insolence. But Trachinus and Trachinus' odious passion will have a bitter blow, forestalled and thwarted by my death. My lamenting arose from the thought that I shall be parted from you and Theagenes before my death." "The facts are as you surmise," I said; "Trachinus intends, after the sacrifice, to turn the customary banquet into your marriage feast. He has explained his purpose to me as your father. I have long known the frantic ardour of his feeling towards you, ever since a conversation that I had with Tyrrhenus in the isle of Zacynthus. But I said no word about it to either of you, that your minds might not be distressed by fears of impending troubles while there was a possibility of our evading the plot laid against us. But, my children, since the divine power has worked against us in this affair, and we are now bound on a course through a sea of dangers, come, let us make a gallant, an impetuous attempt, and advance to meet the onset of our danger, resolved either to achieve life with gallantry and freedom or to gain death with probity and valour."

(30) 'They promised to do whatever I bade them, and after informing them of the steps we were to take I left them busied with their preparations. I then went to the pirate who was second-in-command to Trachinus—his name, I think, was Pelorus—and told him that I had something greatly to his advantage to impart to him. He readily gave me his attention, and took me apart, where none could overhear us. "You shall be told it, my son," I said, "in concise form, since limits of time prevent our talking at large. My daughter is in love with you, and no wonder: she has been captivated by your superior character. She suspects that the chief of your band is preparing this feast to celebrate his marriage with her; indeed he has intimated as much by ordering her to appear in attire of special elegance. So look to it and, if you can, avert this event, and rather get possession of the girl

for yourself; for she says that she will die sooner than be married to Trachinus." "Have no fear," he said. "I myself have for some time past had a tender feeling for her, and have been longing to hit on some expedient; so now Trachinus shall either freely resign his bride to me as the prize to which I am entitled for having led the boarding party on to the merchant ship, or he shall find that he has had a woeful wedding, when this right hand has dealt him his deserts." I ran off after hearing his words, to avoid raising any suspicion, and went and reassured my children with the good news that the scheme was making some progress.

(31) 'A little after that we were at dinner; and when I perceived that the men were far gone in liquor and were tending to be in in a roistering mood, I said softly to Pelorus, close to whom I had taken care to be placed: "Have you seen how the girl has arrayed herself?" "No, I have not," he replied. "Well, you could do so," I went on, "if you crept secretly into the ship: you know that this is what Trachinus has forbidden. There you will behold Artemis herself, seated before your eyes. But at present be prudent in your looking, lest you draw down death on both yourself and her." He made not a moment's delay; as though pressed by some necessity, he arose and hurried unobserved on board the vessel, where he saw Chariclea wearing a garland of laurel on her head and glittering in her gold-inwoven robe. For she had dressed herself in her sacred vesture brought from Delphi, so as to be in fitting garb for either a triumph or a tomb. Her whole attire was radiant, and had an aspect well adapted to the bridal chamber. He, fired, as was natural, by this sight, and assailed at once by desire and jealousy, plainly showed in his eyes, when he returned from his visit, that he meditated some frantic act. Hardly had he resumed his seat when he said: "And I, why do not I obtain the reward due to the man who led the boarding party?" "Because", said Trachinus, "you have not asked for it. Besides, the time for distributing the booty has not yet been fixed." "Then I demand", he said, "the girl who is among the prisoners." When Trachinus answered "Take anything you please except her," Pelorus rejoined: "Then you are violating the pirates' law which assigns to the first man who boards an enemy ship—to him who has been foremost in facing the danger of a combat fought for all the rest—the choice of

whatever he desires." "That law, my gallant friend," replied
Trachinus, "I am not violating. I rely on another which requires
subordinates to give way to their leaders. True, I have a certain
affection for this girl, and in taking her as my wife I lay claim to
precedence. If you disobey my command you will soon howl for
it—feeling the weight of this wine-bowl!" Then Pelorus,
glancing round at the company, said: "You see, this is the wage
of all my labours![1] Thus each man among you will be cheated
of his reward, and know the quality of this tyrannical law."

(32) 'What a scene then ensued, Nausicles! Just like a sea
convulsed by a sudden squall, those men were stirred up by an
unreasoning impulse to an indescribable commotion, crazed as
they were with wine and wrath. Taking sides with one or the other
of the disputants, some clamoured for deference to their chief,
and some against infringement of their law. At length Trachinus
made a threatening motion, as though about to strike Pelorus
with the wine-bowl; but he, already holding himself on the alert,
forestalled the blow by stabbing the other in the breast with his
dagger. Trachinus fell, mortally wounded; the rest of them were
grappled in a truceless conflict, fighting hand to hand and raining
blows without stint, some to avenge their chief, and others in
defence of Pelorus and the right. With the sound of one dismal
outcry they struck and in turn were stricken with billets of wood,
stones, bowls, torches and tables. I had removed myself as far
away as I could, and from a rising ground I treated myself to a
spectacle void of danger. But Theagenes, for his part, did not
refrain from fighting, nor did Chariclea. Acting as had been
agreed, he from the start plied his sword in support of one side,
appearing for all the world like one possessed; and she, when she
perceived that the fighting had broken out, shot from the ship
well-directed arrows that spared only Theagenes. She did not
strike at one party only in the struggle, but brought down whoever first came into her view. Herself unseen, she easily descried
the enemy by the light of their blazing fire, while they were
unable to tell what was wreaking the mischief, and some suspected that these strokes were dealt them by some superhuman
power. In time all of them were laid low, except that Theagenes
was left fighting in single combat with Pelorus, who was a man

[1] Apparently a quotation from some tragedy.

of boundless valour, since he had practised his hand in a vast number of butcheries. And Chariclea's archery was now no longer able to give its aid: her heart ached with longing to assist, but she was afraid of missing her mark, as the fight had now come to close quarters, the two men pressing each other hard in hand to hand combat. At last, however, Pelorus could bear up no longer. Chariclea, though without power of giving active support to Theagenes, sent a volley of words to his aid, calling out: "Bravely now, dearest one!" From that moment Theagenes clearly had the upper hand of Pelorus, as though her voice supplied him with fresh strength and courage, and indicated that the prize for which they fought was still alive. Rousing up his spirit from the stress of his now numerous wounds, he leapt upon Pelorus and drove his blade at the man's head, which he missed as the other bent his body aside, but grazing the top of his shoulder he cut off his arm at the elbow joint; whereupon the man took to flight, pursued by Theagenes.

(33) 'I am unable to relate what happened next, except that I could see no sign of Theagenes' return, since I had stayed where I was on the rising ground, and had shrunk from making my way by night through the battle area. With Chariclea it was quite otherwise. When the dawn came I saw Theagenes lying prostrate like a dead man, and Chariclea seated by his side, lamenting and making as though she intended to slay herself over his body, yet restrained by a faint hope that the youth might haply survive. By ill fortune I had no time to speak to them and hear from them, or to relieve their distress with comforting words, or to tend them in any way practicable; for our calamities at sea were now so immediately succeeded by others on land. At the moment when, on seeing daylight, I was descending the hillock, a band of Egyptian brigands came running down, as it seemed, from the mountain range that overlooked the area. They at once laid hold on the young pair, and shortly after led them away, carrying with them as much as they could of the ship's cargo. As for me, I tried in vain to follow after them at a distance bewailing my own and my children's fate: I could neither protect them nor think it well that I should join them, since I had rather reserve myself for some better prospect of assisting them. In truth, I had not the strength to do it; how could I? At that

moment I was forlorn, and my age prevented me from rushing along with the Egyptians over the mountain heights; and now I owe it to the grace of the gods and your kindness, Nausicles, that I have meanwhile recovered my daughter. To this I have contributed nothing, but have been liberal only in bestowing tears and laments for her.' With these words he wept himself and his hearers wept with him, and so the banqueting was changed to lamenting, mingled with a certain pleasure; for wine disposes one somewhat to tears.[1] At length Nausicles, to encourage Calasiris, said to him: 'Father, from now onwards at least you can be in good spirits: you have already recovered this daughter of yours, and only the night time hinders you from seeing your son. At daybreak we shall go to Mitranes and try by all possible means to have the excellent Theagenes released to you.' 'That will be my desire,' said Calasiris; 'but it is now time to break up the party. Let us be mindful of the divine power, and let the libations for deliverance be brought round.'

(34) Thereupon the libations were handed round, and the banquet broke up. Calasiris looked out for Chariclea, and when, as he carefully watched the company passing by, he failed to discover her, he finally made his way on the advice of a woman into the sanctuary. There he found Chariclea clasping close the feet of the statue: her prolonged praying and exhausting grief had caused her to slide into a deep slumber. He wept for a little while at the sight, and implored the god to give a happier turn to her affairs; he then gently roused her and led her to their dwelling, her face blushing, as it seemed, for her inadvertent surrender to sleep. She withdrew into the women's quarters, and lay down with the young daughter of Nausicles, but spent a wakeful night, her mind occupied by the cares that beset her.

---

[1] Cf. Homer, *Od.* xix. 122, where Odysseus says that he must refrain from weeping lest he be taken for a drunkard. Aristotle (*Probl.* iii. 24) mentions the fact that men in liquor are apt to be tearful.

BOOK VI

Cnemon marries the daughter of Nausicles at Chemmis, and Calasiris and Chariclea, disguised as beggars, go in search of Theagenes.

(1) Calasiris and Cnemon had gone to take their rest in a room of the men's quarters. There they passed the remainder of the night, more slowly than they wished, but yet more quickly than they expected, since the greater part of it had been spent at the feast and in the narration whose length gave no feeling of surfeit. Without waiting for full daylight they went to see Nausicles, whom they pressed to tell them where he thought Theagenes might be, and to take them to him with all speed. He agreed to this, and conducted them on their way. Chariclea earnestly begged that she might accompany them, but was prevailed on to stay where she was, Nausicles assuring her that they would not be proceeding any great distance, and would return with Theagenes immediately. So they left her behind, with a heart wavering between sorrow over this separation and joy over its hoped-for outcome. They had just quitted the village, and were passing along by the banks of the Nile, when they saw a crocodile which crawled across their path from right to left, and with a sudden dash plunged into the flowing waters of the river. While the others took this sight with composure as something ordinary —though Calasiris differed in pronouncing it to portend an obstacle awaiting them on their way—Cnemon was greatly alarmed when he saw it. The creature had not shown itself clearly to him, but rather slipped past him like a shadow along the ground, and he was even on the point of taking to flight. At this, while Nausicles laughed consumedly, Calasiris remarked: 'Cnemon, I thought it was only in the night that you had your attacks of cowardice, and only darkness made you start with fright at every sound; and here you are, in broad daylight, showing yourself, it seems, a prodigy of courage! Not only the

141

mention of names, but now sights of a commonplace and harmless kind strike you with dismay.' 'And what god or spirit is it,' asked Nausicles, 'whose naming our gallant friend cannot bear to hear?' 'Whether a god or a spirit might so affect him,' replied Calasiris, 'I cannot say; but a human being and, what is stranger, not even a man or someone renowned for valour, but a woman—and that, as he himself says, a dead one—makes him shudder with fear if one utters her name. On that night, for instance, when you arrived, my good sir, as the deliverer of our Chariclea from the herdsmen, after he had somehow overheard somebody or other mention this name that I tell of, he did not permit me to snatch so much as a wink of sleep: he was continually swooning away with his terror, and I was hard put to it to bring him round. If I could do so without annoying or scaring him, I would have told you the name just now, Nausicles, to make you laugh still more.' And with that he added: 'Thisbe.'

(2) But this time Nausicles did not laugh. Withdrawn into himself at what he had heard, he stood pensive for a long time, at a loss to know for what sort of reason, through what connection or in what degree Cnemon was affected by the name of Thisbe. Observing this, Cnemon broke into a peal of laughter and said: 'My good Calasiris, do you see what mighty power this name possesses, and what a bugbear it is, not only to me, as you yourself, say, but now to Nausicles as well? Or rather, we see here a complete change-over of its effect. It is now my turn to laugh, since I know that she no longer exists; while our doughty friend Nausicles, who so merrily laughs others to scorn, has assumed a gloomy look.' 'Enough of that,' said Nausicles; 'you have your revenge on me in full measure, Cnemon. But by the gods of hospitality and friendship, and by the share of salt and board that you both have received, I think, with kindly courtesy in my house, will you please explain how you know the name of Thisbe, how you have come to fear it, or why you have been making fun of me?' Then Calasiris said: 'It is your turn now, Cnemon, to give us the story which you have so often promised to relate to me, and which will acquaint us with your own adventures, but which you have hitherto put off each time with artful subterfuges. The right moment has now arrived for you to tell it, and so gratify Nausicles here, relieving as well the

tedium of our journey with the welcome aid of its recital.'
Cnemon complied, and related in brief all the events which he
had before described to Theagenes and Chariclea. He told them
that he was a native of Athens, that his father was Aristippus,
and that Demaenete became his stepmother. He then recounted
her illicit love for him, and how on failing of her object she
hatched a plot against him, employing Thisbe as her accomplice;
and he added the circumstances of his exile from his native land,
the people having imposed this penalty upon him as a parricide;
and how, during his stay in Aegina, he first had from Charias, a
youth of his own standing, the news of Demaenete's death, and
the manner of it, Thisbe having set a trap for her also; and that
he later learnt from Anticles how his father had suffered the
confiscation of his estate, through the blood-relations of Demaenete combining against him to arouse in the people a suspicion
of his being her murderer; and that Thisbe eloped from Athens
with her lover, the merchant of Naucratis. Cnemon finally
added that, after taking ship for Egypt with Anticles to search
for Thisbe, in the hope that if he could find her and bring her
to Athens he might clear his father of that calumnious charge,
and at the same time punish her, he had encountered a host of
dangers and happenings, until he was captured by a band of
murderous pirates. From these he managed to escape, and
landed in Egypt, where he was captured again by the robber
herdsmen; and there it was that he met with Theagenes and
Chariclea. He also related the violent end of Thisbe and the
events that ensued, up to those which were all known to Calasiris
and Nausicles.

(3) On hearing this story Nausicles revolved in his mind a
multitude of questions, now being minded to relate what had
passed between him and Thisbe, now thinking it well to defer
the story to some other time. At length, though with an effort,
he refrained, partly because he thought it the better way, and
partly because a fresh incident gave him pause. They had just
travelled about sixty furlongs, and were already approaching the
village where Mitranes was staying, when they met with an
acquaintance of Nausicles, and asked him whither he was bound
in such urgent haste. 'Nausicles,' he answered, 'you question me
on my hurried pace as though you did not know that all my

efforts just now are directed to one object—compliance with the commands of Isias of Chemmis. For her I till the soil, I supply all her needs; because of her I pass sleepless nights and days that I may deny her nothing—though it be at my heavy cost and pains—nothing, great or small that Isias there may demand of me. So now I am running, as you see, to bring this bird, a flamingo of the Nile, which my beloved had demanded of me.' 'What a considerate mistress', said Nausicles, 'you have taken to your bosom! How very slight her requirements are, if she has demanded of you a flamingo, and not the Phoenix [1] itself, which comes to us from Ethiopia or India!' 'That is just her way,' he replied; 'it is her regular practice to make sport of me and my efforts. But you, whither are you bound, and on what business?' 'We are hastening to see Mitranes,' they said. 'You hasten in vain, to no purpose,' he said, 'for Mitranes is not there at present: he has set out this night on an expedition against the herdsmen inhabiting the village of Bessa. For he had dispatched a young Greek prisoner to Oroondates at Memphis, to be forwarded thence, I believe, as a gift to the Great King; and the men of Bessa, led by Thyamis, whom they have lately appointed their chief, captured the youth in a surprise attack, and now have him in their possession.'

(4) He continued, as he started to run past them, with these words: 'But I must hurry on to Isias, who I suppose is all eyes now watching for me, and not let my delay produce a lovers' quarrel: she is a terror for working up, on no good grounds, accusations and a show of indignation against me.' After hearing his words they stood for a long time speechless at this surprising disappointment of their expectations. At length Nausicles rallied their spirits by representing that they should not be led by a passing moment of disappointment to abandon their undertaking altogether; they ought now to return to Chemmis, consider carefully what steps they had to take and, after putting up provisions in quantity for a lengthy excursion, devote them-

---

[1] The early legend (Herod. ii. 73) was that this aquiline bird, with red and gold plumage, visited Egypt once in every five hundred years to inter the body of its predecessor in the temple of the Sun at Heliopolis. A later one was that when the bird reached the age of five hundred years, it built its own funeral pile, was burnt to death on it, and produced from its remains a reborn Phoenix.

selves to the search for Theagenes, whether he might be heard of
among the herdsmen or among some other people, maintaining
everywhere a good hope of discovering him. For at this moment
it seemed to be not without divine aid that they had met with a
man who was an acquaintance and whose report had served to
guide them to the quarter in which they should seek out Theagenes, keeping the course of their journey pointed directly upon
the herdsmen's village.

(5) They were quickly convinced by his words and, methinks,
a fresh hope too was born in them at the hearing of that report;
while Cnemon privately encouraged Calasiris by assuring him
that Thyamis would see to the safety of Theagenes. They therefore decided to return, and did so, and descried Chariclea in the
front porch of the house looking out for them in the distance and
in every quarter. When she saw no sign of Theagenes coming
with them, with a loud and dismal wail she exclaimed: 'Can it
be, father, that you three come back to me alone, as you were
when you set out from here? Theagenes then, it seems, is dead!
If you have something to tell, speak out quickly, for heaven's
sake; do not increase my misfortune by delaying your news. It
is an act of kindly feeling to be prompt in disclosing a calamity:
one's soul is thus made ready to encounter the dread fact, and is
given early relief from its pain.' To cut short her extreme anxiety
Cnemon said: 'What a depressing way this is of yours, Chariclea!
Ever showing yourself prone to presaging the worst, and that too
a delusion—which is just as well. For in fact Theagenes is alive;
he is safe and sound, by the gods' grace.' How this had come
about, and with whom he then was, Cnemon told her briefly.
Then Calasiris said to him: 'You have never yet been in love
by your way of speaking; else you would know that even unfear-
ful things are terrible to lovers, and that they trust only the
evidence of their eyes in regard to their sweethearts, whose
absence is sheer terror and anguish to their amorous souls. The
cause of this is that they have persuaded themselves that their
darlings can never be parted from them save by some grievous
hindrance barring their way. So, my friend, let us indulge
Chariclea in her deep and genuine suffering from the pangs of
love, and ourselves go indoors and bethink us what we are to do.'

(6) So saying he took Chariclea by the hand with the tender

care of a father and led her into the house. Nausicles, who wished from that moment to dispel their anxieties, and had a new purpose astir in his mind, made arrangements for holding a more splendid banquet than usual for a party of themselves only and his daughter, whose appearance he enhanced with a special elegance and choice adornments of great price. When they considered that they had had their fill of feasting, he entered on a parley with them in these words: 'My good guests, the gods be my witness when I tell you that it would suit me well if you chose to remain here, in this very place, and live with me permanently, sharing alike my means and all that I hold most dear. For I have come to regard you, not as guests merely paying me a visit, but as affectionate, genuine friends of mine henceforward; and I shall look upon all the services that I may render to you as anything but a burden. I am ready, should you wish to go in search of your kinsfolk, to assist you with all my power for so long as I may happen to be with you. But you on your part must understand that I lead the life of a merchant; that is the skill that I cultivate. Fair west winds have been blowing now for some time, and have opened the sea to navigation; they give good promise of easy passages to traders, and my business summons me as with a trumpet call to set out for Greece. It would therefore be right and proper for you to impart to me what in time you propose to do, so that I may adapt my plans to suit the end that you have in view.'

(7) Calasiris pondered his words for a moment or two, and then said: 'Nausicles, may your voyaging hence go off with fair auspices; may Hermes the Gaingiver and Poseidon the Safeguarder be your companions and conductors, and speed you on your course through every sea with gentle waves and winds, and render every harbour secure for you and every city accommodating and friendly towards merchants! You treat us so handsomely during our stay, and send us forth so courteously when we wish to depart, with such careful observance of the laws of hospitality and friendship! We feel some pain, it may be, at our parting from you and your house, which your attentions have led us to look upon as our own; but we are under an inexorable necessity of giving our utmost efforts to the discovery of those who are dearest to us. This is the case with me and Chariclea

here; as to Cnemon, and what his purpose may be—whether he is willing to gratify us by sharing in our wanderings or has decided on some other course—he might tell us here and now.' Cnemon was intending to make reply, and was on the point of speaking when suddenly he broke into sobs, and a flood of tears gushed forth and muffled his tongue; until at length he recovered his breath and deeply groaning said: 'O Destiny of man, whose workings abound in continual turns, and are so utterly inconstant! What a huge upsurge of troubles you have determined to raise against me, as indeed you have against many more, time and again! You have bereft me of my family and my father's house, and have banished me from my native land and city which held all that was dearest to me; you have cast me up on the land of Egypt, to say nothing of all that befell me by the way; and you have delivered me into the hands of brigand herdsmen. You have vouchsafed me a gleam of good hope in granting me chance companions, as unfortunate as myself, but yet Greeks, with whom I was hoping to spend the remaining days of my life. And this consolation, it seems, you are now cutting off. Which way am I to turn? What is it my duty to do? Can I desert Chariclea, when she has not yet discovered Theagenes? A monstrous act, O Earth, and criminal! Should I then accompany her and help her in her search? If one could be sure of finding him the labour would be welcome, buoyed up by the hope of success; but if the prospect is uncertain, and the difficulties increase, there is no certainty as to where my wandering steps will come to rest. Why should I not, after begging your indulgence and that of the gods of friendship, propose at this very moment my return to my native land and my family—at this opportune juncture that has occurred, it would seem, by the grace of some god, when Nausicles here, as he has told us, is about to leave for Greece—so that, even if something in the meantime should have happened to my father, his house might not remain bereft of an heir to succeed him? For even if I should have to be a pauper, the survival in my person of at least some relic of my family would be of real value in itself.

'O Chariclea, it is principally to you that I make my excuses, your indulgence that I beg and crave; O grant it to me! I will accompany you as far as the herdsmen's haunt, and will entreat

Nausicles to delay for a little, hard pressed for time though he be. My hope is that by handing you over in person to Theagenes I may prove myself a steadfast guardian of the treasure entrusted to my care, and that I may part from you with a like steadfast confidence in what the future will bring, and a good conscience. If, however, we should fail at that point—which Heaven forbid! —I still should be forgiven, since I should not even then have left you desolate, but would have transferred my charge of you to Calasiris here, as your devoted guardian and father.' Now Chariclea had already guessed from numerous signs that Cnemon had been deeply impressed by the daughter of Nausicles; for a lover is quick to detect the sway of the same strong feeling over another. She had understood from words dropped by Nausicles that this alliance would be agreeable to him, and that he had long been scheming for it and subtly contriving to entice Cnemon into a profitable bit of business. At the same time she did not regard Cnemon as a suitable or trustworthy companion for their intended journey. She therefore said to him: 'As you please; for I am under an obligation to you, which I now acknowledge, for your past good services to us: but as for your help in the future, there is no necessity at all for you to be preoccupied with our interests, or to share against your will the perils attendant on fortunes other than your own. You should go and regain your city of Athens, your family and your home, and not on any account reject Nausicles and the occasion that has presented itself, as you say, for doing all this by his means. Calasiris and I will continue to struggle with events until we reach the end of our wanderings. Even if no human being should strike up with us, we shall be confident of having the gods as companions on our way.'

(8) Nausicles now took part and said: 'May Chariclea's prayers be granted; may the gods accompany her as she desires; and may she regain her kinsfolk—so stalwart a spirit is hers, and so sagacious a mind. And you, Cnemon, must not take it too hard that you are not bringing Thisbe to Athens, now that you have me here as the person responsible for her seizure and abduction from Athens; for the merchant of Naucratis, the lover of Thisbe, is none other than I. Nor should you lament your poverty, or expect any longer to be a beggar; for if you

should find it acceptable, as it would be to me, that I brought you back again, you will there be in possession of ample wealth, and will regain your home and your native land. And if you desire to marry, I affiance to you my daughter here, with the addition on my part of the richest dowry that my means can provide, while I regard the settlement on your part as already discharged since I came to know your family, your home and your nation.' On hearing this Cnemon did not hesitate for a moment: he was obtaining what he had long prayed for and desired without any hope, and what he now unexpectedly found to be more than his prayers had sought. 'I gladly accept at once all that you propose,' he said, and thereupon held out his right hand: Nausicles placed it in that of his daughter and confirmed their espousal. He then called on his kinsfolk to chant the nuptial song and led up the first dance, having designated the banquet of the day as the feast in celebration of this improvised marriage. All the guests were now engaged in dancing and an impromptu performance of the nuptial song about the inner chambers, and all night long the bridal torches lit up the house. But Chariclea alone, apart from the rest, entered her private room and securely closed the door. There, assured of being undisturbed, she raged as in a bacchic frenzy, letting her hair float loose and wild; then, after rending her clothes, she said: 'Come, let us also dance, in honour of the Fate assigned to us, a measure suited to its nature. Let us sing to it dirges, and perform the tragic motions of lamentation. Let gloomy shade overspread us, and rayless night direct our rites, as this lamp has now been dashed to the ground. What kind of bridal bed has Fate devised for me? What nuptial chamber is appointed for me? Here Fate holds me alone, with no husband, widowed, alas! of him who is my husband only in name, Theagenes. Cnemon is marrying; Theagenes is a vagabond, and one who is a prisoner, perhaps even in fetters. This might yet be a piece of good fortune, if only his life could be saved. Nausiclea is being wedded, and is dissevered from me after sharing her bed with me till the past night: but Chariclea is alone and derelict. It is not of their lot, O Fortune and Fates, that I complain; no, let them fare as their hearts desire: it is that in deciding mine you have not put me on a level with them. You have drawn out my drama to such an inordinate length that its story transcends all that are told on any stages in the world. But why do I at such an hour thus rail against the dealings of the gods? Let the issue be determined according to their pleasure. But, O Theagenes, my sole, my darling care, if you are dead, if I should have to believe that which I pray I may never know, I shall not hesitate to join you. Meanwhile I tender you these offerings'—and with that she plucked out some of her hair and threw it on the bed—'and I pour these libations from the eyes that you cherish,' and as she spoke the bedding was all bedewed with her tears. 'But if happily your life is preserved for me, come now, my dear one, and repose yourself by my side, though it be but in the vision of a dream. Yet even so, of your goodness restrain yourself, and reserve your own virgin bride for the lawful bond of marriage. Ah, look now, I do clasp you in my arms, imagining that you are here with me and see me.'

(9) As she spoke these words she suddenly flung herself prone on the bed, and spreading out her arms embraced it with sobs and heavy sighs, until from the excess of her grief a misty dizziness crept upon her, overclouding her mental faculties, and insensibly drawing her into a sleep which held her until broad daylight had come. Calasiris, surprised that he did not see her at the usual time, went in search of her. Coming to her room, he knocked loudly and repeatedly called her name, till he roused her from slumber. Chariclea, alarmed by this sudden call, darted to the door in the state in which she was disturbed, drew back the bolt and opened for the old man to enter. When he saw her dishevelled hair, her dress all tattered on her bosom, and her eyes still swollen and showing traces of the frenzy that held her before she fell asleep, he understood the cause. He led her back to the bed, seated her and put a cloak about her. Having her thus more suitably attired, he asked: 'What is this, Chariclea? Why such excessive, such immoderate dismay? Why this senseless subjection to circumstances? I do not recognize you at this moment, you whom I have hitherto found so gallant always and sagacious under the strokes of Fortune. Come now, have done with this extravagant folly! Recollect that you are human, a thing unstable, wont to swerve of a sudden this way and that. Why hasten to destroy yourself, when better prospects may well be just appearing? And be considerate of us, my child;

be considerate, if not of yourself yet at least of Theagenes, to whom only life with you is desirable, and existence has value only if you survive.' Chariclea blushed as she heard these words, and did so the more when she thought of the state in which she had been surprised. For a long time she was silent; then, as Calasiris kept on pressing her for a reply, she said: 'There is truth in your remonstrances; yet I may perhaps be excused, father; for it is no vulgar or riotous desire that drives me to such behaviour in my misery, but a pure and sober longing for one who, having had no union with me, is yet to me a husband, and who is, moreover, Theagenes. That he is not with me is painful, but more fearful is the doubt whether he survives or not.' 'On that score', said Calasiris, 'take comfort; the gods assent to his living now and rejoining you hereafter, if we are to put faith— and we must—in the predictions of the oracle about you both, and in the man who yesterday reported that Theagenes had been captured by Thyamis as he was being sent up to Memphis. If he has been captured he is evidently safe, because of the friendly terms of acquaintance between him and Thyamis. So the time has now come for us to act without delay, and to go with all possible speed to the village of Bessa and search, you for Theagenes, and me not only for him but for my son also. You are aware, I believe, from what you have surely heard already, that Thyamis is my son.' Chariclea showed some anxiety at this, and said: 'If Thyamis is indeed your son, your own and not another's, a different person, then am I heading straight for a situation of extreme danger.' Calasiris wondered at this, and asked her the meaning of it. 'You know', she replied, 'that I was taken prisoner by the herdsmen. And so in that place Thyamis was drawn into a longing for me by the fresh beauty of my looks, which seems to have brought me nothing but misfortune; and my fear is that, if in our search we should light upon him, he would recognize me as the maiden whom he saw there, and would effect by force the marriage which he then proffered to me and which I artfully contrived to evade.' 'I hope', said Calasiris, 'that his passion would never so overmaster him that he would disregard his father's presence before his eyes, and that the glance of his parent would not shame him into the repression of a longing which, if really felt, is not permissible.

Nevertheless, since there is nothing to hinder you, why not contrive some artifice to circumvent the dangers that alarm you? It seems that you are skilful enough in the invention of evasions and deferments of your assailants' devices.'

(10) Somewhat composed by his words, Chariclea said: 'Whether you are speaking sincerely, or have been making game of me, let it pass for the moment. I did once before devise a scheme with Theagenes, but it was debarred by events that befell at the time. I will have recourse to it now, with better chances of success. When we resolved to escape from the herdsmen's island we decided to change the character of our dress to one of utter squalor, and to go thus disguised as beggars on our visits to villages and towns. So, if you are agreeable, let us assume that character and go abegging, for in this way we shall be less likely to be molested by people who fall in with us. The simple life is a security in such encounters, and "Poverty finds Pity instead of Envy at its side." [1] And we shall the more easily obtain our necessary supply of daily food; for in a strange land it is hard for the unacquainted to find what they can buy, whereas a dole that is asked is readily bestowed out of compassion.'

(11) Calasiris commended her plan, and was for setting out promptly on their travels. Meeting with Nausicles and Cnemon, they made known to them their departure, and two days later they started out, after declining to take a pack-animal, though one was offered to them, or any person as a fellow-traveller. Nausicles and Cnemon, with all the household, escorted them on their way. Nausiclea also, having obtained her father's permission after pressing entreaties, joined in escorting them; for the charm of Chariclea's company had quite overcome the bashfulness of a recent bride. After they had proceeded about five furlongs, they bade a final farewell to one another, those of the same sex embracing each other, shaking hands, shedding abundant tears, and wishing each other the best of fortune as they parted. Cnemon begged to be excused from accompanying the travellers, being newly bound in wedlock, and professed his intention of following and overtaking them at the first opportunity. And so they parted: while the rest returned to Chemmis, Chariclea and Calasiris first changed into their beggars' disguise,

[1] Apparently a quotation from a play.

pauperizing their appearance with rags which they had previously provided; then Chariclea disfigured her face, besmirch-
ing it by rubbing it with soot and smearing it with mud. She
also flung over her head a filthy veil whose hem straggled down
from her forehead and covered one of her eyes. Under her arm
she slung a wallet, seemingly for holding their store of scraps of
meat and bread; but its actual purpose was to be the receptacle
for her sacred robe and her garlands from Delphi, and also the
heirlooms and tokens for identification exposed with her by her
mother. Calasiris carried across his shoulders the quiver of
Chariclea, which he had wrapped in some old, worn sheepskin, as
though it were some ordinary bundle; her bow he unstrung and,
as soon as it straightened itself, grasped it as a staff on which he
leant heavily with much of his weight; and whenever he got sight
in advance of people whom he was about to meet he made himself more of a humpback than was the mere effect of old age,
dragged along one of his legs, and at times had Chariclea leading
him by the hand.

*Calasiris and Chariclea come upon a battlefield strewn with
corpses near the village of Bessa, and witness the gruesome practices
of a nocturnal sorceress.*

(12) When they had quite fitted themselves for the parts that
they were to play, they exchanged a little banter, each flattering
the other on being so becomingly costumed. They then besought
the deity concerned with their fortunes to cease at this point,
if ever, from afflicting them and to be satisfied; and so they
hastened on their way to Bessa, the village in which they hoped
to find Theagenes and Thyamis: but in this they were disappointed. For just as they were nearing Bessa, about sunset,
they saw a multitude of men lying dead who had been but lately
slain: the greater number of them were Persians, as was evident
from their dress and armour, while a few were natives of the
country. They surmised that a battle scene had there been
enacted, but could not tell who were the contending parties.
They moved about among the corpses, looking everywhere in
fear that a relative of their own might be lying among them; for
human souls, apprehensive for their dearest ones, are apt to

forbode the worst. They came upon an elderly woman who was clinging to the body of a native and giving vent to all manner of doleful cries. They therefore resolved to see if they could possibly gather some information from the old dame; so they seated themselves near to her, and tried first to console her and restrain her miserable wailing. Then, as she yielded to their efforts, they asked her for whom she was mourning, and what the fighting was, Calasiris asking his questions in Egyptian. She gave them a brief account of all that had occurred: it was over her son's body that she mourned, and she had purposely come among the corpses in the hope that someone would run her through and rid her of life; but meanwhile she was rendering to her son the customary tribute in the only form left to her, that of her tears and lamentation.

(13) Of the fighting she gave them this account: 'A young stranger, of singular beauty and stature, was being taken to Memphis for Oroondates, the lieutenant-governor of the Great King. He had been dispatched, I believe, by Mitranes, a garrison commander, after being taken prisoner, and was offered as a gift of particular value, so they say. The people of our village here', she went on, pointing to the place near by, 'waylaid the party and carried him off, stating—it may have been the truth, or perhaps just a made-up pretext—that they knew him. Mitranes, learning this and being naturally annoyed, led an expedition against the village two days ago. Now, our villagers are an extremely warlike race, having always made their living by brigandage, and are quite regardless of death; hence it is that they have so often bereft many women, like me in this instance, of husbands or children. When they had reason to expect the coming of this attack, they set well-concealed ambuscades in advance and, meeting the onset of the enemy, they gained the upper hand. While some faced the Persians in direct combat, others assailed them from ambushes in their rear, shouting as they caught them off their guard. Mitranes fell fighting in the front line, and with him fell nearly all the rest, since they were encircled and had no chance even of finding a way of escape. A few of our people fell also; and among those few, by a grievous disposition of Fate, was my son, wounded in the breast, as you see, by a Persian javelin. And now, woe is me! I lament over his

dead body; and seemingly I shall have to lament over my other son, who alone is left to me, since he has joined in the expedition of our remaining men which set out yesterday against the city of Memphis.' When Calasiris inquired what was the cause of this expedition, the old woman went on to tell him—what she had heard from her surviving son—that having killed some soldiers of the Great King and his majesty's garrison commander, they saw full well that the outcome of deeds ill done would be no slight matter for them, but the risk of losing their all. Oroondates, the lieutenant-governor at Memphis, was equipped with abundant forces, and would act on the instant of receiving the news; at the first attack he would make a clean sweep of the village, and would inflict the punishment of complete destruction upon its inhabitants. 'Seeing therefore that they must put their all to the hazard,' she said, 'they decided, if possible, "to remedy ventures brave with braver",[1] and forestall the intended operations of Oroondates by making an unexpected attack on him. Thus they would either destroy him as well as Mitranes, if they should catch him at Memphis or, if he happened to be absent through being engaged, according to report, in an Ethiopian campaign, they would the more easily get possession of the city while it was deprived of its defenders; while they would place themselves out of danger for the present, and could also re-establish Thyamis, their brigand chief, in his sacred office of prophet, which is now illegally held by his younger brother. Otherwise, if they should meet with failure in their enterprise, they would at any rate fall as victims of war, and would avoid the alternative of being captured and subjected to tortures and outrages at the hands of the Persians. But you strangers, what place are you making for now?' 'The village,' said Calasiris. 'It would not be safe for you', she said, 'at this late hour, unknown too as you are, to have dealings with the people who remain there.' 'But if you would conduct us', said Calasiris, 'we should not be without hope of our being in safety.' 'I have not the time,' replied the old woman, 'for I propose during the night to offer up some sacrifices to the departed spirits. But if it is not disagreeable to you—but indeed it is a necessity for you, though you may not like it—retire here a little, where you will be clear

[1] A variation of a proverbial phrase, 'to remedy harm with harm'.

of the corpses: at daybreak I will conduct you, and as my guest friends you will be quite secure.'

(14) Calasiris explained all that the woman had said to Chariclea, and taking her with him he moved away. When they had walked a little distance apart from the corpses, they came upon a low mound; there the sage lay down, resting his head on the quiver, while Chariclea seated herself as well as she could on her wallet. The moon was just coming up, and was shedding a bright light on everything around—it chanced to be the third day after the full moon. Calasiris, advanced in years as he was, felt much fatigued by his journeying, and was overcome by sleep; but Chariclea, kept awake by the anxieties that pressed upon her, became a witness of a scene which, although unholy, was familiar enough to the women of Egypt. The old dame, thinking that she had now secured a quiet time, free from any disturbance or observation, proceeded first to dig a hole in the ground, and then on either side of it to light a fire. Between these she laid the body of her son and, taking an earthenware bowl from a tripod set near by, she poured some honey into the hole; from another bowl she poured some milk, and from a third a libation of wine. Then she took a cake of spelt fashioned in the likeness of a man, and having wreathed it with laurel and fennel she cast it into the hole. Last of all she took up a sword and, in a state of frenzied agitation, uttered outlandish and foreign-sounding words of invocation to the moon. She then made a cut in her arm, smeared some of her blood on a spray of laurel and sprinkled it on the fire. After adding to these a number of other magical acts she crouched down over her son's body and, uttering some incantation in his ear, aroused him, and by the power of her sorcery compelled him to stand upright. Chariclea, who had watched even her first doings with no little alarm, was now trembling with terror at such uncouth proceedings. She awakened Calasiris, and made him a witness of the scene that was being enacted. They themselves remained in darkness and could not be seen; but they could clearly observe what was passing in the light shed by the fires, and could also overhear what was spoken at so little distance from them. For the old woman was now questioning the corpse in louder tones: her inquiry was, whether his brother, the son still left to her, would

return safe and sound. He spoke no word in reply, but only gave a nod which yielded his mother a doubtful hope of contentment; then he suddenly sank down and lay prone on his face. She turned the body over on to its back and, without desisting from her inquiry, but even pouring into his ears what seemed to be still more powerfully compelling incantations, she went leaping about, sword in hand, now to the fire and now to the pit, till she aroused him once more. When he was standing up she plied him with the same question, and was forcing him to impart his occult knowledge, not by merely nodding, but distinctly by word of mouth. While the old dame was thus occupied, Chariclea earnestly entreated Calasiris that they might draw near to her operations and make inquiry for themselves about Theagenes: but he declined, telling her that the scene was an unholy one, although they might be obliged to tolerate its performance. For it was not right for prophets either to perform or to countenance such practices: their divination proceeded from lawful sacrifices and righteous prayers, whereas profane persons obtained theirs by actually crawling about the ground among corpses, after the manner which a fortuitous occasion had revealed to them in the case of this Egyptian woman.

(15) While he was still speaking the corpse muttered out these words in deep and dismal tones, as though from a chasm or the inmost recesses of a cavern: 'I was for sparing you at first, mother, and bore with you when you were offending against human nature, violating the ordinances of the Fates, and moving the immovable by magical arts, because reverence for parents is maintained, so far as may be, even among the departed. But since of your own motion you are destroying that respect, and are pressing on from the impious methods that you used at first to an extravagance of impiety without limit; since you compel my dead body, not merely to stand erect and nod, but also to speak; since you are neglecting my burial and so preventing me from commingling with the other souls of the departed, and are bent only upon your own concerns; hear now what hitherto I have scrupled to declare to you. Your son will not return to you safe and sound, nor will you yourself escape death by the sword. You have continually squandered your years on these unholy practices, and will meet ere long the violent death appointed

for all such offenders, you who, moreover, instead of waiting to perform these abominable mysteries by yourself apart, things which are properly kept in the secrecy of silence and darkness, now disgracefully expose what may be the lot of the deceased before such witnesses as these! One of them indeed is a prophet, and there less harm is done; for he has the wisdom to keep silence on such things, his lips sealed against their disclosure; besides, he is dear to the gods. So, although his two sons are preparing to face the bloody ordeal of the sword in single combat, he will intervene and prevail on them to desist, if he makes haste. But it is a graver matter that a young girl should come to behold and overhear all that has passed in relation to me —this poor woman, distracted with love and wandering the world over, one may say, in search of her beloved; with whom, after she has undergone countless toils and countless perils, and reached "the utmost borders of the earth",[1] she will live united in the splendour of regal state.' Having thus spoken he collapsed and lay prostrate; while the old woman, comprehending that those eye-witnesses must be the two strangers, dashed away after them just as she was, sword in hand and raving mad. She rushed about, wherever the slain were lying, with the suspicion that they had concealed themselves among the corpses, and the determination to dispatch them, if she could discover them, for having spied upon her sorceries with insidious and hostile intent. At length, as she pursued her search among the corpses with the unwary haste of rage, she failed to avoid an upright fragment of a spear-shaft which transfixed her in the groin. There she lay dead, having thus quickly fulfilled her son's prediction of her just punishment.

[1] Evidently quoted from a drama.

BOOK VII

The sons of Calasiris, Thyamis and Petosiris, contend in single combat for the priesthood at Memphis, and are pacified by their father. Chariclea finds Theagenes at Memphis.

(1) Calasiris and Chariclea, after an experience of such grave danger, were eager to remove themselves from the horrors of that scene, while they were also urged on by the prophetic message there received by them; so they went along the road to Memphis in hot haste. And indeed, as they were nearing the city, the events predicted by the corpse were already being brought about there. For when Thyamis arrived at the head of his brigands from Bessa, the people of Memphis had just had enough time to close the gates, upon a warning given to the citizens by a soldier in Mitranes' force who had escaped from the battle at Bessa and had foreseen this attack. Thyamis then ordered his men to ground arms at a certain part of the city wall, and rested them there after the forced march that they had made, while he also produced the impression of being about to besiege the place. The people in the city, who at first were struck with terror from the supposition that the approaching force was a large one, but learnt by looking down from the wall that those who had actually advanced against them were but few in number, hastened immediately to call out the few archers and mounted men who had been left on guard in the city, and also armed the townsfolk with whatever weapons were available, intending to sally forth and join battle with the enemy. But an elderly man of high standing opposed their doing so, explaining that although the satrap Oroondates happened to be absent on the Ethiopian campaign, it would be proper at least to inform his wife Arsace of their proposed action. 'If her consent is given', he said, 'we shall have the more prompt and zealous support of the troops that are to be found in the city.' His advice was approved, and they all proceeded to the royal palace which was used by the satraps as their residence in the absence of the King.

(2) Arsace was a tall and beautiful woman, of lively intelligence and with a spirit that presumed greatly on her high birth, as might be expected in the sister of the Great King. But in general she was given to a disreputable way of life, abandoning herself to illicit and dissolute pleasure; and in fact, among other misdeeds, she had been accessory to the previous exile of Thyamis from Memphis. For shortly after Calasiris, in consequence of the divine warning about his two sons, had migrated in complete secrecy from Memphis, and had disappeared and was even thought to have died, Thyamis as his elder son had been called to the prophetic ministry. While he was solemnizing with public sacrifice his induction into the office, Arsace chanced to meet him at the temple of Isis in all the charming bloom of his youth, made more attractive by the fine vestments of the ceremonial in which he was engaged; and she plied him with immodest glances and signs that darkly hinted at her disgraceful purpose. These advances met with not the slightest response from Thyamis, whose nature and upbringing alike had endowed him with a temperate mind, and he was far from suspecting the drift of her behaviour: he supposed that it might have some other explanation, so preoccupied he was with the sacred rites. His brother Petosiris, however, who had long been consumed with jealousy of his priestly function, had closely observed the overtures of Arsace, and availed himself of her licentious attempt as a means of undermining his brother. He approached Oroondates in secret, and not only informed him of his wife's amorous desire, but went so far as to add the slander that Thyamis was consenting to it. The satrap was the more easily convinced because of some grounds that he already had for suspecting Arsace. He did nothing to disquiet her, since he had no certain proof; and besides, fear and respect for the royal family constrained him to bear patiently any suspicion that he might have on his mind. But Thyamis he openly denounced, with continual threats of taking his life, until he forced him to flee the country and installed Petosiris in the office of prophet.

(3) So much then for that affair, which had occurred in an earlier time. Now when Arsace found the crowd of people pressing into her residence, telling her of the enemy's aggression —of which she already had intelligence—and demanding that

all the available troops be ordered to sally out with them, she stated that she could not give that order offhand, since she had not yet learnt the numbers of the enemy, nor who they were, nor whence they came; neither did she understand the reason of their attack. She advised the people to go over to the walls and from them observe everything; then, with the support of other forces, they could take such measures as might be possible and advantageous. Her proposal was approved, and they all promptly marched off to the walls. There Arsace gave directions for an awning to be set up, formed of purple hangings inwoven with gold: beneath this she sat, richly adorned, on a lofty throne, and round her stood a bodyguard clad in gilded armour; and she displayed a caduceus [1] as the symbol of peaceful parley, and requested the leaders and notables of the enemy to come close up to the wall. When Thyamis and Theagenes, as delegates of the main body, arrived and halted below the wall, fully armed but bareheaded, the herald made this announcement: 'Arsace, wife of Oroondates the premier satrap, and sister of the Great King, sends you word saying: "What would you? Who are you? What reason do you allege for venturing on this aggression?"' They replied that they were a body of Bessans; but Thyamis explained who he was, how he had been unlawfully dispossessed of his prophetic office through the machinations of his brother Petosiris and Oroondates, and that he was to have it restored to him by the Bessans. If he recovered his priesthood peace would be made, and the Bessans would return home without doing the least injury to anyone; if he did not they would commit their cause to the arbitrament of armed conflict. If Arsace had any true conception of what was proper in the case, she ought to seize this opportunity of inflicting on Petosiris the due penalty for his malicious treatment of her and the nefarious slanders of his report to Oroondates, by which falsehoods he had aggrieved her with her husband's suspicion of an illicit and depraved passion and him, Thyamis, with exile from his native land.

(4) At this declaration the people of Memphis were one and all confounded; for they recognized Thyamis, and they had

[1] A short staff with two serpents twined about it, usually borne by heralds and envoys in war, in imitation of Hermes, the messenger of the gods, who was supposed to have borne such a staff on his errands.

never understood, from the first moment of the transaction, what could be the reason of his unexpected exile. This they now began to suspect from what had been said, and they believed his account to be true. More than any of the rest Arsace was perturbed in mind amid the harassing tempest of her reflections. Filled with wrath against Petosiris and, moreover, reviewing in her mind all that had occurred in the past, she set about devising some means of wreaking her vengeance. Looking upon Thyamis and then upon Theagenes, she felt her mind torn asunder by her equal desire for each of them, drawn to both at once, to the one by a love that she was reviving, to the other by a more poignant passion that she was newly implanting in her heart. Her state was such that even those around her perceived her deep discomposure. However, after a short pause, she collected herself, like one coming out of an epilepsy, and said: 'My good friends, war is a madness that has seized all the Bessans, and especially you two young men, so well grown and handsome, and of such good birth, as I apprehend and can readily believe. For the sake of some brigands you have rashly exposed yourselves to manifest danger, and will not be able to withstand the first onset, if it comes to a battle. The forces of the Great King could never be so weak that, even though the satrap happens to be absent, the mere remnant of our army stationed here would not suffice to make a clean sweep of you all. But there is no call, I conceive, for the main mass of you to be cut to pieces. Since the grounds for this aggression are the private concern of certain persons, and not a cause affecting the public in general, why should not their dispute be decided between themselves alone, and they be bound to accept whatever outcome may be determined by the gods and by justice? I accordingly resolve', she said, 'and command that all the people of both Memphis and Bessa shall keep still, and refrain from reasonless hostilities against each other, whilst those who are disputing the position of prophet between themselves shall engage in single combat and contend for the priesthood as the victor's prize.'

(5) As she ended this speech Arsace was acclaimed by the whole population of the city, with full approval of her order, both because they were now strongly inclined to suspect Petosiris of dishonest practices, and also because each man deemed it

expedient to avert an obvious and all but inevitable danger by means of a contest between others than himself. The Bessans, in the main, seemed dissatisfied and unwilling to allow their leader to imperil himself on their behalf; till at length Thyamis persuaded them to give their assent by pointing out Petosiris' lack of strength and military experience, and reassuring them with the solid advantage that this would give him in the fight. It was on this very fact, it would seem, that Arsace had reckoned in proposing the single combat, as she quickly perceived that her object would be successfully attained without suspicion being aroused; it would be a convenient way of taking her revenge on Petosiris, if he had to fight to the death with the much more valiant Thyamis.

Then it could be seen how more swiftly than words can tell her commands were carried out. Thyamis, all eagerness in his haste to meet the challenge, was duly methodical and cheerful in spirit as he completed his equipment of armour, Theagenes the while giving him many words of encouragement and fastening on his head the helmet, which was adorned with a fine crest and ablaze with the glitter of gold, and finally buckling on his other pieces of armour to ensure his full protection. But Petosiris, at Arsace's command, was being pushed by main force outside the gates—loud and long were his shouts of protest—and was being armed under compulsion. At the sight of him Thyamis remarked: 'My dear Theagenes, do you not see how Petosiris is quaking with fear?' 'I see that,' he replied; 'but how are you going to deal with the situation? For it is not just an enemy, but one who is also a brother here opposed to you.' 'You are right,' said Thyamis; '"your words have sped direct to the mark of mine own thought." [1] I have indeed resolved to vanquish him, if the deity permits, but not to kill him; for I trust that wrath and resentment over my past maltreatment would never prevail on me to incur the pollution of the bloodshed of my own brother, the slaughter of one born of the same womb, as the price of requiting the wrongs of the past and gaining a dignity in the future.' 'Your words reveal a noble spirit,' said Theagenes, 'and a mind sensible of the claims of nature. But pray now, what duty do you commit to my care?' 'The combat before me', he

---

[1] Apparently a reminiscence of a line in some drama.

replied, 'is a trifle of little account; but the chances of human life are wont to spring many a strange surprise upon us. So, if I should win, you shall come with me into the city, and shall share my hearth and home on equal terms; but if my hopes should be disappointed, you shall be the leader of these Bessans, who are most kindly disposed towards you; and you shall carry on the struggles of the brigands' way of life until the deity intimates to you some more propitious aim for your activities.'

(6) Thereupon they embraced each other with mingled tears and kisses; and Theagenes sat there, just as he was, on the watch for what should happen. To Arsace he thus unconsciously afforded the luxury of beholding him, as she watched intently his every motion and indulged her eyes for the while in some gratification of her desire. Thyamis advanced upon Petosiris, who, however, did not stand to face his onset, but at his first movement took to flight and made for the gates, his one concern being to gain an entrance into the city. But he was foiled in his purpose, for he was repulsed by the guards at the gates and, finding that the people on the walls were urging them to deny him admission at whatever point he might attempt it, he fled away for a time as fast as he could round the circuit of the city, having already cast away his arms. Theagenes ran along behind, in his anxiety for Thyamis, and from a feeling that he could not bear to miss seeing every incident of the action: but he went quite unarmed, so that he should not be suspected of aiming to support Thyamis in the fight. He had laid down his shield and spear at that part of the wall where he had sat under the eyes of Arsace, and had left them for her to gaze upon, this time instead of himself, before he started to follow the course of the race. Petosiris was neither being overtaken nor getting far ahead in his flight, ever and anon seeming on the point of being caught, yet escaping by just so much as Thyamis in his armour could naturally be outrun by his unarmed rival. In this manner they once, and then twice, sped round the walls; but as they were completing their third circuit, Thyamis lunged downward with his spear at his brother's back and threatened that he would transfix him if he did not stop. The citizens, ranged along the wall as in a theatre, were observing and appraising the spectacle below. At this point either some divine Power or Fortune in

control of human affairs appended a new scene to this tragic performance by introducing, as a counter-interest, the opening of another drama. On that day, and at that moment, it suddenly produced Calasiris, as it were, upon the stage, joining in this race and unhappily beholding the mortal combat of his sons. After enduring so many trials, essaying every expedient, and submitting himself to exile and wanderings among strangers, in order somehow to evade so atrocious a sight, he was now defeated by Destiny, and constrained to see what the gods had long before presaged to him. So, espying from afar the progress of the pursuit, and comprehending from the repeated predictions that these were his own children, he forced even his old age into the effort of running at a pace more strenuous than his years warranted, in the hope of being in time to prevent their final grapple.

(7) Then, as he came up with them, and was running along with them, he kept calling out: 'What is this, Thyamis and Petosiris?' Again and again he cried out to them: 'What is this, my children?' But as yet they did not recognize their father's features, for he was still wearing the beggar's rags: themselves wholly intent on their contest, they disregarded him as some mendicant or poor lunatic. Of the spectators on the walls, some wondered at his flinging himself so recklessly between men committed to armed combat, while others laughed at a madman rushing on a futile errand. But when the old man understood that the meanness of his clothing prevented his recognition, he stripped himself of his ragged attire, loosened and let down his reverend locks, and cast away the burden from his shoulders and the staff from his hand. Standing face to face with them, he was beheld in his own majestic and venerable mien. Then gently he knelt down and stretched forth his hands in entreaty, weeping and sobbing out these words: 'My children, it is I, Calasiris; it is your father! Stop where you are, and stay your fated frenzy! Your parent is before you: show him the reverence that is his due.' At his words they were unnerved and nearly sank to the ground; both threw themselves down before their father, and clasping his knees first gazed at him intently to make sure of their recognizing him. When they perceived that it was he in very truth and not an apparition, a number of contrary feelings

came over them in the same moment. They rejoiced to find their
parent alive, beyond all hope; they were pained and ashamed at
being surprised in such an action; and they were possessed by a
harassing doubt as to what the sequel was to be. Moreover, the
people of the city in their astonishment neither said nor did anything, but, mute from their ignorance, and comparable to figures
in a painting, they were standing there, thrilled by the spectacle
alone, when another person made an appearance on the scene—
Chariclea. Following closely in the footsteps of Calasiris, she had
at some distance recognized Theagenes; for lovers are quick of
sight to perceive one another, and often the movement or the
bearing alone of someone observed at a distance or even from
behind, can impress them·with the resemblance. As though
distracted by the sight of him, she rushed with frantic speed at
Theagenes, enfolded him in her arms, clung tightly about his
neck and, hanging there, greeted him with sobs of anguished
weeping. He, as was natural at the sight of her features all
besmirched and deliberately disfigured, and her attire all thread-
bare and tattered, tried to thrust her off and elbow her aside,
taking her for one of the mendicant tribe, a very vagabond. At
length, when she would not let go, to stop her molesting him and
hindering his view of Calasiris, he cuffed her sharply. 'O
Pythian!' she said softly to him; 'and do you not remember the
torch?' Then Theagenes, as if transfixed by those words, recalled
the torch as one of the emblems agreed between them.[1] He gazed
intently at Chariclea and, enlightened by the rays shot forth
from her eyes as by a sunbeam breaking from a cloud, he clasped
her fondly in his encircling arms. And lastly, all the people at
that part of the walls where Arsace sat in state and was swelling
now with no little jealousy as she observed Chariclea, took their
fill of the wondrous spectacle presented by the scene.

*Arsace, wife of the Persian satrap Oroondates, becomes enam-
oured of Theagenes.*

(8) Thus was composed an impious strife between brothers,
and a contest that was expected to be decided by bloodshed ended
in a change from the tragic to a joyful mood. A father beheld his

[1] As told in v. 5.

sons armed against each other for single combat; after facing the imminent disaster of the children's death occurring before the parental eyes, he himself became the dispenser of peace. He proved indeed unable to evade the conjuncture foreordained by Destiny; but he had the happiness of attending in the nick of time at the issue appointed for it. Sons now regained their parent after his ten years' time of wandering, and him who had been the cause of their sanguinary dispute over the office of prophet they were soon crowning with their own hands and escorting in the dignity of the priestly insignia with which they now invested him. But, above all, the love scene gave the finishing touch of charm to the drama. Chariclea and Theagenes, in all the beauty and grace of their youth, who beyond all hope had found each other again, more than anyone else attracted the gaze of the citizens. Indeed, the whole population poured out through the gates and filled the outlying plain. Persons of every age were there: the adolescents of the city, just entering on their manhood, ran up to Theagenes; while men of mature years, in the full possession of manly vigour, surrounded Thyamis, whom they were of an age to recognize. The young maidens of the city, with minds already envisaging the bride-chamber, attended on Chariclea, while old men and everyone of the religious order escorted Calasiris. Thus a sort of sacerdotal procession was formed on the spur of the moment. Thyamis had dismissed the Bessans with assurances of the gratitude that he felt for their generous support, and a promise to send them, a little later, at the full moon, a hundred oxen, a thousand sheep, and for each man a gift of ten drachmas. He now set his neck beneath his father's arm, so as to lighten the old man's effort in walking and bear up his steps, which were somewhat enfeebled by such an unexpected access of joy. On his other side Petosiris did likewise; and so, by the light of torches, the old man was conducted to the temple of Isis, amid sounds of general applause and felicitation; while the tones of many Panpipes and sacred flutes incited the more impetuous of the young folk to wild transports of dancing. Nor indeed did Arsace lag behind in taking her part in the proceedings. Parading with her bodyguard in a specially pompous progress of her own, she brought necklaces and a quantity of gold into the temple of Isis, making as if she came for the same reason as the rest of the people, but in fact keeping her eyes fixed solely on Theagenes, and feasting more than anybody else on the sight of him. Yet her pleasure was not unalloyed. Theagenes was leading Chariclea with his hand on her arm, and as he cleared their way through the jostling throng he stung Arsace to the quick with jealousy. When Calasiris arrived in the inner sanctuary, he prostrated himself and, clasping the feet of the statue, remained thus for a great length of time, in which he came very near to expiring. The bystanders brought him to himself again; with some difficulty he stood up, poured a libation and offered prayers to the goddess. He then removed from his head the sacerdotal crown and set it on the head of his son Thyamis, telling the assembled people that he was now much advanced in years, and foresaw by other signs that his end was approaching; but that his son, the elder of his children, could lawfully claim the prophet's insignia, and was qualified in both soul and body to undertake the public functions of the priesthood.

(9) The people loudly acclaimed his statement, and praised him in terms intimating their full approval of his action. He then, together with his sons and Theagenes, entered a part of the temple assigned to the prophets for their use, and there they remained. Arsace departed also, after much hesitation: ever and anon she would turn back and vaguely linger, as though intending some further worship of the goddess. However, at long last she did depart, turning round again and again towards Theagenes while he was still visible. When she finally arrived at the royal palace, she went straight to her chamber, threw herself, dressed as she was, upon her bed and lay there uttering no word —a female ever prone to ignoble pleasure, but at that moment fiercely inflamed by the overmastering impression of Theagenes, which outrivalled all others that she had ever experienced. There she lay all night long, continually turning over on this side and on that, and continually sending forth deep groans. Now she sat up, and now she sank down on the bed-sheets, and stripping off part of her clothing flung herself suddenly upon the bed again; at times she summoned her maidservant for no reason, and dismissed her without giving any order. In short, her passion was insensibly descending into eventual madness, had not an old woman named Cybele, one of the attendants of her

bed-chamber who ministered confidentially to her amours, run into the room. There she was able at once to perceive the whole state of affairs, since a lamp revealed everything and seemed to be adding its flame to the fire of Arsace's love. 'What is this, mistress?' she asked; 'what new, what strange passion is it that afflicts you? Who is it this time, the sight of whom distracts my own nursling? Who is so arrogant, so senseless, as to withstand the power of your great beauty, and not to see his happiness in your rapturous embraces, but only to despise your beck and bidding? Do but tell me who, my precious child. No heart is so flinty that it cannot be defeated by my enticements. Tell me, and you can go straight to the achievement of your purpose. My services, I think, have often given you good proof of my skill.'

(10) These and other suchlike words were the burden of her talk as she fawned on Arsace, crouching at her feet and seeking by all manner of flatteries to induce her to confess her trouble. Then Arsace, after a few moments' silence, said: 'I am smitten, mother, as never before. Many a time and oft you have served me well in affairs of this kind, but I doubt if this time I can count on your being successful. For the battle that today was almost joined before the walls, and was then so suddenly arrested, has for those others turned out a bloodless one, and was concluded in peace; but for me it has started a more real sort of battle, in which I have received a wound, not in a mere limb or other part of my body, but in my very soul, through the sight that it unfortunately presented to me of that young stranger who ran along with Thyamis during the single combat. You know quite well, I am sure, dear mother, who it is that I mean. For by such a marked distinction did he far outshine all the other men with his beauty that even a boor devoid of any love of the beautiful must have remarked it, and still more must you, with your wide and expert knowledge. So now you, dear friend, are apprised of the shaft that has pierced me: lose no time in applying every artifice, every magic spell and wheedling address that you have acquired in the long span of your life, if you truly wish your nursling's life to be saved. For it is not possible for me to live, unless by some means or other I can possess that man.' 'I remarked the youth,' said the old dame: 'he was broad in chest and shoulders, and he held his head erect with a gallant

air that singled him out from the rest, while in stature he over-topped everyone else. He had an ardent gleam in his eyes, and his glance was at once amiable and awe-inspiring; he it was, to be sure, with the flowing locks, and cheeks just beginning to show a golden ornament of down. It was at him that a foreign woman, not uncomely but, as it seemed, impetuous in manner, suddenly rushed up and hung upon him, locked in close embrace. Was not this the man whom you mean, mistress?' 'It was he, little mother,' she replied. 'You have done well to remind me of the demonstrative act of that depraved creature from some brothel, so highly presuming on a paltry, a vulgar, a factitious beauty; but yet, more fortunate is she than I, in having had the luck to win such a lover!' At these words the old woman smiled at her in a sly, smirking manner and said: 'Take heart, mistress; until today our stranger has thought her beautiful, but if I could contrive to face him with you and your beauty, he will take gold, as they say, in exchange for bronze,[1] and will thrust aside that little mincing courtesan with all her futile affectations.' 'If you do that, my darling Cybele, you will at one stroke cure me of two diseases, love and jealousy, by satisfying the one and expelling the other.' 'It shall be done,' said the old woman, 'so far as in me lies. Now I would have you revive yourself by keeping quiet for the moment: do not let despondency enfeeble you before-hand; rather cheer yourself with hope.'

Calasiris dies. Arsace endeavours to seduce Theagenes with the aid of her serving-woman Cybele.

(11) So saying, she took away the lamp, closed the door of the room and went off. When she perceived that day was just dawning, she took with her one of the eunuchs of the palace, and also a maidservant whom she ordered to follow along with some cakes and other offerings, and hastened to the temple of Isis. On arriving at the doors, she stated that she wished to offer a sacrifice to the goddess on behalf of her mistress Arsace, who had been much disturbed by certain dreams, and so desired to avert by these offerings the evils revealed to her. One of the sacristans

[1] Alluding to Homer, *Il.* vi. 235–6, where Glaucus exchanges his golden armour for the bronze armour of Diomedes.

objected and sent her away, declaring that the temple was now given up entirely to mourning. For the prophet Calasiris, he said, on returning to his residence after prolonged absence, had on that evening enjoyed a fine feast in company with his dearest ones, and had indulged in complete relaxation and geniality. At the end of the banquet he had offered up libations and a number of prayers to the goddess; he had then told his sons that only up to that hour would they be seeing their father, and he repeatedly adjured them to devote their best efforts to caring for the young Greeks who had arrived there with him, and to give them all possible assistance in whatever plans they might adopt. He retired to take his rest; then, whether it were that by the fullness of his joy the channels of respiration had been too greatly distended and slackened, and so his body, aged as it was, had suddenly broken down, or that the gods had granted him this end at his request, at cock-crow it was discovered that he was dead, while his sons were keeping night-long watch over the old man on the hint of his warning. 'So now', said the sacristan, 'we have issued a summons for the attendance of the rest of the prophets and priests in the town, that they may conduct his funeral with the customary rites of their ancestral tradition. You must therefore depart, since it is not right that anyone except the persons invested with the holy functions should offer sacrifice or even set foot in the temple, during these seven whole days succeeding the decease.' 'Then how will they fare in the meantime, those strangers whom you mentioned?' asked Cybele. 'A lodging has been prepared for them,' he replied, 'near by, just outside the temple, on the order of the new prophet Thyamis; and, as you see, here come those very persons, removing themselves from the holy place for the present, in obedience to the rule.' Then Cybele, seizing on the circumstance like a hunter grasping his quarry, said: 'Well now, sacristan most beloved of the gods, here is your chance to render a service both to these strangers and to us, above all to Arsace, sister of the Great King. You know how she loves the Greeks, and what an aptitude she has for entertaining guests. Tell these young people that by Thyamis' command it is in our house that arrangements for their accommodation have been made.' The sacristan did as Cybele requested, having no suspicion of her deep-laid designs, but only thinking to show kindness to the strangers by introducing them into the satrap's court, and at the same time to concede this favour to the persons desiring it, as one in particular that could entail no harm or penalty. When he saw Theagenes and Chariclea, now close at hand, dejected and tearful, the sacristan said to them: 'This is no lawful behaviour, nor agreeable to our ancestral tradition—indeed, you have been told already of its prohibition—to be weeping and wailing over a prophet. Our duty, enjoined on us by the divine and hallowed teaching, is to attend him to his grave with gladness and felicitation, as having obtained the better portion allotted to him by the higher powers. However, you may be pardoned, since you have been bereft, as you say, of your father, your protector and your only hope. Yet you must not yield utterly to despair, since Thyamis, it seems, is succeeding, not only to his father's priesthood, but also to his regard for you. In fact, he has begun by giving orders for due care to be taken of you, and a lodging has been prepared for you in handsome style, such as might be hoped for by one of the most prosperous persons in our country, and not by mere strangers whose means appear to be so reduced at present. Follow this woman,' he said, pointing to Cybele; 'regard her as a mother to you both, and accept her as your helpful guide.'

(12) Theagenes and his companion did as the man advised; for, while their spirits were sunk to the depths by the unexpected blows that they had sustained, they were thankful to find for the moment some sort of lodging that offered them a refuge. More cautious, no doubt, they would have been, had they suspected the tragic significance of that abode, so imposing and so fraught with mischief for them. At this moment the Fortune that imposed their toils and trials, having allowed them a respite of a few hours and indulged them with a transient joy, was promptly loading them with fresh affliction, and bringing them like self-made slaves into the presence of their enemy. With the pretence of kindly hospitality it was now leading captive a pair of young strangers who were all unwary of what might be in store for them. Thus it is that a wandering life inflict ignorance, like a kind of blindness, on those who visit foreign parts. And so, as soon as they arrived at the residence of the satrap, and faced the

imposing portico, erected on a larger scale than that of any
private dwelling, and thronged with a great parade of bodyguards
and array of domestic servants, the sight of an establishment
so disproportionate to their present condition filled them with
bewilderment and consternation. Nevertheless, they followed
Cybele, who kept urging them to come on and bidding them
have no fear; she continually called them her little children, her
darlings, and insisted that they should look forward with gladness
to the experience that awaited them. At length the old woman,
having brought them into the apartment where she lodged, in a
specially private and retired part of the palace, dismissed the
other persons in it and, sitting alone with the young pair, said
to them: 'My children, I have perceived the cause of the dejection that at present affects you, and how the death of the prophet
Calasiris has filled you with grief, for he had come to be as a
father to you. Now, it is proper that you should tell me who you
are and whence you came. I know that you are Greeks, and
besides, by your looks one may well surmise that you are persons
of good family: the brightness of your eyes, and the comeliness
and charm of your whole appearance, produce a clear impression
of gentle birth. But of what region of Greece, of what city are
you? Who are you, and by what sort of wanderings have you
made your way here? Tell me all this; I wish to learn it for your
own future benefit, that I may be able to give a full account of
you to my mistress Arsace, sister of the Great King, and consort
of Oroondates, greatest of all satraps. She is a lover of the Greeks,
a lover too of their refinement, and a benefactress of foreigners;
and through me you would be treated with the special honour
that is your due. You will be informing a woman who is not
altogether alien to you; for I also, mark you, am a Greek by
birth, a citizen of Lesbos who was brought here as a captive, but
who fares better than my countryfolk at home. I am everything,
I may say, to my mistress; she almost breathes and sees through
me. I am her mind, her ears, her all; I am constantly bringing
her acquainted with persons of the best quality, and am her
trustworthy confidant in all her secret concerns.' Theagenes
then brought up for comparison together in his mind these
words spoken by Cybele and the behaviour of Arsace on the
previous day. He recalled with what an intent, immodest gaze

she had looked upon him, continually and clearly indicative of her unchaste thoughts; and he augured nothing good in what was to ensue. He was about to speak to the old woman, when Chariclea leant over and whispered in his ear: 'Remember "your sister" in what you may say.'

(13) He understood to what she was referring, and said: 'Mother, that we are Greeks you have, it seems, found for yourself the means of knowing. We are brother and sister; our parents were captured by brigands. We set out in search of them, and have met with even worse misfortunes than they; for we fell in with men more cruel still, by whom we were stripped of all our possessions, and they were many. We narrowly escaped with our lives, and by some happy disposition of the deity we happened upon Calasiris of blessed memory. We came here intending to live with him thenceforward; but now, as you see, we are left utterly destitute and alone, having lost, besides those parents of ours, him whom we considered and who was indeed our father. This then is our story: we are most grateful to you for your present welcome and kind attentions; but you would gratify us still more if you would arrange for us to live by ourselves apart and in seclusion, and defer the favour that you proposed for us just now, of introducing us to Arsace, rather than disturb the splendour and wellbeing of her state with the alien and forbidding intrusion of our vagabond existence. For, as you know, it is best to have acquaintance and contact with persons of similar condition to one's own.'

(14) After this speech Cybele could not forbear revealing by the look of relief in her face how highly delighted she was to hear the words 'brother and sister', as she reflected that Chariclea would present no hindrance or impediment to the love-making of Arsace. 'Young man of surpassing beauty', she said, 'you will not speak thus of Arsace when you have had some experience of that lady. She is a person familiar with every sort and condition, and is prompt to assist those who are undeservedly less prosperous. A Persian by birth, she is very much a Grecian at heart, delighting in people from that country and quick to give them a welcome. For the manners and society of Greeks she has an immense affection. Take heart then from the thought that you will be treated as handsomely and honourably as befits a man,

while your sister will give the lady her entertaining companionship. But by what names am I to announce you?' When she had been told that they were Theagenes and Chariclea, she bade them await her there, and hurried away to Arsace, after charging the portress—herself also an old woman—not to admit anyone who might try to gain an entrance, and not to allow the young couple to go out. 'Not even your son Achaemenes, if he should appear?' asked the portress; 'just after you set out for the temple he went away to have his eyes treated for the ailment which still, as you know, is giving him some trouble.' 'Not even him,' replied Cybele. 'Shut the door, keep the key to yourself and tell him that I have taken it with me.' Her order was obeyed. Then, hardly a moment after Cybele had departed, their solitude suggested to Theagenes and Chariclea that they had this opportunity for lamenting and reflecting on their situation. They bewailed themselves, each giving nearly the same expression to the same thoughts; the one continually sighing forth 'O Theagenes!' and the other 'O Chariclea!' He would ask: 'What fresh mischance has overtaken us?' and she: 'What sort of trouble is it that we shall have to face?' And each time they would fondly embrace and weep and kiss each other once more. At length the memory of Calasiris caused a conversion of their lamenting to mourning for him, especially on Chariclea's part, because she had for a longer time experienced his solicitude and kindness. 'O Calasiris,' she exclaimed in woeful tones, 'I am debarred from calling you by the most honoured name of father, since my Destiny has in jealousy cut me off from all hope of addressing you with that word. My natural father I have never known, and him who adopted Chariclea, alas, I have deserted; [1] while him who took charge of me, reared me and preserved me I have lost, and the customary lamentation over his corpse still lying there is denied me by the prophets' rule. But see now, to you, my supporter and saviour—and I will add, my father also, despite the will of Destiny—here at least, where I can, and in such manner as I can, to you I pour libation of my tears, and tender the pious tribute of my locks.' With that she began to tear out large tresses of her hair. Theagenes restrained her, grasping her hands and pleading with her; but she went on

[1] Referring to her flight from Delphi and Charicles (iv. 17).

speaking in tragic vein: 'What call have we now to go on living? On what hope can we turn our eyes? The guide to lead us through a strange land, the staff to aid our wandering steps, our safe conduct to our native country and recognition of our parents, our consolation in calamity, our resource and deliverance in perplexities, the anchor of all our ventures, Calasiris, has perished, and has left us like a lost pair in harness to stumble blind and baffled on this alien soil. To us all wayfaring, all sea-voyaging, are impeded by our ignorance. Gone is the holy and gentle, the wise and truly venerable heart which itself has failed of achieving the fulfilment of its good offices towards us.'

(15) As she was continuing to utter these and other mournful plaints, and as Theagenes, while tending to swell the lamentation with plaints of his own, yet strove to restrain them out of tenderness for Chariclea, Achaemenes arrived and, finding the door bolted and barred, asked the portress what was the meaning of it. When he learnt that it was the doing of his mother, he came up close to the door and, curious to know her motive, caught the sound of Chariclea's lamentation. He stooped down, peered through the holes through which the chains securing the bolts had been passed, and espied the scene within. Again he questioned the portress as to who were the persons in the place. She replied that she knew nothing more of the matter than that they were a girl and a youth, strangers so far as she could guess, who had just been lodged in the house by his mother. He stooped down once more and tried to get a clear impression of the persons who he saw in the room. Chariclea was completely unknown to him; none the less he was utterly amazed at her beauty, and imagined how fine and lovely she would look if she were not weeping, so that his admiration drew him insensibly into the passion of love. Theagenes he fancied that he recognized, in a dim and dubious manner. Then, while Achaemenes was absorbed in his inspection, Cybele arrived, having returned from making a full report of her talk with the young pair. She had warmly congratulated Arsace on her good fortune, which had brought her unsolicited so great a success, beyond anything that could have been looked for from all the planning and contriving in the world—so great, that now she had the beloved one an inmate of her house, where he could see her and be seen by

her with nothing at all to fear. When with many such assurances
she had inflamed Arsace, she had some difficulty in restraining
her mistress's impulse to go at once and gaze on Theagenes:
she told her she would not have her seen by the young man all
pale and swollen-eyed from sleeplessness; she should rather take
a rest for that day and recover her usual beauty. By plying her
with suchlike counsels Cybele at length brought her to a cheerful
and hopeful view of her heart's desire, and went on to prescribe
her most suitable procedure and the demeanour that she should
adopt towards her guests.

(16) After that, when Cybele arrived at her own door, she
said: 'Why this curiosity, child?' 'It is about the strangers in
the house,' he replied, 'to know who and whence they are.'
'That is forbidden, my son,' she told him; 'hold your tongue,
keep this to yourself, tell nobody; and have little or nothing to
do with the strangers. This is my mistress's decision.' He went
away in prompt obedience to his mother, surmising that Theagenes was just an ordinary accessory to one of Arsace's amours.
As he departed he said to himself: 'Is not this the man whom I
received from Mitranes the commandant to take to Oroondates
for dispatch to the Great King, and whom the Bessans under
Thyamis carried off from me, when I came within an ace of
losing my life and was the only one of the escort who succeeded
in getting away? Can it be that my eyes are deceiving me? But I
am recovering my sight, and already it is nearly as clear as it
used to be. What is more, I have heard that Thyamis was here
yesterday, and that after fighting it out in single combat with his
brother he has regained the priestly office. Yes, this is the man.
But for the present I must say no word of my recognition of
him, and must also be on the look-out for what the mistress's
intentions may be regarding these strangers.' Thus did he speak
to himself.

(17) Cybele, running in upon the young pair, detected traces
of their lamenting. For although at the sound of the door being
opened they began to compose themselves and strove to reassume
their normal poise and looks, they yet failed to delude the old
woman, since their eyes were still bedewed with tears. So she
called out: 'Sweetest children, why this untimely lamenting when
you ought to be rejoicing; when you should be congratulating

yourselves on the happy turn in your fortunes? Arsace has the best intentions towards you that your hearts could desire: she has consented to give you an audience tomorrow, and in the meantime she has accorded to you the warmest welcome and kindest attentions. Come now, you must cast aside these silly, these truly childish bewailings; the time has now come for you to bring yourselves to order and comply obediently with the wishes of Arsace.' To this Theagenes answered: 'It was the memory, mother, of the death of Calasiris that aroused in us such anguish, and compelled our tears for the loss of his fatherly concern for our welfare.' 'What nonsense!' she said. 'Calasiris, a merely fictitious father, an old man who had to yield to our common nature and the period of his years. Everything is yours to have, as the gift of a single person—distinction, wealth, luxury and enjoyment of the flowering time of your years; in short, you are to regard her as your Fortune, and do homage to Arsace. Only you must take my advice as to how you should approach and behold her when she gives the command, and how you are to set about any service that she may require of you; for her spirit, as you know, is high and mighty, indeed queenly, being specially exalted by her youth and beauty, and will not brook any slighting of her orders.'

(18) At these words Theagenes remained silent, reflecting on their disagreeable and sinister import. Shortly after, some eunuchs appeared bearing on golden dishes what might seem to be remnants from the satrap's table, but in fact were dainties of surpassing costliness and refinement. 'These dishes', they said, 'Her Highness sends to welcome and honour her guests on this occasion.' They set down the dishes before the young pair and immediately withdrew. Moved not only by the urgings of Cybele but equally by a prudent desire not to appear to flout this courtesy, they tasted a little of the fare set before them. The same thing occurred in the evening and on each following day. On the morrow, however, in the first hour or so, the eunuchs on the same duty stood before Theagenes and said: 'You have been summoned, most fortunate sir, by our mistress, and we have received an order for your presentation. So come now and enjoy that happiness of which she permits but few, and that but rarely, to partake.' For a brief space he made no motion; then, as

though he were haled away by main force, he rose and said to them: 'Is it commanded that I come alone, or with my sister here?' They replied that he was to come alone, and that she would be presented separately; for at present Arsace had with her some Persian officers of state; and besides, it was customary to grant interviews to men by themselves and to women on another occasion. Theagenes leant over to Chariclea and said to her in a low voice: 'This is neither honourable nor above suspicion.' After hearing her answer that they must not run counter but concur at first, and make a show of readiness to do everything to content the lady, he followed his conductors.

Theagenes is received in audience by Arsace.

(19) These men instructed him on the proper manner of meeting and addressing her, and said that it was customary to prostrate oneself on entering: to this he made no response. He entered and found her seated on a lofty throne. She was resplendent in a purple robe shot with gold, and was gorgeously adorned with costly necklaces and a magnificent tiara, while her face had the full luxurious bloom produced by an ample assortment of cosmetics. Close to her stood the bodyguard, and on either side sat the high officers of her council. Theagenes' spirit did not quail. As though unmindful of his agreement with Chariclea to make a pretence of humble service, he was moved to all the prouder defiance by this arrogant Persian display. Without the bending of a knee or any prostration, he held his head high as he said: 'Greetings to the lady of the blood royal, Arsace.' The company were annoyed, and raised a murmur that Theagenes' refusal to prostrate himself showed the seditious spirit of a reckless adventurer; but Arsace smiled and said: 'You must forgive him as an ignorant foreigner—in a word, a Greek, infected with that nation's contempt of us.' And with that she removed her tiara from her head, despite vehement remonstrances from the company, since with the Persians this gesture is the regular sign of returning a salutation. Then she said through an interpreter—for while she understood the Greek language she did not speak it—'Have no fear, stranger: tell us what you would have; you will not be disappointed.' She then dismissed him, indicating

her wish to the eunuchs with a nod of her head. He was being conducted by some of the bodyguard, when Achaemenes, catching sight of him again, recognized him more exactly and, suspecting the cause of the extraordinary honour done to him, was struck with wonder; however, he kept silence, adhering to the course on which he had resolved.

Arsace entertained the Persian dignitaries at a banquet, ostensibly in customary compliment to them, but really in celebration of her meeting with Theagenes. To him and his companion she sent, not merely the usual share of her repast, but also some carpets and embroidered coverlets made by the craftsmen of Sidon and Lydia. She sent besides two slaves to wait upon them—a young girl for Chariclea and a young boy for Theagenes, both being of Ionian race and tender years. Repeatedly she requested Cybele to make haste and achieve her object with all possible speed, as she felt herself no longer able to endure the ardour of her passion; and Cybele was to spare no effort in trying by all possible means to inveigle Theagenes. Cybele, to be sure, did not openly declare Arsace's design, but with circuitous and insinuating talk she sought to draw him into comprehension of it. She made much of her mistress's kindly feeling towards him, and with some fair-sounding representations offered him the sight, not only of her apparent beauty, but also that concealed by her clothing. She spoke of her charming and companionable nature, and how she delighted in young men of specially refined and noble character: in fact, by her whole description she was testing him to see if he were amenable to the lure of love. Theagenes concurred in praising the kindness of Arsace, her affection for the Greeks, and all her other such qualities, and he avowed his gratitude to her; but those which incited him to wantonness he preferred to pass over, as though he had not so much as understood them from the first. The old dame in consequence felt a choking in her throat, and her heart seemed to gasp when, just as she was assuming that he understood her enticements, she perceived him to be so audaciously spurning her temptation. And Arsace, she found, was becoming unbearable; she harassed her with declaring that her patience was exhausted, and demanded fulfilment of the promise made to her. This Cybele each time found some excuse or other for putting off, now asserting that the youth, though desirous, was overawed, and now inventing the sudden attack of some disorder.

(20) When about the next five or six days had passed by, in which Arsace had once or twice summoned Chariclea before her and, to gratify Theagenes, received her with honour and graciousness, Cybele was forced to speak more plainly to Theagenes and declare her mistress's love to him without further disguise, promising him an infinite abundance of benefits if he complied with her desire, and adding: 'What is this timidity? Why are you so averse from love? A man so young and hand-some, in his very prime, to repulse a woman who is his match, and entirely devoted to him! Not to seize on this affair as a prize, as a windfall, when no fear attaches to its doing, and when her husband is away, and you have me who nurtured her and am the keeper of all her secrets, to procure this union! And you, who have no hindrance in your way, with no bride or wife! Yet many a time have numbers of men ignored these impedi-ments, if they were such as had the sense to perceive that their action would in no way harm their kindred, and would advantage themselves by the acquisition of ampler means, along with the enjoyment of that pleasure.' She ended by mingling some threats with her arguments. 'Well-bred women', she said, 'who love young men, become hard-hearted and rancorous from dis-appointment, and avenge themselves, with good reason, on any who slight them, as outrageous offenders. This lady, mark you, is of the Persian race and the blood royal—to use the words of your own greeting to her. Reflect that she is invested with great authority and power, whence she possesses full and free licence to honour the well disposed and chastise the recalcitrant; whereas you are a foreigner, all alone, with no one to protect you. Spare yourself for your sake, spare her for hers. She deserves this indulgence from you, for her misconduct arises from the mad-ness of her longing for you. Be on your guard, and beware of a lover's resentment, the vengeful wrath of a woman spurned. Many a man, to my knowledge, has had to recant: I have more experience than you of the ways of Aphrodite. These white hairs that you see have had their part in many such encounters; but a man so insensible, so uncouth, I have never met before.' She next directed her words to Chariclea—for of necessity she had

the hardihood to argue as she had done in the girl's hearing.
'Add your voice to mine, daughter,' she said, 'in persuading
this man—I know not by what name I ought properly to
call him—your brother. You will have your portion of profit
from this affair: you will be treated with no less affection, and
with greater honour; enriched to your heart's content, you will
procure a brilliant marriage for yourself. These are things to be
envied even by the prosperous; how much more by strangers
who are plainly at present in a state of destitution?'

(21) Chariclea, with a wry smile and glowering eyes, replied:
'It would be desirable, indeed the best thing of all, that the most
excellent Arsace should not be so enthralled. Failing that, the
next best thing would be to endure her trouble with self-restraint.
But since a human weakness has affected her, and she has been
conquered, as you say, and has succumbed to her desire, I too
would advise Theagenes here not to reject the affair, if he could
safely undertake it, and there were no fear of inadvertently
causing some harm to himself and to her, through the facts
coming to light and the satrap by some means learning of their
illicit conduct.' At these words Cybele started up, embraced
Chariclea with repeated kisses, and said: 'Well done, child! You
have not merely taken pity on a woman of like nature to your
own, but have also taken thought for your brother's safety. But
have no fear on that score; for the sun himself, as the saying is,
will not get knowledge of it.' 'Enough of this for the present,'
said Theagenes; 'now leave us to consider.' Cybele thereupon
departed, and Chariclea said: 'O Theagenes, Destiny procures
for us the sort of successes in which there is more of adversity
than any apparent prosperity. Nevertheless, persons of intelligence ought to turn even their misfortunes to the best account
possible in the circumstances. Now, I cannot tell whether your
intention is to carry through this affair to the full; and indeed I
should not have felt greatly upset, if our deliverance depends
entirely on that and on that alone. But if, to your honour, you
find the proposal repugnant, see that you make a pretence of
compliance. Foster with promises this barbarian woman's yearning; frustrate with deferments any sharp measures that she
may meditate against us; soothe with hope, and allay with
assurances, the fiery heat of her indignation. It may well be that

the respite thus gained will even, by the gods' design, bring forth a solution. But, Theagenes, do not let your mere rehearsal send you sliding down to the vileness of performance.' At this Theagnes smiled and said: 'Ha, so you now, even in the midst of danger, have not escaped that innate malady of women, jealousy! I, you may be sure, cannot so much as simulate such things; for shameful words and deeds are equally depraved. Besides, the discomfiture of Arsace brings us at once the boon of an end to her pestering us. If I should have to suffer, my fortune and my judgment have already taught me, in many trials, how to bear whatever may befall.' 'Take care lest you unwittingly plunge us into grievous trouble,' Chariclea replied, and said no more.

(22) While they were engaged in these speculations, Cybele had sent the hopes of Arsace soaring high, by telling her to expect a more favourable turn in the affair, because Theagenes had shown certain signs of this. She then returned to her quarters where, after letting the evening go by, she spent the night in making constant appeals to Chariclea, who had continued from the first to be her bedfellow, to aid her in her task; then, in the morning, she again asked Theagenes what decision he had made. His answer was a point-blank refusal, and a declaration that nothing at all was to be expected of him. In dismay she ran back to Arsace who, on hearing her report of Theagenes' perverseness, ordered the old woman to be hustled headlong out of the room. Then, hastening to her chamber, she lay down on her bed and took to lacerating herself. Hardly had Cybele left the women's apartments when her son Achaemenes, seeing her downcast and tearful, asked her: 'Has something untoward, something vexatious, mother, befallen? Has some report annoyed your mistress? Has news of some disaster arrived from the army? Is it that the Ethiopians in the present campaign are gaining the upper hand of our master Oroondates?' And so he went on, with a string of similar questions. But Cybele merely said 'Your talk is nonsense,' and ran away. But he was not to be so put off: following after her, he grasped her hands, fondled her and begged her to explain to her very own son what it was that distressed her.

Cybele's son Achaemenes seeks Chariclea in marriage.

(23) So then she led him by the hand to a secluded part of the gardens and said: 'To no one else would I have related my own and my lady's misfortunes; but she is in desperate straits, and I expect to be in mortal peril—for I know that Arsace's distress and distraction will swoop down on me—and so I am compelled to speak, on the chance that you can devise some deliverance for her who bore you, brought you forth to the light of day and nurtured you at these breasts. Madam is in love with the young man now staying with us. It is no tolerable or ordinary love, but one that is incurable. We had hopes, she and I till now, that it might prosper, but we have been utterly frustrated. Thus it was that all those kindly thoughts and ingenious courtesies were bestowed on the strangers. But since this young booby has the hardihood and cruelty to set his face against us, she, I know, will lose her life, while I shall be destroyed, as having deluded and deceived her with my promises. That is the position, child. If you can bring some relief, give me your support; if not, then you have to perform the last rites for your deceased mother.' 'And what reward shall I have, mother?' he asked; 'for this is no time for me to mince matters with you, or to use devious circumlocutions in promising you my aid, when you are in such extreme anguish and on the very verge of giving up the ghost.' 'Anything that you desire,' Cybele replied, 'you can count upon. At present she has made you one of the chief cupbearers, to do me honour. If you have in mind some higher dignity, declare it: riches you will gain to an incalculable amount, if you can be the saviour of this unhappy lady.' 'I have long suspected this affair, mother,' he said, 'and have kept my cognizance of it to myself, awaiting the outcome with much concern. But I lay claim to no distinction or riches. Only let Arsace bestow that girl on me in marriage, the so-called sister of Theagenes, and she will accomplish all that she has at heart. I am in love with the girl, mother, very deeply: Madam knows from her own case the force and nature of this passion, and she may fairly lend her aid to one who is labouring under the same infection as herself, and who, moreover, promises her such a gratifying success.' 'Do not hesitate,' said Cybele. 'Madam will show her gratitude to you in

no ambiguous manner for having been her benefactor and saviour; besides, we may well be able by ourselves to persuade the girl. But tell me, by what means can you relieve us?' 'I shall not answer that', he replied, 'until Madam has pledged herself by oath to keep her promise. But you must not make trial of the girl in advance, because I see that she has some high and mighty notions, and you might unwittingly upset the whole business.' 'Everything shall be as you wish,' she said, and then ran in to see Arsace in her chamber. There she fell down at her knees and said: 'Be comforted: everything is turning out well, by Heaven's will; only command that my son Achaemenes be summoned before you.' 'Let him be summoned,' said Arsace, 'if you are not intending to deceive me again.'

(24) Achaemenes entered: Arsace, having now heard all the terms from the old woman, swore that she would procure his marriage with the sister of Theagenes. 'Madam,' said Achaemenes, 'let Theagenes, who is your slave, cease henceforth to play the fine gallant with his chosen mistress.' 'What mean you by that?' she asked. He then related the whole story: how Theagenes was taken prisoner in the ordinary way of war and fell into captivity; how Mitranes had dispatched him to Oroondates for delivery to the Great King; and how he himself, put in charge of the youth for his transmission, had lost him through a daring onslaught of Bessans and Thyamis, from which he himself had barely succeeded in escaping. He ended by showing Arsace the letter of Mitranes to Oroondates, which he had been careful to have ready with him, and said that, if further proof were needed, he would produce Thyamis also as witness. Arsace was greatly inspirited by his words, and without a moment's delay she quitted her chamber, passed into the suite in which she was accustomed to sit in state for official business and ordered that Theagenes be brought in. When he appeared she asked him whether he knew Achaemenes, pointing him out where he stood near at hand. He replied that he did. She then put a second question: 'And did he not take you away as a prisoner in his charge?' Theagenes assented to this also. 'Know then,' she said, 'that you are our slave. You will work as one of our servants, obedient to our beck and call, however much against your will. Your sister I am bestowing in marriage upon

Achaemenes here, who holds one of the highest offices in our household, both for his mother's sake and for his general regard for our interests. This event only awaits the appointment of the day and the arrangements for holding the festivity in duly magnificent style.' Theagenes, though wounded to the quick by her words, nevertheless resolved not to show fight, but to evade the savage creature's onset. 'Mistress,' he said, 'thanks be to the gods that we, who are of the noblest birth, have at least this blessing in our misfortunes, that we are become slaves to you and to none other—you who have looked upon us, mere aliens and strangers in your eyes, with such mildness and kindly favour. As for my sister, she is no prisoner, and hence no slave: but she chooses to attend on you and to go by such designation as you may be pleased to give her. Consider well, and do exactly what you judge to be correct.' 'Let him be placed', she said, 'among the table attendants, and be instructed in the serving of wine by Achaemenes, so as to be well trained in advance for his attendance on the King.'

(25) The two young men accordingly withdrew—Theagenes in gloomy mood and with a look of absorption in thinking of what he had to do, while Achaemenes mocked and jeered at Theagenes, saying: 'So you, sir, who were swaggering of late so haughtily, you who could not bend your neck, who alone were free, who could not bear to bow your head in obeisance, will now perhaps incline it, or else by fisticuffs be disciplined to hold it down.' Arsace then dismissed all the rest of the company, retaining only Cybele, to whom she said: 'You see now, Cybele, every excuse has been stripped off: go, tell the haughty fellow that, if he obeys us and falls in with our purpose, he will be given his freedom, and will have the ample enjoyment of a life of affluence; but if he persists in his opposition to us, he will learn what it is to deal with a woman whose love is spurned, and who is, moreover, his deeply offended mistress, and he will have to submit to the meanest and most ignominious servitude, and suffer every kind of punishment.' Cybele went and delivered Arsace's message, adding not a few such exhortations of her own as seemed expedient. Theagenes requested her to wait a little while. Left alone with Chariclea, he said to her: 'All is over with us, Chariclea: every cable, as they say, has been severed, every

anchor of hope has been completely torn away, and we are unable now even to call ourselves free in our misfortune, but have become slaves once more'—and here he added the kind of slavery that it was. 'Henceforth we are exposed to barbarous cruelties, and we must either subserve the humours of our lords and masters or be numbered amongst the condemned. All this could yet be borne; but, more grievous still, Arsace has promised to bestow you in marriage on Cybele's son, Achaemenes. This event, of a certainty, will not take place, or I shall not see it occur, so long as life can provide me with a sword and armour to prevent it. But what is to be done, what contrivance can we devise, to frustrate these abominable unions, mine with Arsace and yours with Achaemenes?' 'One only,' replied Chariclea; 'assent to yours, and you will prevent mine.' 'Fie on such words!' he said; 'may the persecutions of our Destiny never prevail on me, who have refrained from attempt on Chariclea, to pollute myself by unlawful intimacy with another woman! But I think I have devised an effectual scheme: necessity is indeed an inventor of expedients.' With that he went off to Cybele and said: 'Go, tell your mistress that I wish to see her alone and unattended.'

Theagenes tells Arsace that Chariclea is not his sister, but his affianced bride.

(26) Conceiving that the great point was gained, and that Theagenes had submitted, the old woman went and informed Arsace. She was bidden to fetch the young man after dinner; and this she did. After ordering the retinue to leave Madam undisturbed and to do nothing likely to give serious annoyance to the occupants of the chamber, she privily brought in Theagenes. The rest of the house was plunged in what seemed a nocturnal darkness, which enabled one to pass along unseen, the chamber alone being illuminated by a lamp. She showed him in, and was about to withdraw; but Theagenes stopped her, saying: 'Let Cybele stay here at present, mistress: I know that she is the faithful keeper of your secrets.' So saying he took hold of Arsace's hands and said: 'Mistress, it was in no spirit of insolent defiance of your will that I deferred complying with your order before,

but because I had to deliberate with myself how it could be done in safety. But now that by what seems a happy turn of fortune I have become your slave, I am much more ready to obey you in all things. One boon only be pleased to grant me over and above the many benefits that you have promised me: countermand the marriage of Chariclea to Achaemenes. Not to speak of other reasons, for a girl who prides herself on the noblest birth to cohabit with a menial would be scandalous: otherwise, I swear to you by the Sun, fairest of the gods, and by all the other gods, that I will not yield to your desire; and if any violence should be offered to Chariclea, you will see me first done to death by my own hand.' 'Be in no doubt,' said Arsace, 'of my desire to grant you every favour, prepared as I am to bestow myself on you. But I am pre-engaged, and bound by oath, to bestow your sister upon Achaemenes.' 'Very well, mistress,' he said; 'then bestow on him my sister, whatever she may be; but my affianced bride, in fact no other than my wife—her you will neither wish, I am sure, to bestow on him nor, though you may wish it, will you do so.' 'What do you mean?' she asked. 'The plain fact,' he replied; 'for in Chariclea I have, not a sister, but a bride, as I said, so that you are released from your oath; and it is possible for you, if you choose, to obtain full proof of the fact, by celebrating at your own good time my marriage with her.' Though somewhat pricked with jealousy at hearing that Chariclea was his bride and not his sister, Arsace was yet able to say: 'So shall it be; and we will arrange another marriage for Achaemenes' consolation.' 'And so it shall be, as between me and you,' he said, 'now that the matter is settled'; and with that he advanced to kiss her hands. But she leant forward and, presenting her mouth instead of her hands, she kissed him. Theagenes then departed without having kissed her in return. He took the next opportunity of relating everything to Chariclea, when she also felt some jealousy over one part of what she heard. He went on to explain the purpose of his obnoxious promise, and how much he achieved by it at a single stroke. 'Your marriage with Achaemenes', he said, 'has been scared off, and a pretext has been devised to balk the desire of Arsace for the present. Best of all, it is likely that Achaemenes will raise a mighty commotion in his annoyance at having his hopes frustrated, and in his resentment of my being favoured by Arsace at his expense. He will come to know the whole truth through his mother's disclosures: I purposely took care to have her present at our conversation, because I wished it to be reported to Achaemenes, while I also secured her witness that my interview with Arsace went no further than words. It may suffice a man with no misdeed upon his conscience to count on the kindness of the supernal powers; but it is desirable also that he convince his human associates of his innocence, so as to have open-hearted converse with them in his passage through this mortal life.' He further pointed out that it was to be anticipated for certain that Achaemenes would even plot against Arsace, being a man of servile condition—for in general the subordinate was inimical to the master—and suffering injury as the victim of a broken oath, and being a lover also who found that others had been preferred to himself. Privy to the most depraved and criminal practices, he had no need of any fabrication for the furtherance of his design, such as many a man commonly made bold to use under the smart of injury, but found in the plain facts a ready means for his revenge.

Theagenes serves the wine at Arsace's table, and Achaemenes is prevented from marrying Chariclea.

(27) By these and many other such observations Theagenes succeeded in restoring some degree of confidence in Chariclea's mind. On the next day he was taken by Achaemenes to begin his service at table, as had been directed by Arsace. She had sent him some costly Persian clothing, in which he now attired himself; and he also adorned his person, half willing and half unwilling, with gold torques and necklaces set with gems. When Achaemenes tried to give him some practical guidance in the duties of the wine-servers, Theagenes went quickly to one of the tripods that held the drinking-cups, took up a vessel of great price and said: 'I need no teachers; of my self-taught knowledge I will attend on Madam, without making a foppery of such simple services. You, my good sir, are compelled by your condition to be skilled in them, but the promptings of my nature and the occasion tell me how they are to be performed.' So saying he mixed a delectable draught for Arsace and bore it to

her, moving with graceful ease and holding the vessel with his finger-tips. This drink then excited her more wildly than ever: as she quaffed it she fixed her gaze intently on Theagenes, and imbibed a larger draught of love than of liquor. Instead of draining the cup, she designedly left a little wine within it as an artful toast to Theagenes.' [1] Achaemenes, seated opposite to her, felt the wound thus inflicted on himself, and was filled with mingled wrath and jealousy, so that Arsace herself observed his grim look and his mutterings under his breath to the company. When the party began to break up Theagenes said to her: 'The first favour that I beg, mistress, is that you bid me dress in this costume only for the time of my attendance.' Arsace signed her assent, and after changing into his ordinary clothes he went away. With him went Achaemenes, who heaped reproaches on him for his indiscreet behaviour and his puerile forwardness, which for that first time Madam had overlooked in a foreigner of no experience; but, if he persisted in such presumption, he would be sorry for it. He added that he was giving Theagenes this advice as a friend, but especially because in a short time he was to become his kinsman as the husband of his sister, in accordance with the promise given by Madam. While he kept on talking a great deal more in this strain, Theagenes marched along on his way, seeming not to listen and holding his head bent down, until Cybele met them as she was hastening to put her mistress to bed for her noontide repose. Seeing her son's gloomy looks, she asked him the cause. 'The foreign boy', he replied, 'has been preferred to us. Having crept in here hardly a day ago, he has been appointed a wine-server; he bids us, the stewards of the banquet and the wine-service, go our ways, hands the wine-cup and places himself close to her royal person, thus elbowing us into a position of merely nominal importance. That this fellow should be dignified with superior functions, and participation in even the most confidential business, as a result of our ill-advised silence and collaboration, is not so disastrous, disaster though it be; but it was quite possible for us, assistants and servants in honourable occupations, to be at least exempt from gross insult in the course of such services.

[1] In drinking a health one drank first and then passed the cup to the person toasted.

(28) 'But more on these matters some other time. For the moment, mother, it is my bride, my best and sweetest Chariclea, whom I was wishing to see, in the hope that I might salve the deep wound in my soul with the sight of her.' 'What bride, my child?' said Cybele; 'you seem to me, in your vexation at the most trivial things that affect you, to be blindly unaware of your major grievances. No longer are you to obtain Chariclea in marriage.' 'What is that you say?' he cried; 'am I not worthy to wed a fellow-slave? What is the cause, mother?' 'We are the cause,' she replied, 'with our inordinate kindness and loyalty to Arsace. Esteeming her above our own security, and placing her passion before our preservation, we have assisted her in every fond desire; and then this noble, this brilliant lover of hers, having once found his way into her chamber, has only to be seen to seduce her into violating the oaths sworn to you and betrothing Chariclea to him, while he stoutly alleges that she is not his sister but his bride.' 'And Arsace has given him this promise, mother?' 'She has, dear boy,' replied Cybele, 'in my presence and hearing, and she is to celebrate their wedding in splendid style within the next few days. To you she has promised another to be your spouse.' At this Achaemenes gave a deep groan, and wringing his hands he said: 'I shall make marriage a bitter thing for them all! Only help me to deferment of the wedding for an adequate space of time, and if any should inquire after me, report that I am indisposed by a bad fall somewhere in the country. That fine fellow calls his sister bride, as though one failed to perceive that this is a device aimed solely at ousting me! For if he should embrace her, if he should kiss her as is usual, nay, even if he slept with her, would that be certain proof of her being, not his sister, but his bride? This affair shall be my concern, as it will be also of the oaths and of the gods that have been flouted.'

(29) After he had thus spoken Achaemenes, driven frantic with mingled anger, jealousy, love and frustration—all sufficiently strong to distract any man, let alone a barbarian—took up an idea that crossed his mind and, without any reasoned judgment of it, adopted it on the spur of the moment. When evening had drawn on he contrived to purloin an Armenian horse from the mounts kept in stall for the satrap's use in

processions and public celebrations, and rode off to find Oroondates, who was actively preparing at Great Thebes his campaign
against the Ethiopians; for this he was assembling a mass of
varied war material and all kinds of troops, and he was just
making ready to start on the expedition.

BOOK VIII

The war between Hydaspes, King of Ethiopia, and Oroondates, Persian governor of Egypt, for possession of Philae and the emerald mines. Achaemenes has an interview with Oroondates.

(1) The King of Ethiopia had cunningly circumvented Oroondates, and had gained possession of one of the two prizes of the war: by a sudden advance he had reduced the city of Philae, which was constantly a bone of contention between them. He thus drove Oroondates into the extreme embarrassment of having to launch his expedition in great haste and largely by improvisation. For the city of Philae lies on the Nile, a little above the Lesser Cataracts, and about a hundred furlongs' distance from Syene and Elephantiné. Egyptian exiles had at one time seized and occupied it, thus making it a subject of dispute between Ethiopia and Egypt, since the former set the Cataracts as the boundary of Ethiopia, while the Egyptians claimed that the previous settlement there of exiles from their country gave them possession of the place no less than if it had been taken by force of arms. It changed hands continually, becoming the property of successive victors in surprise attacks, and at this time it was held by a garrison of Egyptians and Persians. The King of Ethiopia dispatched a delegation to Oroondates demanding not only Philae but the emerald mines besides: a long time before, as has been related,[1] he had sent an envoy to make representations, but without avail. He now ordered his envoys to precede him by a few days, and followed after them with a force which he had got ready long before as though for a campaign elsewhere, and had let no one know the purpose of this expedition. When he calculated that his envoys had passed by Philae, and had put the inhabitants and the garrison in a careless mood by a message stating that they

[1] Referring to the envoy who told Charicles the story of Chariclea's exposure and was expelled by Oroondates for presenting the Ethiopian king's demand for the emerald mines, ii. 31–2.

were on an embassy of peace and friendship, he suddenly
appeared and drove out the garrison after it had resisted for two
or three days, but had to yield to superior numbers and the use
of siege engines against the walls. He thus got possession of the
city without injury done to any of the inhabitants. Oroondates,
greatly disconcerted by this action and by full accounts of it from
men who had made their escape, was still further disturbed by
the arrival of Achaemenes, appearing unexpectedly with no
order given for his admission. When he asked whether something
serious had happened to Arsace or his household, Achaemenes
answered that this was so, and that he wished to speak to him in
private. When they had withdrawn to where they were alone, he
gave an account of all that had occurred: how Theagenes, taken
prisoner by Mitranes, had been dispatched to Oroondates for
delivery, at his discretion, as a gift to the Great King, since he
was the sort of young man who was worthy to serve at the royal
court and table; how he was carried off by the Bessans after they
had left Mitranes among the slain; how he had later arrived at
Memphis—and here he inserted the events connected with
Thyamis. Achaemenes ended by recounting the love of Arsace
for Theagenes and his installation in the palace; the kind treatment given to him, and his attendance and cupbearing service;
how up to the present it was probable that no unlawful act had
been committed, as the young man had maintained a resolute
resistance. But it was to be feared that such an act might occur
through forcible coercion of the stranger, or perhaps his weakening under the effect of time, if measures were not quickly taken
to snatch him away forthwith from Memphis and so entirely
eradicate the cause of Arsace's love. It was for these reasons that
he had made haste to slip away unobserved and make this
report; for his loyalty to his master was such that he could not
bear to conceal the injury that was being done to his honour.

(2) When by his account he had filled Oroondates with wrath,
so that the satrap abandoned himself to indignation and thoughts
of vengeance, he sought next to inflame him with a passion for
Chariclea, by adding a description of her in which he exalted
her merits to their real height, and applied all his art to investing
the girl's beauty and grace with a divine charm, such as had
never been seen before nor could ever be seen again. 'Regard as

of little worth compared with her,' he said, 'all your concubines, not merely those at Memphis, but those also who travel in your train'; and much more Achaemenes told him, in the hope that, after having intercourse with Chariclea, Oroondates would, a little later at any rate, grant his request for her as the reward for his information, and would bestow her on him in marriage. The satrap was altogether highly excited now and inflamed, as though entangled in the twofold toils of anger and desire. Without a moment's delay he summoned Bagoas, one of his confidential eunuchs, and dispatched him at the head of fifty horsemen to Memphis, with orders to bring Theagenes and Chariclea to him immediately, wherever Bagoas himself might get hold of them.

On the information given him by Achaemenes, Oroondates sends stern messages to Memphis. Thyamis tries to obtain Theagenes and Chariclea from Arsace, whose passion makes her fiercely resent Theagenes' obduracy.

(3) The man was charged besides with letters, one of which was for Arsace, and was couched in these terms: 'Oroondates to Arsace: send me Theagenes and Chariclea, the brother and sister who are prisoners, and slaves of the King who are to be consigned to the King. Send them willingly, for they will be fetched away, even against your will, and so Achaemenes' information will be credited.' The other letter was for Euphrates, chief of the eunuchs at Memphis, telling him: 'For your disregard of affairs in my house you will be held to account. At this moment hand over the Greek strangers who are prisoners to Bagoas for him to bring to me, whether Arsace is willing or unwilling. Hand them over without fail: otherwise, be it known to you that order has been given that you yourself be brought in fetters to be flayed alive.' Bagoas and his troops set out to execute their commission, with the missives from the satrap bearing his seal, so that the staff at Memphis should be completely convinced of their genuineness, and should readily hand over the young pair. Meanwhile, Oroondates set out on his campaign against the Ethiopians. He had ordered Achaemenes to accompany him, and kept him unawares under secret guard until he should establish the truth of his report.

During these same days affairs at Memphis took the following course. Just after the disappearance of Achaemenes Thyamis, who had now regained the full possession of his prophetic office and held in consequence a leading position in the city, performed the obsequies of Calasiris, and paid to his father all the customary honours during the prescribed number of days.[1] He next bethought him of making a search for Theagenes and Chariclea as soon as he was permitted by the ordinance of the prophets' law to associate with the laity. When by dint of persistent inquiries he learnt of their lodgment in the satrap's palace, he went in hot haste to Arsace and laid claim to the young strangers, stating that on many grounds they were his personal concern, but that his chief reason was that his father Calasiris in his dying words had charged him with the particular guardianship and protection of the pair. He avowed his gratitude to her for having received these young people, foreigners and Greeks though they were, and shown them so much kind attention during the space of those days in which unconsecrated persons were forbidden to frequent the temple; but he considered it his right to regain possession of the wards entrusted to his personal care. 'I wonder', said Arsace, 'that on the one hand you bear witness to our goodness and humanity while on the other you convict us of inhumanity, if we are to be thought unable or unwilling to provide for these strangers and accord them fitting treatment.' 'It is not that,' said Thyamis; 'I know that they will fare more plenteously here than they would with me, if they should choose to stay where they are. But the fact is that, being persons of distinguished family, they have in their life met with such a series of various molestations from Fortune that they are now reduced to mendicancy, and above all things they desire to regain their kin and re-enter their native land. To help them in this aim my father has left me the inheritor of his care; and there are other grounds on which these strangers can rightly claim my friendship.' 'It is well', Arsace said to him, 'that you have done with humble pleading, and put forward the claim of right, which tells the more strongly on my side, since the authority of a lord and master has a firmer hold than that of

---

[1] The number was seven; cf. vii. 11, where the sacristan states that during these days only the officiating priests and ministrants could enter the temple.

an ineffectual guardian.' Surprised at these words, Thyamis asked: 'You, mistress of these persons! How is that?' 'By the law of war,' she replied, 'which declares those taken prisoner to be slaves.'

(4) Then Thyamis, perceiving that she meant to advert to the affair of Mitranes, said: 'But, Arsace, we are now in a state, not of war, but of peace: the one aims to enslave, the other to liberate; one is the pursuit of a tyrant, the other is the decree of a sovereign. The truth about peace and war is to be apprehended, not so much from the accepted meaning of those terms, as from the disposition of the persons employing them. By adding justice to them you would find that you had them better defined. But propriety and advantage do not even enter into the question; for how can it be honourable or profitable for you to appear, and also confess yourself, to be so ardently devoted to a couple of young foreigners?'

(5) At these words Arsace could restrain herself no longer, and her behaviour took a turn which may be seen commonly in lovers; while they believe that their case is unobserved, they blush for it, but when detected they cast away all shame; unnoticed they are quite timid, but discovered they show a bold self-disclosure. Guessing that Thyamis had formed a suspicion of her conduct, she took no account of the prophet and the prophetic distinction, and thrust aside all the modesty of her sex. 'Ah, you people will live to regret what you have done to Mitranes,' she said. 'A time will come when Oroondates will inflict condign punishment on those who murdered him and his party. I will not let these strangers go: for the present they are my slaves, and a little later they will be sent up to my brother, the Great King, in accordance with Persian law. So now bestow your eloquence on vain definitions of justice, propriety and advantage: the possessor of power needs no aid of that kind, for in place of each one of those notions he has his own set purpose. Now, get you gone from our court immediately and willingly, if you would not find yourself made to go, however unwilling.' Thyamis then departed, after calling the gods to witness, and merely protesting that the affair would come to no good in the end; his intention was to divulge it to the citizens and to solicit their support. 'I make no account', said Arsace, 'of your

prophetic function: love recognizes but one prophecy—possession.' She then retired to her chamber. There she sent for
Cybele and consulted with her on the situation. She was now
beginning to suspect the flight of Achaemenes, who was nowhere
to be seen. Cybele, in answer to her insistent inquiries after
Achaemenes, kept inventing one ingenious reason after another,
aimed at inducing her to believe anything rather than the fact
of his visit to Oroondates. But finally she was unable fully to
convince Arsace, for his continued absence was now beginning
to discredit her suggestions. Yet even so Arsace said to her:
'What are we to do, Cybele? How shall I extricate myself from
this contingency? My love, instead of weakening, grows more
intense; the young man is so much fuel for its raging flame. He
is hard and ruthless; he seemed at first to have some kindlier
feeling than he has now, and he sought to console me, at least
for the while, with delusive promises; but now his response is
downright, undisguised refusal. And what disturbs me still more
is that he on his part may have discovered something of what I
suspect regarding Achaemenes, and is thus the more inclined to
shrink from the venture. But Achaemenes above all distresses
me. Has he not gone off to denounce me to Oroondates, or
perhaps to persuade him, or just to make mention of things that
seem not altogether improbable? If only I could see Oroondates!
One caress, a single tear, of his Arsace will be more than he can
withstand. The glances of a woman's, of a helpmate's, eyes have
a magical power of persuading a man. Most awful of all would it
be if, not having had my will of Theagenes, I were forestalled by
the accusation—it might even be by the punishment—of an
intimacy not yet attained, but believed by Oroondates to have
occurred. Go therefore, Cybele, leave no stone unturned or
device untried: you see how things have turned out for me and
have brought me to the very verge, to the decisive turning-point.
Reflect also that, if my case becomes desperate, there is no
possible chance of my sparing others. Why, you will be the first
to share the consequences of your son's enterprises which, I
cannot guess how, you have failed to detect.' To this Cybele
answered: 'Of my son, and my loyalty to you, mistress, you have
formed a false opinion, as you will learn from the facts. You,
who on your part deal so supinely with your love, and show a real

slackness, must not throw the blame on others who are blameless. Unlike a mistress who controls, you make much of this stripling as though you were his slave. At the beginning this was perhaps the right way, when he was thought to be of a tender and tractable disposition; but, as soon as he puts up a resistance to you as his lover, he should feel what it is to have you as his mistress, and by the lash and the rack he should be subdued to your desires. For the nature of young men inclines them to be haughty when they are made much of, but to be submissive when they are coerced. So will this fellow perform, when flagellated, that which he refused when flattered.' [1] 'I believe you are in the right,' said Arsace; 'but how could I bear, ye gods, to behold with my eyes that body of his being lacerated or in any way chastised?' 'There you are again, showing your slackness,' she replied, 'as though it will not be for his good, after some slight tormenting, to choose the wiser course, and for yours, after feeling a little distress, to gain what you have at heart. And you can easily spare your eyes the pain of seeing the thing done: hand him over to Euphrates, with instruction to punish him for some blunder, and so avoid the distressing sight; for hearing affects one less painfully than seeing. Then, if we should see signs of his conversion, you could relent and reprieve him, as having received adequate correction.'

Cruel maltreatment of Theagenes. Cybele accidentally drinks the poisoned wine with which she sought to kill Chariclea.

(6) Arsace was now persuaded; for love that has lost all hope has no mercy on the beloved, and readily turns frustration into vengeance. She sent for the chief eunuch, and ordered him to carry out her resolve. He, naturally infected with the jealousy common among eunuchs, had besides for long been smouldering in spite against Theagenes on account of what he both saw and suspected. He immediately put him in fetters, and oppressed him with starvation and blows in a gloomy cell, where he kept him under lock and key. To Theagenes, who feigned ignorance of

---

[1] A certain similarity in the words 'flagellated' and 'flattered' is intended, as in some other instances, to preserve a marked similarity of words in the Greek.

what he well knew, and made a show of asking the reason of all
this, he made no reply, but each day increased his punishments
to a severity of vengeance beyond what Arsace intended or had
enjoined. He allowed no one to visit the prisoner, except only
Cybele, on particular order given to him. She made frequent
visits, with the pretended purpose of bringing in secret some
additional food, as though she were full of pity for him, and
owing to their late association deeply distressed; but in fact she
came to test Theagenes' state of mind under this treatment, and
to see whether he was giving way and becoming amenable as a
result of his torments. But he played the man more than ever,
and fought still more stoutly against these efforts. With his body
sinking in exhaustion, but his spirit firmly braced in defence of
chastity, he both prided himself and gloried in the Fortune
which, hurtful to him in the extreme, was favouring him with
the happiest of lots, in affording him the means of proving his
faithful attachment to Chariclea. If only she herself could know
of this he would consider it his greatest boon; and he called
aloud on Chariclea as 'his life, his light, his soul'. Cybele,
observing this, and informed though she was of Arsace's desire
that only a mild pressure was to be put on Theagenes, since she
had consigned him, not to destruction, but to compulsion, took
the contrary course of announcing to Euphrates that he was to
increase the young man's punishments. But when she found that
she was achieving nothing, and that even this expedient had
failed to realize her hopes, she perceived the grievous pass to
which she had come. On the one hand she must expect the
undelaying vengeance of Oroondates if he learnt of the affair
from Achaemenes; while on the other Arsace might well strike
first and destroy her for having made game of her mistress in her
advancement of the intrigue. She therefore decided to grapple
with her embarrassments and accomplish some great mischief
by which she would either bring to fruition the desire of Arsace,
and so evade for the present the peril in which she stood with
her, or else abolish the evidences of the whole affair by contriving
the deaths at one swoop of all the persons involved. So she went
to Arsace and said: 'Our labours are of no avail, mistress; that
hard-hearted youth will not give in, but grows ever more
impudent. He has the name of Chariclea continually on his

lips, and comforts himself with his invocations of her, as though
they could relieve his pain. Let us then drop our last anchor, as
they say,[1] and clear from our course her who impedes us. If he
should learn that she was no more, he would probably be converted to our design, having relinquished his desire for her as
hopeless.'

(7) Arsace snatched eagerly at this advice and, her long-
standing jealousy now heightened by annoyance at Cybele's
report, she said: 'You are right; and it is for me now to order the
destruction of that pestilent creature.' 'But who will obey your
order?' asked Cybele. 'All else is within your power; but to take
a life without judgment passed by Persian magistrates is forbidden by the laws. And thus you would be involved in the troublesome business of fabricating charges and accusations against the
girl, with the uncertainty besides of our allegations being believed. But, if you agree, I in my readiness to do and undergo
everything for you will carry out the scheme by means of poison,
and will remove your opponent from your path with a magic
potion.' Arsace approved her proposal and bade her act upon
it. Cybele set out at once, and found Chariclea lamenting and
weeping, utterly abandoned to her grief and to considering how
she could rid herself of her life. For by now she had formed some
notion of what had befallen Theagenes, despite the crafty
beguilements at first tried on her by Cybele and the various
excuses which she invented each time that he failed to appear
for his usual visit to their apartment. 'Wretched girl,' she said,
'will you never cease wasting and exhausting yourself to no
purpose? Theagenes, I tell you, has been released, and will come
here this evening. My mistress, a little irritated by some blunder
of his in his service, ordered him to be locked up; but she
promised to release him today on account of an ancestral festival
which she is about to celebrate, and also in response to my
entreaties. So now arise, pluck up your spirits a little and, for
this occasion at least, take some food with me.' 'How can I
believe you?' said Chariclea. 'Your continual deception of me
undermines all confidence in words that you utter.' To which

---

[1] The meaning is: 'Try our last chance of safety as we drift towards
disaster.' The action in the next phrase seems to be that of hastily clearing a
fairway before moving farther. Heliodorus is not apt to mix metaphors.

Cybele replied: 'I swear by all the gods that your troubles shall all be dispersed this day, and you shall be freed from all anxiety. Only be in less haste to do away with yourself; it is so many days now that you have fasted! Come, be persuaded, and taste the dishes that have been so opportunely provided.' Chariclea complied, though with much hesitation, suspecting as usual some deception, but then again putting her trust in oaths, and gladly welcoming the prospect held out by Cybele; for the heart is apt to believe that which it desires. So they placed themselves at table and partook of the fine fare. The favourite handmaid who waited on them served cups of diluted wine: Cybele signed to her to hand a cup first to Chariclea, and then took one herself and drank after her. Before the old woman had quite drained hers she was seen to grow dizzy: she poured out the few drops of drink that remained, shot a piercing glance at the maid and fell a prey to violent spasms and convulsions.

Chariclea, falsely accused of giving the poison to Cybele which caused her death, is condemned to be burnt, but escapes unhurt from the flames.

(8) Chariclea herself was utterly confounded, and tried to bring her to her senses, while all present were thrown into no less confusion. For the noxious drug, it seemed, working more swiftly than any arrow dipped in deadly venom, and potent enough to kill even a young person in the full vigour of life, had laid hold on a body that in time had become withered, and more swiftly than words could tell had made its way to the more vital parts. The old woman's eyes were aflame; her limbs, after the spasms had passed off, lapsed into immobility, and a sable hue overspread her skin. Yet I conceive that her guileful soul was even more malignant than that baneful potion. Cybele, in fact, even at the moment of death, would not relinquish her villainies, but partly by signs and partly by muttered words she indicated Chariclea as the contriver of the deed. The old dame expired; and at the same instant Chariclea was put in fetters and hurried before Arsace, who asked her whether she was the preparer of the poison, and threatened her, if she declined to avow the truth, with castigation and torture. Then Chariclea surprised the

onlookers with a singular spectacle. Showing no sign of dismay or ignoble temper, she plainly regarded the situation as matter for laughter and jesting. While her clear conscience enabled her to ignore the calumny, she rejoiced that she was to die now that Theagenes was no more, and to be saved the abominable act that she had decided to commit upon herself, since it was to be perpetrated by others. 'Your Highness,' she said, 'if Theagenes is alive I am as guiltless as he is of this murder; but if he has fallen a victim to your pious purposes, you have no need to put me to the torture. Here I am, the poisoner of her who nurtured you and instructed you in exemplary conduct: now slay me out of hand. Nothing could be so pleasing to Theagenes, the loyal contemner of your disloyal designs.'

(9) Infuriated by her words, Arsace ordered her to be smartly cuffed. 'Take the pestilent wretch,' she said, 'fettered as she is, and let her behold her marvellous lover suffering the same treatment, befitting his case. Load her limbs with chains, and deliver her likewise to Euphrates, for him to keep in his custody till tomorrow, when she will be sentenced by the court of Persian magistrates to the punishment of death.' While Chariclea was being taken away, the young girl who had served the wine to Cybele—she was one of the two Ionian maids whom Arsace had at first assigned to the young pair as their personal attendants —whether moved by some kind feeling for Chariclea, derived from familiar association with her, or by divine intent, shed some tears, and moaned, and said: 'Alas, poor lady! She is not to blame.' The bystanders were surprised, and pressed her to explain precisely what she meant by this. She then confessed that it was she who had given the poison to Cybele: she had received it from the old woman herself, with the order to give it to Chariclea; but, either seized with a sudden confusion at the baseness of the proceeding, or else flustered by Cybele's signing to her that she was to hand it first to Chariclea, she had changed over the cups and had presented the one containing the poison to the old woman. She was immediately brought before Arsace, and all present accounted it a godsend that Chariclea was thus cleared of the charge against her; for nobility of character and aspect induces pity in even a barbarous people. The declaration of the handmaid resulted only in Arsace's remarking 'Why, she

is an accomplice, it would seem,' and commanding that she be
fettered and kept under guard for the trial. She then issued an
order for the Persian officers of state, who were empowered to
deliberate on public affairs, judge causes and assess due penalties,
to be convoked for holding the trial on the following day. When
they met the next morning and went into session, Arsace
delivered her accusation. She gave information of the poisoning,
recounting it in every particular: continually she shed tears for
her nurse, in whom she had lost the most precious and affectionate member of her household; and she called on the judges to be
witnesses to this repayment that she had received from the
stranger woman for the welcome that she had given her and the
extreme kindness with which she had treated her. In short, she
couched her accusation in the bitterest terms. Chariclea put
forward nothing in her defence, but again admitted the charge,
and acknowledged that she had administered the poison, adding
that she would gladly have destroyed Arsace also if she had not
been prevented: she even went so far as to abuse Arsace to her
face, and to do everything that she could to provoke the judges
to impose the penalty. For during the night, in the prison, she
had imparted to Theagenes her whole design, and had in turn
been fully informed of his plans. It was agreed between them
that they must voluntarily accept whatever kind of death was
inflicted on them, so that they might be rid once for all of a
desperate existence, endless wandering and an implacably
adverse Fortune. She had then given him what was regarded as
her last fond embrace. Always careful to carry secretly on her
person the necklaces that were exposed with her, she then
fastened them within her clothing about her loins, so as to have
them upon her, in a sort, as her burial ornaments. She admitted
every charge brought against her, and invented others that were
not brought. The judges in consequence made no delay over
their decision, and came very near consigning her to one of the
more savage punishments inflicted in Persia; but affected no
doubt by the sight of her youth and her irresistible beauty, they
condemned her to be burnt to ashes on a pyre. She was immediately seized by the executioners and removed to a little distance
outside the city walls, a herald all the while proclaiming that she
was to be burnt as a poisoner. A large crowd besides followed

after them from the city: some had been eye-witnesses of her being taken along, and others, on hearing the news as it spread swiftly through the town, hurried out to view the spectacle. Arsace also appeared as a spectator on the walls, for it would have been dreadful for her to miss feasting her eyes on Chariclea's punishment.

When the executioners had piled up the pyre to an enormous mass, and when from the flame that they had applied it blazed up brightly, Chariclea begged them, as they dragged her towards it, to allow her a brief delay, promising that she would mount the pyre of her own accord. Then, raising her hands to the quarter of the heavens where the sun sent forth his beams, she cried: 'Sun and Earth and Powers that above and beneath our earth are beholders and avengers of wrongdoing in mankind, ye are witnesses to clear me of the charges brought against me and of my willingness to suffer death on account of the intolerable afflictions laid on me by Fortune. Receive me, therefore, with kindly welcome, and be prompt to punish the accursed, the nefarious, the adulterous Arsace, who doth this to me in order to deprive me of my bridegroom.' As soon as she had spoken, all the people cried out at her declaration, and were for deferring her punishment and holding a second trial: some were getting ready, others had even started, to take action. But she forestalled them by mounting the pyre. She took her stand at its very centre, and remained there for a long time unmoved and unaffected, while the fire surged around her without closing in upon her, and did no harm, but retired wherever she stirred towards it. The flames only served to illuminate her and make her conspicuous; and her beauty shone forth in the bright glare of the blaze, so that she seemed like a bride in a nuptial chamber of fire. She began to dart to one side and another of the pyre, wondering at the strange event, while eagerly seeking her death; but all her attempts were in vain, for the fire each time receded, as though quailing before her advance. The executioners, instead of slackening, increased their efforts, urged on by threatening signs from Arsace. They brought fresh bundles of wood, and piled on reeds from the river, and did their utmost to foment the blaze. But all was of no avail; and the citizens became more and more agitated, conceiving that the girl's deliverance must be wrought by some divine power. 'She is pure, she is guiltless, poor woman!' they cried, and going up close they scared away the fuellers from the pyre. Thyamis led the way, and encouraged the people to come on to the rescue—for he also had come upon the scene, on learning from the mighty outcry what was going forward. They were eager enough to pluck Chariclea from the fire but, not venturing so near it, they urged her to leap out of the blazing pile, since if she could endure to stay within the flames she should have no qualms in deciding to quit them. Seeing and hearing their incitements, and convinced on her own part that it was a god-sent protection that had preserved her, Chariclea thought it best not to appear ungrateful to the higher powers by refusing their benefaction. She leapt forth from the pyre; whereupon the citizens with one voice raised a great shout of mingled joy and amazement, and extolled the mightiness of the gods, while Arsace, losing all control of herself, rushed down from the walls and darted out through a small gate, escorted by a strong guard and the high Persian officers. She seized Chariclea with her own hands and, eyeing the people arrogantly, she said: 'You should be ashamed to attempt the deliverance from punishment of a pestilent woman, a poisoner, who was caught in the very act of committing murder, and has confessed to it! By going to the rescue of a nefarious woman you are thereby revolting against the laws of Persia, the King himself, the satraps, the magistrates and the judges. Doubtless the fact that she has not been consumed by the fire has deluded you into a feeling of pity, and you ascribe this feat to the gods. Will you not come to your senses, and reflect that this only the more plainly proves it a case of poisoning by one who is such an adept in the black arts that she is able to repel the power of fire? Come, all of you, and attend, if you please, at the council meeting to be held tomorrow in public for your satisfaction, when you will witness her confession, and her conviction on the evidence of the accomplices whom I am holding in custody.' With these words she grasped Chariclea tightly by the neck and took her away, giving orders to the bodyguard to keep back the crowd. Some of the people were indignant and inclined to resist, but others drew back, as the suspicion of dark practice was getting a hold on them; and there were some also who were deterred by fear of Arsace and the strong force around her. Chariclea was again handed over to Euphrates, and again she was fettered with chains, but with more this time, and was kept in custody for a second trial and a second punishment.

Chariclea is again fettered and committed to prison, where she confers with Theagenes.

One supreme advantage she found now amid her perils, in having the company of Theagenes and giving him a full account of what had been happening to her. Arsace in fact had devised this very thing from a kind of vengeful derision, supposing that the young pair would be more acutely pained by the sight of each other pent up in the same cell and chained, and harassed with punishments. For she knew that the sufferings of the beloved are more distressing to the lover than his own. But to them it was rather a consolation to be so placed, and they considered it an advantage to be enduring the same sort of distresses: if one of them should be punished more lightly than the other, it was felt to be a defeat and a falling short of a lover's duty. They had besides the chance to converse together, and to advise and encourage one another to sustain with a noble and generous spirit the fortunes that befell them and their struggles to preserve their virtue and their loyalty to each other.

(10) And indeed they had much talk to exchange far into the night, as might be expected of a pair who had given up hope of meeting again after that night was passed, and who sought to make the most that they could of each other's company. At length they came to speculate upon the miracle of the burning pyre. Theagenes attributed its cause to benevolence of the gods, who reprobated the injustice of Arsace's slanders and had compassion on a guiltless woman in no way meriting punishment. But Chariclea seemed to be in some doubt. 'The strange manner of my preservation', she said, 'points of course to some heavenly, some divine beneficence: but our subjection to so many trying misfortunes in close succession, and the manifold and excessive punishments with which we have been tormented, may show that we are pursued by divine displeasure, and are feeling the weight of Heaven's enmity upon us; unless perchance it was

some miraculous act of a deity who meant, while driving us into utter misery, to deliver us from a desperate plight.'

(11) She had hardly ceased uttering these words, and Theagenes was warning her not to speak so rashly, and advising her to observe more reverence and moderation, when she cried out: 'Ye gods, be gracious to us! A strange dream, or perhaps an apparition, has just come to my mind. I saw it last night, and at the time, I know not how, I let it slip from my thoughts: but now it has returned to my memory. My dream was of a poem composed in regular verse, and it was spoken by that divinest of men, Calasiris: either he appeared to me when I had inadvertently fallen asleep, or he came before my eyes in the flesh. The verses, I think, were something of this sort:

> "If thou wear the stone pantarbe,[1] dread not the force of fire,
>   For even the unexpected can the Fates easily achieve."'

A tremor ran through Theagenes, as through one inspired, and so far as his chains permitted he leapt up and exclaimed: 'Ye gods, be gracious to us! I also, through recollection, am revealed a poet. From the same prophet Calasiris, or else from a god appearing in Calasiris' form, I have received an oracle which seemed to say:

> "To the Ethiopian land shalt thou arrive, in company with a maiden,
>   And tomorrow shalt escape from the bonds of Arsace."

I can guess what the oracle portends for me. It seems that "the Ethiopian land" means the subterranean region, and that I shall dwell there with the maiden Persephone, and that the release from bonds is the liberation from this terrestrial body. Now, what do you make of your poem, with that self-contradiction in its verses? For the word "pantarbe" signifies "fearing everything", whereas your message bids you have no fear of the fire.' 'My darling Theagenes,' said Chariclea, 'your habituation with misfortunes has inclined you to conceive and imagine everything in its worst possible aspect; for the human mind is apt to be swayed by the course of events. This prophecy appears to me to give a more favourable intimation than you conclude from it: the

----

[1] See iv. 8.

maiden may well be myself, with whom it is declared that you will set foot on my native land of Ethiopia, after you have escaped from Arsace and the bonds of Arsace. How that is to come about is to us neither clear nor easy to take on trust, but to the gods it is feasible and will be the concern of the beings who have vouchsafed to us these oracles. The prediction regarding me, indeed, you know to have been already fulfilled by their intervention: you see me alive at this moment, after being in utterly desperate straits. I carried upon me then the means of my own salvation, all unawares; but now I seem to understand it. For just as always in the former time I was careful to wear about me the tokens that were exposed with me, I did so especially when the hour of my judgment, which I expected to be my last, was approaching. I chose then to sling them secretly about my loins, so that if I should be saved they should be a means of providing me with the necessaries of life; while, if worse should befall, they should serve as my last adornments at my burial. Now, among these tokens, Theagenes, consisting of costly necklaces and precious stones of India and Ethiopia, there is a ring, presented by my father to my mother on their betrothal. Its bezel is set with a stone called pantarbe, and it bears an inscription in certain sacred characters which, we may believe, is instinct with a celestial sanctity and thus, I imagine, convers on the stone a certain power of repelling fire, and of keeping its wearers unscathed in conflagrations. This it was, most likely, that wrought my deliverance, under divine Providence. This inference and this belief I draw from the admonitions of the divinely inspired Calasiris,[1] who ofttimes informed me that this power was stated and explained in the lettering embroidered on the swathe exposed with me and now wound about my loins.' 'Your surmise is probable, and indeed is true,' said Theagenes; 'it fits so very well with the succour that you received. But from tomorrow's perils what other kind of pantarbe will deliver you? For this one does not promise immortality as well, worse luck, as immunity from burning; while the accursed Arsace, we can guess, is even now devising some other, and more exquisite, form of punishment. Would that she might condemn us both to die together, at the same moment! I should regard that, not as

death, but as a respite from all these troubles.' 'Take heart,' said
Chariclea; 'we have another pantarbe, in that prophecy. Let us
rely upon the gods; then we shall have the greater joy in our
salvation, and amid our sufferings, if they must come, a purer
spirit.'

The messengers from Oroondates arrive at Memphis.

(12) Thus they speculated on their fate, now lamenting and
each professing to feel the greater pain and anguish for the other,
now making their last requests of one another, and swearing by
the gods and their present fortunes to be faithful to their mutual
love until death; and so they passed those hours. Bagoas and his
troop of fifty horsemen arrived at Memphis while the night was
still quite dark and the whole city was fast asleep. They quietly
roused the gatekeepers, stated who they were and were recognized; they then proceeded swiftly and noiselessly to the satrap's
palace. There Bagoas posted his horsemen all round the palace,
so that if he met with any opposition they should be at hand to
assist him. He admitted himself by a postern gate known to only
a few persons, after forcing open its weakly fastened doors. He
gave his name to the porter and ordered him to be silent; he then
hastened to find Euphrates, aided by his practical knowledge of
the building, and also by a faint glimmer of moonlight. He found
the man in his bed and roused him from sleep. In consternation
Euphrates cried out: 'Who is there?' The other quieted him,
saying: 'It is I, Bagoas; order a light to be brought.' Euphrates
summoned a page-boy who was in waiting, and ordered him to
light a lamp without awakening the others. The boy came in,
set the lamp on its stand and withdrew. 'What is it?' Euphrates
asked; 'what message of fresh trouble does your sudden, unexpected appearance bring me?' 'Not a case for much talk,' said
Bagoas; 'only take this letter and read it: but before you do so
recognize the device on the seal, and be assured that this command comes from Oroondates. Act upon his injunctions, availing
yourself of the night time and swiftness as your confederates in
avoiding detection. The question whether it would be prudent
to deliver first to Arsace the missive addressed to her you must
decide for yourself.'

(13) Euphrates received the letters from him, and after reading them both he said: 'Arsace will bewail herself, especially as just now her condition is desperate: a kind of fever, suggesting a divine visitation, seized her yesterday; an extreme heat spread through her and still grips her, allowing scant hope of her survival. I for one would not have handed her this letter even if she had been quite well; for she would rather have died first, and destroyed us with herself, than have consented to give up these young people. Now you, let me tell you, have arrived most opportunely. Take charge of these strangers, fetch them away, and assist them with all the zeal that you can muster. Have pity on them without reserve: wretched unfortunates, they have suffered countless outrages and castigations, by no wish of mine, but on orders given to me by Arsace. In any case they seem to be of good family and, as I can tell from my observation of their behaviour, are perfectly well-conducted persons.' So saying he led him to the prison. When Bagoas saw the young pair, fettered and much wasted though they were by the tortures inflicted on them, he was astonished alike at their stature and their beauty. They, supposing that this was the end, and that Bagoas had come with others in the small hours to take them off for their last breath of life, were for a moment dismayed; then, recovering themselves, they clearly showed to those present by their cheerful and unstrained looks that they felt, not any anxiety, but an increase of joy. Indeed, as Euphrates and his men approached and laid hands on them, and were beginning to release them from the timbers to which their chains were bolted, Theagenes exclaimed: 'Well done, accursed Arsace! She thinks to conceal her nefarious deeds beneath the gloomy shades of night. But the eye of justice is keen to detect and bring to light even the close-kept secrets of criminals. As for you, carry out your orders; and whether it be fire or water or the sword that has been ordained for our execution, indulge us with one and the same death that we shall suffer together.' Chariclea joined with him in making the same request. The eunuchs, moved to tears—for they understood something of what was said—gently led away the young pair, still in chains.

Oroondates' emissary Bagoas takes Theagenes and Chariclea away from Memphis. On their way they learn that Arsace has hanged herself.

(14) On their leaving the palace, Euphrates stayed behind. Then Bagoas and his horsemen relieved the young pair of most of their chains, leaving on them as much as would serve for custody but not for punishment. Each was mounted on a horse, and with the troop guarding them in a ring about them they rode in unremitting haste on their way to Thebes. For the remainder of the night they travelled without a halt, and on the following day they nowhere sat down to rest till about the third hour.[1] The heat of the sun's rays, as it was summer time and in Egypt, became at length unbearable, and they felt languid from lack of sleep; in particular they observed that Chariclea was exhausted by the continuous riding. So they decided to fling themselves down where they were, for recovery of both their own and their horses' breath and for the girl's refreshment. Now the Nile had there an embankment in the form of a headland, at which the river's flow was broken from its direct course, and after being diverted into a semicircular detour, turned about to a course opposite to that taken at its diversion, thus creating in what it enclosed a kind of earthen gulf on the mainland. This tract was rich in spacious meadows, well watered throughout as they were: of its own accord it produced grass in plenty, affording a generous abundance of fodder for flocks and herds, while overhead it was amply shaded with Persian trees, sycamores and other leafy growths that flourish by the Nile. There Bagoas and his troop bivouacked, the trees serving as their tents: he took some food himself, and offered some to Theagenes and Chariclea. At first they refused it, but he forced them to take some; they declared that it was superfluous for those to be fed who had to die so soon. But he disabused them of this belief, assuring them that nothing of the sort was to happen; they were being conducted, he explained, not to their death, but to Oroondates.

(15) The excessive midday heat was now abating, for the sun, no longer standing at the zenith, was sending his rays aslant

[1] i.e. of daylight.

from the occidental quarter. Bagoas and his men were completing
their preparations for proceeding on their journey when a
horseman arrived whose strenuous career, it seemed, had left
him breathless and his horse, which he checked with some
difficulty, streaming with sweat. He went aside with Bagoas,
spoke some words to him and then took his rest. Bagoas stood
for a moment pensive, his mind apparently engrossed by the
news that he had received. 'You strangers,' he said, 'be comforted. Your enemy has paid the penalty: Arsace is dead, having
hanged herself in a strangling noose [1] as soon as she heard of
our departure with you. By her own choice she has forestalled
the death which she was doomed to die; for she could not have
escaped punishment at the hands of Oroondates and of the King,
and must either have been executed or have spent the rest of her
days in the most abject degradation. That is what Euphrates
tells me in the message brought by the man who arrived just
now; so take heart, keep up your spirits, since you on your part
have done no wrong, as I am definitely informed, and you are
quit of the woman who has wronged you.' With these words
Bagoas sought to conciliate them—though faltering in his use
of the Greek tongue and slurring over the words, most of which
he mispronounced—disgusted as he had been by the dissolute
and despotic conduct of Arsace in her lifetime, and also because
he could thus encourage and console the young pair in the hope,
as was true enough, that he would gain great and distinguished
credit with Oroondates if he delivered to him safe and sound a
youth who put into the shade all the other servants of the satrap
and a maiden whose irresistible beauty marked her out to be the
satrap's wife in succession to the departed Arsace. Theagenes
and Chariclea themselves rejoiced when they heard the news:
they acclaimed the might of the gods and of justice, feeling sure
that they had no longer any calamity to fear, even should the
greatest hardships await them, now that their worst enemy was
laid low. So it is that some persons find it pleasant even to perish,
if they can see their enemies perish with them. The shades of
evening were now well advanced, and with their extension came

---

[1] This phrase is an almost exact quotation from Euripides' *Hippolytus*,
802, where the Chorus announces to Theseus that his wife Phaedra, distracted by her futile passion for her stepson Hippolytus, has hanged herself.

a rising breeze that brought some coolness to speed wayfarers on their journey. The party made a start, and rode during that evening and all through the ensuing night and the morning of the next day, making haste to reach Thebes in time to find Oroondates there. Nevertheless, they were disappointed; for on their way they were met by a man from the army who reported that the satrap had set out from Thebes, and that he himself had been dispatched to summon with all speed every soldier and man-at-arms, even detachments posted as town garrisons, and to hurry them away to Syene. The whole country, he said, was filled with alarm, and it was to be feared that the city had been captured, the satrap having arrived too late, and the Ethiopian forces having pressed on faster than news of them could travel. Bagoas thereupon turned aside from Thebes and marched towards Syene.

Theagenes and Chariclea are captured near Syene by a body of Ethiopian troops.

(16) As he was drawing near to this place he fell into an ambush laid by Ethiopians—a body of well-armed youths who had been sent forward to act as scouts and establish by investigation whether the route was secure for the main army. But owing to the night and their ignorance of the locality they lost their way at a point where they had got as far ahead of their comrades as was advisable. They crept into a thicket by the river and kept watch there, holding the thicket as a strong-point which would be at once a protection for themselves and a trap for the enemy. When day was just dawning they espied Bagoas and his horsemen passing by: on discovering that they were but few in number they allowed them to proceed for a little distance, and having ascertained that no other troops were following on, they suddenly emerged with loud cries from the swamp and fell upon them. Bagoas and his company of horsemen were utterly scared by the surprise of this outcry. They inferred from the colour of their assailants that they were Ethiopians, and saw that their numbers were overwhelming; for they were light-armed troops, amounting to a thousand, who had been dispatched on scouting duty. Without waiting to observe them precisely the Persians

beat a retreat, moving less hurriedly at first than they might, that their departure should not have the appearance of a rout. The Ethiopians followed in pursuit, sending on in advance all the Troglodytes in their force to the number of two hundred. The Troglodytes [1] are a section of the Ethiopian people leading a nomad life in lands bordering on those of the Arabs. They excel in swiftness of foot, both by their nature and by training from childhood: they have never at any stage been schooled in bearing heavy arms, but by skirmishing with slings in battle they either strike a sharp blow at their adversaries or, perceiving them to be in superior strength, evade them by flight. The enemy at once abandon pursuit of them, knowing their bird-like fleetness of motion and their skill in creeping into narrow-mouthed holes and secret clefts in the rocks. So it was on this occasion: on foot they outdistanced the horsemen, and they succeeded in wounding some of them by using their slings; but when counter-attacked they made no stand, running back helter-skelter to their comrades whom they had left on the march a long way behind them. The Persians, observing this, and despising the small number of attackers, made bold to counter-attack. They beat off for a little space the men who pressed upon them, and continued their retreat in haste, urging their horses with the spur, giving them the rein, and exerting all the strength and speed of which they were capable. The whole body of them made their escape by keeping close to a bend in the Nile where it formed a kind of promontory and they were screened from the enemy's sight by the projection of the embankment; except that Bagoas was captured after a stumble of his horse had given him a fall and caused an injury to his leg which put him out of action; and Theagenes and Chariclea were also taken, partly because they had not the heart to leave Bagoas in the lurch when he had shown himself to be a man of such kindly disposition towards them as gave them good hopes of him. They had accordingly dismounted to stand by him when they could probably have made their escape. But their chief reason was their willingness to give themselves up; for Theagenes had told Chariclea that his dream was then being realized, and that these Ethiopians were

---

[1] The name means literally 'creepers into holes', and so a kind of 'cave-men'. These people dwelt near the southern shores of the Red Sea.

the people whose country they were destined to enter as prisoners
taken in battle.[1] It was best therefore to surrender and entrust
themselves to an uncertain fortune, rather than to the certain
danger that they must face before Oroondates.

(17) Chariclea's understanding went further than this, in her
submission to the guidance of her Destiny, and she had high
hopes of better things to come: she regarded their assailants as
friends rather than foes, but she expressed nothing of her
thoughts to Theagenes, merely signifying her assent to his
counsel. The Ethiopians, on coming up to them, inferred from
Bagoas' looks that he was a eunuch and a non-combatant and,
seeing that the young pair were unarmed and in chains, and
persons of distinguished beauty and birth, they inquired who
they were, conveying their question through one among them
who was an Egyptian and also spoke the Persian tongue, and
assuming that the young pair would surely comprehend either
one or both of these languages. For scouts and spies, dispatched
to find out what is being said as well as what is being done, have
learnt from expediency to take with them men who can converse
in the languages and accents of local inhabitants and the enemy.
Theagenes, helped alike by the length of his abode among
Egyptians and the brevity of the question, replied that Bagoas
was one of the chief officers of the Persian satrap, but that he and
Chariclea, being Greeks by birth, were previously being taken
along as prisoners of some Persians but had now, by what seemed
a more favourable turn of fortune, passed into the hands of
Ethiopians. These latter then decided to spare their lives and
carry them off as their prisoners. They regarded this as the first
capture made in their hunt, and a grand prize to lay before their
king. For they had, first, that man, the most precious possession
of the satrap—indeed, at the Persian court the eunuch kind are the
eyes and ears of the King, having no children, no family ties, to
seduce them from their faithful allegiance, and their only attachment being to the person who has placed his trust in them—and
they also had this young pair, who would be the handsomest

---

[1] The dream in 11 above foretold only that they would escape from the
bonds of Arsace and come to Ethiopia. Theagenes' present addition, 'as
prisoners taken in battle', is perhaps a natural enlargement, such as is commonly made in noting coincidences or wonderful changes of fortune.

gift that they could bring to adorn their king's service and court. So they took their captives away forthwith, mounting them on horses, one because of his wound, and the others since their chains made it impossible for them otherwise to keep up with the rapid pace of the march. This incident was like the prologue and the prelude of a drama. Strangers, captives in chains, who a little while before had their execution hovering before their eyes, were being not so much carried off as honourably escorted: in the plight of prisoners they were being marched under guard by men who ere long were to be their subjects. This then was their situation.

BOOK IX

Oroondates and his Persian troops are besieged by the Ethiopians in Syene (Assuan), a little below the Lesser Cataracts of the Nile.

(1) Syene by this time was vigorously besieged on every side, and was completely enclosed as with a net, by the Ethiopian forces. For Oroondates, having learnt that the Ethiopians would soon be approaching, since after passing the Cataracts they were making straight for Syene, had succeeded in just outstripping them and swiftly entering the city before them. He had the gates closed and the walls fortified with missiles, arms and machines, and waited on the alert for the issue. The King of Ethiopia, Hydaspes, on receiving at some distance the early intelligence from his scouts that the Persians were about to make their entrance into Syene, had gone at once in pursuit of them with the aim of heading them off by bringing them to battle; but he failed to come up with them in time. He proceeded to launch his forces against the city. Ranging his army all round the walls, he laid siege to the place with numbers which at the mere sight of them seemed irresistible, as countless thousands of men, together with their arms and animals, thronged the Syenean plains. Here the troop of scouts met the King and brought their captives before him. He was delighted with the aspect of the young pair, having immediately a kindly feeling for them as his personal belongings, while unaware of the promptings of his prophetic soul. But still more did he rejoice in the omen of prisoners brought to him in chains. 'Praise be to the gods', he cried, 'for delivering into our hands these enemies in chains as our first spoils of war! These', he said, 'are our first prisoners, and they must be reserved as firstlings of the war for sacrifice in celebration of our victory, according to the traditional custom of the Ethiopians. They are to be kept in custody for a ritual offering to the gods of our country.' He rewarded the scouts with gifts, and sent them with the prisoners to the baggage train. He then appointed a detachment of men who spoke their language to have the special duty of guarding them, giving order that they were

218

to be treated in all respects with the utmost care, supplied with plenty of good food and kept unsullied by any pollution; and their sustenance was now to be as that of devoted victims. He further commanded that their chains be replaced by others of gold; for the Ethiopians are accustomed to employ gold for all purposes which with other peoples are served by iron.

(2) The guards carried out his orders: by releasing the captives from their first chains they kindled in them a hope of freedom; but they brought them no advantage, only fettering them again with links of gold. At this moment Theagenes was moved to laughter and said: 'Ha ha, what a splendid change! See the grand generosity of Fortune towards us! We exchange iron for gold[1] and, growing rich in captivity, gain value as prisoners.' Chariclea herself smiled, at the same time seeking to alter Theagenes' mood by a heartening reminder of the predictions received from the gods, and by the soothing charm of brighter hopes. Hydaspes then launched an attack on Syene, expecting that the first sound of the battle-cry before the walls would place the city at once in his grasp. But he was in a short time repelled by the defenders, who in action put up a gallant resistance, and in speech assailed him with abusive and exasperating taunts. Angered, therefore, at finding that they had resolved from the first to show a defiant front rather than consent to an immediate surrender, he decided against wearing out his army with the tedium of a siege or trying the effect of siege-engines, which might bring down some of the defenders but would probably allow others of them to escape. He preferred to reduce the place by such a mighty and overwhelming operation as would ensure its complete and summary devastation.

(3) He accordingly went to work on the following plan. He divided the circuit of the walls into sections of sixty feet, to each of which he assigned ten men. He then ordered a trench to be dug which he made as wide and deep in its dimensions as he could. The digging was done by some of his men, while others removed the soil, and others again heaped it high so as to form an embankment, thus opposing another wall to that which was being besieged. Nobody tried to prevent them or to hinder this circumvallation; none ventured to sally out from the city against

[1] See note to vii. 10, p. 170.

an army of such immense size, and it was plain to all that arrows
shot from the battlements were ineffectual; for Hydaspes had
provided for this by so regulating the space between the two
walls as to keep his labourers out of range. After completing
this work more quickly than words could tell, because of the
vast number of hands hastening it on, he began one of another
kind. He had left an open space in the circuit, of fifty feet in
breadth, without ditch or dike, and from its two terminal points
he led connecting branches of his dike extended to the Nile, and
made each ascend gradually from the lower ground to the upper
and highest level. One might have compared this work to that of
Long Walls: [1] they continued throughout at an even distance of
fifty feet apart, while lengthways they traversed the space
between the Nile and Syene. When the two dikes had been led
up to the river, he opened a breach in the river-bank and conducted the flow of water into the channel formed by the two
branch-dikes. As the water then passed from a superior to an
inferior level, and as it rushed from the enormous breadth of
the Nile into a narrow conduit and was pent in by those artificial
banks, it produced at the breach a loud, indescribable sort of
roar, and along the channel a noise of splashing that was audible
even to persons at the farthest point from it. When they heard
this sound and began also to observe its cause, the people of
Syene became aware of their evil plight, and perceived that the
purpose of the circumvallation was to drown them in a flood.
They were unable to escape from the city, since they were
hemmed in by the dike and the already encroaching water, and
at the same time saw the peril of staying where they were. They
therefore set about taking such measures for their deliverance as
were available to them. First, they caulked the crevices in the
timbers of their gates with lamp-wicks and bitumen; next, they
strengthened their wall by making its base more secure, some
bringing soil, others stones, others wood, and everyone that
chanced to be at hand. No one remained idle; all alike, children,
women and old men, bent to the work, for mortal danger is no
respecter of sex or age. The more able-bodied and those in their

---

[1] Such pairs of Long Walls provided Greek cities situated a few miles
from the sea with a protected avenue leading to them from the seaport. The
most famous pair were those between the Piraeus and Athens.

prime for bearing arms were allotted the task of excavating a narrow conduit underground from the city to the dike raised by the enemy.

(4) And here the work was carried out in the following manner. Near to the wall they sank a well to a depth of about five fathoms which had an extension beneath the foundations. Then by torchlight they turned and scooped out a mine running straight across to the dike. The men in their rear, and others again behind those, received the soil from the men in front and carried it out to a part of the city which had long been occupied by gardens, and there they heaped it into a mound. By making this conduit they wisely provided an outlet by its vacant course for any overflow of water that might come upon them. Yet, for all that, their endeavours were overtaken by disaster. The Nile, flowing now between the long dikes, rushed forcibly into the circular space about the town and flooded it all the way round, thus forming a lagoon between the two lines of walls. Immediately Syene became an island: an inland tract encompassed by water, with the waves of the Nile surging about it. At first, and for some part of the day, the wall held out; but the heavy pressure of the water as it rose higher and higher enabled it to seep low down through the cracks in the soil, which was black and loamy and fissured by the summer heats, and so it could make its way under the foundations of the wall. Then the groundwork yielded beneath the heavy weight above and, in parts where it became loose and subsided, the wall began to sink, and by its tottering clearly indicated its dangerous state. The battlements were swaying this way and that, and the defenders were being tossed about by their oscillation.

(5) As evening began to draw in one part of the wall between two towers collapsed, though not so much as to fall below the level of the lagoon or to let in the water; but, standing about five ells higher, it still threatened to become at any moment a prey to the inundation. This danger caused a confused cry of lamentation to be sent up throughout the city, loud enough to be heard by the enemy. Raising their hands to heaven, the people made great outcry to their last remaining hope—the saviour gods—and besought Oroondates to send envoys to treat with Hydaspes. To this he consented, becoming now in his own despite a

bond-slave of Fortune; but, blockaded as he was by the water, he saw no possible means of sending anyone through to the enemy. Yet, at the dictate of necessity, he conceived a plan. He wrote his proposal in a letter which he attached to a stone and, using a sling to dispatch his parleying, launched his appeal as a missile over the flood. But in this he had no success, for the projectile failed to achieve the necessary distance, and fell futile into the water. Again he wrote a letter in the same terms and launched it forth, and again he failed; and though all the archers and slingers vied with one another in efforts to attain the range, like men striving to hit a mark for their very lives, all were equally at fault. At last, stretching out their hands towards the enemy, who were standing upon the dikes to view the spectacle of their distress, the people sought by piteous gestures to express what they could of the purport of their missiles—now reaching out with their palms upturned in supplication, and now bringing their hands round behind their backs, as if chained, to show a willing acceptance of slavery. Hydaspes understood that they were suing for their salvation, and he was prepared to grant it; for an enemy who submits induces good-hearted men to deal humanely. But for the moment he was not able to agree, thinking it well to test with more certainty the temper of his opponents. He had in readiness some river ferry-boats which he had arranged to be floated from the Nile on the flood of his canal and which, after they had drifted within his circumvallation, he was keeping moored there. Of these he selected ten new-built boats, manned them with archers and heavy-armed men and, having instructed them in what they were to say, sent them off to the Persians. They crossed over in battle order, so that if any surprise action were taken by the men on the walls they should be prepared to counter it. The spectacle was indeed a strange one: a vessel making a passage from one wall to another; a sailor voyaging over an inland tract; and a ferry-boat travelling over arable ground. War, ever productive of the new and strange, was then particularly and most unusually producing a marvellous event, in thus engaging marines in a conflict with wall defenders, and arming land troops against lake forces.

For when the men in the city saw the boats, with their crews fully armed, making for the ruined section of the wall, they were panic-stricken, being filled now with abject terror by the perils that beset them; and they imagined those to be hostile who came in fact as their saviours, since everything is suspect and fearful to a man in the grip of imminent danger. So they began to fight at long range, launching missiles and shooting arrows; for even men despairing of their lives regard as a gain each moment that passes in deferment of their deaths. They sent their shafts, not in order to wound, but with the object merely of checking the advance of the boats. The Ethiopians sent off volleys in return: shooting with more effective aim, as not yet understanding the Persians' intentions, they transfixed two or three men, and then some more, so that a few, stung by their sudden and unexpected wounding, hurled themselves headlong from the walls into the water outside. And the fighting might have raged with greater heat between the Persians, who were sparing the oncomers and only trying to stop them in their course, and the Ethiopians, who were angrily defending themselves, had not a man of eminence in Syene, already advanced in years, come among the men on the walls and said: 'You crack-brained people, distracted by your sore straits! These men, whom till now we were so persistently entreating and begging to help us, are we going to repulse them, when beyond all hope they are arriving? If they come to us as friends, with a message of peace, they will be our saviours; and if their design is hostile it will be easy enough, even if they effect a landing, to overcome them. And what shall we gain by destroying them when such a vast cloud of others on land and on water encircles our city? No, let us receive them and be fully apprised of their intentions.' Everybody commended his advice, which was approved by the satrap also. They left the ruinous breach, and stationed themselves at each side of it on the wall; then they grounded arms and kept quiet.

(6) When the defenders had evacuated that open space between two towers, and the people signalled by waving white sheets that a landing was permitted, the Ethiopians drew near. From their boats, as though in a public assembly, they spoke thus to their audience of the besieged: 'Persians and Syeneans here present, Hydaspes, King of the Ethiopians in the East and in the West, and now also of you, knows how to wreak havoc on his enemies, but is of his nature disposed to have pity on

suppliants, adjudging the one course to a manly spirit, and the other to humane feeling, and assigning the former to the soldier in action, the latter to his personal decision. Holding now your existence in the balance of his absolute will, he grants to you, as declared suppliants, relief from the peril, so evident to all and unquestionable, which war has brought upon you. As to the conditions on which you would be only too glad to escape from your predicament, he lays down none, but leaves the choice of them to you. For he is not tyrannical in victory, but so regulates the lot of men as not to incur divine resentment.' The Syeneans replied that they yielded themselves, their children and their wives to Hydaspes, to be dealt with as he pleased, and handed over their city to him, if it should survive, though at that moment labouring desperately in the storm, unless some timely intervention of the gods, or of Hydaspes, should deliver it. Oroondates then said that he would renounce the grounds and the prizes of the war, and would surrender the city of Philae and the emerald mines; but for himself he claimed immunity from any compulsion to yield up either himself or his soldiers. If Hydaspes wished to show himself entirely humane, he should allow them, if they refrained from doing any injury or taking any hostile action, to depart to Elephantiné.[1] For he might as well perish at once as accept a seeming survival and then be convicted before the Persian King of the base surrender of his army. Nay, he would fare much worse; for the death now to be suffered by him was likely to be the simple, customary one, whereas that later one would be devised with inventions of extreme cruelty and exquisite forms of torment.

(7) To this proposal Oroondates added a request that two Persians be taken on board the boats with the professed purpose of going to Elephantiné, and he promised that if the people there agreed to submit to servitude, he on his part would hesitate no longer. The envoys received this proposal and returned, taking with them the two Persians, and reported the whole of the parley to Hydaspes. He laughed in scorn, and strongly reprehended the fatuity of Oroondates, a man who discussed terms on a basis of equality when the prospect of his living or dying depended entirely on another and not on himself. 'It

[1] A garrison town in an island oasis of the Nile near Syene.

would be absurd', he said, 'to let the folly of one man bring destruction upon so many.' He then gave permission for Oroondates' messengers to proceed to Elephantiné, since he cared not a whit if they should advise its citizens to resist. To one section of his own troops he assigned the task of blocking up the breach in the Nile bank, and to another that of opening a new breach in his dike, so that by the stoppage of the influx of water and by the drainage of the lagoon water through this outlet the ground about Syene might be quickly reclaimed and made dry enough to be passable on foot. Hardly had they started on their appointed tasks when they had to defer their completion to the morrow, because evening, and then night, closed in upon them shortly after the issue of these orders.

(8) The people in the city were not letting slip any practicable means of salvation available to them, never despairing of the possibility of some quite unexpected deliverance. The men who were digging the subterranean tunnel seemed now to be nearing the dike, on calculation of the distance from wall to dike, as it appeared to the eye and by measurement of the length of their sap with a line. Others were re-erecting the ruined section of the wall, working by lantern light; their building was easily done, since the stones in falling had rolled to the inner side. They considered themselves to be in safety for the time, but not even then did they remain free from alarm. About midnight something happened at that part of the dike where in the evening the Ethiopians had set about cutting their new outlet. Either the soil at that point had been heaped up loosely without being beaten down, so that the under part had become soaked and had given way, or the sappers had also caused that same part to subside into the void that they were creating; or else the new cutting of no great depth, by which the workers had formed a certain depression, had enabled the water, as its level rose during the night, to make its way and overflow, and then, once a passage for it was opened through the breach, insensibly to deepen its course; or again, one might ascribe what happened to divine assistance. Suddenly the dike broke asunder. So great was the resounding rumble which resulted, filling the minds of the hearers with terror, that with no knowledge of what had occurred the Ethiopians and also the Syeneans themselves imagined that

the greater part of the walls and of the city had collapsed. The besiegers, who were not in any danger, remained quietly in their bivouacs, waiting to learn the truth of the matter in the morning; while the besieged ran out to man the whole circuit of the walls, each perceiving his particular part to be intact, and everyone supposing the blow to have fallen at some other point; until daylight came upon the scene and dispersed the fog of terrors that enveloped them. The breach was then revealed, and the water was seen to have suddenly receded. For already the Ethiopians were blocking up the opening through which their channel was fed, by letting down rafts of planks fastened together and strengthened outside with stout logs and consolidated with earth and brushwood: these were laid in position by many thousands of men, some working on the river bank and some on boats. So the water receded; but yet it was not possible for either of the opposing forces to pass across to meet the other. For the ground was all covered with a deep slime: the surface appeared to have dried, but beneath it was spread a liquid mass of mud which lay in wait to engulf both horse and man in stepping upon it.

(9) They continued thus for the space of two or three days. The Syeneans had opened their gates, and the Ethiopians had laid aside their arms, while both sides indicated their peaceful intentions. It was a truce made without actual parley: neither side was any longer concerned to keep watch on the other; furthermore, the citizens had already given themselves up to merrymaking. For just at that time the Nile festival happened to be held, the greatest one in Egypt: it is celebrated round about the summer solstice, when the rise in the river begins to appear, and it is observed by the Egyptians more fervently than any other festival. This is because they deify the Nile, and regard him as the greatest of their divinities. They proudly aver that this river acts in emulation of the heavens, since independently of cloud packs and rainfall from the sky it irrigates their tilth, each year regularly watering the soil; so say the common folk. The things that they reverence as their deities are these: they account the conjunction of the moist and the dry essences to be the principal cause of human existence and life, and they say that the being and manifestation of the other elements are contingent on these, and that whereas the Nile represents moisture their land stands

for dryness. So much for what is given out to the public. But to the initiated authority pronounces that the earth is Isis and the Nile Osiris, bestowing these names on material things. Thus the goddess [1] longs for the god [2] in his absence, and rejoices in his union with her; when he disappears she weeps again and detests Typhon [3] as a hostile power. I conceive that men versed in natural science and theology do not expose to laymen the deeper meanings that lie hidden within these tenets; they merely charm the people into a belief presented in the guise of a myth, but indoctrinate the true initiates more luminously within the sanctuary by the light of the flaming torch of reality.

(10) Thus far may our account of this matter meet with divine approval; but the deeper secrets of the mysteries must be paid the respect of strict silence, and we now proceed with the story of the events at Syene. The festival of the Nile, then, had come on, and the inhabitants were engaged in sacrifices and ceremonies, their bodies fatigued by perils facing them on every side, but their souls not unmindful of performing, so far as their situation allowed, their pious duties towards the deity. Oroondates, however, seizing his opportunity at midnight, when the Syeneans had betaken themselves to a deep slumber consequent upon their feasting, marched his army out of the town. He had previously informed his Persians in secret of the appointed hour and gate at which they were to make their departure: each company commander had instruction to leave horses and beasts of burden where they were, so as to avoid encumbering his movements or causing a disturbance which might lead to their discovery; the men were told to take only their arms with them, and to provide themselves with a beam or a plank of wood.

Oroondates and his Persian troops make their escape in secret from Syene, which is then entirely surrendered to Hydaspes and the Ethiopians.

(11) When they had assembled at the gate to which they had been directed, they flung across the mud the timbers brought

[1] Isis.   [2] Osiris.
[3] Father of the winds, sometimes identified with the whirlwind and its clouds of dust.

along by each company and linked them one to another, the men
behind passing them along to those in front, so that over this sort
of gangway the whole force was enabled to make a quite easy and
rapid crossing. On attaining solid ground Oroondates eluded the
Ethiopians who, instead of taking any precautions or troubling
to set a watch, were sleeping without any apprehension, and he
marched his army at their utmost, breath-taking pace in one long
stretch to Elephantiné. He made his way unhindered into the
city: the two Persians whom he had sent in advance from Syene
were on the look-out each night for his arrival, in accordance
with the order given to them; and when the agreed password was
spoken they immediately threw the gates wide open. As day
began to dawn the Syeneans became aware of their flight. At
first each citizen could no longer find in his own house the
Persians who were billeted on him; then in groups they con-
ferred together; and finally they caught sight of the gangway.
Thus once again they were filled with anguish, feeling themselves
liable this second time to a criminal charge more serious than the
former—that of treachery in return for the signal humanity with
which they had been treated, and of aiding and abetting the
flight of the Persians. They therefore resolved to set forth from
the city in a body and deliver themselves up to the Ethiopians,
attesting with oaths their ignorance of the affair, on the chance
of inducing the besiegers to have mercy on them. So they
assembled all the people of every age, and carrying branches
betokening supplication, lighting candles and torches, and holding before them sacred emblems and images of the gods like
heralds' wands of peace, they passed over the gangway, towards
the Ethiopians. While still at some distance they fell on their
knees in supplication, and in this fixed attitude broke, of one
accord and with one mournful voice, into piteous wailing and
pleading; and the more to move compassion they laid on the
ground before them their infant children, and let them stray at
random, seeking to soften in advance the rancour of the Ethiopians by means of this unsuspected and blameless portion of
their body. The children, in their fright and their ignorance also
of what was going on, were doubtless scared away by the
immense outcry, for they ran off out of reach of their parents
and guardians. They went on in the direction of the enemy, some

crawling, some stumbling in their steps and whimpering as they
went in affecting tones, as though Fortune were enlisting them
for an improvised act of supplication.

(12) Hydaspes, at the sight of all this, supposed that by it the
people meant to reinforce their original supplication with a view
to a full and unreserved admission of defeat; but he sent to ask
what they wanted, and how it was that they came alone, without
the Persians. They gave him an account of everything: the
flight of the Persians, their own innocence of the scheme and
their ancestral celebration; how, occupied with their pious
duties towards the gods, and then overcome by sleep after their
feasting, they had been unaware of what was doubtless a swift
departure; and even had they observed it they were unarmed
and could have done nothing to stop a body of armed men. On
receiving this intelligence Hydaspes suspected—what was the
case—that some insidious ruse would be employed by Oroondates. He summoned the priests alone, prostrated himself before
the images of the gods which they brought along with them to
ensure due respect, and inquired whether they could inform him
more particularly about the Persians—which way they had
marched, on what support they were relying and whom they
were going to attack. The priests replied that they knew nothing
at all of the matter; but they surmised that the Persians had
marched to Elephantiné, as their main army had been assembled
there, and Oroondates relied especially on his armoured cavalry.

(13) Having told him this they besought him to enter the city
as its master, and to lay aside his resentment against them. But
he did not deem it wise to proceed himself into the place for the
present: he sent in, however, two phalanxes of armed men, in
order to test his suspicion of a trap and, if no such danger should
appear, to garrison the city. He then dismissed the Syeneans
with gracious promises, and himself drew up his army in order
of battle, so that he could either receive an onset of the Persians
or else, if they were slow to move, advance against them. The
ranks had not yet been fully formed, when scouts rode up with
news of the approach of the Persians in battle array. For
Oroondates, having arranged for his main army to assemble at
Elephantiné, had been himself obliged, on receiving intelligence
of the unexpected approach of the Ethiopians, to race to Syene

with only a small force. Blockaded there by those earthworks, he had requested, and on giving his parole had been granted, his life by Hydaspes. But he proved to be a man of most untrustworthy character: he arranged to send out two Persians who were to cross the water together with the Ethiopians, pretending that they went to ascertain the inclination of the men in Elephantiné regarding the terms on which they might decide to make their peace with Hydaspes; though in fact the aim was to see if they would rather prepare themselves to do battle as soon as Oroondates might effect his escape. This treacherous plan he proceeded to carry out. Finding that the troops there were fully prepared for action, he led them out forthwith, and advanced without a moment's delay, expecting by his rapid movement to be breaking up the preparations of the enemy.

Oroondates leads an army from Elephantiné to attack Hydaspes at Syene.

(14) And indeed very soon he was visible with his troops in battle array. The brave show of his Persians at once captivated the gaze of all, as their armour, inlaid with silver and gold, flashed across the plain. The sun was just rising and darted his rays upon their front; an indescribable glitter was scattered far and wide as their suits of armour shone resplendent with a lightning all their own. Now, the right wing was formed by the true-born Persians and Medes, with their armoured men in front and the archers close behind, so that, as these wore no full accoutrements, they should the more safely discharge their arrows from the shelter afforded by the shields of the armoured men. The Egyptian, the Libyan and all the foreign contingents were posted in the left wing; they also had supporting forces attached to them, but on their flanks, where javelin-men and slingers had orders to sally out and harry the enemy sideways with their missiles. Oroondates himself took his position in the centre, mounted in splendour on a scythed chariot and escorted by a phalanx on either side to ensure his safety. In front of him he ranged only the armoured cavalry, which gave him especial confidence in boldly facing the hazards of the battle. For in fact it is this brigade of Persians which is always the most formidable

in action; placed in the front line of battle it serves as an unbreakable bulwark.

(15) Their fighting equipment is furnished in this way: a picked man, chosen for his bodily strength, is capped with a helmet which has been compacted and forged in one piece and skilfully fashioned like a mask into the exact shape of a man's face; this protects him entirely from the top of the head to the neck, except where eye-holes allow him to see through it. His right hand is armed with a pike of greater length than a spear, while his left is at liberty to hold the reins. He has a sabre slung at his side, and his corslet extends, not merely over his breast, but also over all the rest of his body. This corslet is constructed thus: plates of bronze and of iron are forged into a square shape measuring a span each way, and are fitted one to another at the edges on each side, so that the plate above overlaps the one below, and laterally one overlaps the next one to it, all forming a continuous surface; and they are held together by means of hooks and loops under the flaps. Thus is produced a kind of scaly tunic which sits close to the body without causing discomfort, and clings all round each limb with its individual casing and allows unhindered movement to each by its contraction and extension. It has sleeves, and descends from neck to knee, with an opening only for the thighs so far as is required for mounting a horse's back. Such a corslet is proof against any missiles, and is a sure defence against all wounds. The greaves reach from above the flat of the foot to the knee, and are joined on to the corslet. The horse is protected by a similar equipment: round his feet greaves are fastened, and his head is tightly bound all about with frontlets. From his back to his belly hangs on either side a housing of plaited strips of iron, serving as armour, but at the same time so pliable as not to impede his more rapid paces. The horse being thus equipped and, as it were, encased, the rider bestrides him, not vaulting of himself into the saddle, but lifted up by others because of his weight. When the moment comes to engage in battle, he gives his horse the rein, applies his spurs, and in full career charges the enemy, to all appearance some man made of iron, or a mobile statue wrought with the hammer. His pike projects with its point thrust far ahead: it is supported by a loop attached to the horse's neck, and has its butt-end suspended by

a strap alongside the horse's haunches; so that it does not recede in the clashes of conflict, but lightens the task of the rider's hand, which only directs the blow. He braces himself and, firmly set so as to increase the gravity of the wound, by his mere impetus transfixes anyone who comes in his way, and may often impale two persons at a single stroke.

(16) Such was the cavalry at the service of the satrap, and thus were the Persian forces disposed with which he advanced to make a frontal attack, always keeping the river in his rear; for, his numbers being much inferior to those of the Ethiopians, he relied on the water to protect him against encirclement. Hydaspes on his part marched to meet him. Facing the Persians and Medes on the right wing he ranged the troops from Meroë—heavy-armed fighters, skilled in close, hand-to-hand combat. To the Troglodytes [1] and the dwellers about the cinnamon-bearing country [2]—light-armed troops, being swift runners and excellent bowmen—he assigned the task of harassing the slingers and javelin-men on the enemy's left. Apprised that the centre of the Persian host vaunted its armoured cavalry, he placed himself and his train of turreted elephants opposite to them, with his heavy-armed Blemmyes [3] and Seres [4] in front, on whom he had enjoined what they should do at the moment of action.

A great battle between the Persians and the Ethiopians at Syene.

(17) Each side raised its standards; the signal for battle was given by the Persians with trumpets, and by the Ethiopians with tambours and drums: Oroondates, after giving a loud shout, set on his phalanxes at the run; but Hydaspes ordered his troops to advance against them, first at a moderate pace, altering it slightly step by step to make sure that the elephants were not left unprotected by the front line, and also that the enemy's cavalry should have the force of its charge already reduced by

[1] See note to viii. 16, p. 215.
[2] Probably some part of Arabia or Ethiopia near the Red Sea: cf. Herod iii. 107–11; Pliny, *N.H.* xii. 19.
[3] A nomad race of Nubia.
[4] A commercial nation to the east of Scythia (in north-west China), especially famous for the production of silk.

the distance between the two armies. As soon as they came within bowshot, and the Blemmyes observed the armoured cavalry stirring on their horses to the charge, they followed the instructions of Hydaspes. Leaving behind them the Seres as a bulwark to protect the elephants, they dashed out at full speed, far in advance of the ranks, and set about the armoured cavalry. The sight of their action gave the beholders an impression of madness, so few were they to make this sudden attack on so much larger numbers of men completely armed. The Persians then with loosened reins accelerated their pace, accounting the hardihood of these men a godsend, and feeling sure of promptly catching them up on their pikes at the first encounter.

(18) Then the Blemmyes, as they were closing in combat with the enemy and were within an ace of being caught on their pikeheads, suddenly at one signal crouched down and crept under the horses with one knee resting on the ground, and with heads and back so bent as barely to avoid being trampled on. But the surprise of their action came as they inflicted injuries with their swords on the horses by stabbing at their bellies as they passed over. Thus no small number of the horsemen fell, because the animals in their anguish took no heed of the bridle and threw their riders. These, as they lay on the ground like logs, the Blemmyes maimed in the thighs, for the Persian armoured cavalryman is unable to move when he is left in this plight without a helping hand. Those whose horses escaped being wounded in the *mêlée* rode on towards the Seres who, while they were only being approached, retired behind the elephants, as though they found in the live beast the refuge of a ridge or a bastion. There a huge slaughter was done upon the cavalry, destroying almost the whole body of them. For the horses, at the unaccustomed sight of the elephants thus suddenly revealed, and in the terror inspired by their great size, either ran back or were jumbled together in confusion, and quickly threw the ranks of their squadrons into disorder. The turret on each elephant was manned by six archers, two shooting from each of its walls except that towards the tail, which alone was left vacant and inactive. So from these battlements, as though on the walls of a citadel, the archers kept up a continual discharge of well-aimed shafts, so dense that the Persians had the sensation of a cloud descending

upon them, especially when the Ethiopians made their enemies' eyes their targets and conducted themselves as men not so much fighting a pitched battle as engaged in a trial of marksmanship. So unerring was their aim that those whom they pierced with their shafts rushed about wildly in the throng with the arrows projecting from their eyes like double flutes. Any who were unable to control their horses in the headlong career of the charge and were perforce carried away into collision with the elephants were, some of them, destroyed thus on the spot, through being tossed and trampled by the elephants, while others were caught by the Seres and the Blemmyes, who sallied out from behind the elephants as from an ambush, and either wounded them with deadly aim or grappled with them and thrust them from their mounts to the ground. Those who escaped made off frustrated, having effected nothing against the elephants; for these beasts go into action with the special protection of iron armour, and besides, they are by nature case-hardened, having a hide in the form of stout scales which extend over the whole surface of their bodies, and are strong enough to break the point of any weapon by their rigid resistance.

(19) As soon as the remnants of the squadron took to flight, the satrap Oroondates, more shamefully than anyone else, abandoned his chariot, and mounting the horse of a Nisaean,[1] fled from the field. These events were unperceived by the Egyptians and Libyans on the left wing, who were prosecuting the fight with the utmost gallantry, and though suffering heavier losses than they inflicted, were bearing up under their ordeal with stubborn determination. The troops from the cinnamon-bearing country, ranged opposite to them, were pressing fiercely upon them and causing them much embarrassment: those troops, when faced with an advance, retreated and, having the great advantage of their superior speed, aimed their arrows backwards and shot their pursuers even while continuing their flight.[2] When their enemies retired they assailed them either by striking at them on their flanks with slings, or by discharging

---

[1] The Nisaean plain, to the south of the Caspian Sea, was noted for its fine breed of horses.

[2] This mode of fighting was known to the Romans as that used particularly by the Parthians.

arrows which, though small in size, were tipped with snake venom and suddenly inflicted an instant death. The men of the cinnamon country use a kind of archery that seems more like a sport than a business. Round their heads they twine a coiled plait in which they fix a circlet of arrows with the feathered ends enclosing their heads and the points projecting outwards like rays. Thus each man in battle has them there ready to his hand, as in a quiver; with an arrogant air and satyr-like prancing he twists and bends his body, crowned with his arrows, and attacks his adversaries quite naked, with shafts that do not have to be pointed with iron. For the spine of a snake is taken and whittled to the length of a cubit, and by sharpening the end to a very fine point a complete arrow, head and all, is produced which probably thus derived its name from the Greek word for bone.[1] For some time the Egyptians maintained their formation, and by locking their shields together withstood the shafts of the archers: they are naturally valorous men who make a trifle of death, not for any material advantage, but rather from an ambition to excel; yet also perhaps from anticipation of the punishment meted out for not standing one's ground.

(20) When, however, they learnt that the armoured cavalry, who were accounted their strongest military arm and hope, had been annihilated; that the satrap had fled away, and that the celebrated armed troops of the Medes and Persians, instead of distinguishing themselves in the battle, had done much less harm to those from Meroë ranged opposite to them than had been done to themselves, and were retreating after the rest, they gave way and in their turn took to headlong flight. Hydaspes, from the watch-tower in which he rode, beheld the now manifest victory; and he sent out heralds to his pursuing troops ordering them to refrain from slaughter and to capture alive any of the foe whom they could seize and bring them in, and above all Oroondates. His order was obeyed. The Ethiopians extended their battalions leftwards, drawing on the ample depth of their ranks to elongate the front at each end; then, wheeling their wings, they compressed the Persian army into an arc, so as to leave the enemy only the single lane to the Nile as an unbarred way of escape.

---

[1] There appears to be no real connection between the words *osteon* (bone) and *oistos* (arrow).

The greater number of them fell into the river, being pushed along by the horses, the scythed chariots and the confused crowding of the whole mass; and they learnt to their cost how adverse to themselves and imprudent was the apparently shrewd manœuvre of the satrap, who from his dread at the outset of their being encircled had in consequence placed them with their backs to the Nile and had unwittingly obstructed his own line of retreat. So he also was captured there. Achaemenes, the son of Cybele, had designed to kill Oroondates offhand in the midst of the tumult, having had intelligence meanwhile of all that had occurred at Memphis, and regretting now the information that he had laid against Arsace, since his means of proving it had perished some time ago; but he failed to deal his man a mortal stroke. However, he was punished on the spot by an Ethiopian who pierced him with an arrow, having recognized the satrap and intending to save his life in accordance with the order given; and he also felt indignant at the criminal attempt of a man who, fleeing before the enemy, should assail his friends and seize on a crisis in their fortunes to pursue what seemed to be a private enmity.

The magnanimous treatment of Oroondates and Syene by the victorious Hydaspes.

(21) So Oroondates was brought by his captor before Hydaspes who, observing that he was at his last gasp and streaming with blood, had its flow checked with a charm applied by his expert practitioners. He was resolved, if he could, to save the satrap's life, and encouraged him with these words: 'Your Excellency, you can count on your safety, so far as the decision rests with me. For it is to one's honour if one conquers one's enemies in prowess while they stand, and in beneficence when they are fallen. But, however, what was your purpose in showing yourself so faithless?' To this the other replied: 'Faithless to you, yet faithful to my master.' Hydaspes then asked him: 'Well, and now that you have been crushed, what punishment do you determine for yourself?' 'That which my King, if he had captured one of your generals,' he said, 'would have inflicted on him for keeping faith with you.' 'Then, to be sure,' said Hydaspes, 'he would

have commended him and sent him on his way with gifts, if yours is a true king and no tyrant, in order to inspire by his praises of foreigners' actions, ambition for similar actions in his own people. But, my good sir, you say that you are faithful; yet you must admit yourself to be stupid, since you took the field in that foolhardy manner against such immense numbers.' 'It was not stupidity, surely,' he replied, 'to have an eye to the mind of my sovereign, which inclines him to go to greater lengths in punishing any act of cowardice in war than in honouring one of courage. So I resolved to go and face the danger, and either to achieve some great, improbable success—some such miracle as a crisis often produces in warfare—or else, should I chance to come out of the struggle alive, to have enough scope left me for justifying my action, on the ground of having done all that it was in my power to do.'

(22) After holding this conversation with him Hydaspes commended him and sent him into Syene with an order to the physicians there to tend him with the greatest possible care. The conqueror then entered the city, together with the flower of his army. All the people, of every age, came out to welcome him; they showered on the troops coronals and flowers of the Nile, and glorified Hydaspes with triumphal hymns of praise. When he had ridden inside the walls, borne on his elephant as on a chariot, he immediately attended to the sacred duty of making thank-offerings to the higher powers. He inquired of the priests concerning the origin of the Nile festival, and whether they had anything to show him in the city that was worthy of admiration or observation. They proceeded to show him the cistern that serves to measure the level of the Nile; it resembles that of Memphis, being constructed of polished ashlar and marked with lines incised at intervals of a cubit. The water of the river percolates into it underground and, as its level reaches the lines, indicates plainly to the inhabitants the augmentations and abatements of the Nile; and, according as so many marks are covered or exposed, they calculate the level of high or low water. They showed him also the indexes of the sundials, which cast no shadow at midday, since in the region of Syene the rays of the sun stand directly overhead at the summer solstice and, by shedding light on the index alike on every side, deprive it of any

incidence of shadow; and so the water also at the bottom of the cistern receives a clear illumination for the same reason. These things held no great surprise of strangeness for Hydaspes, since he knew of similar conditions occurring at Meroë in Ethiopia. They then glorified their festival, highly extolling the Nile, which they entitled Horus,[1] and Life-giver, to whom the whole of Egypt is beholden, the Upper as to its Saviour, and the Lower as to its Father and Creator through his bringing down a fresh silt year by year, whence he derives the name of Nile;[2] he also announces the seasons of the year: the summer by his rising, the autumn by his ebbing, and the spring by the flowers growing by his side, and by the crocodiles laying their eggs. The Nile, they hold, is exactly identical with the year, as is confirmed by his appellation; for the letters of his name, if translated into numerals, will amount to three hundred and sixty-five units, equal to the days in the year.[3] And they further instanced certain plants, flowers and animals which are peculiar to him, and many other attributes besides. 'But all these proud distinctions', said Hydaspes, 'belong not to Egypt but to Ethiopia; for in fact this river, or god according to you, and all the river monsters, are sent along here by Ethiopia, and to her you should rightly give your worship, as being to you the mother of the gods.' 'And so indeed we do worship her', said the priests, 'on many accounts, but especially because she has presented you to us as our saviour and our god.'

(23) Hydaspes advised them to beware of blasphemy in their praises; he then withdrew into his tent and gave the rest of the day to recruiting his strength. He entertained at a banquet the most eminent Ethiopians and the priests of Syene, and granted leave for a like celebration by his troops. The Syeneans supplied the army with numerous herds of oxen, many flocks of sheep, many more of goats, and also droves of pigs, with abundance of wine, partly as gifts and partly as purchases. On the following day, seated aloft in state, Hydaspes distributed among his forces the beasts of burden, the horses and all the material taken as

---

[1] A different version of the myth from that given in 9 above, where the Nile was identified with Osiris, the father of Horus.

[2] The Greek here for 'fresh silt' is *nea ilus*.

[3] $N+e+i+l+o+s = 50+5+10+30+70+200 = 365.$

spoil in the city and in the battle, assigning to each man what was due for his part in the action. When the man who had taken Oroondates prisoner came up: 'Ask what you please,' Hydaspes said to him. 'I have no call to ask for anything,' he replied; 'but if it should agree with your judgment also, I am quite satisfied to keep what I took from Oroondates, and to have saved his life as you commanded.' With that he displayed the sword-belt of the satrap, set with jewels, an article of great value, and of workmanship costing many talents. At this many of the by-standers loudly protested that it was a treasure too fine for an ordinary person, and more suitable for a king. Then Hydaspes smiled and said: 'What could be more kingly than to keep my magnanimity up to the mark of this fellow's cupidity? Besides, the rules of war allow the victor to strip the person of his prisoner; so let him go off with his spoil, which I grant him, and which he could easily have kept in secret, even against my will.'

Theagenes and Chariclea are reserved by Hydaspes as victims for a sacrifice of thanksgiving for his victory.

(24) After him appeared the captors of Theagenes and Chariclea, who said: 'O King, our spoils are not gold nor jewels; those things are of no great price in Ethiopia, where the royal palace has them stored in heaps. But we have brought you a maiden and a youth, brother and sister of Greek birth, who next after yourself surpass all the rest of mankind in stature and beauty; and for this we consider ourselves deserving of your munificent bounty.' 'It is well', said Hydaspes, 'that you have recalled them to my mind. For it was but casually that I had sight of them in that hour of commotion, when you presented them to me. So let someone go and fetch them, and let the rest of the prisoners come here with them.' Immediately they were brought to him, on word given by a runner, who passed outside the walls to the baggage train, ordering the guards to take them with all haste before the King. The young pair asked one of the guards, a half-Greek, where they were being taken this time; he replied that King Hydaspes was reviewing the prisoners. 'Ye gods of salvation!' cried the two together, at the mention of Hydaspes' name; for until that moment they were uncertain whether the

King were he or some other. Then Theagenes said softly to Chariclea: 'Clearly, my dearest, you must tell the King who we are; for mark you, it is Hydaspes, he who, you have so often told me, is your father.' 'Darling,' replied Chariclea, 'great affairs require great prearrangements. A plot, whose beginnings have been laid out by the deity with many complications, must needs be brought to its conclusion through detours of some length; and particularly where a great lapse of time has blurred the story, it is not clarified to advantage at one sharp stroke, above all, when the prime mover in the whole scheme affecting us, she on whom the entire sequence of complication and recognition depends, I mean Persinna, my mother, is missing. That she too is still living, by the will of Heaven, is known to us.' 'Then what if they sacrifice us first,' broke in Theagenes, 'or else make a gift of us as captives, thus cutting off our return to Ethiopia?' 'Not so; quite the contrary,' replied Chariclea. 'You know how you have often heard our guards say that we are being fed as victims for sacrifice to the gods of Meroë; so there is no fear of our being presented or previously put to death, when we have been dedicated to the gods by a vow which it would be criminal for men with a high regard for piety to violate. If, overcome with excess of joy, we should rashly declare the truth about ourselves in the absence of those who could recognize and confirm our story, we might imprudently irritate our hearer and kindle in him a justified anger. He would consider it, very possibly, a piece of insolent mockery, if prisoners consigned to slavery should endeavour by a fictitious and incredible artifice to foist themselves, as in some transformation scene, upon the sovereign as his children.' 'But the tokens of identity,' said Theagenes, 'which I know you carry with you and preserve, will warrant that we are no fiction or fraud.' 'The tokens', said Chariclea, 'are tokens to those who know them or who exposed them with me; but to those who know them not, or cannot recognize them all, they are mere unmeaning keepsakes or, perchance, necklaces that involve their holders in suspicion of theft and brigandage. And if Hydaspes should chance to recognize them in part, who could be found to persuade him that it was Persinna who provided them, and that it was a mother who gave them to her daughter? An indisputable token, Theagenes, resides in the maternal nature, which causes the parent at the first meeting to experience the tender feeling of affection for her offspring, through the impulse of a secret sympathy. So let us not discount this great token which can establish the credit of all the rest.'

(25) While they were thus talking together they had come near to the king, and Bagoas also had been brought there at the same time. When Hydaspes saw them standing before him he started up for a moment from his throne and said: 'Ye gods, be gracious to me!' and then resumed his seat, in deep thought. The officers in attendance asked what it was that troubled him, and he answered: 'I had in mind a fancy that a daughter like this girl was today born to me, and that of a sudden she had come, like her, to the flower of her age: of this dream I made no account, but just now recalled it, because of the resemblance appearing in her at whom I was looking.' His attendants said that it was a kind of imagery in the mind which often prefigured in definite form the things that were to come. He then had less regard to his vision, and asked the young pair who they were and whence they came. Chariclea was silent; Theagenes then stated that they were brother and sister, and Greeks. 'Well done, Greece!' said the King; 'not only does she bring forth persons of fine form and character, but she also provides us with well-bred and auspicious victims for the sacrifices of thanksgiving for our victory. But why in that vision did I not have a son also born to me,' he asked the company with a laugh, 'since this young man, the girl's brother, who was to appear now before me, should surely have been foreshadowed, as you tell me, in my dreams?' He then directed his remarks to Chariclea, and speaking in the Greek tongue, which is held in much respect among the Gymnosophists [1] and the kings of Ethiopia, he said: 'And you, girl, why do you remain silent, making no reply to my inquiry?' 'At the altars of the gods,' she said, 'for which we understand that we are reserved as pious offerings, you will learn who I am and who are my parents.' 'And whereabouts are they to be found?' he asked her. 'They are here present,' she replied, 'and will not fail to be present also at my sacrifice.' Hydaspes smiled again and

[1] Plutarch, *Life of Alexander*, 64, gives an account of Alexander's talk with ten of these 'naked sages' in India.

said: 'Of a truth she is dreaming, this dream-born daughter of mine: she imagines that her parents will be sent over from Greece to the midst of Meroë! Well, let these two be taken and tended with the customary care and liberality, so that they do full honour to our sacrifice. But who is this man beside them, looking so like a eunuch?' One of the servants told him: 'He is in truth a eunuch, Bagoas by name, the most precious possession of Oroondates.' 'He shall go along with them,' said the King, 'not to be sacrificed, but as custodian of one of the victims, this girl whose beauty requires that she be guarded with especial precaution, so that she be kept pure for us until the moment of the sacrifice. The eunuch kind have a certain jealousy ingrained in them; for their appointed office is to debar others from that of which they have been deprived.'

(26) When he had thus spoken he turned to his review of the other prisoners as they passed in line before him, and to examining the quality of each. Those whom Fortune designated from infancy to be slaves he bestowed as gifts, while those of gentle birth he set at liberty. He made a choice of ten youths and as many maidens who were distinguished by their blooming age and beauty, and ordered them to be taken along with Theagenes and Chariclea and reserved for a like purpose. When he had dealt with all the requests submitted by the others, he came finally to Oroondates, who on being summoned was brought forward on a litter. 'I have secured', he said, 'the objects of the campaign, and have placed under my control the primal grounds of our enmity, namely Philae and the emerald mines. I am not moved by the common passion for exploiting a success to the utmost advantage, or using a victory for an immoderate enlargement of dominion: I rather content myself with the frontiers which nature has set for the division between Egypt and Ethiopia from the beginning—the Cataracts. So, having secured that for which I came out, I shall return with reverence for justice. And you, if you survive, shall hold sway as satrap over those whom you governed originally, and shall send this message to the King of the Persians: "Your brother Hydaspes has conquered by his action, but by his judgment he has ceded to you all your property. He solicits your friendship, if you are pleased to give it, as the finest possession known to mankind; while, if you resume

hostilities, he will not decline the challenge. And to the Syeneans I grant release from payment of their prescribed tribute for ten years, and I charge you to do likewise.'''

(27) The effect of this speech was to rouse among those present, both townsfolk and soldiers alike, acclamation and applause that were audible far and wide. Oroondates stretched forth his hands and, crossing his left with his right, bent low in adoration—a form of obeisance not habitually rendered by Persians to any king but their own. Then: 'I aver to all you here present', he said, 'that I do not consider myself to be infringing the usage of my country if I acknowledge as king the man who presents me with my satrapy, or to be transgressing the law when I adore the most law-abiding of mankind; who, with the power to destroy, has the humanity to let live and, in a position to be my lord and master, allows me to continue in my satrapy. In return for all this I undertake, if I am still living, to establish a profound peace and an everlasting friendship between the Ethiopians and the Persians, and to confirm to the Syeneans the edict regarding them. If anything should happen to me, may the gods reward Hydaspes, and the house and kindred of Hydaspes, for his noble treatment of myself.'

BOOK X

The victorious King Hydaspes is welcomed to his capital of Meroë in Ethiopia.

(1) So much then for the relation of events at Syene, a city which had suddenly passed out of a dreadful predicament into a blissful condition, thanks to the rectitude of a single man. Hydaspes, after sending on in advance the greater part of his army, set out himself for Ethiopia, escorted for a very great distance by an acclaiming multitude of all the people of Syene and all the Persians. At first his route kept close to the banks of the Nile and the region bordering on the river; but when he reached the Cataracts, and had sacrificed to the Nile and the deities of the frontiers, he turned off and pursued a more inland course. Arrived at Philae, he rested his army there for about two days, and again sent forward the majority of his troops, who took the prisoners along with them, while he himself remained to strengthen the walls of that city and post a garrison in it. When he marched away he dispatched two picked cavalrymen with orders to go on ahead and change horses at each village or town, so as to perform with all speed their errand of conveying to the people of Meroë his good news of the victory.

(2) To the sages whom they call Gymnosophists, and who are privy councillors and advisers concerned with the King's business, he wrote as follows: 'To the most reverend Council, King Hydaspes: I send you the good news of my victory over the Persians, making no vain boast of my success, since I would not provoke the fitful caprice of Fortune. But your prophetic gift has evinced its accuracy now, as always, and I hasten to salute it with these lines. I therefore invite and adjure you to come to the accustomed place, that by your presence you may enhance in the eyes of the Ethiopian people the sanctity of the sacrifices of thanksgiving for my victory.' To his wife Persinna he wrote: 'This is to let you know that we have conquered and, what is of more moment to you, we are safe and sound. Make preparations

for magnificent processions and sacrifices of thanksgiving for
us, and convoke the sages, giving them also the directions that
we have sent, and hasten them to the meadows fronting the city
which are consecrated to the gods of our fathers—Sun, Moon
and Dionysus.'

(3) On the receipt of these letters Persinna said: 'This must
be the meaning of the dream that I beheld last night. I thought
that I conceived and was at once delivered of a child; it was a
daughter, immediately come to her nubile bloom. The birth
pangs of my dream shadowed forth, it would seem, the ordeals
of the war, and my daughter the victory. Go now and proclaim
the good news throughout the city.' The special messengers
carried out her behest: their heads crowned with lotus of the
Nile, they waved palm branches in their hands as they passed on
horseback through the more important parts of the city, pub-
lishing the victory by the mere guise in which they came. And
Meroë indeed was quickly filled with rejoicing; night and day
each family, street and ward held dances and offered sacrifices in
honour of the gods and decked the temples with garlands. Their
hearts were gladdened not so much by the victory as by the
preservation of Hydaspes, a man who by his rectitude, combined
with his gracious clemency towards his subjects, had instilled
into his people such a love as is felt for a father.

(4) Persinna first sent to the meadows fronting the city herds
of oxen, horses, sheep, gazelles, griffins and every other kind of
beast, in quantity enough to provide the sacrifice of a hecatomb
of each kind, and to furnish besides a feast for the whole population. This done, she went to see the Gymnosophists in the temple
of Pan, where they resided. She handed them the letter from
Hydaspes, and added her own request that they would comply
with the King's appeal to them, and pay herself also the courtesy
of enhancing the festal celebration by their presence. They bade
her wait a little while; they passed into the sanctuary to pray to
the deities according to their practice, and inquire what they
were to do. After a brief interval they returned; then, while the
rest of them kept silence, the president of the council, Sisimithres, said: 'Persinna, we will come, since the gods give us
permission: but the divine voice foretells that the sacrifices will
be attended with some clamour and disturbance, which, however,

will suddenly turn in the end to a good and pleasing issue. For a limb of your body, or a link in the monarchy, has been lost; but Destiny intends to restore at that moment the missing part.' 'Threatened ills of any kind', said Persinna, 'will take on a change for the better if you are present; and when I am informed of the approach of Hydaspes I will give you the word.' 'No need to give us word,' said Sisimithres; 'he will arrive tomorrow morning. A letter will give you news of this in a little while.' And so it fell out. As Persinna was returning and was nearing the palace, a horseman delivered to her a letter from the King advising her that he would arrive on the next day. Heralds immediately made announcement of the message, stating that only those of the male sex were allowed to go and meet him: women were prohibited. For in fact as the sacrifice was to be offered up to the purest and brightest of the gods—Sun and Moon—it was against the accepted rule to let the female sex take part, to the end that the victims should be preserved from even an involuntary defilement. The only woman permitted to attend was the priestess of the Moon, who was Persinna: the king officiated for the Sun and the queen for the Moon, according to the rule and custom of the land. Chariclea also, of course, was to be present at the ceremony, not as a spectator, but as an oblation to the Moon. An uncontrollable impulse then took possession of the city: without waiting for the appointed day the people began that evening to cross over the river Astaborras, some by the pontoon bridge, others in ferry-boats made of reeds which were moored in large numbers at many points along the bank, to provide direct crossings for dwellers at too great a distance from the bridge. These boats move at a high speed owing to their light material and load, since they can carry only a burthen of not more than two or three men. They are made of split reeds, each half of a reed forming a skiff.

(5) Meroë, the capital of Ethiopia, is in the form of a triangular island, round which flow navigable rivers—the Nile, the Astaborras and the Asasobas. One of these, the Nile, where it touches the apex of the triangle, is parted this way and that; the other two rivers, after flowing along either side of the island, rejoin each other to be one with the Nile, to which they yield up their waters and their names. This city is very large, and hence

has the specious appearance of a mainland on an island; for it measures three thousand furlongs in length and a thousand in breadth. It supports various animals of immense size, especially elephants, and is fertile in trees surpassing any of other lands. For besides palms of enormous height bearing succulent dates of extraordinary size, the wheat and barley in the ear stand so tall that anyone mounted on a horse or a camel may sometimes be hidden among them, and the seed sown is multiplied in the harvest by as much as three hundred. The species of reeds growing there has already been mentioned.

(6) So all through that night the people crossed over the river at several points, making haste to meet Hydaspes and welcome him with tributes of praise as though he were a god. While they advanced some way farther on, the Gymnosophists met him a little before he reached the meadow-lands, and there they clasped his hands and saluted him with kisses. After them Persinna greeted him within the portico and precincts of the temple: there they prostrated themselves in adoration of the gods, and offered up their vows of thanksgiving for his victory and his safe return. They then came outside the precincts and gave their attention to the public sacrifice. They had seats of state in the tent that had been specially erected on the plain; it was constructed of four newly cut reeds, one of which stood like a column at each corner of the rectangle, and these supports curved inwards at the top to form a vault, being linked together with palm branches so as to provide a roof over the space below. In a second tent near by were displayed on a lofty plinth statues of the national gods and images of the semi-divine Memnon, Perseus and Andromeda, whom the sovereigns of Ethiopia regard as the founders of their line. On a lower level, in order to have the divinities, as it were, above their heads, the Gymnosophists were seated on a secondary dais. Next to them a phalanx of armoured men was ranged in a ring, leaning on their shields, which were held upright and touching one another for the purpose of pressing back the crowd behind them and keeping the middle space free from any interference with the performance of the sacrifices. Hydaspes first made a brief speech to the people in which, after announcing the victory, he told of the advancement thereby secured for the common weal. He then gave the word

for the officiating priests to begin the sacrifices. Three lofty altars in all had been erected—two standing close together in a separate position, for the Sun and the Moon, and the third in another part by itself, for Dionysus. On this last all sorts of beasts were slaughtered; and I suppose it is because of this god's appeal to the people at large and his gracious favour towards all men that they propitiate him with oblations of every kind and variety. To the other altars they led up, for the Sun a team of four white horses—a natural dedication of the swiftest creature to the swiftest god—and for the Moon an offering of a yoke of oxen, because her nearness to the earth naturally claims for her the consecration of man's fellow-labourers on the land.

The special sacrifice of human victims is demanded by the people.

(7) While these rites were still being performed, a confused, disorderly outcry suddenly arose, such as may come from a huge, promiscuous crowd. 'The traditional ceremonies must be carried out!' was the clamour of the people standing around: 'The customary sacrifice must now be offered for the nation's good; the first-fruits of the war must be presented in oblation to the gods!' Hydaspes understood that they were demanding the human sacrifice which it was their custom to perform, though only on occasions of victory over a foreign enemy, with victims chosen from prisoners that had been taken in the field. He hushed them with a sign of his hand, and indicated by nodding his head that their request would be granted forthwith; and he gave the word for the prisoners already assigned to this purpose to be brought. This was accordingly done, and among them were Theagenes and Chariclea: they had been relieved of their chains and crowned with garlands. They wore a downcast look, as was natural; but Theagenes not so much as the rest, while Chariclea, with a radiant face, was smiling as she kept her gaze fixed so intently on Persinna that she on her part was moved at the sight of her. She heaved a deep sigh and said: 'Husband, what a fine girl you have chosen for the sacrifice! I do not know that I ever saw such beauty. What a noble look in her eyes! What a high spirit in facing her fate! How pitiable, in the fresh

bloom of her age! If it were our fortune to have with us yet the
one and only child that I bore, our unhappily perished daughter,
she would be reckoned to be about the same age as this girl. O
husband, if only it were somehow possible to exempt her, I
should find it a great consolation to have such a girl in my
service! And the poor creature may happen to be a Greek, for
her face is not that of an Egyptian.' 'She is a Greek,' replied
Hydaspes, 'and of parents whom she is just now about to name:
she cannot show them to us—how could she?—though she
promised to do so. However, she cannot be delivered from this
sacrifice: yet I wish that it were possible, because I too am
moved, for some reason, and feel pity for the girl. But, as you
know, the law requires that a male be presented and sacrificed
to the Sun, and a female to the Moon. This girl is the first female
captive brought to me, and she was assigned to this day's
sacrifice; to set her aside would be inexcusable in the eyes of the
people. One thing alone might rescue her: if she should stand
upon the brazier that you know of, and should then be proved
to be not untainted by any intimacy with men; for the law
ordains that she who is brought as an offering to the goddess
shall be pure, as must the victim also that is to be sacrificed to
the Sun; though the law has no such concern in the case of a
sacrifice to Dionysus. Yet it is a question whether it will be
seemly that a girl convicted on the brazier of having had intimacy
with some man should be given a place in your household.'
'Let her be convicted,' said Persinna; 'only let her life be saved!
Captivity, war, long exile from one's native land—these render
such a decision undeserving of blame, especially in her case;
for in her beauty she carries about with her the motive of her
own undoing, if indeed she has undergone anything of the sort.'

(8) While Persinna was yet speaking, her eyes suffused with
tears which she sought to hide from her audience, Hydaspes
ordered the brazier to be brought. The attendants thereupon
collected from the crowd some children of tender age—the only
kind of persons who are able to touch the brazier without taking
harm—and had them carry it out of the temple and set it in the
midst of the assembly. The attendants then bade each of the
prisoners step upon it. As they took their stand in turn, all
immediately had their soles burnt; some could not endure the

first touch of it, however brief. It is constructed of a lattice of gold bars, and is endued with the special power of severely burning whoever is impure or has in some way perjured himself; but it allows those who are innocent to take their stand on it without being hurt. Those prisoners they assigned to Dionysus and other gods, except two or three young women who on mounting the braziers were approved as virgins.

The chastity of both Theagenes and Chariclea is proved by the ordeal of the brazier. The Gymnosophists protest against the human sacrifice.

(9) Then Theagenes, when his turn came to go upon the brazier, was shown to be pure. Everybody marvelled, not merely at his stature and beauty, but especially that a man in the fresh bloom of his age should be without experience of the ways of Aphrodite; and he was held in readiness for the sacrifice to the Sun. 'Fine rewards in Ethiopia', he said softly to Chariclea, 'for those who lead a pure life! Sacrificial slaughter is the prize presented to the chaste! But, dearest one, why do you not declare yourself? For what moment are you still waiting? Till they cut our throats? Speak, I beg you, and disclose the truth about yourself. Perhaps you will save my life also, if you are recognized for what you are, and you then intercede for me. If you fail of that, you will yet for certain escape your own danger: I shall be content, when I have learnt that, to meet my end.' 'The crisis draws near', she said, 'and Fate now holds our future in the balance.' Without waiting for the order of the officials in charge she produced from a wallet which she carried upon her the sacred tunic of Delphi, bespangled with gold-embroidered rays, and put it on. She loosened her hair and, like one possessed, ran forward and leapt upon the brazier. For a long time she stood there unharmed, flashing forth then the light of her beauty in yet greater brightness; observed by all on every side of that high position, and resembling in her attire rather a statue of a deity than a mortal woman. Amazement, in fact, took hold of everyone at once; they all raised a resounding outcry, confused and inarticulate, but eloquent of the wonder and admiration with which they were filled by the scene, and more particularly by the fact

that she could keep unsullied, and manifestly then possessed such superhuman beauty and the perfect bloom of her youth, enhanced as it was by her modest reserve more than by her charms. Yet it gave pain besides to the populace that she showed herself so suitable for the sacrifice and, god-fearing though they were, they still would have rejoiced to see her deliverance procured by means of some contrivance. Greater grief was felt by Persinna, which moved her to say to Hydaspes: 'Poor unfortunate girl! Priding herself for so long, and now so inopportunely, on her virtue, and gaining death in return for earning so fair a fame! Ah, what can be done, husband?' 'It is useless', he replied, 'to pester me thus, and to feel this pity for her who is not to be saved, but because of her extraordinary qualities is reserved for the gods, it would seem, from her earliest days.' He then turned and spoke to the Gymnosophists: 'Most excellent sages,' he said, 'all is now prepared; why do you not begin the rites?' Sisimithres answered him in Greek, so as not to be understood by the crowd: 'Hold your peace: we have incurred up to this moment enough defilement of our sight and hearing. We shall withdraw into the temple, since such an abomination as human sacrifice is both condemned by ourselves and, we believe, unacceptable to the divine nature. And would that it were possible to have sacrifices of all other live creatures prohibited! Heaven, to our thinking, is well satisfied with offerings only of prayers and perfumes. But you must remain here, for a king is at times obliged to comply with even the senseless impulse of a multitude: perform this sacrifice, impious indeed, but unalterably ordained by the long-standing tradition of Ethiopian custom. You will afterwards have need of purifications; though perhaps that need may not arise; for it seems to me that this sacrifice will not come to pass, to judge by sundry signs divinely given, and especially by the light that shines about these strangers, distinguishing them as aided and protected by some higher power.'

(10) With these words he arose, as did the rest of the council also, and was preparing to withdraw with them, when Chariclea leapt down from the brazier and, running to Sisimithres, threw herself down at his knees, despite every effort of the attendants to restrain her, in their belief that her appeal was for a reprieve

from death. 'Excellent sages,' she said, 'stay but a moment: I propose to bring a case for judicial hearing against these sovereign rulers, and you alone, I understand, are the judges of persons in their position. In this trial for my life, be you the arbiters. That I should be slaughtered in sacrifice to the gods is neither possible nor just, as I shall convince you.' They gladly admitted her plea, and said to the King: 'Sire, do you hear the challenge and the allegations of the foreign woman?' Hydaspes laughed and said: 'What sort of suit, and how grounded, can there be betwixt me and her? On what kind of pretext or claim of rights does she take her stand?' Sisimithres then told him: 'Her forthcoming statements will suffice to explain all.' 'Why would not this affair', he said, 'be thought an insult rather than a judgment, if I, a king, should be put on trial by my prisoner?' 'Justice is not overawed by dignities,' replied Sisimithres; 'he alone is king in a court of justice who prevails by having the stronger case.' 'But it is for suits between sovereigns and their countrymen, not foreigners,' he said, 'that the law appoints you to be judges.' 'Just decision', replied Sisimithres, 'is based, for the truly wise, not on one's personal appearance only, but on one's conduct as well.' 'It is obvious', said the King, 'that she can have nothing serious to say, but after the fashion of those who stand in peril of their lives she will give us idle tales, invented to gain time. However, let her speak, since Sisimithres will have it so.'

Chariclea claims immunity from sacrifice, as she is no foreigner, but a daughter of the King himself, and is encouraged by the presence of the Gymnosophist Sisimithres.

(11) Chariclea, besides being cheered by the prospect of relief from her immediate danger, was still more delighted to hear the name of Sisimithres. For it was he who originally found her exposed and took her up, and placed her in the keeping of Charicles, ten years before, when he was sent to the Cataracts on a mission to Oroondates concerning the emerald mines; at that time he was merely one of the order of Gymnosophists, but now he had been appointed president of the council. Chariclea could not recollect the man's appearance, since she was quite young, only seven years of age, when she was parted from him; but she recalled

his name, and was especially delighted with the anticipation of having his advocacy and assistance towards her recognition. Stretching forth her hands to heaven, she cried in resounding tones: 'O Sun, founder of the line of my ancestors, and ye other gods and demigods who are the guiding powers of our family, I call you as witnesses that I shall say nothing that is not true. Be my helpers also in the trial that I have now to enter upon; in it I shall open my plea for the rights that I claim for myself with these words: Are they foreigners, O king, or people of the country, whom the law bids you sacrifice?' 'Foreigners,' he replied. 'Then it is time that you looked about for other victims,' she said, 'for you will find that I am your countrywoman, a native of this land.'

(12) In his surprise at this statement he called it a falsehood. 'You wonder at the lesser things,' she said; 'the greater are yet to come. Not only am I a native of this land; I am also of royal birth, and nearest in the priority of succession.' Again Hydaspes spurned her words as stuff and nonsense. 'Enough now, father,' she said, 'of vilifying your daughter.' The King then began to treat her words, not merely with contempt, but with resentment, taking them as a piece of insolent jesting. 'Sisimithres and the rest of you,' he said, 'do you see the pass to which my forbearance has brought me? To be sure, the girl is completely brainsick, attempting thus to fend off death by her foolhardy inventions. In her desperation she makes an appearance on the scene, as by a stage device, to declare herself my daughter, when never yet, as you know, have I been blessed with the birth of any child, save only once, when I heard at the same moment of one born and lost to me. So let her be taken away, and let her cease contriving to postpone the sacrifice.' 'No one will take me,' cried Chariclea, 'so long as the judges have not ordered it. And you are a party to this present suit, in no position to act as judge. The slaying of foreigners, O King, may be permitted by the law; but to slay your own children is not allowed to you, father, either by law or by nature. That you are a father the gods this day will declare, deny it though you may. Every cause that comes for judgment, O King, admits these two surest proofs—written affidavits and witnesses' affirmations. I shall produce to you evidence of both these kinds that I am your

daughter, by citing as witness, not just a member of the public,
but the judge himself—and no stronger testimony, I conceive,
could a pleader have than what is in the knowledge of the judge,
while for written evidence I present here a narrative of both my
and your fortunes.'

*Hydaspes by various signs is at length convinced of Chariclea's
identity, but doubts whether she ought not to be sacrificed.*

(13) As she spoke these words she drew forth the swathe
which was exposed with her and which she wore about her loins,
unfolded it and handed it to Persinna. At her first glance the
Queen stood dumbfounded and stunned, and for long she kept
gazing by turns on the script in the swathe and on the girl. She
was seized with a fit of trembling and throbbing, and sweated
profusely, from her gladness at the discovery, but also from
bewilderment at the incredible happening of what was beyond all
hope, and from fear lest Hydaspes should feel suspicion and mis-
trust—even, it might be, anger and vengefulness—at these revel-
ations. Hydaspes in consequence, observing for himself her
astonishment and overpowering anguish, said to her: 'Wife, what
means this? What disturbs you so in this writing that she is
showing you?' 'O King,' she replied; 'my lord and husband, I
can speak not a word more; take it and read it; this swathe will
inform you of everything.' She handed it to him, and relapsed
into a sorrowful silence. Hydaspes took it in his hands, and
invited the Gymnosophists to stand by and read it with him. As
he made out the words he was himself filled with wonder, and
was aware besides of the deep amazement of Sisimithres, whose
looks betrayed a multitude of various thoughts passing through
his mind, as he continually turned his gaze on the swathe and
on Chariclea. At length Hydaspes, having learnt of the exposure
and the reason of it, said: 'That a girl was born to me I know;
that she died I was informed at the time by Persinna herself; I
now learn that she was exposed. But who took her up, saved her
life and reared her? Who conveyed her into Egypt, where she
was taken prisoner? And what proof is there, after all, that this
girl here is that same one; that the exposed child has not
perished; and that some person, chancing upon these tokens

of recognition, did not turn his chance discovery to fraudulent use? Some deity perhaps, to make game of us, has furnished the girl with these tokens as a sort of mask and, mocking at our desire for children, would foist upon us a bastard or suppositious succession, overcasting the truth with this swathe as with a cloud.'

(14) In answer to his words Sisimithres said: 'The first matters that you call in question can be cleared up for you. He who took up the exposed child, who reared her in secret, and who brought her to Egypt when you sent me there as your envoy is myself; and that we are forbidden to lie you know from past experience of us. I recognize this swathe: it is inscribed, as you see, with the royal lettering of Ethiopia, thus precluding any question of its production elsewhere; and that the pricking out is the actual handiwork of Persinna you of all people must recognize. But there were other tokens exposed with the girl, which I gave to the man who received her from me, a Greek and, as was evident, a person of excellent character.' 'Those also are preserved,' said Chariclea, displaying the necklaces as she spoke. The sight of these astounded Persinna still more; and when Hydaspes asked her what they were and whether she had any further explanation to make, her only reply was that she recognized them, but that it would be best to examine them within doors. Again Hydaspes appeared to be much disturbed; then Chariclea told him: 'These should be the tokens of recognition for my mother, but this ring is one particular to you'; and she showed the pantarbe. Hydaspes recognized it as his gift to Persinna at their betrothal. 'My dear lady,' he said, 'this token I recognize as mine; but that you who have the use of it are my child, and have not just happened to acquire it, I still am not sure. For, apart from other reasons, your complexion is of a bright fairness foreign to the Ethiopian colour.' Sisimithres then told him: 'White was she taken up whom I myself then took up; and in particular, the period of years tallies with the present age of this girl: between it and her exposure the time amounts in all to about seventeen years. And to me the very glances of her eyes are convincing; I recognize the whole cast of her features, her miraculous beauty—everything apparent in her now corresponding to what she showed at that time.' 'Your words are excellent,

Sisimithres,' said Hydaspes; 'they are more in the style of a most ardent advocate than in that of a judge. But take care that in clearing up one part of the problem you may not be raising up a fresh question: one of such difficulty and gravity that it would be no light matter for my life's partner to clear herself of its import. How could we two Ethiopians have begotten such an unlikely child as a white girl?' Sisimithres looked askance at him, with a smile that had a touch of irony, and said: 'I wonder what has come over you, that you belie your own character by reproaching me now with an advocacy in which I can see nothing base. For I define a genuine judge as the advocate of justice. Why should I not appear as your advocate rather than the girl's? With the gods' aid I prove to you your fatherhood, and this your daughter, whom I saved for you in her swaddling clothes, I cannot desert, now that she is being restored to you in the bloom of her age. Well, hold what opinion you please of us, we take no account of that; for we do not live for complaisance to others, but are content with teaching ourselves to strive after absolute goodness and virtue. However, the solution of the difficulty presented by the girl's colour lies in the message of the swathe. Persinna here acknowledges that she contracted certain shapes or impressions of likeness from looking upon the figure of Andromeda during her union with you. If you still required some further assurance, the original is there before us. Look carefully, and see if Andromeda is not unmistakably manifest in the girl as in the picture.'

(15) The servants were ordered to take down the picture, and they brought it and set it up beside Chariclea. The result was a great burst of applause and clamour from the onlookers, as they explained to one another such fragments as they could gather of what was being said and done, and were struck with an amazement mingled with high delight at the exactness of the resemblance; so true it was that Hydaspes himself could no longer be in doubt, but stood for a long time lost in both joy and wonder. 'One matter still remains,' said Sisimithres; 'the question of the monarchy, of the legitimate succession to the throne and, above all, of the truth itself. Bare your arm, girl: it was discoloured with a black device above the elbow. There is nothing unseemly in laying bare the evidence of your parentage and lineage.' At once

Chariclea bared her left arm, and on it was what seemed like a ring of ebony smirching the ivory of its skin.

(16) Persinna now could no longer contain herself. She started up on a sudden from her throne, and running to the girl embraced her, clung about her weeping and, in the wild transport of her joy, uttered a loud moaning like that of a lowing heifer; for an excess of pleasure will at times produce even wailing, and she came near collapsing with Chariclea on to the ground. Hydaspes was moved with pity at the sight of his wife lamenting, and his mood was swayed to compassion; yet he kept his eyes fixed, as though they were of horn or iron,[1] upon the scene before him, and stood still, fighting down the travail-anguish of his tears: and while his soul tossed on the surges of paternal affection and manly spirit, his judgment was parted in a dissension betwixt these two, being alternately swung over to one and the other as by an ocean swell. He finally gave in to all-conquering Nature: not only was he convinced of his fatherhood but he also proved himself to have all a father's feelings. Persinna now had sunk to the ground with her daughter, and was holding her in a close embrace. In the sight of everyone he raised her up, took Chariclea in his arms and poured forth on her a flood of tears as a libation solemnizing his paternity. Nevertheless he was not to be deflected from the full discharge of his immediate duties. For a moment he paused, and observed how the people were stirred by the same emotions, and were weeping with mingled joy and pity at the dramatic turn that Fortune had given to events; how they sent up a mighty cry to the heavens without hearkening to the heralds' calls for silence, or indicating clearly what they meant with all this uproar. He then, with a wave of his outstretched hand, subdued to a calm the stormy tumult of the people. 'You who are here present,' he said, 'you see and hear how the gods beyond all expectation have declared me to be a father, and how this girl is by many proofs discovered to be my daughter. But so extreme is my affection for you and for my native land that, making light of the succession of my line and the appellation of father, although I was like to obtain all this

---

[1] A clear reminiscence of Homer, *Od.* xix. 209–12, where Odysseus, unrecognized by Penelope, gazes fixedly at her as she laments over his long absence from her.

through her, I am intent for your sake on performing the sacrifice to the gods. For, while I see you weeping and yielding to an impulse of human emotion in your pity for the untimely fate of this girl, and also for the frustration of my hopes for the succession, it is nevertheless necessary, though it be against your will, that I obey our country's law and set the claims of our fatherland above any personal advantage. Whether it is in truth the pleasure of the gods that she should be given to me and at the same time taken away—a blow which I suffered once before at her birth, and which I suffer now on her discovery—this I cannot tell; but I leave it to your consideration. Nor do I know whether those gods, having banished her from her native land to the uttermost ends of the earth, and having miraculously restored her to my arms in the plight of a captive, will welcome an offering of the girl this time as a sacrifice upon their altar. When I saw her as an enemy I did not slay her, and when she became my prisoner I did not maltreat her. Yet now that she is found to be my daughter I will not put off her sacrifice, believing it to be your will also that this oblation shall be made; nor will I give way to a feeling that might perhaps be pardoned in another father, and flinch or resort to entreating your indulgence for an unholy breach of the law in this present case, because of your attaching more weight to nature and the feelings that spring therefrom, and pretending that there is some other way in which the deity may be duly served. Just as you have openly shown your sympathy with me, and the grievous pain that you suffer from my affliction as though it were your own, so in like measure it behoves me to set your interests above mine, and to take little account of my loss of an heir, and as little of the lamenting of my unhappy Persinna here, who finds herself at once a mother for the first time and childless. Cease therefore, if you please, your vain weeping and commiseration of us, and let us proceed to the sacrifice.

'To you, my daughter—for it is now for the first, and the last, time that I address you by that longed-for name—let me say this: in vain are you lovely, in vain have you discovered your parents. A hard fate has made your own country more baneful to you than a foreign land; you have come safely through your sojourn on an alien soil, only to meet destruction on entering

your native land. Do not perturb my heart with wailing,[1] but
now more than ever display that gallant, that royal spirit which is
yours. Follow now the father that begot you; who has not been
able to attire you in your bridal garments, nor has led you to the
nuptial chamber and bed, but adorns you for sacrifice, lights
torches not of the marriage rite but of an altar offering, and
presents this peerless flower of beauty as a sacrificial victim.
And O ye gods, forgive of your grace those words—it may be,
impious words—that I have spoken, overborne by the pain of
having called one my child only to become that child's slayer!'

*Hydaspes bows to the people's demand that Chariclea's life be
spared.*

(17) As he ended this speech he took hold of Clariclea, making
as if to lead her to the altar and the pyre upon it; but smouldering
in his heart was the stronger fire of his grief, and he prayed that
the words which he had speciously addressed to the public
assembly might be of none effect. The great throng of Ethiopians
had been deeply disturbed by his speech; they would not suffer
even the least effort to remove Chariclea, and suddenly cried
out in loud protest: 'Save the girl! Save the blood-royal! Save
her whom the gods have saved! We are grateful: for us the law
has been sufficiently observed; we have acknowledged you to be
our king; acknowledge yourself to be a father. May the gods
look leniently upon the seeming breach of the law: we shall
more truly break it if we set ourselves against their purposes.
Let no one destroy her whose life they have preserved! Father
of our people, be now a father in your home!' And uttering a
multitude of other such cries they ended by making an active
demonstration also against his intention, standing in his way,
and in fact withstanding him, and demanding that the deity be
propitiated by offering up the other victims. Hydaspes not only
willingly but gladly accepted defeat, submitting of his own
accord to this wished-for compulsion. When he saw that the
masses were continuing overlong to revel in repeated clamouring,

[1] A reminiscence of Achilles' words to Phoenix, who tried to persuade him
to lay aside his wrath and help the Acheans to save their ships from being
destroyed by the Trojans. (Homer, *Il.* ix. 612.)

and were somewhat insolently sportive in their chanting of his praises, he allowed them to take their fill of delight and waited for them to settle down in time of themselves to calmness.

(18) He then moved close to Chariclea and said: 'My darling, that you are my daughter has been revealed by the tokens of recognition and testified by the sage Sisimithres and, above all, declared by the gods' benevolence. But who may this man be who has been captured with you and has been reserved as a thanksgiving oblation to the gods for our victory, and is now stationed at the altars in readiness for the sacred rite? How came you to call him your brother,[1] when you were first brought to me at Syene? Surely he will not be discovered to be our son, since you are the one and only child conceived by Persinna.' At this Chariclea blushed, hung her head and answered: 'I lied in calling him my brother; necessity framed the fiction. Who he really is he can tell better than I, for he is a man, and will not be ashamed to explain the truth more boldly than is fitting for a woman like me.' Hydaspes, unable to understand the meaning of her words, then said: 'Forgive me, little daughter, for having made you blush by facing you with a question about a young man which was distasteful to your maiden modesty. But go now and rest yourself in the tent with your mother: you will not only fill her heart with gladness, for she labours now more with yearning for the enjoyment of your company than with pain when she was bearing you; but you will also soothe her with the relation of your adventures. It will be for me now to attend to the sacrifice, after selecting the other female victim who is to be slain together with the young man as an offering in your place, if by our best endeavours we can find a worthy substitute.'

(19) Chariclea almost gave utterance to a cry of woe, so sorely was she distressed by this mention of the slaughter of Theagenes: yet with a great effort she turned to what was expedient, and forced herself to hold out against the maddening power of her passion for the sake of her most practical course. Quietly she crept on in pursuit of her purpose and said: 'Sire, perhaps it became no longer necessary for you to seek another girl when once the people had on my account foregone the offering of a

---

[1] In ix. 25 it was Theagenes who told this falsehood to the King, while Chariclea remained silent, in seeming agreement.

NAME

ID NUMBER

BOOK TO BE SENT TO

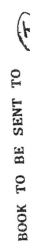

female victim. If, however, some should contentiously insist on taking a pair of victims, one from each sex, for a due performance of the sacrifice, you must hasten to find, not only a girl, but another youth also; or, failing that, to lead, not another girl, but me after all to the slaughter.' 'Do not speak so,' he said; and when he asked her reason for saying this she answered: 'Because this young man is destined by Heaven to live with me while I live, and die with me when I die.'

(20) At these words Hydaspes, having not yet grasped the truth of the matter, said: 'I commend your humane heart, daughter, your goodness in pitying and seeking to save a Greek stranger of your own age, who has shared your captivity and has acquired familiarity with you through the events of your exile; but there is no possibility of delivering him from the sacrifice. For, besides the impiety of an outright rejection of the traditional thank-offering for victory, the people themselves would not tolerate it, after they have been hardly induced, by the gods' grace, to make the concession in your favour.' [1] To this Chariclea rejoined: 'O King—for it seems that I may not call you father— if by the gods' grace my body has been saved alive, it would be expected of the same grace that my soul [2] should be saved like- wise, since the gods know that in allotting my destiny they decreed that soul to be truly mine own. But if this consequence should be found unacceptable to the Fates, and it will be neces- sary to enhance the sacred ritual with the slaughter of this foreign youth, grant me this one boon at least: command that I myself, with my own hand, shall perform the sacrifice, and that having received the sword as a precious keepsake I shall be celebrated and admired throughout Ethiopia for my manly resolution.'

(21) Deeply disturbed by her words, Hydaspes said: 'But I do not understand this reversal of your purpose. A moment ago you were trying to shield this stranger; and now you request that you may slay him with your own hand, as though he were an enemy. No, I can see in such an action nothing noble or glorious redounding to you or any girl of your age; and even if

[1] The King's religious zeal leads him to misrepresent the inclination of the people as shown in 9 and 17 above.
[2] By the words 'my soul' she apparently means Theagenes.

it were to your honour, it is quite impossible. Only to persons consecrated to the Sun and the Moon has the performance of this service been assigned by ancient tradition, and then not to any of these at random, but only to such as cohabit with wife or husband. Thus your virginity debars your request, put forward I know not with what intent.' 'But there is no impediment on that score,' said Chariclea, leaning over to Persinna and speaking aside in her ear; 'for I myself have one, mother, who has the right to such a name, if you should both give your consent.' 'We shall consent,' said Persinna with a smile, 'and with the gods' blessing we shall bestow on you one whom we may select as worthy both of you and of ourselves.' Then Chariclea said, in a louder tone: 'No need to select one who is mine already.'

(22) She was about to speak more openly—for she was compelled by the pressing emergency to be bold, and by the peril of Theagenes with which she was faced, to ignore her maidenly modesty—when Hydaspes, no longer able to restrain himself, said: 'Ye gods, how you seem to mingle evil with good! The unhoped for happiness that you have vouchsafed to me you partly withhold; you present me with a daughter beyond all expectation, but one out of her mind! How can she not be demented, when she gives vent to such inconsequent statements? She named one a brother who was not; when asked about him, who this stranger was, she said she did not know. Next, she sought to save the life of this unknown man as if he were a friend; and when she learnt that her request could not be granted, she begged that she might sacrifice him herself, as though he were her worst enemy. She was told that this was not lawful, since that kind of sacrifice has been solemnly committed to one woman alone, and that a wedded one; whereupon she declares that she has a husband, without going on to tell who he is. How indeed could she, when she has none, nor ever has had one, as was proved in the ordeal of the brazier? Unless it be that in her case alone an untruth is told us by that trial, ever found truthful by the Ethiopians, as to the purity of persons subjected to it, and it allows her to come off unburnt from treading upon it, and favours her with a spurious virginity. And to her alone it is given to count the same persons in one instant her friends and her enemies, and to invent brothers and sisters who do not

exist! Go then, wife, into the tent, and soothe her into a sober
mood. Either some god on a visit to our sacred rite has smitten
her with frenzy, or an excess of joy over unhoped for felicity
has driven her out of her wits. I go now to order someone to
search for and find the female victim whom it is our duty to
sacrifice to the gods instead of her; and, until that has been
arranged, I shall proceed with interviewing the embassies from
various nations and receiving the gifts that they have brought me
in honour of my victory.' With these words he took his seat in
state on an eminence near the tent, and commanded that the
ambassadors should approach and present whatever gifts they
might be bringing with them. The announcer, Hermonias, then
asked whether he wished them to be introduced all at once, or
by turns, taking each nation separately, one envoy at a time.

*Hydaspes, bewildered by the apparently insane behaviour of
Chariclea, gives audience to a number of ambassadors. Theagenes
skilfully recaptures a runaway bull.*

(23) He replied that they should come in order, individually,
so that each should be treated with the distinction due to him.
The announcer went on to say: 'Then the first to come will be
your brother's son, Meroebus; he has just arrived, and is waiting
outside the encampment to have himself announced.' 'So, you
utterly stupid fool,' exclaimed Hydaspes, 'you did not immediately inform me? This is no ambassador who has come, but
a king, as you are well aware. He is the son of my brother lately
deceased; it was I who established him on his father's throne, and
I now treat him as my son.' 'So I understood,' said Hermonias;
'but I understood also the prime importance of catching the
right moment—a point of particular concern to considerate
announcers. Forgive me, therefore, if while you were conversing
with the princess I took care not to interrupt your sweetest
pleasures.' 'Well, now at any rate let him come to me,' said the
King; and the man charged with the errand ran off and returned
with his charge the next moment. Meroebus appeared, a comely
figure of a youth just passing out of his adolescent years at the
age of seventeen. In stature he overtopped almost everybody
present and, when he entered with a splendid troop of armed

bodyguards preceding him, the Ethiopian soldiery standing around showed their admiration and respect by drawing aside to clear the way for his advance.

(24) Hydaspes on his part could not remain seated on his throne, but went to meet his visitor, enfolded him in his arms with a paternal warmth of affection, and seated him by his side; then, giving him his right hand, he said: 'You have come just in time, my son, to join in the festival of victory and the sacrificial celebration of a marriage. For the gods and demigods of our fathers, the founders of our line, have produced for us a daughter and for you, as it seems, a bride. But you shall be given a fuller account later on. If you have any request to make of me for the people of your kingdom, pray state it to me.' Meroebus, when he heard the word 'bride', was filled with feelings at once of such pleasure and of such delicacy that even his black complexion could not conceal his blushes, as when a sparkle has run over some soot. He was silent for some moments and then said: 'The other ambassadors, father, who have come will compliment you with gifts of choice offerings brought by each from his country to crown your illustrious victory; but I, thinking it right that the noble and valiant spirit that you have evinced in war should be suitably matched with a present of similar character, bring here for you a man who is as invincible a combatant in fields of battle and in bloodshed as he is irresistible when he wrestles and boxes in the dust of the arena.' And with that he intimated with a nod that this person should come forward.

(25) The man then advanced into their midst and prostrated himself before Hydaspes. His frame was of such a size, so much on the scale of the men of old time, that as he bent to kiss the King's knee he appeared almost to rival in height the persons seated on the upper stage. Without even waiting to be bidden, he undressed and stood there naked, challenging anyone who might wish to meet him in combat, either armed or weaponless. When no one came forward after repeated summons from the King by mouth of a herald, Hydaspes said to the man: 'You shall receive at my hands the victor's prize in due proportion.' So saying he ordered an elephant of many years and huge size to be brought before him. When the creature had arrived the man received it gladly, while the people gave way to a sudden

outburst of laughter, in their delight at the witty comment of the
King, and with a sense of the consolation that they derived from
this mockery of the man's arrogant behaviour for their own
apparent intimidation. After him were introduced the ambassadors of the Seres, who brought materials of thread spun and
woven from the cobwebs [1] of their country, made up in the
forms of one robe of purple dye and another of purest white.

(26) When the King had received these gifts, and had granted
their request for the release of some men who had been condemned and imprisoned a long time before, the envoys from
Arabia Felix advanced with sweet-smelling leaves of cassia,
cinnamon and other aromatic plants with which Arabia abounds;
there was a good hundredweight of each sort, and they filled the
whole place with a delicious fragrance. These were followed by
the envoys from the Troglodytes, bringing gold from ant-hills
and a pair of griffins [2] in double harness of gold chains. Next
came the embassy of the Blemmyes, carrying bows and arrows
pointed with python's bone, which they had interlaced so as to
form a crown.[3] 'These,' they said, 'O King, are the gifts that we
present to you; they do not compare in costliness with those of
the other missions; but along the riverside, as you have witnessed, they have shown their worth in war against the Persians.'
'Indeed they are more precious', said Hydaspes, 'than compli-
mentary gifts of many talents' value; for it is owing to them that
all the others are brought to me today.' With that he invited
them to inform him of any request that they would like to make.
They asked for a reduction of their tribute, and he granted them
a complete exemption for a period of ten years.

(27) Nearly all of the several embassies had been received,
and the King had presented to each of them in return gifts which
were equal to and, in most cases, more valuable than those
brought by them, when the envoys of the Auxomites [4] appeared.
They were in the position, not of tributaries, but of friends and

[1] See note on the Seres, ix. 16, p. 232.
[2] These legendary animals, mentioned by Herodotus (iii. 13; 27) as 'gold-
guarding griffins', appear as ornaments on Scythian tombs. Scythia (Siberia)
was famed for its production of gold.
[3] The idea of this crown seems to have been borrowed by the Blemmyes
from the people of the cinnamon country: cf. ix. 3.
[4] An Ethiopian race dwelling to the south-east of Meroë, between the
River Astaboras and the Red Sea.

allies under a treaty with the King, and they showed their gratification at his success by offering gifts like the others; but among these in particular was a strangely shaped animal, of a wonderful kind. Its stature equalled that of a camel in height, while its hide was coloured and marked with vivid spots like that of a leopard. Its hindquarters and parts about its flanks were low-built, like those of a lion; but its shoulder-parts, front legs and breast rose up to a height out of all proportion to its other parts. Its neck was slender, and protruded a great way from the main bulk of its body after the fashion of a swan's throat. Its head, shaped like that of a camel, was nearly twice the size of that of a Libyan ostrich; and it rolled its eyes, the rims of which seemed to be pigmented, with a grim expression. Its uncouth, swaying gait differed from the motion of any other land or water animal: its legs did not step forward alternately, one after another, but the two right legs moved together as one, and then the left legs together took their turn as a distinct pair, each side of the body thus being heaved up by their action. With this lumbering motion, and a gentle disposition, it could be led by its keeper using a slender cord twined about its head, and was kept on its path by his will as surely as if he employed an un-breakable chain. The appearance of this animal astounded the whole multitude, and its form then suggested its name: impressed by its more striking features, the people called it offhand a 'camelopard'. Nevertheless, it filled the whole assembly with trepidation.

(28) Now this is what happened next. At the altar of the Moon stood a pair of bulls, and at that of the Sun a team of four white horses, duly held ready for the sacrifice. The appearance of that alien, unfamiliar, unheard-of monster caused a great commotion among the victims, as though they beheld some spectre. They were filled with terror and broke the halters by which the attendants held them. One of the bulls—which alone, it seems, had caught sight of the wild beast—and two of the horses sped away in headlong flight. Unable to force their way out of the ring of soldiers, who with a wall of close-locked shields formed a circular barrier of heavy-armed men, they dashed about in distraction, careering and wheeling about the middle space, and upsetting everything that came in their way, whether lifeless

object or living creature. Mingled cries of two kinds arose as this was happening—some of fright from people towards whom the animals were rushing, and some of pleasure from those who, as the animals dashed at others, were stirred to amusement and laughter by seeing these people knocked down and trampled on. At this noise Persinna and Chariclea themselves were unable to remain quiet in their tent; drawing the curtains a little aside, they obtained a view of what was occurring. At that moment Theagenes, either impelled by the manly spirit that was born in him, or acting on the instigation of some god, observed that the guards posted round him had been dispersed by the impact of the tumult. Suddenly he stood upright: until then he had been crouching on one knee by the altar, and was expecting instant slaughter. He snatched up a piece of cleft wood that lay upon the altar, seized hold of one of the horses that had not bolted, vaulted on to its back, grasped the hair on its neck and used its mane as a bridle. Stirring on his mount with his heel, and continually urging it on with the piece of wood in place of a whip, he rode after a runaway bull. At first the onlookers supposed this action to show that Theagenes was taking to flight, and each man shouted to his neighbour that the youth must not be allowed to force his way out of the fence of armed soldiers. But as he proceeded in his exploit they had to change their opinion, and to understand that it was no case of cowardice or evasion of the sacrifice. For he speedily caught up with the bull and for a little drove it along from behind, prodding the beast and thus inciting it to run more swiftly. Whichever way it dashed he pursued it closely as it turned about, cautiously eluding it when it swung round to attack him.

(29) When he had brought it to be accustomed to the sight of himself and his procedure, he began to ride alongside it, flank grazing flank, and horse and bull mingling their breath and their sweat together. He regulated his pace so evenly with the bull's that people at a distance could fancy that the heads of the two animals grew upon a single body; and they sang the praises of Theagenes, glorifying him for this novel manner of driving a pair composed of horse and bull. This then was the effect that he produced upon the multitude. But Chariclea at this sight was seized with trembling and palpitation. She was at a loss to know

the purpose of his exploit and, fearing that he might come by a fall, was feeling the pangs of the wounds that he might receive as though they were those of her own slaughterer; so that Persinna, observing her trouble, asked: 'My child, tell me what is the matter. You seem to be taking the stranger's peril upon yourself. I for my part am affected also, and feel pity for his youth. I pray indeed that he may escape this danger and be preserved for the sacrifice, so that our service to the gods may not be left entirely unperformed and abandoned.' Chariclea replied to this: 'How ridiculous, to pray that he may not die, in order that he may die! But, mother, if it be possible for you, save the man's life, as a favour to me.' Persinna, surmising not the true reason but an ordinary amorous one, said: 'It is not possible to save his life; however, if you have some attachment to this man which gives you such an anxious concern, do not hesitate hereafter to unbosom yourself to me, as your mother. Even if you have acted on some youthful impulse, even if your conduct has been unbecoming to a maiden, a mother's nature knows how to come to her daughter's aid, and feminine sympathy is able to draw a veil over a woman's lapse.' Upon this Chariclea wept for a great while, and then said: 'This additional misfortune I have to bear, that when I speak to understanding persons I am not understood, and in telling my particular misadventures I am thought to be withholding the tale. From now onward I am compelled to deliver my own indictment, stark and undisguised.'

(30) After making this statement she was intending to reveal the truth, when she was again distracted by an outcry, resounding far and wide, which arose from the multitude. For when Theagenes incited his horse to put forth its utmost speed so as slightly to outpace the bull and bring its breast level with the animal's head, he let the horse run on free while he leapt off it and threw himself on to the bull's neck. He then laid his face down between its horns and, encircling them with his arms as with a coronal, locked his fingers together on the bull's forehead. The rest of his body was slung over the beast's right shoulder, and thus suspended from it he was borne along, only slightly tossed by the bounding of the bull. But when he felt it beginning to gasp beneath its burden and its muscles to relax their extreme tension, at the moment when it came round to the point where

Hydaspes sat in state, he swung himself over to the front, thrust
his feet against its legs, and so by knocking repeatedly against its
hoofs he artfully hampered its progress. Finding itself impeded
in its onward course, and overborne by the young man's strength,
it gave way at the knees and suddenly lurched headlong; then
tumbling on to its shoulders it rolled over on its back, and for a
long time lay stretched out, upside-down, with its horns stuck
fast in the ground and so implanted there that its head became
immovable. Its legs stirred in futile prancing, and beat the empty
air in the wild anguish of its defeat. Leaning upon it, Theagenes
made use of his left arm alone for his support, while he raised
his right hand heavenward and waved it again and again. On
Hydaspes and the whole assembly he cast joyous looks, with a
smile that seemed to be inviting them to share his gladness; while
the bellowing of the bull served him as a trumpet to proclaim
his victory. In response then came the resounding outcry of the
people, conveying no articulate words of definite praise, but
from wide-open mouths expressing their admiration as from a
single throat, and wafting it in a prolonged and uniform tone to
heaven. At the King's command servants ran up: some of them
raised up Theagenes and brought him to Hydaspes, while others
threw a noosed cord over the horns of the bull and drew it along,
sadly crestfallen. They then tethered both it and the horse, which
they had caught, once more to the altar.

As Hydaspes was about to speak to Theagenes and be concerned with him, the people, who had been delighted with the
youth, having felt kindly towards him since his first appearance,
and were now moreover astonished at his bodily strength, but
above all were stung with jealousy against the Ethiopian athlete [1]
brought by Meroebus, all cried out with one accord: 'Let him
be matched with Meroebus' man! Let him who received the
elephant contend with him who subdued the bull!' Thus they
continued calling out. Their prolonged insistence induced
Hydaspes to give his assent, and the Ethiopian was brought into
the assembly. He came glancing about with a disdainful, swaggering air; his paces were long and trailing, and he swung up each
forearm in turn to meet his other outstretched elbow.

[1] Because none of them had accepted his challenge (above, 25).

Theagenes wrestles with a gigantic Ethiopian and defeats him.

(31) When the man had drawn near to the royal circle Hydaspes looked towards Theagenes and said in Greek: 'Stranger, you must contend with him; the people demand it.' 'Their will be done,' replied Theagenes, 'but what kind of contest is it to be?' 'Wrestling,' said Hydaspes. To which the youth rejoined: 'Why not a combat with swords and in armour, that by some great stroke given or received I may thrill Chariclea, her who has hitherto maintained a steady silence about me, nay, has utterly dismissed me, it would seem, from her thoughts?' 'For what purpose', said Hydaspes, 'you drag in the name of Chariclea may be known to yourself; but it is in wrestling and not in duelling with swords that you have to contend: for the sight of bloodshed before the moment of the sacrifice is against the law.' Theagenes then, perceiving that Hydaspes feared that he might be killed before the sacrifice, said: 'You do right to reserve me for the gods, who will not be unmindful of us.' With these words he took up some dust and scattered it over his shoulders and arms, which were still moist with sweat from his bull hunt; he shook off what did not adhere, stretched out his hands before him, took his stand on firmly planted feet, bent his knees, curved his shoulders and back, slightly inclined his neck, braced in his whole frame and stood chafing to be at grips in the wrestling. The Ethiopian eyed him with a sneering smile, and nodded ironically as if he made light of his opponent. Suddenly he ran forward and heaved his arm like a crowbar on to the neck of Theagenes: the noise of the blow was audible afar, and again he swaggered and laughed complacently to himself. Theagenes, as a man trained from early years in the exercises of the gymnasiums, and thoroughly versed in Hermes' art of athletic contests, decided to give way at first, and having tested the power of his adversary, not to fling himself upon this monstrous bulk of a man exasperated to the point of savagery, but to rely on his own practised skill to outwit his mere boorish strength. Immediately then, while somewhat shaken by the blow, he pretended to be in greater distress than he was, and offered the other side of his neck, fully exposed, to meet another stroke. As the Ethiopian launched a second blow Theagenes at once gave

way under its force, and feigned to be on the point of falling prostrate on his face.

(32) The Ethiopian, deeming him beaten, was now full of confidence, and made a third onslaught, this time without any caution. Again he raised his outstretched arm, and was about to swing it down, when Theagenes suddenly crouched and darted in beneath him, thus avoiding the downward stroke. With his right forearm he thrust up his opponent's left arm, and staggered him as he was at the same time partly pulled to the ground by the downward sweep of his own hand, which struck only empty air. Theagenes then came up beneath his armpits and got a firm hold around him from behind. Straining hard he just engirdled the man's bulky middle with his hands, upset his footing by hard and repeated hammering with his heel at the joints and bones of the other's ankles, and so forced him to crouch down on one knee. He then, bestriding him with feet apart, thrust his legs into the region of the Ethiopian's groin, dislodged the wrists on which he was relying to uphold his chest, brought the man's forearms round to meet on his brows, drew them over to his back and shoulders, and so compelled him to sprawl with his belly on the ground. Thereupon the multitude sent forth one great shout, even more resounding than the former, and the King himself could not forbear to spring up from his throne. 'O hard necessity!' he said; 'what a man it is that under our law is appointed to be sacrificed!' At once he called the young man to him and said: 'A crown is reserved by custom for you at the altar; but take your crown now for this victory, glorious indeed, yet fruitless to you and fleeting. Since it is not possible for me to deliver you—would that I might!—from your appointed fate, I will grant you at least what boons lie in my power. If you have in mind anything that could give you pleasure while life is still yours, pray request it.' With these words he placed on Theagenes' head a golden crown set with jewels, and as he did so was observed to shed some tears. 'Well then,' said Theagenes, 'I will make you my request; and I call on you to grant it, as you promised. If it is beyond the bounds of possibility for me to escape the sacrifice, command that it be performed by your newly discovered daughter.'

(33) Startled by these words, as he recalled to mind the

similar request of Chariclea, Hydaspes did not think fit, however, in the hurry of the moment, to trace out their exact
meaning. 'They were possible things, stranger,' he said, 'that
I both invited you to ask and agreed to give you. She who
slaughters the victim must be a married woman, not a maiden
so the law declares.' 'But she herself too has a husband,' replied
Theagenes. 'This is the talk of an idle babbler,' said Hydaspes;
'of one, in truth, at the point of death. This girl has been proved
by the brazier to be a stranger to marriage or intercourse with
any man; unless perchance Meroebus be this husband that you
mention—I know not on what authority. I have named him, not
yet as her husband, but only as her betrothed.' 'Add now that
he will never be hers in marriage,' said Theagenes, 'if I have
any insight into the mind of Chariclea; and it will be only right
to believe me, as a victim moved to prophecy.' At this Meroebus
said to him: 'Good sir, it is not in their life, but after their
slaughter and dissection that victims intimate to the diviners the
signs revealed by their entrails. Thus you were correct, father,
in saying that the stranger is speaking wildly at the point of
death. Now, if you please, give order that this man be led to the
altars, and yourself, when you have settled any business that
awaits your attention, proceed to the sacrifice.' So Theagenes
was conducted to the appointed place. Chariclea, who had felt a
little relief at the moment of his victory and had built high
hopes upon it, at the sight of him being led away relapsed into
lamentation. Persinna did all that she could to console her,
saying: 'The young man may well be saved, if you will consent
to recount to me the yet untold parts of your story, and make
everything quite clear.' Then Chariclea, under stress of the
occasion, which she saw admitted of no delay, prepared to relate
the more important passages in her story.

(34) Hydaspes next inquired of the announcer whether any
ambassadors were still waiting to be received. 'Those only from
Syene, Sire,' replied Hermonias. 'They bring a letter and
friendly gifts from Oroondates, and have just arrived but a
moment ago.' 'Let them also come here,' said Hydaspes: they
then appeared and handed to him the letter. He opened it and
read its contents, as follows: 'To the humane and prosperous
King of the Ethiopians, Hydaspes, from Oroondates, satrap of

the Great King. Seeing that, conquering me in battle, you have conquered me even more in judgment,[1] and have freely conceded to me my satrapy entire, I should not be surprised if you were to grant me now a small request. A girl who was being brought to me from Memphis has become involved in the warfare: taken prisoner, she was sent on your order to Ethiopia, as I learnt from those who were with her at the time and escaped from that danger. I ask that she be released to me and bestowed on me as a gift, since I have myself some affection for the child, and particularly wish to deliver her safe and sound to her father, who has wandered far and wide over the earth and, while searching for his daughter, was caught up in the fighting at the garrison town of Elephantiné. As I was afterwards reviewing the survivors I saw him, and he demanded to be sent off to your gracious presence. You have the man there with the other envoys: his behaviour suffices to declare his noble birth, and his mere appearance inspires respect. Gladden him, Sire, by returning him to me as a father now not in name only but also in actual fact.' The King, after reading the letter, asked: 'Who among this company is the man searching for his daughter?' They pointed out an old man, to whom he said: 'Stranger, I am prepared to do all this, as Oroondates requests; but I have had only ten young female prisoners brought to me. One so far has been identified as being other than your daughter: inspect the rest and if, in observing them, you can find her, take her.' The old man prostrated himself and kissed the King's feet. The girls were then fetched; he inspected them and failed to find her whom he sought. Dejected again, he said: 'O King, none of these is she.' 'My mind is wholly yours,' said Hydaspes; 'you must blame Fortune if you do not find her whom you are seeking. That no other girl was brought here, or is in the camp, you can satisfy yourself by looking all around.'

Charicles appears and denounces Theagenes as the abductor of his daughter.

(35) The old man smote his brow and shed tears; then, after raising his head and scanning the throng round about him, he

---

[1] See ix. 26.

ran off suddenly like one in a frenzy, and on reaching the altars
he rolled up the border of his coarse cloak—for that was what
he wore—into a loop, flung it about Theagenes' neck and haled
him along, calling out in resonant tones: 'I have got you, ah, my
enemy! I have got you, ah, you pernicious villain!' The guards
strove to oppose and detach him, but he held on fast and, as
though grown into one person with the youth, succeeded in
bringing him into the presence of Hydaspes and the council.
'O King,' he said, 'this is the man who has abducted my
daughter, who has made my house childless and desolate, and
snatched her, my life and soul, from the sanctuary of the altars of
Pythian Apollo; and now I find him seated, as one undefiled, by
the altars of the gods!' All present were profoundly shocked by
this proceeding, and all were astonished, some by what they could
gather from his words, and the rest by the sight of his action.

(36) When Hydaspes bade him explain his meaning more
clearly, the old man, who was in fact Charicles, concealed
the real truth of Chariclea's kinship,[1] apprehending that he
might possibly provoke the enmity of her true parents if she
should have previously disappeared during her flight into the
interior. He therefore curtailed his account to what could do no
harm and said: 'I had a daughter, O King, and only by beholding her could you be convinced of the justice of my description
of what she was in mind and in body. She was a virgin and a
ministrant of Artemis at Delphi. This fine fellow, a native of
Thessaly, had come to Delphi, my city, at the head of a sacred
mission for the performance of some national solemnity. Unobserved he abducted this girl from the very sanctuary, the
sanctuary of Apollo. Thus he should in justice be deemed to
have committed a sacrilege that affects you also; for he has
profaned your national god, Apollo, who is the same as the Sun,
and his temple. He had an accomplice in this abominable act, a
certain false prophet of Memphis. I went in chase of him through
Thessaly, and requested the people of Oeta, his fellow-citizens,
to deliver him up, but nowhere could I find him; though they
were ready enough to hand him over, even to be slain, wherever
he might be found, as an accursed villain. I then guessed that

---

[1] Heliodorus has nowhere explained how Charicles came to know the
parentage of Chariclea.

the chief haunt of the fugitives was Memphis, to which city
Calasiris belonged. I arrived there, and discovered that Calasiris,
as he deserved, had died. From his son Thyamis I received full
information about my daughter and, among other things, that
she had been dispatched to Oroondates at Syene. I failed to find
Oroondates at Syene; for I went on there, and was caught by
the warfare at Elephantiné. So I have come here now, and I
appeal to you in the terms set forth in that letter. You hold the
robber; take up now the search for my daughter; and in doing
a kindness to me, a long-suffering man, give yourself the satisfaction of showing your regard for the satrap who intercedes
for us.'

(37) He said no more, only adding to his words a mournful
lamentation. Hydaspes then asked Theagenes: 'What can you
answer to that?' He replied: 'His accusations are all true. I
have offended against him by robbery, rapine, violence and
injustice; but to you I am a benefactor.' 'Then restore', said
Hydaspes, 'her who belongs to another. Since you are already
dedicated to the gods, you shall suffer a slaughter glorified by
the sacrifice, and not one of just retribution for wrongdoing.'
'But it is not the wrongdoer,' said Theagenes, 'but the holder of
the wrongful spoil who should rightly restore it. You are yourself the holder of it: restore it, unless this man himself should
acknowledge that Chariclea is your daughter.' The suspense was
now more than anyone could bear; all at the same moment felt
confounded. Sisimithres had restrained himself for some time:
while he had all along been acquainted with what was being
spoken and done, he was still waiting for the revelation from on
high to come full circle. But now he ran to Charicles and enfolded
him in his arms, saying: 'She is saved, you see, she whom since
the day when you took her into your care from me you regarded
as your daughter; but she is in truth the daughter, as has been
discovered, of parents that you know.'

*The evidence of Charicles and Sisimithres convinces Hydaspes
of the divinely ordained betrothal of Theagenes and Chariclea.*

(38) Upon this Chariclea ran out of the tent and, casting aside
all the reserve belonging to her sex and age, rushed in a kind of

bacchic frenzy to Charicles and fell down at his knees, saying:
'Father, whom I reverence no less than my true parents, punish
me as you will; I am a guilty wretch who struck down my father!
Even though deeds in the past might be ascribed to the design
or ordinance of the gods, pay no heed to that.' Persinna, where
she stood apart, embraced Hydaspes, saying: 'It is all as she
states, husband; do not doubt it. This Greek youth, be assured,
is affianced to our dear daughter, for she has just now, though
with some reluctance, told me all.' The people on their part
exulted with shouts of congratulation; persons of every age and
condition rejoiced in unison over the turn of events. Most of
what was being said they could not comprehend; but they
conjectured the facts from what had previously transpired
concerning Chariclea; or it might be that they were led to
surmise the truth by the influence of some divine power that
had designed the whole of this dramatic scene, and by whose
means extreme contraries were now composed into a harmony.
Joy and grief were intertwined, tears were mingled with laughter,
and the most baleful proceedings were converted into festivity.
Laughing while they wept, rejoicing as they lamented, finding
those whom they were not seeking, and losing those whom they
thought to have found—in fine, they saw the expected slayings
transformed into holy sacraments.

(39) Hydaspes then inquired of Sisimithres: 'What is to be
done, my wise friend? To deny the gods their sacrifice is
impious; to slaughter those whom they have bestowed on us is
unholy: we must devise what course we are to take.' Sisimithres
replied, not in Greek, but in Ethiopian, so as to be understood
by everyone: 'O King, excess of joy, it would seem, beclouds
the minds of even the most sagacious of men. Thus you should
long ere now have concluded that the gods do not welcome this
sacrifice that is being prepared for them. At this moment, as the
most blessed Chariclea stood by the very altar, they have mani-
fested her to be your daughter, and have sent up here from the
depths of Greece her foster-father, as though dropped from the
sky; and again, they struck the horses and the bulls held ready
at the altars with that alarm and disorder, by which they meant
to intimate that what is regarded as the crowning ritual was to be
interrupted. And now, to consummate their beneficence and, as

it were, bring the drama to a joyous climax, they have produced
this foreign youth here as the betrothed of the maiden. Come,
let us recognize the divine miracle that has been wrought, and
become collaborators in the gods' design. Let us proceed to the
holier oblations, and exclude human sacrifice for all future time.'

*Theagenes and Chariclea are married and invested with the in-
signia of the priesthood, and proceed amid popular acclamation to
the celebration of their marriage in Meroë.*

(40) When Sisimithres had delivered this speech in loud, clear
tones that were audible to all, Hydaspes, himself now also speaking in the language of the country, and laying hold of Chariclea
and Theagenes, said: 'And therefore to all present I say that,
since these events have been thus brought about by the direction
of the gods, it would be criminal to run counter to their will.
Calling as witnesses, then, the very powers who have thus
ordained, and you who are evidently disposed to comply with
their behests, I declare this couple to be duly joined in matri-
mony, and I sanction their union under the ordinance for the
begetting of children. And, if you think fit, let this decision be
confirmed by sacrifice, and so let us proceed with the sacred
rites.'

(41) His speech was greeted with a chorus of approval from
the army, and with hand-clapping in loud applause, as though
the marriage were already being celebrated. Hydaspes then
moved up to the altars, and before beginning the sacrifice he
said: 'O Sun, our Lord, and O Moon, our Lady, if indeed it has
been by your design that Theagenes and Chariclea have been
declared man and wife, it follows that they are fitted to render
you priestly service.' With these words he removed his mitre and
that of Persinna, the insignia of their priesthood, and set his
upon Theagenes' head and Persinna's upon that of Chariclea.
As soon as this was done Charicles called to mind the oracle at
Delphi, and recognized that the divine prediction [1] of long ago
was being fulfilled in actual fact. For it had stated that the young
pair, after fleeing from Delphi,

[1] In ii. 35.

' Shall arrive at the swarthy land of the Sun.
There they shall win and wear about their temples, as the
   noble prize of virtuous lives,
A white coronal from darkling brows.'

Thus crowned with the white mitres, they were invested with all
the priestly insignia, and themselves performed a propitious
sacrifice. Then, with torches lit and tuneful fluting and piping,
they were all escorted to the city—Theagenes with Hydaspes
on a horse-drawn chariot, Sisimithres and Charicles on another,
and Chariclea and Persinna on a car drawn by white bulls. And
so, amid congratulations, plaudits and dances the procession
passed on to Meroë, where the city was to be gladdened by the
more splendid celebration of the holier marriage rites.

   This is the conclusion of the Ethiopian Story of Theagenes
and Chariclea, composed by a Phoenician of Emesa, of the line
of the descendants of Helios (the Sun), namely Heliodorus, son
of Theodosius.

EVERYMAN'S LIBRARY: A Selected List

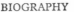

BIOGRAPHY

Baxter, Richard (1615–91).
THE AUTOBIOGRAPHY OF RICHARD BAXTER.   868

Boswell, James (1740–95). *See* Johnson.

Brontë, Charlotte (1816–55).
LIFE, 1857. By *Mrs Gaskell.* Introduction by *May Sinclair.* (*See also* Fiction.) 318

Burns, Robert (1759–96).
LIFE, 1828. By *J. G. Lockhart* (1794–1854). With Introduction by *Prof. James Kinsley*, M.A., PH.D.   (*See also* Poetry and Drama.) 156

Byron, Lord (1788–1824).
LETTERS. Edited by *R. G. Howarth*, B.LITT., and with an Introduction by *André Maurois.*   (*See also* Poetry and Drama.) 931

Canton, William (1845–1926).
A CHILD'S BOOK OF SAINTS, 1898.   (*See also* Essays.) 61

Cellini, Benvenuto (1500–71).
THE LIFE OF BENVENUTO CELLINI, written by himself. Translated by *Anne Macdonell.* Introduction by *William Gaunt.*   51

Cowper, William (1731–1800).
SELECTED LETTERS. Edited, with Introduction, by *W. Hadley*, M.A.   774
(*See also* Poetry and Drama.)

Dickens, Charles (1812–70).
LIFE, 1874. By *John Forster* (1812–76). Introduction by *G. K. Chesterton.* 2 vols.
(*See also* Fiction.) 781–2

Evelyn, John (1620–1706).
DIARY. Edited by *William Bray*, 1819. Intro. by *G. W. E. Russell.* 2 vols.   220–1

Fox, George (1624–91).
JOURNAL, 1694. Revised by *Norman Penney*, with Account of Fox's last years. Introduction by *Rufus M. Jones.*   754

Franklin, Benjamin (1706–90).
AUTOBIOGRAPHY, 1817. With Introduction and Account of Franklin's later life by *W. Macdonald.* Reset new edition (1949), with a newly compiled Index.   316

Goethe, Johann Wolfgang von (1749–1832).
LIFE, 1855. By *G. H. Lewes* (1817–78). Introduction by *Harelock Ellis.* Index.
(*See also* Poetry and Drama.) 269

Hudson, William Henry (1841–1922).
FAR AWAY AND LONG AGO, 1918. Intro. by *John Galsworthy.*   956

Johnson, Samuel (1709–84).
LIVES OF THE ENGLISH POETS, 1781. Introduction by *Mrs L. Archer-Hind.* 2 vols.
(*See also* Essays, Fiction.) 770–1
BOSWELL'S LIFE OF JOHNSON, 1791. A new edition (1949), with Introduction by *S. C. Roberts*, M.A., LL.D., and a 30-page Index by Alan Dent. 2 vols.   1–2

Keats, John (1795–1821).
LIFE AND LETTERS, 1848. By *Lord Houghton* (1809–85). Introduction by *Robert Lynd.* Note on the letters by Lewis Gibbs.   (*See also* Poetry and Drama.) 801

Lamb, Charles (1775–1834).
LETTERS. New edition (1945) arranged from the Complete Annotated Edition of the Letters. 2 vols.   (*See also* Essays and Belles-Lettres, Fiction.) 342–3

Napoleon Buonaparte (1769–1821).
HISTORY OF NAPOLEON BUONAPARTE, 1829. By *J. G. Lockhart* (1794–1854).   3
(*See also* Essays and Belles-Lettres.)

Nelson, Horatio, Viscount (1758–1805).
LIFE, 1813. By *Robert Southey* (1774–1843).   (*See also* Essays.) 52

Outram, General Sir James (1803–63), 'the Bayard of India.'
LIFE, 1903. Deals with important passages in the history of India in the nineteenth century. By *L. J. Trotter* (1827–1912).   396

Pepys, Samuel (1633–1703).
DIARY. Newly edited (1953), with modernized spelling, by *John Warrington*, from the edition of Mynors Bright (1875–9). 3 vols.   53–5

Plutarch (46?–120).
LIVES OF THE NOBLE GREEKS AND ROMANS. Dryden's edition, 1683–6. Revised, with Introduction, by *A. H. Clough* (1819–61). 3 vols.   407–9

Rousseau, Jean Jacques (1712–78).
CONFESSIONS, 1782. 2 vols. Complete and unabridged English translation. New Introduction by *Prof. R. Niklaus*, B.A., PH.D., of Exeter University.   859–60
(*See also* Essays, Theology and Philosophy.)

Scott, Sir Walter (1771–1832).
LOCKHART'S LIFE OF SCOTT. An abridgement by *J. G. Lockhart* himself from the original 7 volumes. New Introduction by *W. M. Parker*, M.A.   39

Swift, Jonathan (1667–1745).

JOURNAL TO STELLA, 1710–13. Deciphered by *J. K. Moorhead*. Introduction by *Sir Walter Scott*. Sir Walter Scott's essay 'Swift, Stella and Vanessa' is included. 757
(See also Essays, Fiction.)

Walpole, Horace (1717–97).

SELECTED LETTERS. Edited, with Introduction, by *W. Hadley*, M.A. 775

Wellington, Arthur Wellesley, Duke of (1769–1852).

LIFE, 1862. By *G. R. Gleig* (1796–1888). 341

CLASSICAL

Aeschylus (525–455 B.C.).

PLAYS. Translated into English Verse by *G. M. Cookson*. New Introduction by *John Warrington*, and notes on each play. 62

Aristophanes (450 ?–385 ? B.C.).

THE COMEDIES. Translated by *J. Hookham Frere*, etc. Edited, with Introduction, by *J. P. Maine* and *J. H. Frere*. 2 vols. (Vol. 1 temporarily out of print.) 516

Aristotle (384–322 B.C.).

POLITICS and THE ATHENIAN CONSTITUTION. Edited and translated by *John Warrington*. 605
METAPHYSICS. Edited and translated by *John Warrington*. Introduction by *Sir David Ross*, K.B.E., M.A., D.LITT. 1000

Caesar, Julius (102 ?–44 B.C.).

WAR COMMENTARIES. 'The Gallic Wars' and 'The Civil War.' Newly translated and edited by *John Warrington*. 702

Cicero, Marcus Tullius (106–43 B.C.).

THE OFFICES (translated by *Thomas Cockman*, 1699); LAELIUS, ON FRIENDSHIP; CATO, ON OLD AGE; AND SELECT LETTERS (translated by *W. Melmoth*, 1753). With Note on Cicero's Character by De Quincey. Introduction by *John Warrington*. 345

Demetrius (fl. late first century A.D.). (See under Aristotle.)

Demosthenes (384–322 B.C.). (See under Oratory, p. 11.)

Epictetus (b. c. A.D. 60).

MORAL DISCOURSES. THE ENCHIRIDION AND FRAGMENTS. Translated by *Elizabeth Carter* (1717–1806). Edited by *W. H. D. Rouse*, M.A. 404

Euripides (484 ?–407 B.C.).

PLAYS. New Introduction by *John Warrington*. Translated by *A. S. Way*, D.LITT. 2 vols. 63, 271

Herodotus (484 ?–425 ? B.C.).

HISTORY. The 'History' deals with the period covering the Persian invasion of Greece, 492–480 B.C. Rawlinson's Translation, additional notes and Introduction, by *E. H. Blakeney*. 2 vols. (Vol. II temporarily out of print.) 405–6

Homer (? ninth century B.C.).

ILIAD. New verse translation by *S. O. Andrew* and *Michael Oakley*. 453
ODYSSEY. The new verse translation (first published 1953) by *S. O. Andrew*. Introduction by *John Warrington*. 454

Juvenal (c. A.D. 50–c. 130).

SATIRES; with THE SATIRES OF PERSIUS. Introduction by *Prof. H. J. Rose*, M.A., F.B.A. William Gifford Translation, 1802. Revised by *John Warrington*. 997

Lucretius (c. 99 ?–50 ? B.C.).

ON THE NATURE OF THINGS. Metrical Translation by *W. E. Leonard*. 750

Ovid (43 B.C.–A.D. 18).

SELECTED WORKS. Chosen by *J. C.* and *M. J. Thornton*. Selections from the *Metamorphoses*, *Heroical Epistles*, the *Festivals*, the *Ibis*, and his epistles written in exile: also his *Art of Love*. 955

Persius (34–62). See Juvenal.

Plato (427–347 B.C.).

THE REPUBLIC. Translated, with an Introduction, by *A. D. Lindsay*, C.B.E., LL.D. The greatest achievement of the Greek intellect in philosophy. 64
SOCRATIC DISCOURSES OF PLATO AND XENOPHON. Introduction by *A. D. Lindsay*, C.B.E., LL.D. 457
THE LAWS. The last of Plato's dialogues is here printed in the A. E. Taylor (1869–1945) Translation. 275

Sophocles (496 ?–406 B.C.).

DRAMAS. This volume contains the seven surviving dramas. 114

Thucydides (c. 460–401 B.C.).

HISTORY OF THE PELOPONNESIAN WAR. Translation by *Richard Crawley*. Introduction by *John Warrington*. Index and five plans. 455

Virgil (70–19 B.C.).

AENEID. Verse translation by *Michael Oakley*. Introduction by *E. M. Forster*. 161
ECLOGUES AND GEORGICS. Verse Translation by *T. F. Royds*. The 'Eclogues' were inspired by Theocritus; the 'Georgics' describe a countryman's life. 222

Xenophon (430 ?–360 ? B.C.). (See under Plato.)

ESSAYS AND BELLES-LETTRES

3

Lamb, Charles (1775–1834).
ESSAYS OF ELIA AND LAST ESSAYS OF ELIA, 1823–33. Introduction by *Augustine Birrell*. Includes the first and the last Essays of Elia. 14
(See also Biography, Fiction.)

Landor, Walter Savage (1775–1864).
IMAGINARY CONVERSATIONS, AND POEMS, 1824–9, 1853. Edited, with Introduction, by *Havelock Ellis*. 890

Lawrence, David Herbert (1885–1930).
STORIES, ESSAYS AND POEMS. Selected by *Desmond Hawkins*. Poetry, Essays, Travel Sketches and Letters. 958
(See also Fiction.)

Locke, John (1632–1704).
AN ESSAY CONCERNING HUMAN UNDERSTANDING, 1690. Abridged and edited by *Raymond Wilburn*, presenting the whole sweep of the work. 984
(See also Theology and Philosophy.)

Lynd, Robert (1879–1949).
ESSAYS ON LIFE AND LITERATURE. Introduction by *Desmond MacCarthy*. 990

Macaulay, Thomas Babington, Lord (1800–59).
CRITICAL AND HISTORICAL ESSAYS, 1843. New Introduction by *Douglas Jerrold*. 2 vols. 225–6
MISCELLANEOUS ESSAYS, 1823–59; LAYS OF ANCIENT ROME, 1842; and MISCELLANEOUS POEMS, 1812–47. Introduction by *Prof. G. M. Trevelyan*, O.M. 439
(See also History.)

Machiavelli, Niccolò (1469–1527).
THE PRINCE, 1513. New Introduction by *Prof. H. Butterfield*, M.A., HON. D.LITT. Translated by *W. K. Marriott*. 280

Mazzini, Joseph (1805–72).
THE DUTIES OF MAN (translated by *Miss E. Noyes*); and OTHER ESSAYS. New Introduction by *Dr Thomas Jones*, C.H., LL.D. 224

Milton, John (1608–74).
PROSE WRITINGS. Introduction by *K. M. Burton*, M.A. The contents of this volume include 'Areopagitica,' 1644, and other important prose works. 795
(See also Poetry, etc.)

Mitford, Mary Russell (1787–1855).
OUR VILLAGE, 1824–32. Edited, with an Introduction, by *Sir John Squire*. 927

Modern Humour. An Anthology in Prose and Verse from over sixty authors. 957

Montaigne, Michel de (1533–92).
ESSAYS, 1580–8. John Florio's version, 1603. Edited (from the third edition, 1632), with Intro. by *A. R. Waller*, 3 vols. *(Vol. I temporarily out of print.)* 440–2

Napoleon Buonaparte (1769–1821).
LETTERS. Some 300 of the most interesting of the Emperor's letters, chosen and translated by *J. M. Thompson*, F.B.A., F.R.HIST.S. *(See also Biography.)* 995

Nelson, Horatio, Viscount (1758–1805).
NELSON'S LETTERS. Compiled by *Geoffrey Rawson*. *(See also Biography.)* 244

Newman, John Henry (1801–90).
ON THE SCOPE AND NATURE OF UNIVERSITY EDUCATION; and CHRISTIANITY AND SCIENTIFIC INVESTIGATION, 1852. Introduction by *Wilfrid Ward*. 723
(See also Theology and Philosophy.)

Poe, Edgar Allan (1809–49).
ESSAYS. *(See Poetry.)*

Quiller-Couch, Sir Arthur (1863–1944).
CAMBRIDGE LECTURES, from 'Q.'s' well-known books *The Art of Reading*, 1920; *The Art of Writing*, 1916; *Studies in Literature*, 1918; and *Shakespeare's Workmanship*, 1918. *(See also Fiction.)* 974

Rousseau, Jean Jacques (1712–78).
ÉMILE; OR, EDUCATION. Translated by *Barbara Foxley*, M.A. Intro. (1955) by *Prof. André Boutet de Monvel*. *(See also Biography, Theology and Philosophy.)* 518

Ruskin, John (1819–1900).
SESAME, AND LILIES, 1864; THE TWO PATHS, 1859; and THE KING OF THE GOLDEN RIVER; OR THE BLACK BROTHERS, 1851. Introduction by *Sir Oliver Lodge*. 219
THE SEVEN LAMPS OF ARCHITECTURE, 1849. With an Introduction (1956) by *Sir Arnold Lunn*. Illustrated with 14 plates of engravings. 207

Sévigné, Marie de Rabutin-Chantal, Marquise de (1626–96).
SELECTED LETTERS. Selected and translated by *H. T. Barnwell*, M.A. 98

Spectator, The, 1711–14. By Joseph Addison (1672–1719), Sir Richard Steele (1672–1729) and Others. Edited by *Prof. Gregory Smith*. New Introduction by *P. Smithers*, D.PHIL., M.P., and a Biographical and General Index by *Prof. Gregory Smith*. Reset with minor revisions, 1945. 4 vols. *(See also Essays under Steele.)* 164–7

Spencer, Herbert (1820–1903).
ESSAYS ON EDUCATION, 1861. Introduction by *C. W. Eliot*. 504

Steele, Sir Richard (1672–1729).
THE TATLER, 1709–11. 993

Sterne, Laurence (1713–68).
A SENTIMENTAL JOURNEY THROUGH FRANCE AND ITALY, 1768; JOURNAL TO ELIZA, written in 1767; and LETTERS TO ELIZA, 1766–7. Introduction by *Daniel George*. *(See also Fiction.)* 796

4

FICTION

Manzoni, Alessandro (1785–1873).

THE BETROTHED (*I Promessi Sposi*, 1840, rev. ed.). Translated (1951) from the Italian by *Archibald Colquhoun*, who also adds a preface.   **999**

Marryat, Frederick (1792–1848).

MR MIDSHIPMAN EASY. New Introduction by *Oliver Warner*.   **82**

THE SETTLERS IN CANADA, 1844. Introduction by *Oliver Warner*.   **370**

Maugham, W. Somerset (*b.* 1874).

CAKES AND ALE, 1930. The finest novel of the author's inter-war period.   **932**

Maupassant, Guy de (1850–93).

SHORT STORIES. Translated by *Marjorie Laurie*. Intro. by *Gerald Gould*.   **907**

Melville, Herman (1819–91).

MOBY DICK, 1851. Intro. by *Prof. Sherman Paul*.   **179**

TYPEE, 1846; and BILLY BUDD (*published* 1924). South Seas adventures. New Introduction by *Milton R. Stern*.   **180**

Meredith, George (1828–1909).

THE ORDEAL OF RICHARD FEVEREL, 1859. Introduction by *Robert Sencourt*.   **916**

Mickiewicz, Adam (1798–1855).

PAN TADEUSZ, 1834. Translated into English prose, with Introduction, by *Prof. G. R. Noyes*. Poland's epic of Napoleonic wars.   **842**

Modern Short Stories. Selected by *John Hadfield*. Twenty stories.   **954**

Moore, George (1852–1933).

ESTHER WATERS, 1894. The story of Esther Waters, the servant girl who 'went wrong.' Introduction by *C. D. Medley*.   **933**

Mulock [Mrs Craik], Maria (1826–87).

JOHN HALIFAX, GENTLEMAN, 1856. Introduction by *J. Shaylor*.   **123**

Pater, Walter (1839–94).

MARIUS THE EPICUREAN, 1885. Introduction by *Osbert Burdett*.   **903**

Poe, Edgar Allan (1809–49).

TALES OF MYSTERY AND IMAGINATION. Introduction by *Padraic Colum*.   **336**
(*See also* Poetry and Drama.)

Priestley, J. B. (*b.* 1894).

ANGEL PAVEMENT, 1931. A finely conceived novel of London.   **938**

Quiller-Couch, Sir Arthur (1863–1944).

HETTY WESLEY, 1903. Introduction by the author.   (*See also* Essays.) **864**

Radcliffe, Mrs Ann (1764–1823).

THE MYSTERIES OF UDOLPHO, 1794. Intro. by *R. A. Freeman*. 2 vols.   **865–6**

Reade, Charles (1814–84).

THE CLOISTER AND THE HEARTH, 1861. Introduction by *Swinburne*.   **29**

Richardson, Samuel (1689–1761).

PAMELA, 1740. Introduction by *George Saintsbury*. 2 vols.   **683–4**

CLARISSA, 1747–8. Introduction by *Prof. W. L. Phelps*. 4 vols.   **882–5**

Russian Short Stories. Translated, with Introduction, by *Rochelle S. Townsend*. Stories by Pushkin, Gogol, Tolstoy, Korolenko, Chehov, Chirikov, Andreyev, Kuprin, Gorky, Sologub.   **758**

Scott, Sir Walter (1771–1832).

The following Waverley Novels each contain an Introduction, biographical and bibliographical, based upon Lockhart's *Life*:

THE ANTIQUARY, 1816. Introduction by *W. M. Parker*, M.A.   **126**

THE BRIDE OF LAMMERMOOR, 1819. A romance of life in East Lothian, 1695. New Introduction by *W. M. Parker*, M.A.   **129**

GUY MANNERING, 1815. A mystery story of the time of George III. New Introduction by *W. M. Parker*, M.A.   **133**

THE HEART OF MIDLOTHIAN, 1818. Period of the Porteous Riots, 1736. New Introduction by *W. M. Parker*, M.A.   **134**

IVANHOE, 1820. A romance of the days of Richard I.   **16**

KENILWORTH, 1821. The tragic story of Amy Robsart, in Elizabeth I's time. New Preface and Glossary by *W. M. Parker*, M.A.   **135**

OLD MORTALITY, 1817. Battle of Bothwell Bridge, 1679. New Introduction by *W. M. Parker*, M.A.   **137**

QUENTIN DURWARD, 1823. A tale of adventures in fifteenth-century France. New Introduction by *W. M. Parker*, M.A.   **140**

REDGAUNTLET, 1824. A tale of adventure in Cumberland, about 1763. New Introduction by *W. M. Parker*, M.A.   **141**

ROB ROY, 1818. A romance of the Rebellion of 1715.   **142**

THE TALISMAN, 1825. Richard Cœur-de-Lion and the Third Crusade, 1191. New Preface by *W. M. Parker*, M.A.   (*See also* Biography.) **144**

Shchedrin (M. E. Saltykov, 1826–92).

THE GOLOVLYOV FAMILY. Translated by *Natalie Duddington*. Introduction by *Edward Garnett*.   **908**

Shelley, Mary Wollstonecraft (1797–1851).

FRANKENSTEIN, 1818. With Mary Shelley's own Preface.   **616**

Shorter Novels.

Vol. I: ELIZABETHAN. Introduction by *George Saintsbury* and Notes by *Philip Henderson*. Contains: Deloney's 'Jack of Newberie' and 'Thomas of Reading'; Nashe's 'The Unfortunate Traveller'; Green's 'Carde of Fancie.'   **824**

POETRY AND DRAMA

REFERENCE

ROMANCE

SCIENCE

Robinson, Wade (1838–76).
THE PHILOSOPHY OF ATONEMENT, AND OTHER SERMONS, 1875. Introduction l
F. B. Meyer.   6$

Rousseau, Jean Jacques (1712–78).
THE SOCIAL CONTRACT, 1762; and OTHER ESSAYS. Introduction by *G. D. H. Cc*
(See also Biography, Essays.) 6(

Saint Augustine (353–430).
CONFESSIONS. Dr Pusey's Translation, 1838, with Introduction by *A. H. Arm
strong*, M.A.   20
THE CITY OF GOD. Complete text of John Healey's Elizabethan Translation, 161
Edited by *R. V. G. Tasker*, M.A., B.D., with an Introduction by *Sir Ernest Barke*
2 vols.   982-

Saint Francis (1182–1226).
THE LITTLE FLOWERS; THE MIRROR OF PERFECTION (by Leo of Assisi); and TH
LIFE OF ST FRANCIS (by St Bonaventura). Introduction by *Thomas Okey.*   48

Spinoza, Benedictus de (1632–77).
ETHICS, 1677; and ON THE CORRECTION OF THE UNDERSTANDING, 1687. Translate
by *Andrew Boyle.* New Introduction by *T. S. Gregory.*   4

Swedenborg, Emanuel (1688–1772).
THE TRUE CHRISTIAN RELIGION, 1771. New and unabridged translation by *J
Bayley.* Introduction by *Dr Helen Keller.* 960 pages.   8(

Thomas à Kempis (1380 ?–1471).
THE IMITATION OF CHRIST, 1471.   4

Thomas Aquinas (1225–74).
SELECTED WRITINGS. Selected and edited by *Father M. C. D'Arcy.*   95

TRAVEL AND TOPOGRAPHY

Borrow, George (1803–81).
THE BIBLE IN SPAIN, 1842. Introduction by *Edward Thomas.*   15
WILD WALES: the People, Language and Scenery, 1862. Introduction by *Dav.
Jones*, C.B.E., the painter and Borrovian.   (See also Fiction.) 4

Boswell, James (1740–95).
JOURNAL OF A TOUR TO THE HEBRIDES WITH SAMUEL JOHNSON, 1786. Edited, wit
a new Introduction, by *Lawrence F. Powell*, M.A., HON. D.LITT.   3$

Calderón de la Barca, Mme (1804–82).
LIFE IN MEXICO, 1843. Introduction by *Manuel Romero De Terreros.*   6(

Cobbett, William (1762–1835).
RURAL RIDES, 1830. Introduction by *Asa Briggs*, M.A., B.SC. 2 vols.   638-

Cook, James (1728–79).
VOYAGES OF DISCOVERY. Edited by *John Barrow*, F.R.S., F.S.A. Introduction b
Guy Pocock, M.A.   9

Crèvecœur, J. Hector St John de (1735–1813).
LETTERS FROM AN AMERICAN FARMER, 1782. Intro. and Notes by *W. Barton Blai*
6

Darwin, Charles (1809–82).
THE VOYAGE OF THE 'BEAGLE,' 1839.   (See also Science.) 1(

Defoe, Daniel (1661 ?–1731).
A TOUR THROUGH ENGLAND AND WALES, 1724–6. Intro. by *G. D. H. Cole.* 2 vol
(See also Fiction.) 820-

Kinglake, Alexander (1809–91).
EOTHEN, 1844. Introduction by *Harold Spender.*   3$

Lane, Edward William (1801–76).
MANNERS AND CUSTOMS OF THE MODERN EGYPTIANS, 1836. With a new Introductio
by *Moursi Saad el-Din*, of the Egyptian Ministry of Education.   31

Park, Mungo (1771–1806).
TRAVELS. Introduction (1954) by *Prof. Ronald Miller*, M.A., PH.D.   2(

Polo, Marco (1254–1324).
TRAVELS. Introduction by *John Masefield.*   30
Portuguese Voyages, 1498–1663. Edited by *Charles David Ley.*   98

Stevenson, Robert Louis (1850–94).
AN INLAND VOYAGE, 1878; TRAVELS WITH A DONKEY, 1879; and THE SILVERAD
SQUATTERS, 1883. New Introduction by *M. R. Ridley*, M.A.   7(
(See also Essays, Poetry, Fiction.

Stow, John (1525 ?–1605).
THE SURVEY OF LONDON. The fullest account of Elizabethan London.   58

Wakefield, Edward Gibbon (1796–1862).
A LETTER FROM SYDNEY, AND OTHER WRITINGS ON COLONIZATION. Introductio
by *Prof. R. C. Mills.*   82

Waterton, Charles (1782–1865).
WANDERINGS IN SOUTH AMERICA, 1825. Introduction by *Edmund Selous.*   77

49 ¹⁶ 6